Story-Wallah

A Celebration of South Asian Fiction

Story-Wallah

Edited by

Shyam Selvadurai

HOUGHTON MIFFLIN COMPANY

2005 • NEW YORK • BOSTON

First published in Canada by Thomas Allen Publishers in 2004

Introduction, notes, and selection copyright © 2004
by Shyam Selvadurai

Visit our Web site: www.houghtonmifflinbooks.com.

Library of Congress Cataloging-in-Publication Data
Story-Wallah : short fiction from South Asian
writers / edited by Shyam Selvadurai.
p.   cm.   ISBN 0-618-57680-0
1. American fiction — South Asian American authors.
2. South Asia — Social life and customs — Fiction. 3. South
Asian Americans — Fiction. 4. Short stories, American.
I. Selvadurai, Shyam, 1965–
PS508.S67S76 2005 813'.01088911 — dc22 2004060937

Printed in the United States of America

MP 10 9 8 7 6 5 4 3 2 1

Page 431 constitutes a continuation of this copyright page.

For Loku (Rishika Williams),

> because *"Good friends are like good books —
> a perpetual delight"* (TIRUKKURAL 783)

For Andrew,

> because *life would be simply unimaginable
> without him*

Contents

Introducing Myself in the Diaspora   I

SAM SELVON (1923–1994, Trinidad)
Cane Is Bitter   15

MENA ABDULLAH (1930, Australia)
The Time of the Peacock   29

CHITRA FERNANDO (1935–1998, Sri Lanka)
The Perfection of Giving   39

ZULFIKAR GHOSE (1935, Pakistan)
The Marble Dome   59

ANITA DESAI (1937, India)
Winterscape   69

BHARATI MUKHERJEE (1940, India)
The Management of Grief   91

K.S. MANIAM (1942, Malaysia)
Haunting the Tiger   109

RAYMOND PILLAI (1942, Fiji)
The Celebration   121

FARIDA KARODIA (1942, South Africa)
Crossmatch   129

MICHAEL ONDAATJE (1943, Sri Lanka)
The Passions of Lalla   157

ROOPLALL MONAR (1947, Guyana)
Bahadur   171

SALMAN RUSHDIE (1947, India)
The Courter   181

RUKHSANA AHMAD (1948, Pakistan)
The Spell and the Ever-Changing Moon   205

KIRPAL SINGH (1949, Singapore)
Jaspal   219

M.G. VASSANJI (1950, Tanzania)
In the Quiet of a Sunday Afternoon   225

ROHINTON MISTRY (1952, India)
The Collectors   235

HANIF KUREISHI (1954, England)
We're Not Jews   263

ROMESH GUNESEKERA (1954, Sri Lanka)
Captives   273

AAMER HUSSEIN (1955, Pakistan)
Karima   291

SHANI MOOTOO (1957, Canada)
Out on Main Street   303

GINU KAMANI (1962, India)
Just Between Indians 315

SHYAM SELVADURAI (1965, Sri Lanka)
Pigs Can't Fly 343

SANDIP ROY (1966, India)
Auld Lang Syne 373

JHUMPA LAHIRI (1967, USA)
This Blessed House 391

MONICA ALI (1967, Bangladesh)
Dinner with Dr. Azad 411

NUMAIR CHOUDHURY (1975, Bangladesh)
Chokra 425

Acknowledgements 429

Copyright Acknowledgements 431

Biographies 433

Introducing Myself in the Diaspora

I am often invited to read from my novels in public, and, if there is a question period afterwards, someone inevitably stands up to ask the following: "What kind of a writer do you consider yourself to be? Are you a Canadian writer or a Sri Lankan writer?"

It is perplexing, this matter of cultural identity, and I am tempted, like some other writers of multiple identities, to reply grumpily, "I'm just a bloody writer. Period."

Yet this response would be disingenuous. I suppose I could answer, "Sri Lankan-Canadian writer," or "Canadian-Sri Lankan writer." But this also does not get to the heart of what I consider my identity to be as a writer (and we are talking of my *writing* identity here). For, in terms of being a writer, my creativity comes not from "Sri Lankan" or "Canadian" but precisely from the space between, that marvellous open space represented by the hyphen, in which the two parts of my identity jostle and rub up against each other like tectonic plates, pushing upwards the eruption that is my work. It is from this space between that the novels come. From a double-visionness, a bi-culturalism.

For the majority of people, a dual identity is a burden forced on them by the fact that their bodies, or their skins to be precise, do not represent the nation-state they are in, thus compelling them to constantly wear their difference on their sleeve and carry it around on their back. In my day-to-day interactions with the world outside, I share the irritation, the burden, the occasional danger of this visible otherness. But when I close the door to my study and sit at my computer, that biculturalism becomes the site of great excitement, of great marvel, the very source of my creativity. It is from this space in-between, represented by the hyphen, that I have written what I consider Canadian novels set exclusively in Sri Lanka. For though the material may be Sri Lankan, the shaping of that material and the inclusion, for example, of themes of gay liberation or feminism are drawn from the life I have lived in Canada. Homosexuality is illegal in Sri Lanka and the very real threat of physical violence and intimidation might have stopped me from exploring this theme had I lived there (being not of a particularly brave disposition). My thoughts and attitudes, indeed my craft as a writer, have been shaped by my life here in Canada. It is from the clash of these cultures, which occurs in the space between, that the conflicts in my plot lines arise. Without them my novels would be deathly boring to read.

Not to write from the space in-between would diminish me.

For the first nineteen years of my life, questions of cultural identity never troubled me. I was born and raised in Sri Lanka, and it was clear to me who I was. That "I" was manifested in being a member of my immediate and extended family, the generations before us lying in the graveyard. It was manifested in my school. Various grand-uncles, older cousins, and even my older brother had gone there before me and the teachers saw me in the context of this continuity (though negatively, always expressing their disappointment at my lack of sportiness, compared to my forbearers). This "I" was embodied in the landscape, the place names, rivers, lakes, stretches of beach that were tied to the narrative of, not just my life, but that of my parents and grandparents before me. This sense of identity remained curiously unshaken by the fact that, growing up, I listened exclusively to Western pop music and read Western books. The rise of ethnic nationalism and tensions between the majority Sinhalese and the minority Tamils (of whom I am a member because of my father, even though my mother is Sinhalese) did not shake my identity. Even the growing violence, the spilling over of that violence into our lives, which would ultimately force us to leave Sri Lanka, did not disturb that sense of who I was.

It was the arrival in Canada that shook it. Here, for the first time, I found myself forced, like almost all new immigrants, to ask myself those questions about who I was: What did it mean to be Sri Lankan? What aspects of my culture made me Sri Lankan, what aspects didn't? What was the essence of Sri Lankanness?

The answers readily furnished themselves and had actually been with me all along through my life in Sri Lanka. I had just not known it.

All colonial societies, in their struggle for independence and the forming of a new nation, reshape and redefine their identity. This drive for a cultural identity involves the establishment of a collective, essential self that is shared by people with a common ancestry and common history. This essential identity is seen to be unchanging, eternal; it provides a common frame of reference to a newly emerged nation. The goal of these new nations, released from colonialism, is to bring to light this identity that has been suppressed and distorted and disfigured by the colonial masters; to express this identity through a retelling of the past. At the core of this restored identity lies the idea that, beyond the mess and contradictions of today, is a resplendent past whose existence, when it is discovered, will restore a people as a culture, as a society.

My problem in embracing this notion of an essential, pure cultural identity was that its contradictions almost immediately bedevilled me. Where, for example, did someone like me, with a Sinhalese mother and a Tamil father, fit in? And what to do with that much-adored grandmother of mine with her blue eyes and white skin who never thought of herself as anything but, well, Sri Lankan? What also to do with the pesky fact that a piece of pop music by the Bee Gees or Olivia Newton-John could take me back to my teenage years, and those long tropical afternoons spent lying on my bed, listening to the radio, in a way no Sri Lankan song could?

In the quest for my cultural identity, I was also discovering that, within Sri Lanka itself, opposition had been mounted by writers and thinkers against this notion of a pure, eternal, fixed Sri Lankan identity. Through reading these writers, I became aware that it was the very idea of a pure, essential culture that had led to the rise of both Sinhalese and Tamil nationalism and violence — the inability of both communities to accept that they shared a crossbred culture where there was more in common than different; the insistence by each that their culture was superior; the refusal by each to acknowledge that we are a little island nation to whose shores, over the centuries, have come the winds of other cultures that have been integrated into what was now being hailed as a pure culture. I could not ignore that it was this very notion of purity that had ultimately brought such violence to my family and forced us out of Sri Lanka.

On a personal level, I was also beginning to come to terms with being gay, beginning to live out another very important part of my identity. It was very clear to me that the pure sense of being Sri Lankan was based on rigid heterosexual and gender roles. Where did someone like me belong then? By being gay, was I no longer Sri Lankan? And if that was not the case, what did it mean to be both Sri Lankan and gay; how to live out this combination of identities?

Some of the answers to these questions came through my understanding the concept of diaspora.

The word "diaspora" (a term unfamiliar to many who are diasporic themselves) comes from Greek and implies a "scattering of seeds." In its most classical sense, diaspora was used to define the experience of Jews expelled from Palestine and forced to disperse to the various parts of the earth. It is now broadly used to define other groups that have, through forced or voluntary migration, taken up abode in places other than the original centre. The Chinese, Irish, Turkish, Armenian, South Asian, and Greek diasporas are examples of this dispersal.

"Immigrant" is often used to identify these groups (and, indeed, the writers coming from these groups). The problem with this term is that the emphasis is on the act of arrival in a new land; it conveys a sense that someone is a perpetual newcomer, a perpetual outsider. The term "immigrant" does not leave much room for the process of becoming and changing and the dynamic cultural mixing that "diaspora" suggests. "Diaspora" also allows for the encompassing of a wider range of people and experiences.

On the one hand, the idea of diaspora acknowledges that the history and culture from which we have come is not an illusion. Histories are real, they have produced concrete and symbolic results. The past still informs who we are. And the truth is that the discovery of hidden histories has played a very important function in many social movements of our time — feminist, gay, anti-colonial, anti-racist. As such, it should not be dismissed outright. A collective identity can be very effective as a tool of resistance and empowerment and freedom.

On the other hand, the idea of diaspora acknowledges the act, the trauma, of migration and the fact that one cannot but be transformed in the new land. The emphasis must shift to a sense of cultural identity that is eclectic and diverse, a sense of cultural identity that is transforming itself, making itself new over and over again. A continuous work in progress. This sense of cultural identity, while taking into account that a group or a culture might have many important points of similarity, also acknowledges that there are many points of difference between its people, and that these differences, such as sexuality and gender and class, also define who we are. This sense of cultural identity stresses not just who one was in the past, but who one might be in the process of becoming.

In embracing the idea of diaspora, South Asian diaspora in my case, I am not blind to its shortcomings.

To start with, the notion of a South Asian diaspora is very questionable really when you take into account the differences, not to mention strife, between India, Pakistan, Bangladesh, and Sri Lanka, which constitute South Asia (yet one cannot deny that it is a useful concept that has been effectively employed in the West to lobby for political and social change, for creating venues and spaces for artistic expression).

While in theory diasporic identity is supposed to be fluid and encompassing of difference, in practice it is often quite the opposite, as we see in the violent expression of purity by some members of the South Asian diaspora to Salman Rushdie's *The Satanic Verses*. Another problem with the idea of diaspora is that despite its best intentions it tends to homogenize a group on a global level, whereas in practice, within that very group, immigration or expulsion might have taken place at different points in history and under different circumstances. Then, depending on the country of destination and interaction with the cultures there, these groups might have evolved in very different ways. In the South Asian context, this is seen clearly in the cultural difference between South Asians who migrated to the Caribbean in the nineteenth century as indentured labourers and South Asians who migrated directly from the subcontinent to the West in the latter half of the twentieth century. The former group, through cultural interaction with the emancipated African slave population, has evolved a very distinct culture. In Shani Mootoo's short story "Out on Main Street," this difference is played out with great humour in the clash between an Indo-Caribbean woman in Canada and more recent immigrants from Asia. In the story, the woman is referred to as a "bastardized Indian," which points to another problem with the concept of diaspora — privileging the point of origin in forming a diasporic identity at the expense of cross-cultural experiences. This privileging of the point of origin becomes even more of an issue for children of mixed marriages.

The concept of diaspora by suggesting an essential point of origin can, despite its best efforts, end up inadvertently suggesting an essential culture as well, with punishing consequences for women or gays and lesbians of that diasporic community. In reality, that is often the way it is played out in the diaspora. For example, one's authenticity within the South Asian diaspora, the sense that one is a true member of the group, is often determined by one's conformity to gender roles and expectations. The burden of femininity is foisted on women, the expectation that ultimately they are the keepers and upholders of the culture. There is the very real threat of expulsion from the community for refusal to conform. The burden of these expectations is played out in Ginu Kamani's story "Just Between Indians." Strict heterosexual expectations, with a similar threat of expulsion, are also present for gay and lesbian members of the South Asian diaspora. The concept of diaspora, based on cultural identity, does not take into account that for women or gays and lesbians there might be strong identity bonds forged with other women and gays and lesbians across cultural communities; that these bonds might ultimately be equal, if not more important, than the ones they hold with members of a similar cultural identity. The concept of diaspora does not take into account that for children of mixed marriages there may be much stronger identification with the culture of the parent who is not (in this case) a member of the South Asian diaspora.

All of the writers in this anthology then are, to various degrees, members of the South Asian diaspora. Some, like Sam Selvon and Rooplall Monar, are of the second, third or even fourth generation born in the diaspora. Others, like Hanif Kureishi and Jhumpa Lahiri, are the first generation born in the diaspora, their parents being immigrants. Salman Rushdie, Anita Desai, Chitra Fernando, Rukhsana Ahmad, and many of the other writers featured in this anthology left South Asia as children, adolescents, or adults. They or their families migrated for purposes of safety, marriage, studies, or employment, and stayed on. Farida Karodia, after a long sojourn outside, has returned to South Africa. Some of these writers might never have visited South Asia; others might visit intermittently; others might have homes in both worlds and frequently travel back and forth. Many of the writers in this anthology have been re-diasporized, moving like Shani Mootoo or Sam Selvon from the Caribbean to the West, or like Salman Rushdie from India to England to the United States.

The other thread that ties these writers together is that they all work in English which, like Urdu (the language of the pre-British colonizers), has become another South Asian language. This is not to discredit work done in the various other languages of South Asia. In fact, there is an important and dynamic body of literature coming from the diaspora in these other languages. It merits great attention and regard; it requires a separate study. What I am addressing here is literature written in English, which is also a legitimate way of talking about experience in the South Asian diaspora (we *do*, after all, have this body of work written in English). But perhaps, more to the point, English is the major link, the lingua franca, of the "South Asian" diaspora (as opposed to "Tamil" or "Gujerati" or "Bengali" diasporas). It is the language around which South Asians organize in professional, social, and artistic groups to demand a share of power and wealth and cultural presence in their new land. On a more personal note, English is the only language in which I can read and write and so my greatest interest lies in seeing what else is being written by South Asian writers in English.

A brief history lesson now:

The South Asian diaspora numbers over nine million and migrated in roughly two waves.

The first began in the 1830s when, following the abolition of slavery, vast numbers of South Asian indentured labourers were shipped off to the sugar plantations of Trinidad, Guyana, Surinam, Mauritius, fiji, and South Africa to replace the old slave populations. There was also a movement of labour to British East Africa and Malaya to work on the railways and in the rubber plantations, respectively. Some also went to these two colonies as low-ranking civil servants, traders, and professionals. The indentured labourers were transported three to four hundred in a ship. The journey lasted three months and seventeen percent of them died on the way. The conditions under which they worked on the plantations were harsh, their wages dismally low, their accommodations former slave huts. Though they were technically free to leave after the period of indentureship (usually five years), their masters, who were after all ex-slave owners, sought to keep them on through a system of fines and other punitive measures, including laws controlling their freedom of movement and rights to own land. The harsh life of these indentured labourers is poignantly captured in Sam Selvon's "Cane Is Bitter." In Rooplall Monar's "Bahadur," the attempts by the main character to rise from his position of field labourer to night watchman, while hilarious, at the same time shines a light on the extremely narrow possibilities of life on the plantations.

The poverty of the labourers, their contract of indenture, the difficulty and expense of travel and the lack of modern forms of communication that we take for granted today meant that these older diasporas were, for the most part, cut off from South Asia and lost contact with their relatives. As a result, they evolved a culture that was unique but also cohesive, as it was based on certain commonalities. The first such commonality was that moment when the labourers climbed out of the boats that had brought them to shore and waded through knee-deep water to the new land. This moment of common initiation created a sense of community often referred to as *jahaji bhai*, the ship brotherhood. Another commonality was that all indentured labourers throughout the colonies had the same set of food rations — rice, dhal, sugar, tea, dried fish, flour, salt, oil, and half a pound of mutton on weekends. This produced a cuisine that has survived into modern times. The dhal-puri (a roti made of two layers of rolled-out dough with dhal sandwiched between them) quintessentially represents this cuisine.

Cut off from South Asia, these indentured labourers were forced to recreate little self-contained South Asias and to draw meaning from their landscape. In doing so, they transformed the new world into which they had been brought. Place names, the vocabulary of local languages, the bringing in of exotic plants and animals (mangos, jackfruit, mynahs) meant that they have left a permanent mark on the landscape.

I must hasten to add that there was variance in terms of assimilation in the new land and the amount of contact that was maintained with South Asia. Those who went as traders or civil servants or professionals tended to resist hybridization more, as well as keep closer ties with South Asia. The colonial power also made a difference to how much of the original culture was kept; the British, for example, were more tolerant of South Asian cultural practices than say the Germans, or the Boers of South Africa. Religious background also affected assimilation, some religions being more insular and resistant to hybridization than others. Demographics also played a part. Large numbers of South Asians in a single place obviously meant that more of the original culture was maintained.

The history of this old diaspora is a complex one and I have not meant to homogenize here. I am just using broad strokes of history to contextualize a literature. But perhaps, more to the point, I want to show that East Africa, Malaysia, Singapore, Fiji, and the Caribbean, as we know these regions today, would be unimaginable without the vital contribution of this old South Asian diaspora. Stories such as Raymond Pillai's "The Celebration," Kirpal Singh's "Jaspal," M.G. Vassanji's "In the Quiet of a Sunday Afternoon," and K.S. Maniam's "Haunting the Tiger" capture the incredible diversity of this first wave of the South Asian migration.

The second movement from South Asia began in the mid- to late twentieth century and consisted of migration to the metropolitan centres of the West. This movement began in the mid-1950s due to the expansion of the motor car industry, when large numbers of workers were needed in Britain. It continued on to the early 1970s with the British government encouraging businesses to import cheap labour from abroad. The aim was to get people in as guest workers who, even after they acquired citizenship, would continue to function as "passive citizens" as opposed to "active citizens" who participated and represented the nation-state of Britain. Most of these early migrants were men who lived in crowded accommodations and worked long hours under poor conditions. They had intended to be sojourners but gradually they extended their stay; wives and children were brought over and a South Asian community started to develop. The early 1970s also brought a more moneyed, professional group of South Asians from Africa (Uganda in particular), who were the victims of a new, vicious brand of African nationalism. Hanif Kureishi's

"We're Not Jews" captures the racism these immigrants to England were often subjected to, and the hard lives they lived (the father in the story works as a packer in a factory).

Though there had been a trickle of South Asian immigrants to the New World (America, Canada, Australia) at the beginning of the twentieth century, the passing of immigration laws in the 1920s and '30s that barred all non-white migration to the New World put a stop to this. Mena Abdullah's "The Time of the Peacock" captures this early migratory experience through its charming portrayal of an Indian family's life on an Australian farm in the 1930s.

It was only when these repressive and discriminatory laws were lifted in the mid- to late 1960s that the great wave of South Asian migration to the New World began. By 1990, nearly one million South Asians had migrated to the United States, and about half a million to Canada. There was a significant community in Australia as well.

While the old South Asian diaspora was characterized by its creation of self-contained communities, the new South Asian diaspora is characterized by mobility. While the old diaspora lost contact with its point of origin, the new diaspora maintains an ongoing and continuous relationship with South Asia. This is mostly due to the enormous strides forward in technology and communication. In the last century, and even in the early decades of this one, long-distance communication and travel were either impossible or too expensive. One couldn't just take a plane "home"; one couldn't just make a long-distance phone call to keep track of how loved ones were faring at "home" and also find out what new cultural and political developments were taking place over "there." Now, communications and technology have made that possible.

The result is that the members of the new diaspora keep constant contact with their point of origin, not just through travel and the Internet and telephones, but through other forms of technology as well. Videotapes, CDs, and cassettes mean that South Asia is ever present visually and aurally in the new land. These members of the new diaspora travel back and forth carrying cultural and political trends in both directions. An increasing number of them lead a dual life, signified by the dual citizenship that many of them maintain. Some of them own two homes and have economic, political, and cultural interests in both places. The easy mobility of this existence is captured in stories like Bharati Mukherjee's "The Management of Grief," Farida Karodia's "Crossmatch," and Sandip Roy's "Auld Lang Syne." In each of these stories, it is precisely this mobility, this ability to travel back and forth, that allows the characters to resolve their dilemmas and inner conflicts.

The dual existence that members of the new diaspora lead has led to an embracing of the idea of the hyphen, the space between the two identities. The rush to adopt the hyphen is seen most clearly in the first wave of South Asians born in the United States or Canada or Britain, particularly those in colleges and universities and the professions. Most of them were raised by parents who were migrants from South Asia, often in a cultural climate in which there was little or no access to other South Asian friends, music, films, etc. Yet precisely because of this, they are keen to embrace hyphenated identities (Indian-Americans, Hindu-Americans, Muslim-Britons), which signal their desire to belong simultaneously "here" and "there."

This dual identity, this double allegiance, does not seem to have hindered members of this newer diaspora from having a growing impact on the cultural, social, and political landscape of Britain and the New World. South Asian writers, visual artists, and filmmakers of the diaspora are using their unique position of the in-between to express the new and critique the old. It is yet to be seen, however, if — like their counterparts in the old diaspora — members of this new diaspora will have such a vital effect on Britain, Canada, the United States, and Australia that these countries, as we will know them in the future, would be unimaginable without them.

It would have been impossible for me to read and make selections for this anthology as anything but a writer. Thus, the stories I chose drew on the same values I aspire to in my own writing — stories that take you into their world by the strength of their voice and hold you there by offering multi-dimensional characters with interesting dilemmas and conflicts; plot turns that surprise and delight; a finely honed use of language; a well-captured sense of place. I was not interested in including message-driven or propagandist stories at the expense of literary quality. This is not to make an argument of art for art's sake. The majority of stories in this anthology do deal with serious social and political issues. It was just that the experience being portrayed, while important, had to be enshrined in a form that would bring that experience to life through the creative use of character and plot. Though my major criterion for selecting one story over another was artistic quality, at the same time I wanted the reader to close this book with a greater awareness of all the regions and experiences that make up the South Asian diaspora. To this end, fine stories from a region that was overrepresented might have been left out to make room for equally good stories from a region that was under-represented.

I tried to adhere very strictly to the rule of including only short stories (linked ones were also permissible as long as they were self-sufficient), but in the end I made one exception: Monica Ali's "Dinner with Dr. Azad" is an excerpt from her novel *Brick Lane*, but it stands on its own as a story. Besides being an excellent piece of fiction, it is one of the only examples I could find of a diasporic Bangladeshi writer working in English. This anthology would have been poorer without it. V. S. Naipaul is a notable absence in this collection; permission could not be secured for his story "My Aunt Gold Teeth."

The critic Vijay Mishra has commented on the "hawker-like capacity" of South Asians to carry their ancestral and cultural baggage around, to lay it out in new contexts. This notion of the hawker stuck with me as I read through the anthology.

There was an eclectic quality to the way the stories jostled up against each other — a story of life on a sugar plantation in Trinidad next to a story of a childhood in rural Australia, next to a story that looked ironically at Buddhist values in Sri Lanka next to a story of immigrants in Canada. The effect created was a marvellous cacophony that reminded me of nothing so much as one of those South Asian bazaars, with their bargaining, carnival-like milieu. The goods on sale in this instance being stories hawked by story-traders: Story-Wallahs.

— *Shyam Selvadurai*

Sam Selvon

Cane Is Bitter

In February they began to reap the cane in the undulating fields at Cross Crossing estate in the southern part of Trinidad. "Crop time coming boy, plenty work for everybody," men in the village told one another. They set about sharpening their cutlasses on grinding stones, ceasing only when they tested the blades with their thumbnails and a faint ping! quivered in the air. Or they swung the cutlass at a drooping leaf and cleaved it. But the best test was when it could shave the hairs off your leg.

Everyone was happy in Cross Crossing as work loomed up in the way of their idleness, for after the planting of the cane there was hardly any work until the crop season. They laughed and talked more and the children were given more liberty than usual, so they ran about the barracks and played hide and seek in those canefields which had not yet been fired to make the reaping easier. In the evening, when the dry trash was burnt away from the stalks of sweet juice, they ran about clutching the black straw which rose on the wind: people miles away knew when crop season was on for the burnt trash was blown a great distance away. The children smeared one another on the face and laughed at the black streaks. It wouldn't matter now if their exertions made them hungry, there would be money to buy flour and rice when the men worked in the fields, cutting and carting the cane to the weighing-bridge.

In a muddy pond about two hundred yards east of the settlement, under the shade of spreading *laginette* trees, women washed clothes and men bathed mules and donkeys and hog-cattle. The women beat the clothes with stones to get them clean, squatting by the banks, their skirts drawn tight against the back of their thighs, their saris retaining grace of arrangement on their shoulders even in that awkward position. Naked children splashed about in the pond, hitting the water with their hands and shouting when the water shot up in the air at different angles, and trying to make brief rainbows in the sunlight with the spray. Rays of the morning sun came slantways from halfway up in the sky, casting the shadow of trees on the pond, and playing on the brown bodies of the children.

Ramlal came to the pond and sat on the western bank, so that he squinted into the sunlight. He dipped his cutlass in the water and began to sharpen it on the end of a rock on which his wife Rookmin was beating clothes. He was a big man, and in earlier days was reckoned handsome. But work in the fields had not only tanned his skin to a deep brown but actually changed his features. His nose had a slight hump just above the nostrils, and the squint in his eyes was there even in the night, as if he was peering all the time, though his eyesight was remarkable. His teeth were stained brown with tobacco, so brown that when he laughed it blended with the colour of his face, and you only saw the lips stretched wide and heard the rumble in his throat.

Rookmin was frail but strong as most East Indian women. She was not beautiful, but it was difficult to take any one feature of her face and say it was ugly. Though she was only thirty-six, hard work and the bearing of five children had taken their toll. Her eyes were black and deceptive, and perhaps she might have been unfaithful to Ramlal if the idea had ever occurred to her. But like most of the Indians in the country districts, half her desires and emotions were never given a chance to live, her life dedicated to wresting an existence for herself and her family. But as if she knew the light she threw from her eyes, she had a habit of shutting them whenever she was emotional. Her breasts sagged from years of suckling. Her hands were wrinkled and calloused. The toes of her feet were spread wide from walking without any footwear whatsoever: she never had need for a pair of shoes because she never left the village.

She watched Ramlal out of the corner of her eye as he sharpened the cutlass, sliding the blade to and fro on the rock. She knew he had something on his mind, the way how he had come silently and sat near to her pretending that he could add to the keenness of his razor-sharp cutlass. She waited for him to speak, in an oriental respectfulness. But from the attitude of both of them, it wasn't possible to tell that they were about to converse, or even that they were man and wife. Rookmin went on washing clothes, turning the garments over and over as she pounded them on a flat stone, and Ramlal squinted his eyes and looked at the sun.

At last, after five minutes or so, Ramlal spoke.

"Well, that boy Romesh coming home tomorrow. Is six months since last he come home. This time, I make up my mind, he not going back."

Rookmin went on scrubbing, she did not even look up.

"You see how city life change the boy. When he was here the last time, you see how he was talking about funny things?"

Rookmin held up a tattered white shirt and looked at the sun through it.

"But you think he will agree to what we going to do?" she asked. "He must be learning all sorts of new things, and this time might be worse than last time. Suppose he want to take creole wife?"

"But you mad or what? That could never happen. Ain't we make all arrangement with Sampath for Doolsie to married him? Anyway," he went on, "is all your damn fault in the first place, wanting to send him for education in the city. You see what it cause? The boy come like a stranger as soon as he start to learn all those funny things they teach you in school, talking about poetry and books and them funny things. I did never want to send him for education, but is you who make me do it."

"Education is a good thing," Rookmin said, without intonation. "One day he might come lawyer or doctor, and all of we would live in a big house in the town, and have servants to look after we."

"That is only foolish talk," Ramlal said. "You think he would remember we when he come a big man? And besides, by that time you and me both dead. And besides, the wedding done plan and everything already."

"Well, if he married Doolsie everything might work out."

"How you mean if? I had enough of all this business. He have to do what I say, else I put him out and he never come here again. Doolsie father offering big dowry, and afterwards the both of them could settle on the estate and he could forget all that business."

Rookmin was silent. Ramlal kept testing the blade with his nail, as if he were fascinated by the pinging sound, as if he were trying to pick out a tune.

But in fact he was thinking, thinking about the last time his son Romesh had come home . . .

It was only his brothers and sisters, all younger than himself, who looked at Romesh with wonder, wanting to ask him questions about the world outside the canefields and the village. Their eyes expressed their thoughts, but out of some curious embarrassment they said nothing. In a way, this brother was a stranger, someone who lived far away in the city, only coming home once or twice a year to visit them. They were noticing a change, a distant look in his eyes. Silently, they drew aside from him, united in their lack of understanding. Though Romesh never spoke of the great things he was learning, or tried to show off his knowledge, the very way he bore himself now, the way he watched the cane moving in the wind was alien to their feelings.

When they opened the books he had brought, eager to see the pictures, there were only pages and pages of words, and they couldn't read. They watched him in the night, crouching in the corner, the book on the floor near to the candle, reading. That alone made him different, set him apart. They thought he was going to be a pundit, or a priest, or something extraordinary. Once his sister had asked: "What do you read so much about, *bhai*?" and Romesh looked at her with a strange look and said, "To tell you, you wouldn't understand. But have patience, a time will come soon, I hope, when all of you will learn to read and write." Then Hari, his brother, said, "Why do you feel we will not understand? What is wrong with our brains? Do you think because you go to school in the city that you are better than us? Because you get the best clothes to wear, and shoes to put on your feet, because you get favour from *bap* and *mai*?" Romesh said quickly, "*Bhai*, it is not that. It is only that I have left our village, and have learned about many things which you do not know about. The whole world goes ahead in all fields, in politics, in science, in art. Even now the governments in the West Indies are talking about federating the islands, and then what will happen to the Indians in this island? But we must not quarrel, soon all of us will have a chance." But Hari was not impressed. He turned to his father and mother and said: "See how he has changed. He don't want to play no games anymore, he don't want to work in the fields, he is too much of a bigshot to use a cutlass. His brothers and sisters are fools, he don't want to talk to them because they won't understand. He don't even want to eat we food again, this morning I see he ain't touch the *baghi*. No. We have to get chicken for him, and the cream from all the cows in the village. Yes, that is what. And who it is does sweat for him to get pretty shirt to wear in Port of Spain?" He held up one of the girls' arms and spanned it with his fingers. "Look how thin she is. All that is for you to be a big man, and now you scorning your own family?" Romesh got up from the floor and faced them. His eyes burned fiercely, and he looked like the pictures of Indian gods the children had seen in the village hall. "You are all wrong!" he cried in a ringing voice, "surely you, *bap*, and you, *mai*, the years must have taught you that you must make a different life for your children, that you must free them from ignorance and the wasting away of their lives? Do you want them to suffer as you have?" Rookmin looked like she was going to say something, but instead she shut her eyes tight. Ramlal said: "Who tell you we suffer? We bring children in the world and we happy." But Romesh went on, "And what will the children do? Grow up in the village here, without learning to read and write? There are schools in San Fernando, surely you can send them there to learn about different things besides driving a mule and using a cutlass? Oh *bap*, we are such a backward people, all the others move forward to better lives, and we lag behind believing that what is to be, will be. All over Trinidad, in the country districts, our people toil on the land and reap the cane. For years it has been so, years in the same place, learning nothing new, accepting our fate like animals. Political men come from India and give speeches in the city. They speak of better things, they tell us to unite and strive for a greater goal. And what does it mean to you? Nothing. You are content to go hungry, to see your children run about naked, emaciated, grow up dull and stupid, slaves to your own indifference. You do not even pretend an interest in the Legislative Council. I remember why you voted for Pragsingh last year, it was because he gave you ten dollars — did I not see it for myself? It were better that we returned to India than stay in the West Indies and live such a low form of existence." The family watched Romesh wide-eyed. Ramlal sucked his clay pipe noisily. Rookmin held her youngest daughter in her lap, picking her head for lice, and now and then shutting her eyes so the others wouldn't see what she was thinking. "There is only one solution," Romesh went on, "we must educate the children, open up new worlds in their minds, stretch the horizon of their thoughts . . ." Suddenly he stopped. He realized that for some time now they weren't listening, his words didn't make any sense to them. Perhaps he was going about this the wrong way, he would have to find some other way of explaining how he felt. And was he sufficiently equipped in himself to propose vast changes in the lives of the people? It seemed to him then how small he was, how there were so many things he didn't know. All the books he'd read, the knowledge he'd lapped up hungrily in the city, listening to the politicians making speeches in the square — all these he mustered to his assistance. But it was as if his brain was too small, it was like putting your mouth in the sea and trying to drink all the water. Wearily, like an old man who had tried to prove his point merely by repeating, "I am old, I should know," Romesh sat down on the floor, and there was silence in the hut, a great silence, as if the words he'd spoken had fled the place and gone outside with the wind and the cane.

And so after he had gone back to the city his parents discussed the boy, and concluded that the only thing to save his senses was to marry him off. "You know he like Sampath daughter from long time, and she is a hard-working girl, she go make good wife for him," Rookmin had said. Ramlal had seen Sampath and everything was fixed. Everybody in the village knew of the impending wedding . . .

Romesh came home the next day. He had some magazines and books under his arm, and a suitcase in his hand. There was no reception for him; everyone who could work was out in the fields.

He was as tall as the canes on either side of the path on which he walked. He sniffed the smell of burning cane, but he wasn't overjoyful at coming home. He had prepared for this, prepared for the land on which he had toiled as a child, the thatched huts, the children running naked in the sun. He knew that these were things not easily forgotten which he had to forget. But he saw how waves of wind rippled over the seas of cane and he wondered vaguely about big things like happiness and love and poetry, and how they could fit into the poor, toiling lives the villagers led.

Romesh met his sisters at home. They greeted him shyly but he held them in his arms and cried, "*Beti*, do you not know your own brother?" And they laughed and hung their heads on his shoulder.

"Everybody gone to work," one girl said, "and we cooking food to carry. Pa and Ma was looking out since early this morning, they say to tell you if you come to come in the fields."

Romesh looked around the hut in which he had grown up. It seemed to him that if he had come back home after ten years, there would still be the old table in the centre of the room, its feet sunk in the earthen floor, the black pots and pans hanging on nails near the window. Nothing would change. They would plant the cane, and when it grew and filled with sweet juice cut it down for the factory. The children would waste away their lives working with their parents. No schooling, no education, no widening of experience. It was the same thing the man had lectured about in the public library three nights before in Port of Spain. The most they would learn would be to wield a cutlass expertly, or drive the mule cart to the railway line swiftly so that before the sun went down they would have worked sufficiently to earn more than their neighbours.

With a sigh like an aged man Romesh opened his suitcase and took out a pair of shorts and a polo shirt. He put these on and put the suitcase away in a corner. He wondered where would be a safe place to put his books. He opened the suitcase again and put them in.

It was as if, seeing the room in which he had argued and quarrelled with the family on his last visit, he lost any happiness he might have had coming back this time. A feeling of depression overcame him.

It lasted as he talked with his sisters as they prepared food to take to the fields. Romesh listened to how they stumbled with words, how they found it difficult to express themselves. He thought how regretful it was that they couldn't go to school. He widened the thought and embraced all the children in the village, growing up with such little care, running naked in the mud with a piece of *roti* in their hands, missing out on all the things that life should stand for.

But when the food was ready and they set off for the fields, with the sun in their eyes making them blind, he felt better. He would try to be happy with them, while he was here. No more preaching. No more voicing of opinion on this or that.

Other girls joined his sisters as they walked, all carrying food. When they saw Romesh they blushed and tittered, and he wondered what they were whispering about among themselves.

There were no effusive greetings. Sweating as they were, their clothes black with the soot of burnt canes, their bodies caught in the motions of their work, they just shouted out, and Romesh shouted back. Then Ramlal dropped the reins and jumped down from his cart. He curved his hand like a boomerang and swept it over his face. The soot from his sleeves smeared his face as he wiped away the sweat.

Rookmin came up and opened tired arms to Romesh. "*Beta*," she cried as she felt his strong head on her breast. She would have liked to stay like that, drawing his strength and vitality into her weakened body, and closing her eyes so her emotions wouldn't show.

"*Beta*," his father said, "you getting big, you looking strong." They sat down to eat on the grass. Romesh was the only one who appeared cool, the others were flushed, the veins standing out on their foreheads and arms.

Romesh asked if it was a good crop.

"Yes *beta*," Ramlal said, "is a good crop, and plenty work for everybody. But this year harder than last year, because rain begin to fall early, and if we don't hurry up with the work, it will be too much trouble for all of us. The overseer come yesterday, and he say a big bonus for the man who do the most work. So everybody working hard for that bonus. Two of my mules sick, but I have to work them, I can't help. We trying to get the bonus."

After eating Ramlal fished a cigarette zoot from his pocket and lit it carefully. First greetings over, he had nothing more to tell his son, for the time being anyway.

Romesh knew they were all remembering the last visit, and the things he had said then. This time he wasn't going to say anything, he was just going to have a holiday and enjoy it, and return to school in the city refreshed.

He said, "Hari, I bet I could cut more canes than you."

Hari laughed. "Even though I work the whole morning already is a good bet. You must be forget to use *poya*, your hands so soft and white now."

That is the way life is, Ramlal thought as Romesh took his cutlass. Education, school, chut! It was only work put a *roti* in your belly, only work that brought money. The marriage would change Romesh. And he felt a pride in his heart as his son spat on the blade.

The young men went to a patch of burnt canes. The girls came too, standing by to pile the fallen stalks of sweet juice into heaps, so that they could be loaded quickly and easily on to the carts and raced to the weighing-bridge.

Cane fell as if a machine were at work. The blades swung in the air, glistened for a moment in the sunlight, and descended on the stalks near the roots. Though the work had been started as a test of speed, neither of them moved ahead of the other. Sometimes Romesh paused until Hari came abreast, and sometimes Hari waited a few canes for Romesh. Once they looked at each other and laughed, the sweat on their faces getting into their mouths. There was no more enmity on Hari's part: seeing his brother like this, working, was like the old days when they worked side by side at all the chores which filled the day.

Everybody turned to in the field striving to outwork the others, for each wanted the bonus as desperately as his neighbour. Sometimes the women and the girls laughed or made jokes to one another, but the men worked silently. And the crane on the weighing-bridge creaked and took load after load. The labourer manipulating it grumbled: there was no bonus for him, though his wage was more than that of the cane-cutters.

When the sun set all stopped work as if by signal. And in Ramlal's hut that night there was laughter and song. Everything was all right, they thought. Romesh was his natural self again, the way he swung that cutlass! His younger sisters and brother had never really held anything against him, and now that Hari seemed pleased, they dropped all embarrassment and made fun. "See *bhai*, I make *meetai* especially for you," his sister said, offering the sweetmeat.

"He work hard, he deserve it," Hari agreed, and he looked at his brother almost with admiration.

Afterwards, when Ramlal was smoking and Rookmin was searching in the youngest girl's head for lice ("put pitch-oil, that will kill them," Ramlal advised) Romesh said he was going to pay Doolsie a visit.

There was a sudden silence. Rookmin shut her eyes, the children stopped playing, and Ramlal coughed over his pipe.

"Well, what is the matter?" Romesh asked, looking at their faces.

"Well, now," Ramlal began, and stopped to clear his throat. "Well now, you know that is our custom, that a man shouldn't go to pay visit to the girl he getting married . . ."

"What!" Romesh looked from face to face. The children shuffled their feet and began to be embarrassed at the stranger's presence once more.

Ramlal spoke angrily. "Remember this is your father's house! Remember the smaller ones! Careful what you say, you must give respect! You not expect to get married one day, eh? Is a good match we make, boy, you will get good dowry, and you could live in the village and forget them funny things you learning in the city."

"So it has all been arranged," Romesh said slowly. "That is why everybody looked at me in such a strange way in the fields. My life already planned for me, my path pointed out — cane, labour, boy children, and the familiar village of Cross Crossing." His voice had dropped lower, as if he had been speaking to himself, but it rose again as he addressed his mother: "And you, *mai*, you have helped them do this to me? You whose idea it was to give me an education?"

Rookmin shut her eyes and spoke. "Is the way of our people, is we custom from long time. And you is Indian? The city fool your brains, but you will get back accustom after you married and have children."

Ramlal got up from where he was squatting on the floor, and faced Romesh. "You have to do what we say," he said loudly. "Ever since you in the city, we notice how you change. You forgetting custom and how we Indian people does live. And too besides, money getting short. We want help on the estate. The garden want attention, and nobody here to see about the cattle and them. And no work after crop, too besides."

"Then I can go to school in San Fernando," Romesh said desperately. "If there is no money to pay the bus, I will walk. The government schools are free, you do not have to pay to learn."

"You will married and have boy children," Ramlal said, "and you will stop answering your *bap* . . ."

"Hai! Hai!" Drivers urged their carts in the morning sun, and whips cracked crisply on the air. Dew still clung to the grass as workers took to the fields to do as much as they could before the heat of the sun began to tell.

Romesh was still asleep when the others left. No one woke him; they moved about the hut in silence. No one spoke. The boys went to harness the mules, one of the girls to milk the cows and the other was busy in the kitchen.

When Romesh got up he opened his eyes in full awareness. He could have started the argument again as if no time had elapsed, the night had made no difference.

He went into the kitchen to wash his face. He gargled noisily, scraped his tongue with his teeth. Then he remembered his toothbrush and toothpaste in his suitcase. As he cleaned his teeth his sister stood watching him. She never used a toothbrush: they broke a twig and chewed it to clean their mouths.

"You going to go away, *bhai*?" she asked him timidly.

He nodded, with froth in his mouth.

"If you stay, you could teach we what you know," the girl said.

Romesh washed his mouth and said, "*Baihin*, there are many things I have yet to learn."

"But what will happen to us?"

"Don't ask me questions, little sister," he said crossly.

After he had eaten he left the hut and sulked about the village, walking slowly with his hands in his pockets. He wasn't quite sure what he was going to do. He kept telling himself that he would go away and never return, but bonds he had refused to think about surrounded him. The smell of burnt cane was strong on the wind. He went to the pond, where he and Hari used to bath the mules. What to do? His mind was in a turmoil.

Suddenly he turned and went home. He got his cutlass — it was sharp and clean, even though unused for such a long time. Ramlal never allowed any of his tools to get rusty.

He went out into the fields, swinging the cutlass in the air, as if with each stroke he swept a problem away.

Hari said: "Is time you come. Other people start work long time, we have to work extra to catch up with them."

There was no friendliness in his voice now.

Romesh said nothing, but he hacked savagely at the canes, and in half an hour he was bathed in sweat and his skin scratched from contact with the cane.

Ramlal came up in the mule cart and called out, "Work faster! We a whole cartload behind!" Then he saw Romesh and he came down from the cart and walked rapidly across. "So you come! Is a good thing you make up your mind!"

Romesh wiped his face. "I am not going to stay, *bap*." It was funny how the decision came, he hadn't known himself what he was going to do. "I will help with the crop, you shall get the bonus if I have to work alone in the night. But I am not going to get married. I am going away after the crop."

"You are mad, you will do as I say." Ramlal spoke loudly, and other workers in the field stopped to listen.

The decision was so clear in Romesh's mind that he did not say anything more. He swung the cutlass tirelessly at the cane and knew that when the crop was finished, it would be time to leave his family and the village. His mind got that far, and he didn't worry about after that . . .

As the wind whispered in the cane, it carried the news of Romesh's revolt against his parents' wishes, against tradition and custom.

Doolsie, working a short distance away, turned her brown face from the wind. But women and girls working near to her whispered among themselves and laughed. Then one of the bolder women, already married, said, "Well girl, is a good thing in a way. Some of these men too bad. They does beat their wife too much — look at Dulcie husband, he does be drunk all the time, and she does catch hell with him."

But Doolsie bundled the canes together and kept silent.

"She too young yet," another said. "Look, she breasts not even form yet!"

Doolsie did not have any memories to share with Romesh, and her mind was young enough to bend under any weight. But the way her friends were laughing made her angry, and in her mind she too revolted against the marriage.

"All-you too stupid!" she said, lifting her head with a childish pride so that her sari fell on her shoulder. "You wouldn't say Romesh is the only boy in the village! And too besides, I wasn't going to married him if he think he too great for me."

The wind rustled through the cane. Overhead, the sun burned like a furnace.

Mena Abdullah

The Time of the Peacock

When I was little everything was wonderful; the world was our farm and we were all loved. Rashida and Lal and I, Father and our mother, Ama: we loved one another and everything turned to good.

I remember in autumn, how we burned the great baskets of leaves by the Gwydir and watched the fires burning in the river while Ama told us stories of Krishna the Flute-player and his moving mountains. And when the fires had gone down and the stories were alive in our heads we threw cobs of corn into the fires and cooked them. One for each of us — Rashida and Lal and I, Father and our mother.

Winter I remember, when the frost bit and stung and the wind pulled our hair. At night by the fire in the warmth of the house, we could hear the dingoes howling.

Then it was spring and the good year was born again. The sticks of the jasmine vine covered themselves with flowers.

One spring I remember was the time of the peacock when I learnt the word *secret* and began to grow up. After that spring everything somehow was different, was older. I was not little any more, and the baby came.

I had just learnt to count. I thought I could count anything. I counted fingers and toes, the steps and the windows, even the hills. But this day in spring the hills were wrong.

There should have been five. I knew that there should have been five. I counted them over and over — *"Ek, do, tin, panch"* — but it was no good. There was one too many, a strange hill, a leftover. It looked familiar, and I knew it, but it made more than five and worried me. I thought of Krishna and the mountains that moved to protect the cow-herds, the travellers lost because of them, and I was frightened because it seemed to me that our hills had moved.

I ran through the house and out into the garden to tell Ama the thing that Krishna had done and to ask her how we could please him. But when I saw her I forgot all about them; I was as young as that. I just stopped and jumped, up and down.

She was standing there, in her own garden, the one with the Indian flowers, her own little walled-in country. Her hands were joined together in front of her face, and her lips were moving. On the ground, in front of the Kashmiri rosebush; in front of the tuberoses, in front of the pomegranate-tree, she had placed little bowls of shining milk. I jumped to see them. Now I knew why I was running all the time and skipping, why I wanted to sing out and to count everything in the world.

"It is spring," I shouted to Ama. "Not nearly-spring! Not almost-spring! But really-spring! Will the baby come soon?" I asked her. "Soon?"

"Soon, Impatience, soon."

I laughed at her and jumped up and clapped my hands together over the top of my head.

"I am as big as that," I said. "I can do anything." And I hopped on one leg to the end of the garden where the peacock lived. "Shah-Jehan!" I said to him — that was his name. "It is spring and the baby is coming, pretty Shah-Jehan." But he didn't seem interested. "Silly old Shah-Jehan," I said. "Don't you know anything? I can count ten."

He went on staring with his goldy eye at me. He *was* a silly bird. Why, he had to stay in the garden all day, away from the rooster. He couldn't run everywhere the way that I could. He couldn't do anything.

"Open your tail," I told him. "Go on, open your tail." And we went on staring at one another till I felt sad.

"Rashida is right," I said to him. "You will never open your tail like the bird on the fan. But why don't you try? Please, pretty Shah-Jehan." But he just went on staring as though he would never open his tail, and while I looked at him sadly I remembered how he had come to us.

He could lord it now and strut in the safety of the garden, but I remembered how the Lascar brought him to the farm, in a bag, like a cabbage, with his feathers drooping and his white tail dirty.

The Lascar came to the farm, a seaman on the land, a dark face in a white country. How he smiled when he saw us — Rashida and me swinging on the gate. How he chattered to Ama and made her laugh and cry. How he had shouted about the curries that she gave him.

And when it was time to go, with two basins of curry tied up in cloth and packed in his bag, he gave the bird to Ama, gave it to her while she said nothing, not even "thank you." She only looked at him.

"What is it?" we said as soon as he was far enough away. "What sort of bird?"

"It is a peacock," said Ama, very softly. "He has come to us from India."

"It is not like the peacock on your Kashmiri fan," I said. "It is only a sort of white."

"The peacock on the fan is green and blue and gold and has a tail like a fan," said Rashida. "This is not a peacock at all. Anyone can see that."

"Rashida," said Ama, "Rashida! The eldest must not be too clever. He is a white peacock. He is too young to open his tail. He is a peacock from India."

"Ama," I said, "make him, make him open his tail."

"I do not think," she said, "I do not think he will ever open his tail in this country."

"No," said Father that night, "he will never open his tail in Australia."

"No," said Uncle Seyed next morning, "he will never open his tail without a hen-bird near."

But we had watched him — Rashida and Lal and I — had watched him for days and days until we had grown tired of watching and he had grown sleek and shiny and had found his place in the garden.

"Won't you ever open your tail?" I asked him again. "Not now that it's spring?" But he wouldn't even try, not even try to look interested, so I went away from him and looked for someone to talk to.

The nurse-lady who was there to help Ama and who was pink like an apple and almost as round was working in the kitchen.

"The baby is coming soon," I told her. "Now that it's spring."

"Go on with you," she laughed. "Go on."

So I did, until I found Rashida sitting in a windowsill with a book in front of her. It was the nurse-lady's baby-book.

"What are you doing?"

"I am reading," she said. "This is the baby-book. I am reading how to look after the baby."

"You can't read," I said. "You know you can't read."

Rashida refused to answer. She just went on staring at the book, turning pages.

"But you can't read!" I shouted at her. "You can't."

She finished running her eye down the page. "I am not reading words," she said. "I know what the book tells. I am reading things."

"But you know, you know you can't read." I stamped away from her, cranky as anything, out of the house, past the window where Rashida was sitting — so cleverly — down to the vegetable patch where I could see Lal. He was digging with a trowel.

"What are you doing?" I said, not very pleasantly.

"I am digging," said Lal. "I am making a garden for my new baby brother."

"How did you know? How did you all know? I was going to tell *you*." I was almost crying. "Anyway," I said, "it might not be a brother."

"Oh yes, it will," said Lal. "We have girls."

"I'll dig, too," I said, laughing, and suddenly happy again. "I'll help you. We'll make a big one."

"Digging is man's work," said Lal. "I'm a man. You're a girl."

"You're a baby," I said. "You're only four." And I threw some dirt at him, and went away.

Father was making a basket of sticks from the plum-tree. He used to put crossed sticks on the ground, squat in the middle of them, and weave other sticks in and out of them until a basket had grown up round him. All I could see were his shoulders and the back of his turban as I crept up behind him, to surprise him.

But he was not surprised. "I knew it would be you," he said. I scowled at him then, but he only laughed the way that he always did.

"Father —" I began in a questioning voice that made him groan. Already I was called the Australian one, the questioner. "Father," I said, "why do peacocks have beautiful tails?"

He tugged at his beard. "Their feet are ugly," he said. "Allah has given them tails so that no one will look at their feet."

"But Shah-Jehan," I said, and Father bent his head down over his weaving. "Everyone looks at his feet. His tail never opens."

"Yes," said Father definitely, as though that explained everything, and I began to cry: it was that sort of day, laughter and tears. I suppose it was the first day of spring.

"What is it, what is it?" said Father.

"Everything," I told him. "Shah-Jehan won't open his tail, Rashida pretends she can read, Lal won't let me dig. I'm nothing. And it's spring. Ama is putting out the milk for the snakes, and I counted —"

But Father was looking so serious that I never told him what I had counted.

"Listen," he said. "You are big now, Nimmi. I will tell you a secret."

"What is secret?"

He sighed. "It is what is ours," he said. "Something we know but do not tell, or share with one person only in the world."

"With me!" I begged. "With me!"

"Yes," he said, "with you. But no crying or being nothing. This is to make you a grown-up person."

"Please," I said to him, "please." And I loved him then so much that I wanted to break the cage of twigs and hold him.

"We are Muslims," he said. "But your mother has a mark on her forehead that shows that once she was not. She was a Brahmin and she believed all the stories of Krishna and Siva."

"I know that," I said, "and the hills —"

"Monkey, quiet," he commanded. "But now Ama is a Muslim, too. Only, she remembers her old ways. And she puts out the milk in the spring."

"For the snakes," I said. "So they will love us, and leave us from harm."

"But there are no snakes in the garden," said Father.

"But they drink the milk," I told him. "Ama says —"

"If the milk were left, the snakes would come," said Father. "And they must not come, because there is no honour in snakes. They would strike you or Rashida or little Lal or even Ama. So — and this is the secret that no one must know but you and me — I go to the garden in the night and empty the dishes of milk. And this way I have no worry and you have no harm and Ama's faith is not hurt. But you must never tell."

"Never, never tell," I assured him.

All that day I was kind to Lal, who was only a baby and not grown up, and I held my head up high in front of Rashida, who was clever but had no secret. All of that day I walked in a glory full of my secret. I even felt cleverer than Ama, who knew everything but must never, never know this.

She was working that afternoon on her quilt. I looked at the crochet pictures in the little squares of it.

"Here is a poinsettia," I said.

"Yes," said Ama. "And here is —"

"It's Shah-Jehan! With his tail open."

"Yes," said Ama, "so it is, and here is a rose for the baby."

"When will the baby come?" I asked her. "Not soon, but when?"

"Tonight, tomorrow night," said Ama, "the next."

"Do babies always come at night?"

"Mine, always," said Ama. "There is the dark and the waiting, and then the sun on our faces. And the scent of jasmine, even here." And she looked at her garden.

"But, Ama —"

"No questions, Nimmi. My head is buzzing. No questions today."

That night I heard a strange noise, a harsh cry. "Shah-Jehan!" I said. I jumped out of bed and ran to the window. I stood on a chair and looked out to the garden.

It was moonlight, the moon so big and low that I thought I could lean out and touch it, and there — looking sad, and white as frost in the moonlight — stood Shah-Jehan.

"Shah-Jehan, little brother," I said to him, "you must not feel about your feet. Think of your tail, pretty one, your beautiful tail."

And then, as I was speaking, he lifted his head and slowly, slowly opened his tail — like a fan, like a fan of lace that was as white as the moon. O Shah-Jehan! It was as if you had come from the moon.

My throat hurt, choked, so that my breath caught and I shut my eyes. When I opened them it was all gone: the moon was the moon, and Shah-Jehan was a milky-white bird with his tail drooping and his head bent.

In the morning the nurse-lady woke us. "Get up," she said. "Guess what? In the night, a sister! The dearest, sweetest, baby sister. . . . Now, up with you."

"No brother," said Lal. "No baby brother."

We laughed at him, Rashida and I, and ran to see the baby. Ama was lying, very still and small, in the big bed. Her long plait of black hair stretched out across the white pillow. The baby was in the old cradle and we peered down at her. Her tiny fists groped on the air towards us. But Lal would not look at her. He climbed onto the bed and crawled over to Ama.

"No boy," he said sadly. "No boy to play with."

Ama stroked his hair. "My son," she said. "I am sorry, little son."

"Can we change her?" he said. "For a boy?"

"She is a gift from Allah," said Ama. "You can never change gifts."

Father came in from the dairy, his face a huge grin, he made a chuckling noise over the cradle and then sat on the bed.

"Missus," he said in the queer English that always made the nurse-lady laugh, "this one little fellow, eh?"

"Big," said Ama. "Nine pounds." And the nurse-lady nodded proudly.

"What wrong with this fellow?" said Father, scooping Lal up in his arm. "What wrong with you, eh?"

"No boy," said Lal. "No boy to talk to."

"Ai! Ai!" lamented Father, trying to change his expression. "Too many girls here," he said. "Better we drown one. Which one we drown, Lal? Which one, eh?"

Rashida and I hurled ourselves at him, squealing with delight. "Not me! Not me!" we shouted while the nurse-lady tried to hush us.

"You are worse than the children," she said to Father. "Far worse." But then she laughed, and we all did — even the baby made a noise.

But what was the baby to be called? We all talked about it. Even Uncle Seyed came in and leant on the doorpost while names were talked over and over.

At last Father lifted the baby up and looked into her big dark eyes. "What was the name of your sister?" he asked Uncle Seyed. "The little one, who followed us everywhere? The little one with the beautiful eyes?"

"Jamila," said Uncle Seyed. "She was Jamila."

So that was to be her first name, Jamila, after the little girl who was alive in India when Father was a boy and he and Uncle Seyed had decided to become friends like brothers. And her second name was Shahnaz, which means the Heart's Beloved.

And then I remembered. "Shah-Jehan," I said. "He can open his tail. I saw him last night, when everyone was asleep."

"You couldn't see in the night," said Rashida. "You dreamt it, baby."

"No, I didn't. It was bright moon."

"You dreamt it, Nimmi," said Father. "A peacock wouldn't open his tail in this country."

"I didn't dream it," I said in a little voice that didn't sound very certain: Father was always right. "I'll count Jamila's fingers," I said before Rashida could say anything else about the peacock. *"Ek, do, tin, panch,"* I began.

"You've left out *cha*," said Father.

"Oh yes, I forgot. I forgot it. *Ek, do, tin, cha, panch* — she has five," I said.

"Everyone has five," said Rashida.

"Show me," said Lal. And while Father and Ama were showing him the baby's fingers and toes and telling him how to count them, I crept out on the veranda where I could see the hills.

I counted them quickly. *"Ek, do, tin, cha, panch."* There were only five, not one left over. I was so excited that I felt the closing in my throat again. "I didn't dream it," I said. "I couldn't dream the pain. I did see it, I did. I have another secret now. And only five hills. *Ek, do, tin, cha, panch."*

They never changed again. I was grown up.

Chitra Fernando

The Perfection of Giving

In my family, everyone regarded my father's elder sister as a very good and generous woman. I thought so too; in those days I had great respect for the opinions of my elders. Father said, "Now try to be like Big Auntie, Mahinda. She's an example to us all." Mother said, "Big Auntie has more *shradda* than all of us." Big Auntie never killed anything, not even a mosquito. And once I saw her saving some ants that had fallen into a basin of water; even the most insignificant creature benefited from Big Auntie's attentions. Big Auntie never stole; she had a large house and garden, a lot of jewellery and a small coconut property in Matara. She had everything she wanted. She never lied. She often said she never did, and of course, we all believed her. Big Auntie's conduct was always irreproachable. She was a broad woman, a bit on the short side and very dark; her nose and lips were thick, her skin coarse. She had a large mole on the tip of her nose and another with a hair in it on her chin. At the back of her head was a very small knot of hair. Unless they were her relations Big Auntie kept all men at a safe distance; and they kept her at an equally safe distance. She had never married. As for drinking or smoking — even the thought of her doing either of these things made me want to laugh.

Once Small Auntie caught Siripala and me sharing a cigarette in the back garden and the first thing she said was, "How disappointed Big Auntie will be, Mahinda. You two boys are only fifteen, but you're already doing all these bad things!" Then she told Father about it. Father said, "I will not have smoking, I will not have drinking in this house." And then he told Big Auntie about it. Big Auntie looked at me in silence. She said, "Mahinda, there's no need for me to tell you anything. Why should I say anything? Your own actions, your karma will deal with you. Smoke as much as you like. When you get lung cancer, you'll know all about it. This gratification of the senses brings only disease, death and *samsara*. Don't say I didn't warn you!"

Small Auntie, who was listening, nodded vigorously and said, "I hope you've taken all this in, Mahinda. No need to look the other way! We're advising you for your own good."

I often wished they were less concerned with my own good but I could say nothing. So I continued to look the other way.

Small Auntie was also unmarried and so had no household of her own. But though she was always singing Big Auntie's praises, she had a strange preference for living in our house. At the time of the cigarette-smoking incident, she was always talking about yet another instance of Big Auntie's generosity and compassion. Big Auntie's good deeds were uncountable so everyone was quite certain that at the very least she could be sure of a place in the Tusitha heaven. But this instance of Big Auntie's generosity was not an alms-giving; it was not a special pooja; it was not donating a loudspeaker to the temple for the relay of the daily sermon so that all the Payagala townsfolk could not but benefit from the loudness of Big Auntie's piety. This was a meritorious deed which was much better. Big Auntie was going to adopt a little girl from Matara! Not, of course, as a daughter. No one expected even Big Auntie to go to such lengths. It was unthinkable that a toddy tapper's child could be Big Auntie's daughter and, therefore, our relative. Big Auntie had too much consideration, too much common sense for that. She was a very practical woman. Kusuma was to come to her house as a servant.

Mala, my young sister, and I were at Big Auntie's house the morning she arrived. Kusuma, her father said, was twelve, but she looked about nine. She was small and skinny and her huge dark eyes half-filled her little face. Lice crawled in her curly black hair. There was a sore on her knee. In the village she had lived in a hut, one of eight children, half-starved, beaten and bullied. In Big Auntie's spacious house there was the comfort of good food, good clothes and a suitable wage deposited in a post office savings account. As Mother said, what more could any sane servant expect! It was, we all felt, the perfect sum total of a servant's happiness.

Father said: "That girl must have done a lot of merit in her past lives. Just imagine! After living like an animal in that hut to come to a house like Big Sister's!"

"Must be like heaven to her!" was Mother's contribution.

"She's not bad looking, and with all the good food she'll be eating she'll soon fill out. I hope she's not going to be greedy and steal. That must be firmly stopped, right from the start." Small Auntie did her best to see that everyone observed the Second Precept.

"Don't worry. Big Sister knows how to deal with stealing. She gives her servants so much! For them to misbehave is just raw wickedness, nothing else. As she always says so rightly, 'No one can escape the karmic law,'" Father said firmly.

A week later, Big Auntie came to our house with Kusuma. Already we noticed an improvement in her appearance. Her hair was clean and lice-free. When she'd arrived she had been wearing a badly sewn shabby frock. Now she wore a close-fitting white cotton blouse and a pretty-flowered red-and-white cloth. Everyone complimented Big Auntie on the good work. She looked very satisfied.

"I know how to treat my servants. That's why they never leave my house. Salpi has been with me for fifteen years now." This was perfectly true. Big Auntie did treat her servants well. They enjoyed a fair bit of comfort in her house. The full effect of Big Auntie's generosity to Kusuma appeared in about three months time. In that time she seemed to have grown taller, fairer and certainly much fuller. Big Auntie often said there was nothing wrong with her appetite. "She eats as much as Salpi, and doesn't she love sweets!"

Small Auntie said, "Now don't spoil her. I hope she won't steal. Have you caught her at it ever?"

"No. She's a bit greedy but I give her plenty to eat. So she really has no need to steal."

"If she steals, will you beat her, Big Auntie?" asked Mala with interest.

"No, Mala. I don't beat anyone. You know that. I'll know what to do. I believe in the karmic law — it's my constant guide."

I was sometimes puzzled by Big Auntie's way of talking about "the karmic law." Of course we all knew about karma. I remembered very well what the monk in the temple used to say: everyone had to take the consequences of his actions in one way or another. If you wanted too many things your desires would make you linger in *samsara*; you would be a prisoner of your desires. That's what the monk said. But I wasn't sure that I understood. Because Big Auntie, who was so wise, seemed to want a lot in return for whatever she did. But in those days I didn't bother too much about such things. I had so many more important things to think about like how to dodge *Pali* classes, or ways and means of smoking without being caught and lectured to.

Big Auntie was pleased with Kusuma. She was intelligent and learnt quickly. She soon learnt to be neat and clean. She was very helpful in the house. She dusted the furniture — all of Big Auntie's carved ebony chairs and couches in the sitting-room. She cleaned all the brass trays, lamps and vases. She was very good at fetching and carrying. Big Auntie wondered whether she should teach Kusuma to read and write. She thought about it a bit. Then she told us that to teach Kusuma how to crochet would be far more useful. Lace table-mats were in great demand and fetched a very good price. Big Auntie was a very practical woman.

After Kusuma's arrival, Mala began to visit Big Auntie almost every day. Kusuma knew very little. So Mala began to feel very wise, though she knew very little herself. I was, of course, the really wise one among the younger lot. In those days, we all thought ourselves very wise. But everyone acknowledged Big Auntie to be the wisest. This was her own opinion as well — naturally.

It seemed to me that Mala liked showing off a bit. She would sit with Kusuma on the veranda steps and tell her all about the wonders of the world. Had Kusuma ever been to Colombo? No. Then she wouldn't ever have been in a lift, would she? No. Had she ever been on an escalator? No. Kusuma's ignorance was so satisfying to Mala! Had she ever been to the zoo? No. What was a zoo? Mala was in her element. She told Kusuma all about the zoo: the tigers, the lions, the bears, the giraffes, the kangaroos, the zebras, the red-backed baboon, the elephants. Kusuma had seen an elephant! Oh! Mala was quite dis-appointed. Where had Kusuma seen an elephant? In a religious pro-cession. That wasn't so bad. The zoo elephants didn't do anything so ordinary. They balanced on little stools or skipped round the arena, and then all the people laughed and clapped. Kusuma longed to go to Colombo to see all those marvels. She asked Mala a thousand-and-one questions. Mala brought her picture books. Kusuma had never held a book in her hands before. She turned over the pages carefully. Mala lent her the books for a few days. She couldn't read, of course, but she loved looking at the pictures. Then Big Auntie ordered Mala to take the books away. Kusuma looked at the pictures too often. That very afternoon she was looking at pictures when she should have been polishing the brass. Of course, Big Auntie didn't mind Mala talking to Kusuma. But she must not spoil her. So Mala took the books away. But Kusuma talked and talked about the ani-mals in the zoo.

"The cat is like the tiger," said Kusuma. "It's a little tiger," she added and cuddled the household cat.

"Yes," I said, "the cat is a kind of tiger." And I told her all about cats and tigers and leopards. She listened to me with her great black eyes wide open. She had a great longing for learning, for knowledge, in those days.

The New Year drew closer. We were going to spend the New Year in Colombo with Fair Auntie and all our cousins. Mala asked, "Can we take Kusuma too?"

Mother looked surprised. It was such a — such a new idea! She didn't know what to say.

"She's never been to Colombo. She's never been in a lift. She's never been on an escalator. And she's never seen a lion or a tiger or a giraffe, or a zebra or a kangaroo or a . . ." Mala had to stop for breath.

"Big Auntie . . . Big Auntie . . ." began Mother.

"I'll ask her," said Mala.

I decided Mala was a lot wiser than I had thought her. We went to Big Auntie's the next day. Mala carried a dish in her hand.

"What's that?" I asked.

"Um . . . nothing," said Mala.

"Nothing! Let me see, let me see." I lifted the cover of the dish and saw the mangoes inside. I laughed. I understood all.

"There's nothing to laugh about," she said a bit huffily.

"Ah, Mala, what's that?" Big Auntie eyed the dish with great interest.

"We had a lot of mangoes at home. And I said you liked mangoes. So Mother sent it."

Big Auntie smiled. She loved getting presents. Mala said tomorrow she would bring her some mangosteens. Tomorrow Banda would come from Kalutara and he always brought mangosteens at this time of the year. As we were leaving Mala said, "We're going to Colombo for the New Year. Can Kusuma come too? Please, please, Big Auntie, please let her come. I always feel so bored at Fair Auntie's. Everyone's bigger than me and they don't play with me. Please, Big Auntie."

Mala's pleading, almost tearful face — the mangoes of today, the mangosteens of tomorrow! How could Big Auntie refuse? She did not refuse. So it was settled. Kusuma would go to Colombo with us. Mala raced to the back of the house. Kusuma was sweeping the garden.

"You're coming with us to Colombo! You're coming with us!" Mala jumped up and down. She was mad with joy.

Kusuma stood where she was, quite still.

"You're coming to Colombo! To Colombo!"

Kusuma stared. Then all at once she understood. She smiled. A little dimple appeared for a moment. I had never seen that dimple before; I never saw it again. Her teeth were very small like gleaming grains of polished rice. And all the stars in the sky tumbled right into her great black eyes.

We were to go to Colombo the following week. The day before we left, Mala and I went over to Big Auntie's with the two bottles of honey that she had wanted. We were to leave for Colombo by the train the next morning. As we stepped on to the veranda we could hear Big Auntie's angry voice from inside.

"Aren't you thoroughly ashamed, girl? You eat a mountain of rice every day. Yet you steal! Greedy, disgusting, filthy girl! *Chee! Chee!*"

Salpi said something but we couldn't hear her very clearly. Thoroughly curious now, we went into the pantry where all the noise was. The moment Big Auntie saw us she said angrily, "Kusuma is not going to Colombo. She's not going. Don't I give her enough to eat? Do you know what she's been doing? Quietly eating my oil cakes. They were here in this airtight tin. I caught her stealing — caught her red-handed!"

It was true, Kusuma was clutching a cake in her hand. She stared at the floor.

"Half the cakes have been eaten! She's been stuffing herself these last two-three days. The greedy thing! Mala, you've been spoiling her with all this talk of Colombo — all these lions and zebras. She's getting quite disobedient. No Colombo for her, no new cloth and jacket. I give and give and give and is this my reward? This creature steals my cakes! Now what shall I do?"

"You can make some more, Big Auntie," said Mala timidly. "Look, we've brought you some really fine honey." She held out the bottles eagerly.

Big Auntie ignored the bottles. "Make some more! Oh! It's easy for you to talk! Will you make them for me? This fine young lady hopes to go to Colombo. And I'm to sweat over a fire making more cakes to replace those she's gobbled up! Oh, no! The karmic law is my constant guide. No Colombo, no zebras and kangaroos for this creature here. She'll stay behind and help to make more cakes!"

Kusuma didn't look up, didn't utter a word. The cake held tight in her clenched fist crumbled and the bits fell on the floor. Mala and I left quietly a few minutes later. We could still hear Big Auntie shouting at Kusuma. Tears of disappointment were streaming down Mala's cheeks; yet Kusuma hadn't shed even a single tear.

We saw her in the garden the next morning as we walked past Big Auntie's house to the railway station. Mala tried to speak to her but she ran inside. Mother said, "Now, Mala, leave her alone. You'll only make Big Auntie angrier. It was very wrong of her to steal. She has to be punished."

"Big Auntie's always talking about giving but she's not going to give Kusuma even a New Year present. And Kusuma isn't going to get any cakes, biscuits or sweets! Big Auntie is very mean!"

"Enough, Mala, enough. You talk far too much! Kusuma has stolen. She has to be punished. I agree completely with Big Auntie," said Father severely. Mala pouted. She was glum all the way to Colombo. But when we arrived at Fair Auntie's, we found that our cousin Leela had come down from Kandy and then Mala forgot all about Kusuma.

After the cake incident, Big Auntie kept Kusuma very busy; she was always cleaning, polishing, sweeping or crocheting. There was little time for play.

In the months that followed I too began to be increasingly busy. At the end of the year, I sat for my first public examination and passed. After that, I went to live with Fair Auntie in Colombo and went to the university there.

I still spent my holidays in Payagala — that small dull town! I remember that last long vacation in my final year at the university very well. Big Auntie was just the same — still full of *shradda*, still busy collecting meritorious acts. But there was now about her an air of relaxation! The air of someone who could rest a bit after a hard life of meritorious toil and labour. Big Auntie knew that she was still a long way from nirvana but she was in no special hurry to get there. She had no objection to remaining in *samsara* for a couple of eons or so, and she was determined to spend those eons as comfortably as possible. She had always been a very practical woman.

A week before my vacation ended we were all invited to a big chanting and alms-giving at her house. Big Auntie's chantings and alms-givings were always a great success. Everyone enjoyed themselves. For at least two days before, the house was full of people, bustle, talk, laughter, the smell of food. There was friendliness and good humour everywhere. This chanting and alms-giving was to be a really grand affair. Twenty-five monks had been invited. Kusuma, who was very artistic, was helping with the decoration of the chanting pavilion. I watched her as she worked. She was at this time about nineteen — tall, slender, light-skinned. Her hair was tied back in a big knot at the nape of her neck. Her face was fuller, rounder but her eyes were as huge as ever. She moved quickly, lightly. And then all at once I realized that Kusuma was a very beautiful woman. So I looked at her often. So did Big Auntie, but for very different reasons. During a chanting and alms-giving there were a lot of young men around. Big Auntie took her responsibilities very seriously. Seeing that everyone behaved in the proper way was the most serious of these responsibilities. Kusuma, in particular, was a special responsibility.

Kusuma wasn't even in the least bit frivolous. Salpi was quite old now, and Kusuma was beginning to have an increasingly important place in Big Auntie's household. She valued that importance very much. She moved gracefully but efficiently from kitchen to veranda, supervising, organizing, advising. One young man in particular was very willing to obey her instructions and orders. He always managed to find work where she was likely to be. If Kusuma was in the kitchen, he was there too, eager to cut, chop, sift or pound. If she was in the sitting-room, now cleared for the chanting pavilion, there he was eager to hammer in nails, paste paper, move tables and chairs. Kusuma spoke to him very briskly, sometimes even severely. There was never the slightest softness in her voice or face. But once I saw her look around as if searching for someone. She looked anxious. Then she spotted him among all the other young men and smiled, a quick, tiny smile. Big Auntie did not see that smile, but I did. I asked Mala who he was. "Ah, that's Piyadasa. He works in Martin Mudalali's shop." I looked at him again. He was tall and light-skinned and had a kind face. I liked him.

On the night of the chant, the twenty-five monks arrived in all their yellow-robed splendour, and took their places in the white pavilion. Its walls were made of cutwork paper; its canopy a dazzling white cloth. If the monks, who were seated inside the pavilion, looked up, they would have seen that the canopy had little bunches of young coconut leaves hanging from it at intervals. They had been placed there by Kusuma.

We sat around the pavilion on mats and listened to the monks chanting the sacred texts. I looked around me and noticed Piyadasa seated behind Kusuma. They were right at the back of the room. Big Auntie, who was the chief supporter of the temple and donor of everything, sat by herself on a special little mat right in front. She held her clasped hands high, almost at forehead level. She was the picture of perfect *shradda* and we all admired her greatly.

After the Great Chant, I went off to bed. Big Auntie sat listening to the chanting all night, I was told. This was nothing less than we expected. Yet she was the most energetic of us all the next morning. After the morning meal, the chief monk preached a short sermon. I still remember that sermon very well. It was on *danaparamita*, the perfection of giving. We had heard lots of Buddha's rebirth stories on the perfection of giving before: the story of Vessantara, of Siri Sanghabo, and of course the story of the little self-sacrificing hare whose image God Sakra placed high up in the bright moon for all to see. These stories we all knew. But not the story the chief monk told us that morning; this was new to us.

"Good people," he began, "of the ten perfections no one perfection is better than another. All these ten equal perfections reside in the Buddha, brighter than a thousand suns. Bearing this in mind, today I shall discourse on the perfection of giving. The perfection of giving shows itself in one key way: in generosity. Giving of alms is generosity. And those who seek the Supreme Goal must ceaselessly practise such generosity. Our good Payagala Hamine and all you others who have participated in this ceremony have shown your devotion to the Doctrine by your liberality and by your presence here. Yet, hard is the way to Enlightenment. Listen to this:

"Once a *bodisathva* was born a king, Manicuda by name. He was compassionate, generous, a giver and donor of all things. Being so, Manicuda wished to perform the great sacrifice, *nirargada*. Various heretics, Brahmins, mendicants, beggars, princes gathered for the great sacrifice. The *bodisathva*, Manicuda, addressed the assembly: 'Sirs, I wish to perform the great sacrifice, *nirargada*, at which no doors are closed, no living being killed. Accept with minds full of sympathy these sacrificial gifts.' And gifts were given to all those who came to suit their desires. Then, on the twentieth day, at sunrise, Sakra, the lord of all the gods, wishing to test the *bodisathva*, took the form of a terrible demon and arose suddenly from the great sacrificial fire. He cried out, 'Fortunate and compassionate lord, deliver me who suffer severe pain by a quick gift of food.'

"'Fear not, fear not, dear one, here is as much food as you desire.'

"'It is not this kind of food I eat, great king, but the flesh and blood of the newly killed.'

"'The kind of food you eat, dear one, cannot be had without injury to others. I abstain from killing. Therefore, eat my flesh and drink my blood to your content. Today, giving away my flesh and blood, I shall place my foot on the head of Mara. Thus will I delight the whole world that yearns for liberation.'

"As the *bodisathva* spoke, the whole earth trembled like a boat in the ocean. Gods, demons and deities, hearing of that wonderful gift, were alike spellbound.

"Taking a knife, the *bodisathva* opened a vein in his brow. The demon drank, quenching his thirst. The *bodisathva* filled with delight, next cut off his flesh and gave it to the demon to eat. And he thought,

'My wealth has been fruitful, my flesh, my blood, my life has been fruitful.'

"As they read his thoughts, the gods assembled in the air cried aloud with joy. Sakra assumed his own form saying, 'Great king, I am Sakra. What do you wish to gain by this deed, by this most strenuous effort?'

"The *bodisathva* replied, 'Kausika, by this gift I do not wish to be a Sakra, a Mara or a Brahma or gain sovereignty over the universe or birth in the heavens. But by this deed may I attain perfect Enlightenment to release the unreleased, to console the unconsoled, to liberate the unliberated. This is my wish.'

"This, good people is *danaparamita*, the perfection of giving."

The monk stopped. The sermon was over. For a moment we were all silent. Then people stirred, joints cracked, and Big Auntie with hands clasped high above her head cried out in a voice trembling with *shradda*, "*Sadhu! Sadhu! Sadhu!*" All who were there took up the cry. The monks bowed their heads and gazed steadfastly at their fans. After giving the people his blessing, the chief monk, followed by the others, left.

Big Auntie, her face beaming, came up to Mother and Small Auntie.

"This is the most successful chanting and alms-giving I've ever given — everything went off beautifully! Did you notice how Mrs. Welikala was eyeing the pavilion? It's ten times nicer than hers!"

Small Auntie laughed. "She asked me who had made it and where we had got all that white paper from. I muttered something, but didn't tell."

Both aunts laughed gleefully, almost like little girls.

Two days later, when I arrived home after a sea-bath, I found Big Auntie, Small Auntie, Mother and Mala all seated on the veranda talking. It seemed a very serious conversation. Big Auntie looked agitated, angry.

"Kusuma wants to marry Piyadasa!" Mala burst out when she saw me.

"Good idea!" I said approvingly.

Big Auntie stared at me as if I had suddenly turned into a serpent. "Kusuma, marry Piyadasa?" she exploded.

"What's wrong with that?" I really couldn't see what all the fuss was about.

"That's what I thought too," said Mala boldly. Mala had just got engaged to our second cousin, Nihal, and felt that everyone should be encouraged to marry as quickly as possible.

We both looked at Big Auntie. In spite of being a final year student at the university, I felt a bit afraid. Big Auntie's chest heaved, her lips trembled, her eyes seemed to shoot sparks of fire.

"The selfishness — the ingratitude of — everybody. After all I've — after all I've done. . . ."

Small Auntie said, "You people — you young people these days don't think of anything serious. Only your own selfish desires matter. Do you ever think of your duty?" She spoke very severely.

"Lust, lust, lust, they're all filled with lust. When I think of what I've done for that girl! She was like a wild animal when she came to me. Covered with sores and lice! I cleaned her, fed her, clothed her, civilized her . . . Piyadasa came to me and said he wanted to marry her . . . said she was willing. I couldn't believe it . . . to do this thing behind my back!"

Big Auntie's chest began to heave again.

I said, "Now, Big Auntie, don't be angry with me, but they haven't done anything behind your back. Piyadasa came and asked you, didn't he? They haven't run away or anything. As Freud says. . . ."

"Mahinda, what do you know about these things! After you went to that university, your head is stuffed full of useless foreign ideas. Who is this Freud, ah? Who is this Marx you're now always trying to talk about? What do these foreigners know of our ancient Sinhalese culture? I've given Kusuma so much! I've been a mother to her. Is it too much to ask for a little gratitude in return!"

"It's her duty to stay with Auntie. Big Auntie didn't bring her up for nothing!" said Mother.

"But she says Piyadasa and she will live close to Big Auntie. She says she'll continue to work for Big Auntie," argued Mala.

"I know what those promises are worth!" Big Auntie sounded very sour.

"Will Kusuma have to live with Big Auntie forever then?" asked Mala.

"Why not?" snapped Small Auntie. "Much better for her to stay with Big Auntie than go off with that Piyadasa and have ten children!"

"I'm not selfish. I'll arrange a marriage for Kusuma to the right person at the right time. But she can't marry Piyadasa." Big Auntie was very firm about that.

"Arrange a marriage for her! No wonder she's so selfish. You've spoilt her thoroughly, Sister," said Small Auntie.

"I'm going to ask Martin Mudalali to send Piyadasa away to his brother's shop in Galle. I've done a lot for Martin Mudalali. That man has a lot of respect for me."

"What if Kusuma runs away?" I asked.

"She'll never do that," said Mala. "She's very loyal to Big Auntie."

"Loyal! Fine loyalty!" snapped Big Auntie.

Kusuma did not run away. She continued to live in Big Auntie's household exactly as before. After a few months, Big Auntie forgot all about the Piyadasa incident. He eventually married a girl in Galle and, as far as we knew, never even visited Payagala again. Kusuma, of course, never married. I never heard Big Auntie talk about arranging a marriage for her again. But she gave over the running of the house entirely to Kusuma. This left her free to study Higher Philosophy. It was Kusuma who arranged for the sale of all garden produce like coconuts and yams. It was Kusuma who bought all the necessities for the household. It was Kusuma who organized all the chanting ceremonies and the alms-givings. She became almost as keen as Big Auntie in the performance of such duties. They seemed to give her an ever-increasing pleasure. She talked a lot about how the accumulation of merit would give a person a better life in the future. She often said that she must have been very wicked in a past life and was determined to be better in this, her present one. Big Auntie was very pleased with her. Small Auntie began to be almost jealous.

I was in Payagala for a few weeks before leaving to study further at London University. "Mahinda," said Small Auntie, "I think Big Auntie gives Kusuma too much to do in the house. That woman is more the mistress of the house than Big Auntie herself. You should listen to her talking! I don't like the way she talks to me! She's turned into a very bossy woman. But Big Auntie listens to everything she says and does everything the way she wants it done. I don't like it."

It was true that Kusuma occupied a very special place in Big Auntie's household. It was true that she spoke to us all as if she were our equal. There was nothing menial about Kusuma. But I didn't see why she should be menial. And I told Small Auntie so.

"You understand nothing, Mahinda, for all your book learning," said Small Auntie. She sounded a bit annoyed. But since this is what everybody at home had always been telling me for a long time, I took no notice. I just smiled as I now always did, when they talked to me like that.

It was a very long time before I returned home again. Many things had happened during my absence. Big Auntie had a stroke which paralyzed both her legs. She now used a wheelchair. After Small Auntie's death of a heart attack, Mother had sold our house and gone to live with Mala in Kandy. Mala urged me to go and see Big Auntie, who still lived in Payagala. "Kusuma looks after her very well — Big Auntie is so lucky to have her — but she's very lonely. I haven't been to Payagala for over a year. I'm tied to the house with all these children."

"Yes, yes, go, Mahinda," said Mother. "I went to see her last year when I was in Colombo, but you know how difficult travelling is these days. The trains are jam-packed. And I'm too old to knock about now. Go, Mahinda, she'll be so happy to see you. She's very fond of you."

Big Auntie's house was still the same. The garden looked flourishing. The coconut trees were loaded with nuts, the mango trees with fruit. The orchids just beside the veranda were all blooming. Big Auntie was in her wheelchair on the veranda. She saw me, tried to speak, but couldn't. Her face quivered. I went up to her and took her hand. She held it tightly. Her hair was completely white, the skin of her neck and arms hung down in loose folds. In the years I'd been away, she had shrunk into an old, old woman.

"I thought I'd never see you again, *putha*," she said at last. Her voice was all quavery. "When did you return?"

"About three weeks ago. Payagala is exactly the same." We talked for a bit. I gave her news of Mother and Mala. She listened. There was a pause. I said, "So, tell me what you've been doing all these years, Big Auntie."

She brightened up. She told me she'd bought half an acre of land next to the temple grounds and had built a new preaching hall there. Kusuma had paid for the whitewashing with the money she earned from crocheting table-mats and pillow lace.

"She's a good girl — doesn't spend her money on clothes and powder like some women. Her one aim in life is to do meritorious acts."

"Because she wants to be born a rich woman in her next life?" I asked, smiling.

"What's wrong with that? We all want to better ourselves, don't we?"

I couldn't argue with that. "Well, what other good deeds has Kusuma done?" I asked, mainly to soothe Big Auntie, who was now looking troubled again.

She said that two years ago Kusuma had donated a magnificent brass lamp to the temple. Big Auntie had wanted to contribute something towards it but Kusuma had refused very firmly. The merit from this act had to be hers and hers alone; she didn't want to share it with anyone.

"You must be very proud of all the good things Kusuma's been doing. You brought her up, so the credit is all yours."

"Yes," she said quietly. She looked down at her hands. I felt something was wrong.

"Aren't you happy with Kusuma, Big Auntie?"

"Yes, yes, I am, Mahinda. Very happy. It's a great joy for me to see how good she is." There was a pause. "Kusuma — Kusuma is building a new shrine-room."

"Kusuma building a shrine-room! Kusuma! But where does she get the money from?" I asked, quite thunderstruck.

"She gets some money from the sale of her table-mats and pillow lace. Then there's the coconut money."

"But the coconuts belong to you?"

"I asked her to use — to use the money," said Big Auntie uncomfortably.

We were silent. I looked around. I could see into the sitting-room from where I was. It seemed strangely bare. Something was missing. Suddenly it came to me. Big Auntie's antique ebony furniture!

"What has happened to your ebony furniture?"

Big Auntie looked even more uncomfortable. "I asked Kusuma to sell it — to sell it for — for the shrine-room."

"But Big Auntie, that — that furniture — you loved that furniture! You said you'd never sell it." In fact, she had always said that the furniture was for me because it had belonged to my grandfather. I wondered whether she remembered. I looked at her. She was twisting her hands nervously. "Kusuma has been like a daughter to me. She does everything for me."

"Where is Kusuma?"

"She's at the temple. She goes every day to see how the building is going on. Don't say anything — don't scold her, Mahinda. She's like my daughter. Her one desire in life is to build that shrine-room."

"But at your expense! Did you really want to sell that furniture?"

Big Auntie began to weep. "That furniture was my father's. I wanted you to have it."

I had never seen Big Auntie weep before. Great rivers of tears streamed down her shrunken cheeks. I noticed she wasn't wearing her ruby earrings. I didn't need to ask what had happened to them. I supposed all Big Auntie's jewellery would be gradually sold to pay for the shrine-room and other meritorious acts.

"I don't want the furniture. I live in a tiny two-roomed flat in London, the size of your sitting-room. What could I do with ebony furniture there?"

"I don't want to cling to my possessions. But that ebony furniture was my father's. I didn't want to sell it."

"Never mind, never mind, Big Auntie. Building a shrine-room is a very good thing, a very meritorious act." It seemed strange to be talking like that. But I couldn't really console Big Auntie, though she stopped weeping.

It was almost lunch-time when Kusuma returned from the temple. She was not at all pleased to see me. I could see that. She was now a middle-aged woman — broad, strong, determined, hard. Lunch was served almost immediately. I wheeled Big Auntie's chair to the dining-table. Big Auntie had loved good food in the old days. I looked at the rice, the coconut *sambol* and the bit of dried fish on the table. Kusuma stared at me defiantly, as if daring me to criticize. I was silent. Big Auntie said, "If only I'd known you were coming, *putha*! I'd somehow have got some seer fish and prawns for you. You used to like them so much!"

"Now I like dried fish better than anything else," I said, giving her a bright, false smile.

It was a very silent meal. I wondered whether I should tell Mother and Mala about Big Auntie's plight. But what good would it do? It was impossible for Big Auntie to live in Kandy. There was no room for her in Mala's house. And who would look after her? I just could not see Kusuma living in Mala's household.

As Kusuma was clearing away the dishes and plates I said, "So, Kusuma, I hear you're building a shrine-room. It must be a very expensive business."

Big Auntie looked at me pleadingly, fearfully.

Kusuma glared at me. "I have found the money for it. It's a very meritorious deed. No one should interfere with such a good thing."

"When will it be completed?"

"The building will be complete in about a month's time. But I need more money for the image and the wall-paintings inside. My name will be inscribed outside because I am the donor," she said smiling, proudly, for the first time. "Would you like to donate something, Mahinda Mahattaya?" she asked.

I was surprised. Big Auntie looked at me appealingly. I pulled out my purse and gave her fifty rupees. She took it eagerly and put the notes into her purse.

I wheeled Big Auntie back to the veranda. "Tell me about London, *putha*. Is it a big city? England must be a very advanced country, no? Who cooks for you?"

She laughed when I told her that I cooked for myself.

"Fine meals you must be cooking! No wonder you look so thin. So why don't you get yourself a wife? Then she can cook for you."

I ignored these suggestions and got up saying I had to leave. Her face changed. "*Arre, putha*, what's the hurry? Stay the night, stay the night."

I said I couldn't. I had to be in Colombo for a lecture at the university that evening. And I'd promised Mother to be in Kandy the next day.

Big Auntie gave a little sigh. "When shall I see you again, *putha*? Next time you come, I'll be dead."

"Don't talk like that! Next time I see you, you'll be on your feet and running this house yourself!" But neither of us believed in that extravagant lie even for a second.

She tried to smile, then said, "No, I'll die in this wheelchair. It's my karma. But I'm very lucky to have Kusuma — she's like my own daughter. It's my karma," she repeated.

I said goodbye. She clung to my hand and kissed it. "Come and see me again before you leave, *putha, Tun sarane Pihitai!*" And she said once again, "It's my karma." A commonplace, almost meaningless phrase mouthed by so many. And yet, as I looked back for one last wave, there seemed to be a truth in it — a truth reflected in that heavy, sullen woman standing in the doorway, so like the other feebly waving a loose-skinned hand.

Zulfikar Ghose

The Marble Dome

It was Friday and the Sharif family was just finishing lunch when the call to prayer from the nearby mosque burst into the room. The priest's voice uttered the melodious Arabic over the powerful loud-speakers attached to one of the minarets, not reciting the words in a mellifluous intonation but expressing them in a combative, challenging tone as if the populace had fallen into a deep sleep and needed to be woken up. The high, ear-splitting amplification made the voice sound harshly aggressive.

Murad, the thirteen-year-old son, was the first to spring up from the table. He abandoned a half-eaten mango and ran to his room where he first quickly closed the window and drew the thick curtain across it. Next, he leaped towards the air conditioner and switched it on high so that the room sounded as if it were the interior of an old propeller-driven aircraft. A quick left turn and two rapid strides brought him to his stereo system. He jabbed at the power button and thrust a tape of rock music into the cassette player. Sealing his ears with headphones, he sat back comfortably in an easy chair, looking briefly at the geometry homework lying on his small desk that he had been naive enough to think he could work on uninterrupted on a Friday afternoon, and closed his eyes. He leaned his head back and let the music relieve the irritation that sprang in him so acutely each time the priest's voice burst from the loudspeakers that he became incapable of studying or performing any valuable activity.

Parvez Sharif had risen from the table at the same time as his son, though he had not moved with Murad's speed. Wearily and sadly, he went about the house closing the windows and switching on the air conditioners. The priest's voice was still pounding upon the walls of the house and echoing through it when Parvez finally stifled it to a bearably low volume by switching on the VCR in his bedroom. The picture that appeared on the monitor at the foot of the bed in which Parvez comfortably arranged himself showed a man seated at a desk speaking a precisely enunciated French to an attractive female secretary and then cut to the face of another man who repeated certain words spoken by the first man. It was a language tape. By letting the French words come loudly at him, Parvez concentrated on the vocabulary, so that he could gain a superior command of the foreign language to help in his export business, and repeating the words aloud he succeeded in distracting himself from the high-pitched sounds from the loudspeakers.

Fatimah had remained at the table when her husband and son, responding as usual to the suddenly violent bursting into the house of the priest's voice by seeking their own auditory distraction, had abandoned their unfinished lunch. She continued to eat her mango. Though the call to prayer boomed insistently into the room in spite of the air conditioner's throbbing whine, she sat determined not to hear it. She deliberately listened to the priest's high-pitched voice so that she would not hear it, just as a person stares hard at an unpleasant sight in order not to see it or chews with slow deliberation before a zealous host a mouthful of food the taste of which disgusts him.

She picked up a second mango and began to slice it slowly, her head bowed over the plate, her ears fixed on the priest's shrieking call. She could hear that Razia, the maid servant, had begun washing up the dishes in the kitchen. There was a clattering of cutlery under the splashing water, and Razia seemed to be furiously making a succession of noisy movements, knocking the lids of the aluminium pans against the sink after she had dropped the rinsed cutlery onto the draining board. Fatimah smiled as she heard poor Razia's efforts to escape the priest's piercing voice which was louder in the kitchen than elsewhere in the house. She herself could not, whatever method she tried, escape from the voice and abandoned the futile attempt to force herself to listen to it in order not to hear it.

She had already instructed Razia to vacuum the carpet in the sitting room in preparation for that evening's party, but decided to do so herself. Quickly, she brought out the Hoover, plugged it in and switched it on the higher of its two settings although the carpet had little dirt on it and the quieter lower setting would have been more than adequate. Fatimah kept working with the Hoover until there was a brief silence from the loudspeakers on the mosque.

Then began the sermon. Fatimah put away the Hoover and went to the kitchen where Razia was drying the cutlery. She could not help hearing the priest's voice and remarking that he had chosen as his subject the evil influence of the West. He had launched into a lurid description of sinful women who flaunted their naked bodies on the cinema screen. His voice was bursting with accusatory anger at the local population which rented videos of foreign films. The video stores should be closed, their contents destroyed, and whoever undertook this holy task would go to heaven. The priest's tone reminded Fatimah of a similarly brutally charged voice but she could not remember whose.

She spoke to Razia about the arrangements for the evening and asked her to remind the gardener to cut an assortment of flowers from the garden so that she could prepare a bouquet to place at the centre of the long table from where the drinks and the food would be served. And Razia must not forget to starch and iron the beige linen cloth for the table. Razia nodded her head and said something that was inaudible over the sermon. Fatimah left the kitchen. The priest was now launched on an attack against people who broke the prohibition against drink.

Fatimah went to the bedroom. Just as she entered and was closing the door behind her she remembered what that brutally charged tone of the priest's voice had reminded her of. She had recently seen a documentary on television about the rise of a white supremacist party in South Africa. Its leader, standing in front of a flag that had upon it a symbol that resembled the swastika, spat out angry words at the microphone. The amplified flow of his violent speech had the crowd of his followers roaring for the blood of anyone who disagreed with their raving leader's ideas.

The TV monitor at the foot of the bed showed a man summarizing a vocabulary related to accountancy. Parvez had fallen asleep. Fatimah was amused to see that though he seemed to have fallen into a deep sleep his lips were silently forming the words, repeating them after the man on the monitor. She climbed into the bed and lay next to her husband. She turned on her side, pressing her ear against the pillow. Placing a hand over the other ear, she too tried to go to sleep.

They woke to a loud static from the TV monitor. The tape had run out and was being rewound in the VCR. Parvez switched off the sound. There was a nearly total silence in the room. The sermon had ended some time earlier. Fatimah went to ask Razia to make tea, but walking down the passage towards the kitchen she saw the maid in the utility room ironing the table cloth, and decided to make the tea herself.

Murad joined his parents for tea at the kitchen table. He said that some senior boys at his school had petitioned the headmaster to let them use a classroom on Fridays and other holidays so that they could study without being disturbed. Parvez doubted if the headmaster would be allowed to open the school on a Friday. Fatimah suggested that the parents should get together and petition the government. It had become so impossible for children to study.

After tea, Parvez went for his daily walk in the neighbourhood park. It was a small oval-shaped park with a brick path laid out like the figure eight. Several men and women were walking on the path in a staggered line, in the same direction as if by common consent. Parvez gradually warmed up to his brisk stride. Each complete circuit of the figure eight was half a mile in length and he went round five or six times daily. As he turned at the top round bend of the path, he faced the direction of his own house (at that distance a quarter of a mile away) lost behind a line of poplars in a nearby street. Beyond it rose the magnificent red sandstone wall of the mosque crowned by a white marble dome.

Light from the late afternoon sun fell unobstructed upon the mosque and seemed to make the sandstone throb with pinpricks of light. The large marble dome and the smaller domes on the four minarets were dazzlingly white against the blue sky. The top part of the arch framing the entrance could be seen above the poplars. The border of yellow glazed tiles with the blue calligraphic pattern could be distinguished from where Parvez walked, almost half a mile away, the light that afternoon being miraculously free of pollution.

The beautiful curvature of the large dome caught the light in a silvery glow just as Parvez, walking on along the bend, was about to face away from the mosque. Involuntarily, he stopped, and stared amazedly at what seemed almost a revelation of perfect beauty. The two outer curving lines of the dome so caught the light that they looked like mirrored crescents illuminating two ends of a globe. A couple of people walked past Parvez and looked at the direction in which he stared and fleetingly wondered what was so curious. A curve created out of slabs of marble, suspended in the air as a brilliant line of light against an unpolluted sky: in this rare moment of time and in this fragment of space, man and nature had combined to create an image that made one's blood leap to the brain.

Parvez began to walk away but stopped again. The smaller domes struck him as even more perfect in their miniaturized rendering of the classical curve which had been shaped by centuries of culture. He was momentarily filled with a great happiness. Taking a deep breath as if more profoundly to savour the thrill pulsing within his blood, he again began to walk away but just then saw what he had hitherto unconsciously excluded from his vision — the four large loudspeakers attached to the front right minaret. The lovely vertical grace of the minaret was transformed into an obscenity by the black tumorous projections just below the marble dome which, once noticed, interfered with, and then negated, one's aesthetic contemplation of the curving marble dome.

He glanced away from the minaret with the speakers and briefly fixed his eyes on the large central dome, and, holding the image of its perfection in his mind, continued his walk. His breath came easily as he marched along filled with a sense of exhilaration. He recalled images of Hindu and Buddhist temples. The gaudy riot of idols in the former possessed a sensuous charm while the figure of the Buddha in the latter always evoked an awed respect. He remembered too the power of the great European cathedrals that made one feel so humble in the presence of God's majesty that the vast Gothic structures so compellingly suggested. It was pure theatre, with the organ, the enchanting choir and the priests dressed in magnificent robes. But nothing in the cathedrals, nor in the temples, sent the sharp current of supreme delight that went racing through his veins as did the simple curving form of the large marble dome on the mosque next to his own house.

The gardener was squatting in front of the flower bed and cutting stalks of zinnias when Parvez returned home from his walk. He was still filled with the pleasure that the contemplation of the dome had aroused in him, and he praised the gardener for the handsome bouquet he was gathering. "Pomegranate flowers!" he exclaimed with enthusiastic approval, seeing the branches of the small green leaves and the deep orange-red blossoms that the gardener had placed in an earthen jar beside him.

Inside the house, Fatimah had spread the linen cloth over the table and was placing upon it a variety of crystal glasses, heaps of china plates (the cream-coloured ones with the gold border), and the silver cutlery. "Have you checked the ice?" she asked. She knew he did not need to, but it was her way of reminding him that he was responsible for seeing to the drinks, a reminder which was, of course, redundant but was expressed as part of the mechanical routine of preparing for a party. The gardener came in with a mass of flowers in his jar. Fatimah had readied three crystal bowls for them and taking the gardener's jar she began to distribute the flowers to the bowls in an arrangement that, when completed, looked like a large tiara with the pomegranate blossoms at the top centre of the pyramid shape.

Parvez waited until he had changed into his evening clothes and it was almost time for the guests to arrive before he brought out the bottles of liquor from where he kept them concealed in the utility room, behind the piled-up towels and sheets in the cupboard with the louvered doors. His supplier from the embassy of one of the Scandinavian countries used a laundryman to deliver the illicit stock, and the clean laundry therefore seemed the appropriate place behind which to keep the bottles. Parvez brought out six bottles of whisky and six other bottles of gin, vodka and vermouth. With a couple of dozen bottles of club soda and tonic water, as well as some of soft drinks, and the glinting array of china and silver, the table presented a most pleasing sight.

The guests began to arrive. The initial awkwardness of coping with the embarrassment of the earliest arrivals soon passed with more people coming in quick succession and it seemed that a most enjoyable party had been going on for a long time. There was a clinking of glasses. The silver forks tinkled against the china plates. A murmur of male voices was frequently pierced by the warm, rising soprano of women talking animatedly. Parvez listened to Zarina Kassim, fascinated as much by her rich voice as by her ideas while she related some developments in the commerce ministry in which she worked as an economics adviser. He heard her describe a forthcoming trade agreement with the European Community and interrupted the flow of her melodious voice only to state that such an agreement would be wonderful for the depressed southern region. "Oh, the whole country!" she remarked eagerly.

Across the room, Fatimah was mixing among the guests, and had paused to hear the novelist Sadiq Aslam describe some of his experiences on a tour of Latin America that he had recently made on a grant from an American foundation. He was in the middle of a story about meeting a Cuban poet in Mexico City. Admired the world over, the poet had been labelled a dangerous dissident in Cuba and thrown into jail. "He'd have been tortured to death for criticizing the dictator," Sadiq Aslam was saying, "if he hadn't been able to get out." And then Sadiq Aslam said something which Fatimah would remember afterwards. "Exile seems the fate of independent minds, for nationalism invariably becomes perverted to a tyranny."

All the guests had long arrived and the house was filled with the warmth of human voices engaged in serious conversation or idle chatter. Remarkably in the circumstances everyone heard the door bell ring. It was as if everyone had been listening for some telltale signal and receiving a distant pulsation of it had suddenly become silent for a moment to confirm it was not merely an imaginary sound. Some people resumed their conversation after hearing the bell ring. They presumed that a servant would answer the door and then summon Parvez to deal with the situation. Other guests remained silent a while longer and looked at Parvez and Fatimah, hoping to see from their faces that the bell had been rung only by some very late-arriving guest and that there was nothing to be apprehensive about. But the hosts both looked puzzled, if not also a little alarmed.

The shadow of a servant was noticed by some, going past the hall to the front door. A moment later, there was a very loud yell, almost a scream from the servant. Then a loud cry of "Allah-ho akbar!" shouted in unison by several voices burst through the rooms. Five men with white, tightly wound turbans on their heads, with the turban ends drawn across the face to below the eyes as a mask, came rushing through, brandishing cricket bats over their shoulders. The crowd of guests fell back, some stepping behind sofas and chairs, some moving closer to the walls as the five frenzied men, shouting verses from the Koran, dashed about wildly in the room. A few of the guests fell to the ground. There were cries from people who were stepped upon by the men jumping this way and that in their wild frenzy. Confusion, shouts and cries, interspersed with two or three screams, raged for three minutes until the men saw where the liquor bottles stood upon the table.

Two of the men leaped towards the table, brandishing the cricket bats like sabres in some sacrificial ceremony, and as if they performed a choreographed scene, the two simultaneously brought the cricket bats smashing down upon the bottles, one swinging down from his left shoulder and the other from his right, again and again, yelling loudly as they did so, sending the bottles crashing across the table and down the floor with what liquor they contained flying in the air and spilling to the ground.

The other three leaped wildly about the room pouncing upon the guests who held a glass of liquor in their hands and smashing the bats down upon their hands. Now there was panic and some of the guests began to run out of the house while some, with their hands bleeding or dangling limply, ran around screaming or looking completely stunned.

Just as the men had come, so they departed, in a fury of movement, and shouting aloud, "Allah-ho akbar!"

It was a long night for Parvez and Fatimah. An ambulance was sent for, the police were called. More saddened than angry, Parvez gave a statement to the police officer. He expected no action would be taken against the priests who employed young thugs to terrorize people who did not accept their fundamentalist views. The home of the owner of a video store had been set on fire a few months earlier by a similar group, and though there were witnesses the police did nothing. They did nothing when three young men charged into an art gallery waving butchers' knives in the air and slashed the canvases on which an artist had painted nudes.

All the guests had gone by the time Parvez completed his statement and the police officer left. Fatimah, severely shocked and then distraught, took a tranquillizer and went to bed. Parvez quietly roamed the deserted rooms, avoiding the sitting room where the carpet was covered with broken glass, soggy with spilled liquor and stained with blood. Finally, he switched off the lights, deciding to go to bed.

He noticed that it was nearly dawn outside and he stood at a window staring at the grey light. Without thinking of it, he found himself going out and walking to the park. Head bowed, he began to walk upon the brick path shaped in the figure eight. When he reached the top bend of the figure, he instinctively looked up in the direction of the mosque. The large dome and the minarets could just be discerned as grey silhouettes against the sky slowly filling with light. Parvez walked on, his head again bowed. It was a slow, pained walk, as if he were constitutionally incapable of proceeding but was compelled nevertheless to do so. His body felt heavy.

He arrived again at the top of the figure eight. Now what he saw created in his mind a moment's ecstasy that seemed timeless. The sun had risen and was precisely behind the large marble dome. An intense brightness seemed to be flooding up from behind the rear of the mosque. The large dome and the four minarets had never looked more perfectly correct in their proportions to one another. Quickly, the light was becoming more brilliant and a blueness was spreading in the sky. And quickly too the sun was climbing up. Suddenly, the left curve of the dome was strikingly lit up, and it looked as if a bright crescent had risen in the clear sky and for a moment all else seemed obliterated and there was only the perfect curving form of the crescent that shone in the sky.

But the sun moved higher and now the light caught the four loudspeakers on the front right minaret. The image of the crescent vanished from Parvez's mind and at that moment there was a sound in the air. "Phooh, phooh." Parvez knew the sound. It was the priest blowing his breath at the microphone before a moment later, as he was now beginning to do, shouting out the call to prayer. The loud, aggressive, almost brutal, tone of the priest's voice reminded him of an image he had seen in several films that contained a reference to a dark era in human history. It was the image of Nazi rallies where a mass of humanity responded with mindless uniformity to a voice that screamed at it from a loudspeaker.

Anita Desai

Winterscape

She stands with the baby in her arms in front of the refrigerator, and points at the pictures she has taped on its white enamel surface, each in turn, calling out the names of the people in the photographs. It is a game they play often to pass the time, the great stretches of time they spend alone together. The baby jabs his short pink finger at a photograph, and the mother cries, "That's Daddy, in his new car!" or "Susan and cousin Ted, on his first birthday!" and "Grandma by the Christmas tree!" All these pictures are as bright and festive as bits of tinsel or confetti. Everyone is smiling in them, and there are birthday cakes and Christmas trees, the shining chrome of new cars, bright green lawns and white houses. "Da-dee!" the baby shouts. "Soo-sun!" The bright colours make the baby smile. The mother is happy to play the game, and laughs: her baby is learning the names of all the members of the family; he is becoming a part of the family.

Then the baby reaches out and waves an ineffectual hand at a photograph that is almost entirely white, only a few shades of grey to bring out the shapes and figures in it. There are two, and both are draped in snow-white clothes which cover their shoulders, exposing only the backs of their heads which are white too, and they are standing beside the very same white refrigerator in the same white-painted kitchen, in front of a white-framed window. They are looking out of it, not at the camera but at the snow that is falling past the windowpanes, covering the leafless tree and the wooden fence and the ground outside, providing them with a white snowscape into which they seem nearly to have merged. Nearly.

The baby's pink finger jabs at the white photograph. The mother says nothing immediately: she seems silenced, as if she too has joined the two figures at the window and with them is looking out of the white kitchen into a white world. The photograph somehow calls for silence, creates silence, like snow.

The baby too drops his hand, lowers his head on his mother's shoulder, and yawns. Snow, silence and sleep: the white picture has filled him with sleep, he is overcome by it. His mother holds him and rocks him, swaying on her feet. She loves the feel of the baby's head on her shoulder; she tucks it under her chin protectively. She swivels around to the window as if she sees the two white figures there now, vanishing into the green dusk of a summer evening. She sings softly into the baby's dark hair: "Ma and Masi — Ma and Masi together."

"Two?" Beth turned her head on the pillow and stared at him over the top of her glasses, lowering the book she was reading to the rounded dome of her belly under the blue coverlet. *"Two* tickets? For *whom?"* because she knew Rakesh did not have a father, that his mother was a widow.

"For my mother and my aunt," he said, in a low, almost sullen voice, sitting on the edge of the bed in his pyjamas and twisting his fingers together. His back was turned to her, his shoulders stooped.

Because of the time difference, he had had to place the call to the village in India in the middle of the night.

"Your *aunt*?" Beth heard her own voice escalate. "Why do we have to pay for your aunt to visit us? Why does *she* have to visit us when the baby is born? I can't have so many guests in the house, Rakesh!"

He turned around towards her slowly, and she saw dark circles under his eyes. Another time they might have caused her to put her finger out to touch those big, bluish pouches, like bruises, but now she felt herself tense at the thought of not just one, but two strangers, foreigners, part of Rakesh's past, invading their house. She had already wished she had not allowed Rakesh to send for his mother to attend to the birth of their child. It had seemed an outlandish, archaic idea even when it was first suggested; now it was positively bizarre. "Why both of them? We only asked your mother," she insisted.

Rakesh was normally quick with his smile, his reassuring words, soft and comforting murmurs. He had seemed nervous ever since she became pregnant, more inclined to worry about what she took as a natural process. But she could see it was not that, it was something else that made him brood, silently, on the edge of the bed, the blue pouches hanging under his eyes, and his hands twisted.

"What's the matter?" she said sharply, and took off her glasses and turned over her book. "What's wrong?"

He roused himself to shake his head, attempted to smile, and failed. Then he lifted up his legs and lay down on the bed, beside her, turning to her with that same brooding expression, not really seeing her. He put out his hand and tried to stroke the hair at her temple. It annoyed her: he was so clearly about to make a request, a difficult request. She tensed, ready to refuse. He ought not to be asking anything of her in her condition. Two guests, two foreigners — at such a time. "Tell me," she demanded.

So he began to tell her. "They are both my mothers, Beth," he said. "I have two mothers."

There were three years between them and those seemed to have made all the difference. Asha was the first child in the family. So delighted was her father that it never crossed his mind she should have been a son. He tossed her up and caught her in his arms and put his face into her neck to make growling sounds that sent her into squeals of laughter. That she was fair-skinned, plump and had curly hair and bright black eyes all pleased him. He liked his wife to dress the child in frilly, flounced, flowered dresses and put ribbons in her hair. She was glad and relieved he was so pleased with his daughter: it could have been otherwise, but he said, "A pretty daughter is an ornament to the home."

So Asha grew up knowing she was an ornament, and a joy. She had no hesitation ever in asking for a toy or a sweet, in climbing onto her parents' laps or standing in the centre of a circle to sing or skip.

When Anu was born, three years later, it was different. Although her father bent over her and fondled her head and said nothing to express disappointment, disappointment was in the air. It swaddled baby Anu (no one even remembered her full name, the more majestic Annapurna), and among the first things she heard were the mutterings of the older people in the family who had no compunction about pronouncing their disappointment. And while her mother held her close and defended her against them, baby Anu knew she was in a weak position. So one might have thought, watching her grow. Although she stayed close to her elder sister, clinging to the hem of her dress, shadowing her, and Asha was pleased to have someone so entirely under her control, there remained something hesitant, nervous and tentative about Anu's steps, her movements and speech. Everything about her expressed diffidence.

While Asha proved a natural housekeeper and joined, with gusto, in the cooking, the washing, the sweeping, all those household tasks shared between the women, pinning her chunni back behind her ears, rolling up the sleeves of her kameez, and settling down to kneading the dough, or pounding spices, or rolling out chapatis with a fine vigour, Anu proved sadly incompetent. She managed to get her hand burnt when frying pakoras, took so long to grind chillies that her mother grew impatient and pushed her out of the way, and was too weak to haul up a full bucket of water from the well, needing to do it half a bucket at a time. When visitors filled the house and everything was in an uproar, Anu would try to slip away and make herself invisible and only return when summoned — to be scolded soundly for shirking work. "Look at your sister," she was always counselled, and she did, raising her eyes with timid admiration. Asha, used to her sister's ways, gave her a wink and slipped her one of the snacks or sweets she had missed. An understanding grew between them, strengthened by strand upon strand upon strand of complicity.

Later, sons were born to their parents, and the pressure, the tension in their relationships with their daughters was relieved. Good-naturedly, the father allowed both of them to go to school. "What is the harm?" he asked the elderly critics of this unusual move. "These days it is good for girls to be educated. One day, who knows, they may work in an office — or a bank!"

That certainly did not happen. Another generation would be born and raised before any girl in that Punjab village became an office clerk or a bank teller. Asha and Anu had a few years in the local government school where they wore blue cotton kameezes with white chunnis, and white gym shoes, and sat on benches learning the Punjabi alphabet and their numbers. Here the scales may well have tipped the other way, because Asha found the work ferociously difficult and grew hot and bothered as she tried to work out problems in addition and subtraction or to read her lessons from the tattered, illustrated textbooks, while Anu discovered an unexpected nimbleness of mind that skipped about the numbers with the agility of a young goat, and scampered through the letters quite friskily. Asha threw her sister exasperated looks but did not mind so much when Anu took over her homework and did it for her in her beautiful hand. Anu drew praise when she wrote essays on "The Cow" and "My Favourite Festival" — but, alas, the latter proved to be her swan song because at this point Asha turned fifteen and the family found her a bridegroom and married her off and Anu had to stay home from then on to help her mother.

Asha's bridegroom was a large man, not so young, but it did not matter because he owned so much land and cattle. He had a great handlebar moustache and a turban and Anu was terrified for Asha when she first saw him, but was later to find no cause for terror: he was a kindly, good-natured man who clearly adored his bright-eyed, quick-tongued, lively young wife and was generous to her and to her entire family. His voice was unexpectedly soft and melodious, and he often regaled his visitors, or a gathering in the village, with his songs. Asha — who had plenty of talents but not artistic ones — looked at him with admiration then, sitting back on her haunches and cupping her chin in her hands which were bedecked with the rings and bracelets he had given her.

They often asked Anu to come and stay with them. Asha found she was so accustomed to having her younger sister at her heels, she really could not do without her. She might have done, had she had children, but, though many were born to her, they were either stillborn or died soon after birth, none living for more than a few days. This created an emptiness in the big house so full of goods and comforts, and Asha grew querulous and plaintive, a kind of bitterness informing her every gesture and expression, while her husband became prone to depression which no one would have predicted earlier. Anu often came upon him seated in an armchair at the end of the veranda, or up on the flat roof of the house in the cool evenings, looking out with an expression of deep melancholy across his fields to the horizon where the white spire and the golden dome of the Sikh temple stood against the sky. He left the work on the farm to a trusted headman to supervise and became idle himself, exasperating Asha who tended to throw herself into every possible activity with determined vigour and thought a man should too.

After yet another miscarriage, Asha roused herself with a grim wilfulness to join in the preparation for Anu's wedding, arranged by the parents to a clerk in a neighbouring town, a sullen, silent young man with large teeth and large hands that he rubbed together all the time. Anu kept her face and her tears hidden throughout the wedding, as brides did, and Asha was both consoling and encouraging, as women were.

Unexpectedly, that unpromising young man who blinked through his spectacles and could scarcely croak one sentence at a time showed no hesitation whatsoever when it came to fathering a child. Nor did Anu, who was so slight of frame and mousy in manner, seem to be in any way handicapped as a woman or mother — her child was born easily, and it was a son. A round, black-haired, red-cheeked boy who roared lustily for his milk and thrashed out with his legs and grabbed with his hands, clearly meant for survival and success.

If Anu and her husband were astonished by him, it could scarcely have matched Asha and her husband's wonder. They were enthralled by the boy: he was the child of their dreams, their thwarted hopes and desires. Anu lay back and watched how Asha scooped Rakesh up into her large, soft arms, how she cradled and kissed him, then how her husband took him from her, wrapped in the candy pink wool shawl knitted by Asha, and crooned over him. She was touched and grateful for Asha's competence, as adept at handling the baby as in churning butter or making sweets. Anu stayed in bed, letting her sister fuss over both her and the baby — making Anu special milk and almond and jaggery drinks in tall metal tumblers, keeping the baby happy and content, massaging him with mustard oil, feeding him sips of sweetened milk from a silver shell, tickling him till he smiled.

Anu's husband looked on, awkwardly, too nervous to hold his own child: small creatures made him afraid; he never failed to kick a puppy or a kitten out of his way, fiercely. Anu rose from her bed occasionally to make a few tentative gestures of motherhood but soon relinquished them, one by one, first letting Asha feed the baby and dress him, then giving up attempts to nurse the boy and letting Asha take over the feeding.

At the first hint of illness — actually, the baby was teething which caused a tummy upset — Asha bundled him up in his blanket and took him home, promising, "I'll bring him back as soon as he is well. Now you go and rest, Anu, you haven't slept and you look sick yourself."

When Anu went to fetch him after a week, she came upon Asha's husband, sitting on that upright chair of his on the veranda, but now transformed. He had the baby on his knee and was hopping him up and down while singing a rhyme, and his eyes sparkled as vivaciously as the child's. Instead of taking her son from him, Anu held back, enjoying the scene. Noticing her at last, the large man in the turban beamed at her. "A prince!" he said, "and one day he will have all my fields, my cattle, the dairy, the cane-crushing factory, everything. He will grow up to be a prince!"

Rakesh's first birthday was to be celebrated at Asha's house — "We will do it in style," she said, revealing how little she thought Anu and her husband were capable of achieving it. Preparations went on for weeks beforehand. There was to be a feast for the whole village. A goat was to be slaughtered and roasted, and the women in the family were busy making sweets and delicacies with no expense spared: Asha's husband was seeing to that. He himself went out to shoot partridges for the festive dinner, setting out before dawn into the rippling grainfields and calling back to the women to have the fire ready for his return.

Those were his last words — to have the fire ready. "As if he knew," wept Asha's mother, "that it was the funeral pyre we would light." Apparently there had been an accident with the gun. It had gone off unexpectedly and the bullet had pierced his shoulder and a lung: he had bled to death. There were no birthday festivities for one-year-old Rakesh.

Knowing that the one thing that could comfort Asha was the presence of the baby in her arms, Anu refrained from suggesting she take him home. At first she had planned to leave the boy with her widowed sister for the first month of mourning, then drew it out to two and even three months. When her husband, taunted by his own family for his failure to establish himself as head of his household, ordered her to bring their son home, Anu surprised herself by answering, "Let him be. Asha needs him. We can have more sons for ourselves." Their house was empty and melancholy — it had always been a mean place, a narrow set of rooms in the bazaar, with no sunlight or air — but she sat in its gloom, stitching clothes for her rapidly growing son, a chunni drawn over her head, a picture of acceptance that her husband was not able to disturb, except briefly, with fits of violence.

After one of these, they would go and visit the boy, with gifts, and Rakesh came to look upon his parents as a visiting aunt and uncle, who offered him sweets and toys with a dumbly appeasing, appealing air. No one remembered when he started calling them Masi and Masa. Asha he already addressed as Ma: it was so clearly her role.

Anu had been confident other children would follow. She hoped for a daughter next time, somehow feeling a daughter might be more like her, and more likely to stay with her. But Rakesh had his second and third birthday in Asha's house, and there was no other child. Anu's husband looked discouraged now, and resentful, his own family turning into a chorus of mocking voices. He stayed away at work for long hours; there were rumours — quickly brought to Anu's attention — that he had taken to gambling, and drugs, and some even hinted at having seen him in quarters of the town where respectable people did not go. She was not too perturbed: their relationship was a furtive, nocturnal thing that never survived daylight. She was concerned, of course, when he began to look ill, to break out in boils and rashes, and come down with frequent fevers, and she nursed him in her usual bungling, tentative way. His family came to take over, criticizing her sharply for her failings as a nurse, but he only seemed to grow worse, and died shortly before Rakesh's fifth birthday. His family set up a loud lament and clearly blamed her for the way he had dwindled away in spite of their care. She packed her belongings — in the same tin trunk in which she had brought them as a bride, having added nothing more to them — and went to live with Asha — and the child.

In the dark, Beth found it was she who was stroking the hair at Rakesh's temple now, and he who lay stretched out with his hands folded on his chest and his eyes staring at the ceiling.

"Then the woman you call Ma — she is really your aunt?" Beth queried.

Rakesh gave a long sigh. "I always knew her as my mother."

"And your aunt is your real mother? When did they tell you?"

"I don't know," he admitted. "I grew up knowing it — perhaps people spoke of it in the village, but when you are small you don't question. You just accept."

"But didn't your *real* mother ever tell you, or try to take you away?"

"No!" he exclaimed. "That's just it, Beth. She never did — she had given me to her sister, out of love, out of sympathy when her husband died. She never tried to break up the relationship I had with her. It was out of love." He tried to explain again, "The love sisters feel."

Beth, unlike Rakesh, had a sister. Susan. She thought of her now, living with her jobless, worthless husband in a trailer somewhere in Manitoba with a string of children. The thought of handing over her child to her was so bizarre that it made her snort. "I know I couldn't give my baby to Susan for anything," she declared, removing her hand from his temple and placing it on her belly.

"You don't know, you can't say — what may happen, what things one may do —"

"*Of course* I know," she said, more loudly. "Nothing, no one, could make me do that. Give my baby away?" Her voice became shrill and he turned on his side, closing his eyes to show her he did not wish to continue the conversation.

She understood that gesture but she persisted. "But didn't they ever fight? Or disagree about the way you were brought up? Didn't they have different ideas of how to do that? You know, I've told Susan —"

He sighed again. "It was not like that. They understood each other. Ma looked after me — she cooked for me and fed me, made me sit down on a mat and sat in front of me and fed me with her own hands. And what a cook she is! Beth, you'll love —" he broke off, knowing he was going too far, growing foolish now. "And Masi," he recovered himself, "she took me by the hand to school. In the evening, she lit the lamp and made me show her my books. She helped me with my lessons — and I think learned with me. She is a reader, Beth, like you," he was able to say with greater confidence.

"But weren't they jealous of each other — of one for cooking for you and feeding you, and the other for sharing your lessons? Each was doing what the other didn't, after all."

He caught her hand, on the coverlet, to stop her talking. "It wasn't like that," he said again, and wished she would be silent so he could remember for himself that brick-walled courtyard in the village, the pump gushing out the sweet water from the tube well, the sounds of cattle stirring in the sheaves of fodder in the sheds, the can of frothing milk the dairyman brought to the door, the low earthen stove over which his mother — his aunt — stirred a pan in the smoky dimness of dawn, making him tea. The pigeons in the rafters, cooing, a feather drifting down —

"Well, I suppose I'll be seeing them both, then — and I'll find out for myself," Beth said, a bit grimly, and snapped off the light.

"Never heard of anything so daft," pronounced her mother, pouring out a cup of coffee for Beth who sat at her kitchen table with her elbows on its plastic cover and her chin cupped in her hands. Doris was still in her housecoat and slippers, going about her morning in the sunlit kitchen. Beth had come early.

When Beth did not reply, Doris planted her hands on the table and stared into her brooding face. "Well, isn't it?" she demanded. "Whoever heard of such a thing? Rakesh having two mothers! Why ever didn't he tell us before?"

"He told me about them both of course," Beth flared up, and began to stir her coffee. "He talked of them as his mother and aunt. I knew they were both widows, lived together, that's all."

Doris looked as if she had plenty more to say on the subject than that. She tightened the belt around her red-striped housecoat and sat down squarely across from Beth. "Looks as if he never told you who his mother was though, or his father. The real ones, I mean. I call that peculiar, Beth, pec-u-liar!"

Beth stirred resentfully. "I s'pose he hardly thinks of it that way — he was a baby when it happened. He says he grew up just accepting it. They *love* each other, he said."

Doris scratched at her head with one hand, rattled the coffee cup in its saucer with the other. "Two sisters loving each other — that much? That's what's so daft — who in her right mind would give away her baby to her sister just like that? I mean, would you hand yours over to Susan? And would Susan take it? I mean, as if it were a birthday present!"

"Oh, Mum!"

"Now you've spilt your coffee! Wait, I'll get a sponge. Don't get up. You're getting big, girl. You OK? You mustn't mind me."

"I'm OK, Mum, but now I'm going to have *two* women visiting. Rakesh's mum would be one thing, but two of 'em together — I don't know."

"That's what I say," Doris added quickly. "And all that expense — why's he sending them tickets? I thought they had money: he keeps talking about that farm as if they were landlords —"

"Oh, that's where he grew up, Mum. They sold it long ago — that's what paid for his education at McGill, you know. That *costs*."

"What — it cost them the whole farm? He's always talking about how big it was —"

"They sold it a bit at a time. They helped pay for our house, too, and then set up his practice."

"Hmm," said Doris, as she shook a cigarette out of a packet and put it in her mouth.

"Oh, Mum, I can't stand smoke now! It makes me nauseous — you know that —" Beth protested.

"Sorry, love," Doris said, and laid down the matchbox she had picked up but with the cigarette still between her lips. "I'm just worried about you — dealing with two Indian women — in your condition —"

"I guess they know about babies," Beth said hopefully.

"But do they know about Canada?" Doris came back smartly, as one who had learned. "And about the Canadian *winter*?"

They thought they did — from Rakesh's dutiful, although not very informative, letters over the years. After Rakesh had graduated from the local college, it was Asha who insisted he go abroad "for further studies." Anu would not have had the courage to suggest it, and had no money of her own to spend, but here was another instance of her sister's courage and boldness. Asha had seen all the bright young people of the village leave and told Anu, "He" — meaning her late husband — "wanted Rakesh to study abroad. 'We will give him the best education,' he had said, so I am only doing what he told me to." She tucked her widow's white chunni behind her ears and lifted her chin, looking proud. When Anu raised the matter of expense, she waved her hand — so competent at raising the boy, at running the farm, and now at handling the accounts. "We will sell some of the land. Where is the need for so much? Rakesh will never be a farmer," she said. So Rakesh began to apply to foreign universities, and although his two mothers felt tightness in their chests at the prospect of his leaving them, they also swelled with pride to think he might do so, the first in the family to leave the country "for further studies." When he had completed his studies — the two women selling off bits and pieces of the land to pay for them till there was nothing left but the old farmhouse — he wrote to tell them he had been offered jobs by several firms. They wiped their eyes with the corners of their chunnis, weeping for joy at his success and the sorrowful knowledge that he would not come back. Instead, they received letters about his achievements: his salary, his promotion, and with it the apartment in the city, then his own office and practice, photographs accompanying each as proof.

Then, one day, the photograph that left them speechless: it showed him standing with his arm around a girl, a blonde girl, at an office party. She was smiling. She had fair hair cut short and wore a green hairband and a green dress. Rakesh was beaming. He had grown rather fat, his stomach bulging out of a striped shirt, above a leather belt with a big buckle. He was also rather bald. The girl looked small and slim and young beside him. Rakesh did not tell them how old she was, what family she came from, what schooling she had had, when was the wedding, should they come, and other such particulars of importance to them. Rakesh, when he wrote, managed to avoid almost all such particulars, mentioning only that the wedding would be small, merely an official matter of registration at the town hall, they need not trouble to come — as they had ventured to suggest.

They were hurt. They tried to hide it from their neighbours as they went around with boxes of tinsel-spread sweets as gifts to celebrate the far-off occasion. So when the letter arrived announcing Beth's punctual pregnancy and the impending birth, they did not again make the mistake of tactful enquiries: Anu's letter stated with unaccustomed boldness their intention to travel to Canada and see their grandchild for themselves. That was her term — "our grandchild."

Yet it was with the greatest trepidation that they set out on this adventure. Everyone in the village was encouraging and supportive. Many of them had flown to the US, to Canada, to England, to visit their children abroad. It had become almost commonplace for the families to travel to New Delhi, catch a plane and fly off to some distant continent, bearing bundles and boxes full of the favourite pickles, chutneys and sweets of their far-flung progeny. Stories abounded of these goodies being confiscated on arrival at the airports, taken away by indignant customs officers to be burnt: "He asked me, 'What is *this*? What is *this*?' He had never seen mango pickle before, can you believe?" "He didn't know what is betel nut! 'Beetle? You are bringing in an insect?' he asked!" — and of being stranded at airports by great blizzards or lightning strikes by airline staff — "We were lucky we had taken our bedroll and could spread out on the floor and sleep" — and of course they vied with each other with reports of their sons' and daughters' palatial mansions, immense cars, stocked refrigerators, prodigies of shopping in the most extensive of department stores. They brought back with them electrical appliances, cosmetics, watches, these symbols of what was "foreign."

The two mothers had taken no part in this, saying, "We can get those here too," and contenting themselves by passing around the latest photographs of Rakesh and his wife and their home in Toronto. Now that they too were to join this great adventure, they became nervous — even Asha did. Young, travelled daughters and granddaughters of old friends came around to reassure them: "Auntie, it is not difficult at all! Just buy a ticket at the booth, put it in the slot, and step into the subway. It will take you where you like," or "Over there you won't need kerosene or coal for the stove, Auntie. You have only to switch on the stove, it will light by itself," or "You won't need to wash your clothes, Auntie. They have machines, you put everything in, with soap, it washes by itself." The two women wondered if these self-confident youngsters were pulling their legs: they were not reassured. Every piece of information, meant to help, threw them into greater agitation. They were convinced they would be swallowed up by the subway if they went out, or electrocuted at home if they stayed in. By the time the day of their departure came around, they were feverish with anxiety and sleeplessness. Anu would gladly have abandoned the plan — but Asha reminded her that Rakesh had sent them tickets, his first present to them after leaving home, how could they refuse?

It was ten years since Rakesh had seen his mothers, and he had forgotten how thinly they tended to dress, how unequipped they might be. Beth's first impression of them as they came out of the immigration control area, wheeling a trolley between them with their luggage precariously balanced on it, was of their wisps of widows' white clothing — muslin, clearly — and slippers flapping at their feet. Rakesh was embarrassed by their skimpy apparel, Beth unexpectedly moved. She had always thought of them as having so much; now her reaction was: they have so little!

She took them to the stores at once to fit them out with overcoats, gloves, mufflers — and woollen socks. They drew the line at shoes: they had never worn shoes, could not fit their feet into them, insisting on wearing their sandals with thick socks instead. She brought them back barely able to totter out of the car and up the drive, weighed down as they were by great duffle coats that kept their arms lifted from their sides, with their hands fitted into huge gloves, and with their heads almost invisible under the wrappings of woollen mufflers. Under it all, their white cotton kameezes hung out like rags of their past, sadly.

When Doris came around to visit them, she brought along all the spare blankets she had in her apartment, presciently. "Thought you'd be cold," she told them. "I went through the war in England, and I know what that's like, I can tell you. And it isn't half cold yet. Wait till it starts to snow." They smiled eagerly, in polite anticipation.

While Beth and Doris bustled about, "settling them in," Rakesh stood around, unexpectedly awkward and ill at ease. After the first ecstatic embrace and the deep breath of their lingering odour of the barnyard and woodsmoke and the old soft muslin of their clothing, their sparse hair, he felt himself in their way and didn't know quite what to do with himself or with them. It was Beth who made them tea and tested their English while Rakesh sat with his feet apart, cracking his knuckles and smiling somewhat vacantly.

At the table, it was different: his mothers unpacked all the foods they had brought along, tied up in small bundles or packed in small boxes, and coaxed him to eat, laughing as they remembered how he had pestered them for these as a child. To them, he was still that: a child, and now he ate, and a glistening look of remembrance covered his face like a film of oil on his fingers, but he also glanced sideways at Beth, guiltily, afraid of betraying any disloyalty to her. She wrinkled her nose slightly, put her hand on her belly and excused herself from eating on account of her pregnancy. They nodded sympathetically and promised to make special preparations for her.

On weekends, Beth insisted he take them out and show them the sights, and they dutifully allowed themselves to be led into his car, and then around museums, up radio towers and into department stores — but they tended to become carsick on these excursions, foot-weary in museums and confused in stores. They clearly preferred to stay in. That was painful, and the only way out of the boredom was to bring home videos and put them on. Then everyone could put their heads back and sleep, or pretend to sleep.

On weekdays, in desperation, Beth too took to switching on the television set, tuned to programmes she surmised were blandly innocent, and imagined they would sit together on the sofa and find amusement in the nature, travel and cooking programmes. Unfortunately these had a way of changing when her back was turned and she would return to find them in a state of shock from watching a torrid sex scene or violent battle taking place before their affronted and disbelieving eyes. They sat side by side with their feet dangling and their eyes screwed up, munching on their dentures with fear at the popping of guns, the exploding of bombs and grunting of naked bodies. Their relief when she suggested a break for tea was palpable. Once in the kitchen, the kettle whistling shrilly, cups standing ready with the threads of tea bags dangling out of them, they seemed reluctant to leave the sanctuary. The kitchen was their great joy, once they had got used to the shiny enamel and chrome and up-to-date gadgetry. They became expert at punching the buttons of the microwave although they never learned what items could and what could not be placed in it. To Rakesh's surprise it was Anu who seemed to comprehend the rules better, she who peered at any scrap of writing, trying to decipher some meaning. Together the two would open the refrigerator twenty times in one morning, never able to resist looking in at its crowded, illuminated shelves; that reassurance of food seemed to satisfy them on some deep level — their eyes gleamed and they closed the door on it gently, with a dreamy expression.

Still, the resources of the kitchen were not limitless. Beth found they had soon run through them, and the hours dragged for her, in the company of the two mothers. There were just so many times she could ask Doris to come over and relieve her, and just so many times she could invent errands that would allow them all to escape from the house so crowded with their hopes, expectations, confusion and disappointments. She knew Rakesh disappointed them. She watched them trying to re-create what he had always described to her as his most warmly close and intimate relationship, and invariably failing. The only way they knew to do this was to cook him the foods of his childhood — as best they could reproduce these in this strange land — or retail the gossip of the village, not realizing he had forgotten the people they spoke of, had not the slightest interest in who had married whom, or sold land or bought cattle. He would give embarrassed laughs, glance at Beth in appeal, and find reasons to stay late at work. She was exasperated by his failure but also secretly relieved to see how completely he had transformed himself into a husband, a Canadian, and, guiltily, she too dragged out her increasingly frequent escapes — spending the afternoon at her mother's house, describing to a fascinated Doris the village ways of these foreign mothers, or meeting girlfriends for coffee, going to the library to read child-rearing manuals — then returning in a rush of concern for the two imprisoned women at home.

She had spent one afternoon at the library, deep in an old stuffed chair in an undisturbed corner she knew, reading — something she found she could not do at home where the two mothers would watch her as she read, intently, as if waiting to see where it would take her and when she would be done — when she became aware of the light fading, darkness filling the tall window under which she sat. When she looked up, she was startled to see flakes of snow drifting through the dark, minute as tiny bees flying in excited hordes. They flew faster and faster as she watched, and in no time they would grow larger, she knew. She closed the magazine hastily, replaced it on the rack, put on her beret and gloves, picked up her bag and went out to the car. She opened the door and got in clumsily; she was so large now it was difficult to fit behind the steering wheel.

The streets were very full, everyone hurrying home before the snowfall became heavier. Her windscreen wiper going furiously, Beth drove home carefully. The first snowfall generally had its element of surprise; something childish in her responded with excitement. But this time she could only think of how surprised the two mothers would be, how much more intense their confinement.

When she let herself into the house with her key, she could look straight down the hall to the kitchen, and there she saw them standing, at the window, looking out to see the snow collect on the twigs and branches of the bare cherry tree and the tiles of the garden shed and the top of the wooden fence outside. Their white cotton saris were wrapped about them like shawls, their two heads leaned against each other as they peered out, speechlessly.

They did not hear her, they were so absorbed in the falling of the snow and the whitening of the stark scene on the other side of the glass pane. She shut the door silently, slipped into her bedroom and fetched the camera from where it lay on the closet shelf. Then she came out into the hall again and, standing there, took a photograph.

Later, when it was developed — together with the first pictures of the baby — she showed the mothers the print, and they put their hands to their mouths in astonishment. "Why didn't you tell us?" they said. "We didn't know — our backs were turned." Beth wanted to tell them it didn't matter, it was their postures that expressed everything, but then they would have wanted to know what "everything" was, and she found she did not want to explain, she did not want words to break the silent completeness of that small, still scene. It was as complete, and as fragile, after all, as a snow crystal.

The birth of the baby broke through it, of course. The sisters revived as if he were a reincarnation of Rakesh. They wanted to hold him, flat on the palms of their hands, or sit crosslegged on the sofa and rock him by pumping one knee up and down, and could not at all understand why Beth insisted they place him in his cot in a darkened bedroom instead. "He has to learn to go to sleep by himself," she told them when he cried and cried in protest and she refused to give them permission to snatch him up to their flat bosoms and console him.

They could not understand the rituals of baby care that Beth imposed — the regular feeding and sleeping times, the boiling and sterilizing of bottles and teats, the cans of formula and the use of disposable diapers. The first euphoria and excitement soon led to little nervous dissensions and explosions, then to dejection. Beth was too absorbed in her child to care.

The winter proved too hard, too long for the visitors. They began to fall ill, to grow listless, to show signs of depression and restlessness. Rakesh either did not notice or pretended not to, so that when Beth spoke of it one night in their bedroom, he asked if she were not "over-reacting," one of his favourite terms. "Ask them, just ask them," she retorted. "How can I?" he replied. "Can I say to them 'D'you want to go home?' They'll think I want them to." She flung her arms over her head in exasperation. "Why can't you just talk to each other?" she asked.

She was restless too, eager to bring to an end a visit that had gone on too long. The two little old women were in her way, underfoot, as she hurried between cot and kitchen. She tried to throw them sympathetic smiles but knew they were more like grimaces. She often thought about the inexplicable relationship of these two women, how Masi, small, mousy Masi, had borne Rakesh and then given him over to Ma, her sister. What could have made her do that? How could she have? Thinking of her own baby, the way he filled her arms and fitted against her breast, Beth could not help but direct a piercing, perplexed stare at them. She knew she would not give up her baby for anything, anyone, certainly not to her sister Susan who was hardly capable of bringing up her own, and yet these two had lived their lives ruled by that one impulse, totally unnatural to her. They looked back at her, questioningly, sensing her hostility.

And eventually they asked Rakesh — very hesitantly, delicately, but clearly after having discussed the matter between themselves and having come to a joint decision. They wanted to go home. The baby had arrived safely, and Beth was on her feet again, very much so. And it was too much for her, they said, a strain. No, no, she had not said a thing, of course not, nothing like that, and nor had he, even inadvertently. They were happy — they had been happy — but now — and they coughed and coughed, in embarrassment as much as on account of the cold. And out of pity he cut short their fumbling explanations, and agreed to book their seats on a flight home. Yes, he and Beth would come and visit them, with the baby, as soon as he was old enough to travel.

This was the right thing to say. Their creased faces lifted up to him in gratitude. He might have spilt some water on wilting plants: they revived; they smiled; they began to shop for presents for everyone at home. They began to think of those at home, laugh in anticipation of seeing home again.

At the farewell in the airport — he took them there while Beth stayed at home with the baby, who had a cold — they cast their tender, grateful looks upon him again, then turned to wheel their trolley with its boxes and trunks away, full of gifts for family and neighbours. He watched as their shoulders, swathed in their white chunnis, and their bent white heads, turned away from him and disappeared. He lifted a fist to his eyes in an automatic gesture, then sighed with relief and headed for his car waiting in the grey snow.

At home Beth had put the baby to sleep in his cot. She had cooked dinner, and on hearing Rakesh enter, she lit candles on the table, as though it were a celebration. He looked at her questioningly but she only smiled. She had cooked his favourite pasta. He sat at the table and lifted his fork, trying to eat. Why, what was she celebrating? He found a small, annoying knot of resentment fastened onto the fork at her evident pleasure at being alone with him and her baby again. He kept the fork suspended to look at her, to demand if this were so, and then saw, over her shoulder, the refrigerator with its array of the photographs and memos she liked to tape to its white enamel surface. What caught his eye was the photograph she had newly taped to it — with the view of the white window, and the two widows in white, and the whirling snow.

He put down his forkful of pasta. "Rakesh? Rakesh?" Beth asked a few times, then turned to look herself. Together they stared at the winterscape.

"Why?" he asked.

Beth shrugged. "Let it be," she said.

Bharati Mukherjee

The Management of Grief

A woman I don't know is boiling tea the Indian way in my kitchen. There are a lot of women I don't know in my kitchen, whispering, and moving tactfully. They open doors, rummage through the pantry, and try not to ask me where things are kept. They remind me of when my sons were small, on Mother's Day or when Vikram and I were tired, and they would make big, sloppy omelets. I would lie in bed pretending I didn't hear them.

Dr. Sharma, the treasurer of the Indo-Canada Society, pulls me into the hallway. He wants to know if I am worried about money. His wife, who has just come up from the basement with a tray of empty cups and glasses, scolds him. "Don't bother Mrs. Bhave with mundane details." She looks so monstrously pregnant her baby must be days overdue. I tell her she shouldn't be carrying heavy things. "Shaila," she says, smiling, "this is the fifth." Then she grabs a teenager by his shirttails. He slips his Walkman off his head. He has to be one of her four children, they have the same domed and dented foreheads. "What's the official word now?" she demands. The boy slips the headphones back on. "They're acting evasive, Ma. They're saying it could be an accident or a terrorist bomb."

All morning, the boys have been muttering, Sikh Bomb, Sikh Bomb. The men, not using the word, bow their heads in agreement. Mrs. Sharma touches her forehead at such a word. At least they've stopped talking about space debris and Russian lasers.

Two radios are going in the dining room. They are tuned to different stations. Someone must have brought the radios down from my boys' bedrooms. I haven't gone into their rooms since Kusum came running across the front lawn in her bathrobe. She looked so funny, I was laughing when I opened the door.

The big TV in the den is being whizzed through American networks and cable channels.

"Damn!" some man swears bitterly. "How can these preachers carry on like nothing's happened?" I want to tell him we're not that important. You look at the audience, and at the preacher in his blue robe with his beautiful white hair, the potted palm trees under a blue sky, and you know they care about nothing.

The phone rings and rings. Dr. Sharma's taken charge. "We're with her," he keeps saying. "Yes, yes, the doctor has given calming pills. Yes, yes, pills are having necessary effect." I wonder if pills alone explain this calm. Not peace, just a deadening quiet. I was always controlled, but never repressed. Sound can reach me, but my body is tensed, ready to scream. I hear their voices all around me. I hear my boys and Vikram cry, "Mommy, Shaila!" and their screams insulate me, like headphones.

The woman boiling water tells her story again and again. "I got the news first. My cousin called from Halifax before six A.M., can you imagine? He'd gotten up for prayers and his son was studying for medical exams and he heard on a rock channel that something had happened to a plane. They said first it had disappeared from the radar, like a giant eraser just reached out. His father called me, so I said to him, what do you mean, 'something bad'? You mean a hijacking? And he said, *behn*, there is no confirmation of anything yet, but check with your neighbours because a lot of them must be on that plane. So I called poor Kusum straightaway. I knew Kusum's husband and daughter were booked to go yesterday."

Kusum lives across the street from me. She and Satish had moved in less than a month ago. They said they needed a bigger place. All these people, the Sharmas and friends from the Indo-Canada Society had been there for the housewarming. Satish and Kusum made homemade tandoori on their big gas grill and even the white neighbours piled their plates high with that luridly red, charred, juicy chicken. Their younger daughter had danced, and even our boys had broken away from the Stanley Cup telecast to put in a reluctant appearance. Everyone took pictures for their albums and for the community newspapers — another of our families had made it big in Toronto — and now I wonder how many of those happy faces are gone. "Why does God give us so much if all along He intends to take it away?" Kusum asks me.

I nod. We sit on carpeted stairs, holding hands like children. "I never once told him that I loved him," I say. I was too much the well brought up woman. I was so well brought up I never felt comfortable calling my husband by his first name.

"It's all right," Kusum says. "He knew. My husband knew. They felt it. Modern young girls have to say it because what they feel is fake."

Kusum's daughter, Pam, runs in with an overnight case. Pam's in her McDonald's uniform. "Mummy! You have to get dressed!" Panic makes her cranky. "A reporter's on his way here."

"Why?"

"You want to talk to him in your bathrobe?" She starts to brush her mother's long hair. She's the daughter who's always in trouble. She dates Canadian boys and hangs out in the mall, shopping for tight sweaters. The younger one, the goody-goody one according to

Pam, the one with a voice so sweet that when she sang *bhajans* for Ethiopian relief even a frugal man like my husband wrote out a hundred dollar cheque, *she* was on that plane. *She* was going to spend July and August with grandparents because Pam wouldn't go. Pam said she'd rather waitress at McDonald's. "If it's a choice between Bombay and Wonderland, I'm picking Wonderland," she'd said.

"Leave me alone," Kusum yells. "You know what I want to do? If I didn't have to look after you now, I'd hang myself."

Pam's young face goes blotchy with pain. "Thanks," she says, "don't let me stop you."

"Hush," pregnant Mrs. Sharma scolds Pam. "Leave your mother alone. Mr. Sharma will tackle the reporters and fill out the forms. He'll say what has to be said."

Pam stands her ground. "You think I don't know what Mummy's thinking? *Why her*? that's what. That's sick! Mummy wishes my little sister were alive and I were dead."

Kusum's hand in mine is trembly hot. We continue to sit on the stairs.

She calls before she arrives, wondering if there's anything I need. Her name is Judith Templeton and she's an appointee of the provincial government. "Multiculturalism?" I ask, and she says, "partially," but that her mandate is bigger. "I've been told you knew many of the people on the flight," she says. "Perhaps if you'd agree to help us reach the others . . . ?"

She gives me time at least to put on tea water and pick up the mess in the front room. I have a few samosas from Kusum's housewarming that I could fry up, but then I think, why prolong this visit?

Judith Templeton is much younger than she sounded. She wears a blue suit with a white blouse and a polka dot tie. Her blonde hair is cut short, her only jewellery is pearl drop earrings. Her briefcase is new and expensive looking, a gleaming cordovan leather. She sits with it across her lap. When she looks out the front windows onto the street, her contact lenses seem to float in front of her light blue eyes.

"What sort of help do you want from me?" I ask. She has refused the tea, out of politeness, but I insist, along with some slightly stale biscuits.

"I have no experience," she admits. "That is, I have an MSW and I've worked in liaison with accident victims, but I mean I have no experience with a tragedy of this scale —"

"Who could?" I ask.

"— and with the complications of culture, language and customs. Someone mentioned that Mrs. Bhave is a pillar — because you've taken it more calmly."

At this, perhaps, I frown, for she reaches forward, almost to take my hand. "I hope you understand my meaning, Mrs. Bhave. There are hundreds of people in Metro directly affected, like you, and some of them speak no English. There are some widows who've never handled money or gone on a bus, and there are old parents who still haven't eaten or gone outside their bedrooms. Some houses and apartments have been looted. Some wives are still hysterical. Some husbands are in shock and profound depression. We want to help, but our hands are tied in so many ways. We have to distribute money to some people, and there are legal documents — these things can be done. We have interpreters, but we don't always have the human touch, or maybe the right human touch. We don't want to make mistakes, Mrs. Bhave, and that's why we'd like to ask you to help us."

"More mistakes, you mean," I say.

"Police matters are not in my hands," she answers.

"Nothing I can do will make any difference," I say. "We must all grieve in our own way."

"But you are coping very well. All the people said, Mrs. Bhave is the strongest person of all. Perhaps if the others could see you, talk with you, it would help them."

"By the standards of the people you call hysterical, I am behaving very oddly and very badly, Miss Templeton." I want to say to her, *I wish I could scream, starve, walk into Lake Ontario, jump from a bridge.* "They would not see me as a model. I do not see myself as a model."

I am a freak. No one who has ever known me would think of me reacting this way. This terrible calm will not go away.

She asks me if she may call again, after I get back from a long trip that we all must make. "Of course," I say. "Feel free to call, anytime."

Four days later, I find Kusum squatting on a rock overlooking a bay in Ireland. It isn't a big rock, but it juts sharply out over water. This is as close as we'll ever get to them. June breezes balloon out her sari and unpin her knee-length hair. She has the bewildered look of a sea creature whom the tides have stranded.

It's been one hundred hours since Kusum came stumbling and screaming across my lawn. Waiting around the hospital, we've heard many stories. The police, the diplomats, they tell us things thinking that we're strong, that knowledge is helpful to the grieving, and maybe it is. Some, I know, prefer ignorance, or their own versions. The plane broke into two, they say. Unconsciousness was instantaneous. No one suffered. My boys must have just finished their breakfasts. They loved eating on planes, they loved the smallness of plates, knives and forks. Last year they saved the airline salt and pepper shakers. Half an hour more and they would have made it to Heathrow.

Kusum says that we can't escape our fate. She says that all those people — our husbands, my boys, her girl with the nightingale voice, all those Hindus, Christians, Sikhs, Muslims, Parsis and atheists on that plane — were fated to die together off this beautiful bay. She learned this from a swami in Toronto.

I have my Valium.

Six of us "relatives" — two widows and four widowers — choose to spend the day today by the waters instead of sitting in a hospital room and scanning photographs of the dead. That's what they call us now: relatives. I've looked through twenty-seven photos in two days. They're very kind to us, the Irish are very understanding. Sometimes understanding means freeing a tourist bus for this trip to the bay, so we can pretend to spy our loved ones through the glassiness of waves or in sun-speckled cloud shapes.

I could die here, too, and be content.

"What is that, out there?" She's standing and flapping her hands and for a moment I see a head shape bobbing in the waves. She's standing in the water, I, on the boulder. The tide is low, and a round, black, head-sized rock has just risen from the waves. She returns, her sari end dripping and ruined and her face is a twisted remnant of hope, the way mine was a hundred hours ago, still laughing but inwardly knowing that nothing but the ultimate tragedy could bring two women together at six o'clock on a Sunday morning. I watch her face sag into blankness.

"That water felt warm, Shaila," she says at length.

"You can't," I say. "We have to wait for our turn to come."

I haven't eaten in four days, haven't brushed my teeth.

"I know," she says. "I tell myself I have no right to grieve. They are in a better place than we are. My swami says I should be thrilled for them. My swami says depression is a sign of our selfishness."

Maybe I'm selfish. Selfishly I break away from Kusum and run, sandals slapping against stones, to the water's edge. What if my boys aren't lying pinned under the debris? What if they aren't stuck a mile below that innocent blue chop? What if, given the strong currents . . .

Now I've ruined my sari, one of my best. Kusum has joined me, knee-deep in water that feels to me like a swimming pool. I could settle in the water, and my husband would take my hand and the boys would slap water in my face just to see me scream.

"Do you remember what good swimmers my boys were, Kusum?"

"I saw the medals," she says.

One of the widowers, Dr. Ranganathan from Montreal, walks out to us, carrying his shoes in one hand. He's an electrical engineer. Someone at the hotel mentioned his work is famous around the world, something about the place where physics and electricity come together. He has lost a huge family, something indescribable. "With some luck," Dr. Ranganathan suggests to me, "a good swimmer could make it safely to some island. It is quite possible that there may be many, many microscopic islets scattered around."

"You're not just saying that?" I tell Dr. Ranganathan about Vinod, my elder son. Last year he took diving as well.

"It's a parent's duty to hope," he says. "It is foolish to rule out possibilities that have not been tested. I myself have not surrendered hope."

Kusum is sobbing once again. "Dear lady," he says, laying his free hand on her arm, and she calms down.

"Vinod is how old?" he asks me. He's very careful, as we all are. *Is,* not was.

"Fourteen. Yesterday he was fourteen. His father and uncle were going to take him down to the Taj and give him a big birthday party. I couldn't go with them because I couldn't get two weeks off from my stupid job in June." I process bills for a travel agent. June is a big travel month.

Dr. Ranganathan whips the pockets of his suit jacket inside out. Squashed roses, in darkening shades of pink, float on the water. He tore the roses off creepers in somebody's garden. He didn't ask anyone if he could pluck the roses, but now there's been an article about it in the local papers. When you see an Indian person, it says, please give him or her flowers.

"A strong youth of fourteen," he says, "can very likely pull to safety a younger one."

My sons, though four years apart, were very close. Vinod wouldn't let Mithun drown. *Electrical engineering,* I think, foolishly perhaps: this man knows important secrets of the universe, things closed to me. Relief spins me light-headed. No wonder my boys' photographs haven't turned up in the gallery of photos of the recovered dead. "Such pretty roses," I say.

"My wife loved pink roses. Every Friday I had to bring a bunch home. I used to say, why? After twenty odd years of marriage you're still needing proof positive of my love?" He has identified his wife and three of his children. Then others from Montreal, the lucky ones, intact families with no survivors. He chuckles as he wades back to shore. Then he swings around to ask me a question. "Mrs. Bhave, you are wanting to throw in some roses for your loved ones? I have two big ones left."

But I have other things to float: Vinod's pocket calculator; a half-painted model B-52 for my Mithun. They'd want them on their island. And for my husband? For him I let fall into the calm, glassy waters a poem I wrote in the hospital yesterday. Finally he'll know my feelings for him.

"Don't tumble, the rocks are slippery," Dr. Ranganathan cautions. He holds out a hand for me to grab.

Then it's time to get back on the bus, time to rush back to our waiting posts on hospital benches.

Kusum is one of the lucky ones. The lucky ones flew here, identified in multiplicate their loved ones, then will fly to India with the bodies for proper ceremonies. Satish is one of the few males who surfaced. The photos of faces we saw on the walls in an office at Heathrow and here in the hospital are mostly of women. Women have more body fat, a nun said to me matter-of-factly. They float better.

Today I was stopped by a young sailor on the street. He had loaded bodies, he'd gone into the water when — he checks my face for signs of strength — when the sharks were first spotted. I don't blush, and he breaks down. "It's all right," I say. "Thank you." I had heard about the sharks from Dr. Ranganathan. In his orderly mind, science brings understanding, it holds no terror. It is the shark's duty. For every deer there is a hunter, for every fish a fisherman.

The Irish are not shy; they rush to me and give me hugs and some are crying. I cannot imagine reactions like that on the streets of Toronto. Just strangers, and I am touched. Some carry flowers with them and give them to any Indian they see.

After lunch, a policeman I have gotten to know quite well catches hold of me. He says he thinks he has a match for Vinod. I explain what a good swimmer Vinod is.

"You want me with you when you look at photos?" Dr. Ranganathan walks ahead of me into the picture gallery. In these matters, he is a scientist, and I am grateful. It is a new perspective. "They have performed miracles," he says. "We are indebted to them."

The first day or two the policemen showed us relatives only one picture at a time; now they're in a hurry, they're eager to lay out the possibles, and even the probables.

The face on the photo is of a boy much like Vinod; the same intelligent eyes, the same thick brows dipping into a V. But this boy's features, even his cheeks, are puffier, wider, mushier.

"No." My gaze is pulled by other pictures. There are five other boys who look like Vinod.

The nun assigned to console me rubs the first picture with a fingertip. "When they've been in the water for a while, love, they look a little heavier." The bones under the skin are broken, they said on the first day — try to adjust your memories. It's important.

"It's not him. I'm his mother. I'd know."

"I know this one!" Dr. Ranganathan cries out suddenly from the back of the gallery. "And this one!" I think he senses that I don't want to find my boys. "They are the Kutty brothers. They were also from Montreal." I don't mean to be crying. On the contrary, I am ecstatic. My suitcase in the hotel is packed heavy with dry clothes for my boys.

The policeman starts to cry. "I am so sorry, I am so sorry, ma'am. I really thought we had a match."

With the nun ahead of us and the policeman behind, we, the unlucky ones without our children's bodies, file out of the makeshift gallery.

From Ireland most of us go on to India. Kusum and I take the same direct flight to Bombay, so I can help her clear customs quickly. But we have to argue with a man in uniform. He has large boils on his face. The boils swell and glow with sweat as we argue with him. He wants Kusum to wait in line and he refuses to take authority because his boss is on a tea break. But Kusum won't let her coffins out of sight, and I shan't desert her though I know that my parents, elderly and diabetic, must be waiting in a stuffy car in a scorching lot.

"You bastard!" I scream at the man with the popping boils. Other passengers press closer. "You think we're smuggling contraband in those coffins!"

Once upon a time we were well brought up women; we were dutiful wives who kept our heads veiled, our voices shy and sweet.

In India, I become, once again, an only child of rich, ailing parents. Old friends of the family come to pay their respects. Some are Sikh, and inwardly, involuntarily, I cringe. My parents are progressive people; they do not blame communities for a few individuals.

In Canada it is a different story now.

"Stay longer," my mother pleads. "Canada is a cold place. Why would you want to be all by yourself?" I stay.

Three months pass. Then another.

"Vikram wouldn't have wanted you to give up things!" they protest. They call my husband by the name he was born with. In Toronto he'd changed to Vik so the men he worked with at his office would find his name as easy as Rod or Chris. "You know, the dead aren't cut off from us!"

My grandmother, the spoiled daughter of a rich *zamindar*, shaved her head with rusty razor blades when she was widowed at sixteen. My grandfather died of childhood diabetes when he was nineteen, and she saw herself as the harbinger of bad luck. My mother grew up without parents, raised indifferently by an uncle, while her true mother slept in a hut behind the main estate house and took her food with the servants. She grew up a rationalist. My parents abhor mindless mortification.

The *zamindar*'s daughter kept stubborn faith in Vedic rituals; my parents rebelled. I am trapped between two modes of knowledge. At thirty-six, I am too old to start over and too young to give up. Like my husband's spirit, I flutter between worlds.

Courting aphasia, we travel. We travel with our phalanx of servants and poor relatives. To hill stations and to beach resorts. We play contract bridge in dusty gymkhana clubs. We ride stubby ponies up crumbly mountain trails. At tea dances, we let ourselves be twirled twice round the ballroom. We hit the holy spots we hadn't made time for before. In Varanasi, Kalighat, Rishikesh, Hardwar, astrologers and palmists seek me out and for a fee offer me cosmic consolations.

Already the widowers among us are being shown new bride candidates. They cannot resist the call of custom, the authority of their parents and older brothers. They must marry; it is the duty of a man to look after a wife. The new wives will be young widows with children, destitute but of good family. They will make loving wives, but the men will shun them. I've had calls from the men over crackling Indian telephone lines. "Save me," they say, these substantial, educated, successful men of forty. "My parents are arranging a marriage for me." In a month they will have buried one family and returned to Canada with a new bride and partial family.

I am comparatively lucky. No one here thinks of arranging a husband for an unlucky widow.

Then, on the third day of the sixth month into this odyssey, in an abandoned temple in a tiny Himalayan village, as I make my offering of flowers and sweetmeats to the god of a tribe of animists, my husband descends to me. He is squatting next to a scrawny sadhu in moth-eaten robes. Vikram wears the vanilla suit he wore the last time I hugged him. The sadhu tosses petals on a butter-fed flame, reciting Sanskrit mantras and sweeps his face of flies. My husband takes my hands in his.

You're beautiful, he starts. Then, *What are you doing here?*

Shall I stay? I ask. He only smiles, but already the image is fading. *You must finish alone what we started together.* No seaweed wreathes his mouth. He speaks too fast just as he used to when we were an envied family in our pink split-level. He is gone.

In the windowless altar room, smoky with joss sticks and clarified butter lamps, a sweaty hand gropes for my blouse. I do not shriek. The sadhu arranges his robe. The lamps hiss and sputter out.

When we come out of the temple, my mother says, "Did you feel something weird in there?"

My mother has no patience with ghosts, prophetic dreams, holy men and cults.

"No," I lie. "Nothing."

But she knows that she's lost me. She knows that in days I shall be leaving.

Kusum's put her house up for sale. She wants to live in an ashram in Hardwar. Moving to Hardwar was her swami's idea. Her swami runs two ashrams, the one in Hardwar and another here in Toronto.

"Don't run away," I tell her.

"I'm not running away," she says. "I'm pursuing inner peace. You think you or that Ranganathan fellow are better off?"

Pam's left for California. She wants to do some modelling, she says. She says when she comes into her share of the insurance money she'll open a yoga-cum-aerobics studio in Hollywood. She sends me postcards so naughty I daren't leave them on the coffee table. Her mother has withdrawn from her and the world.

The rest of us don't lose touch, that's the point. Talk is all we have, says Dr. Ranganathan, who has also resisted his relatives and returned to Montreal and to his job, alone. He says, whom better to talk with than other relatives? We've been melted down and recast as a new tribe.

He calls me twice a week from Montreal. Every Wednesday night and every Saturday afternoon. He is changing jobs, going to Ottawa. But Ottawa is over a hundred miles away, and he is forced to drive two hundred and twenty miles a day. He can't bring himself to sell his house. The house is a temple, he says; the king-sized bed in the master bedroom is a shrine. He sleeps on a folding cot. A devotee.

There are still some hysterical relatives. Judith Templeton's list of those needing help and those who've "accepted" is in nearly perfect balance. Acceptance means you speak of your family in the past tense and you make active plans for moving ahead with your life. There are courses at Seneca and Ryerson we could be taking. Her gleaming leather briefcase is full of college catalogues and lists of cultural societies that need our help. She has done impressive work, I tell her.

"In the textbooks on grief management," she replies — I am her confidante, I realize, one of the few whose grief has not sprung bizarre obsessions — "there are stages to pass through: rejection, depression, acceptance, reconstruction." She has compiled a chart and finds that six months after the tragedy, none of us still reject reality, but only a handful are reconstructing. "Depressed Acceptance" is the plateau we've reached. Remarriage is a major step in reconstruction (though she's a little surprised, even shocked, over *how* quickly some of the men have taken on new families). Selling one's house and changing jobs and cities is healthy.

How do I tell Judith Templeton that my family surrounds me, and that like creatures in epics, they've changed shapes? She sees me as calm and accepting but worries that I have no job, no career. My closest friends are worse off than I. I cannot tell her my days, even my nights, are thrilling.

She asks me to help with families she can't reach at all. An elderly couple in Agincourt whose sons were killed just weeks after they had brought their parents over from a village in Punjab. From their names, I know they are Sikh. Judith Templeton and a translator have visited them twice with offers of money for air fare to Ireland, with bank forms, power-of-attorney forms, but they have refused to sign, or to leave their tiny apartment. Their sons' money is frozen in the bank. Their sons' investment apartments have been trashed by tenants, the furnishings sold off. The parents fear that anything they sign or any money they receive will end the company's or the country's obligations to them. They fear they are selling their sons for two airline tickets to a place they've never seen.

The high-rise apartment is a tower of Indians and West Indians, with a sprinkling of Orientals. The nearest bus stop kiosk is lined with women in saris. Boys practice cricket in the parking lot. Inside the building, even I wince a bit from the ferocity of onion fumes, the distinctive and immediate Indianness of frying ghee, but Judith Templeton maintains a steady flow of information. These poor old people are in imminent danger of losing their place and all their services.

I say to her, "They are Sikh. They will not open up to a Hindu woman." And what I want to add is, as much as I try not to, I stiffen now at the sight of beards and turbans. I remember a time when we all trusted each other in this new country, it was only the new country we worried about.

The two rooms are dark and stuffy. The lights are off, and an oil lamp sputters on the coffee table. The bent old lady has let us in, and her husband is wrapping a white turban over his oiled, hip-length hair. She immediately goes to the kitchen, and I hear the most familiar sound of an Indian home, tap water hitting and filling a teapot.

They have not paid their utility bills, out of fear and the inability to write a cheque. The telephone is gone; electricity and gas and water are soon to follow. They have told Judith their sons will provide. They are good boys, and they have always earned and looked after their parents.

We converse a bit in Hindi. They do not ask about the crash and I wonder if I should bring it up. If they think I am here merely as a translator, then they may feel insulted. There are thousands of Punjabi-speakers, Sikhs, in Toronto to do a better job. And so I say to the old lady, "I too have lost my sons, and my husband, in the crash."

Her eyes immediately fill with tears. The man mutters a few words which sound like a blessing. "God provides and God takes away," he says.

I want to say, but only men destroy and give back nothing. "My boys and my husband are not coming back," I say. "We have to understand that."

Now the old woman responds. "But who is to say? Man alone does not decide these things." To this her husband adds his agreement.

Judith asks about the bank papers, the release forms. With a stroke of the pen, they will have a provincial trustee to pay their bills, invest their money, send them a monthly pension.

"Do you know this woman?" I ask them.

The man raises his hand from the table, turns it over and seems to regard each finger separately before he answers. "This young lady is always coming here, we make tea for her and she leaves papers for us to sign." His eyes scan a pile of papers in the corner of the room. "Soon we will be out of tea, then will she go away?"

The old lady adds, "I have asked my neighbours and no one else gets *angrezi* visitors. What have we done?"

"It's her job," I try to explain. "The government is worried. Soon you will have no place to stay, no lights, no gas, no water."

"Government will get its money. Tell her not to worry, we are honourable people."

I try to explain the government wishes to give money, not take. He raises his hand. "Let them take," he says. "We are accustomed to that. That is no problem."

"We are strong people," says the wife. "Tell her that."

"Who needs all this machinery?" demands the husband. "It is unhealthy, the bright lights, the cold air on a hot day, the cold food, the four gas rings. God will provide, not government."

"When our boys return," the mother says. Her husband sucks his teeth. "Enough talk," he says.

Judith breaks in. "Have you convinced them?" The snaps on her cordovan briefcase go off like firecrackers in that quiet apartment. She lays the sheaf of legal papers on the coffee table. "If they can't write their names, an X will do — I've told them that."

Now the old lady has shuffled to the kitchen and soon emerges with a pot of tea and two cups. "I think my bladder will go first on a job like this," Judith says to me, smiling. "If only there was some way of reaching them. Please thank her for the tea. Tell her she's very kind."

I nod in Judith's direction and tell them in Hindi, "She thanks you for the tea. She thinks you are being very hospitable but she doesn't have the slightest idea what it means."

I want to say, humour her. I want to say, my boys and my husband are with me too, more than ever. I look in the old man's eyes and I can read his stubborn, peasant's message: *I have protected this woman as best I can. She is the only person I have left. Give to me or take from me what you will, but I will not sign for it. I will not pretend that I accept.*

In the car, Judith says, "You see what I'm up against? I'm sure they're lovely people, but their stubbornness and ignorance are driving me crazy. They think signing a paper is signing their sons' death warrants, don't they?"

I am looking out the window. I want to say, *In our culture, it is a parent's duty to hope.*

"Now Shaila, this next woman is a real mess. She cries day and night, and she refuses all medical help. We may have to —"

"— Let me out at the subway," I say.

"I beg your pardon?" I can feel those blue eyes staring at me.

It would not be like her to disobey. She merely disapproves, and slows at a corner to let me out. Her voice is plaintive. "Is there anything I said? Anything I did?"

I could answer her suddenly in a dozen ways, but I choose not to. "Shaila? Let's talk about it," I hear, then slam the door.

A wife and mother begins her new life in a new country, and that life is cut short. Yet her husband tells her: Complete what we have started. We, who stayed out of politics and came halfway around the world to avoid religious and political feuding have been the first in the New World to die from it. I no longer know what we started, nor how to complete it. I write letters to the editors of local papers and to members of Parliament. Now at least they admit it was a bomb. One MP answers back, with sympathy, but with a challenge. You want to make a difference? Work on a campaign. Work on mine. Politicize the Indian voter.

My husband's old lawyer helps me set up a trust. Vikram was a saver and a careful investor. He had saved the boys' boarding school and college fees. I sell the pink house at four times what we paid for it and take a small apartment downtown. I am looking for a charity to support.

We are deep in the Toronto winter, grey skies, icy pavements. I stay indoors, watching television. I have tried to assess my situation, how best to live my life, to complete what we began so many years ago. Kusum has written me from Hardwar that her life is now serene. She has seen Satish and has heard her daughter sing again. Kusum was on a pilgrimage, passing through a village when she heard a young girl's voice, singing one of her daughter's favourite *bhajans*. She followed the music through the squalor of a Himalayan village, to a hut where a young girl, an exact replica of her daughter, was fanning coals under the kitchen fire. When she appeared, the girl cried out, "Ma!" and ran away. What did I think of that?

I think I can only envy her.

Pam didn't make it to California, but writes me from Vancouver. She works in a department store, giving make-up hints to Indian and Oriental girls. Dr. Ranganathan has given up his commute, given up his house and job, and accepted an academic position in Texas where no one knows his story and he has vowed not to tell it. He calls me now once a week.

I wait, I listen and I pray, but Vikram has not returned to me. The voices and the shapes and the nights filled with visions ended abruptly several weeks ago.

I take it as a sign.

One rare, beautiful, sunny day last week, returning from a small errand on Yonge Street, I was walking through the park from the subway to my apartment. I live equidistant from the Ontario Houses of Parliament and the University of Toronto. The day was not cold, but something in the bare trees caught my attention. I looked up from the gravel, into the branches and the clear blue sky beyond. I thought I heard the rustling of larger forms, and I waited a moment for voices. Nothing.

"What?" I asked.

Then as I stood in the path looking north to Queen's Park and west to the university, I heard the voices of my family one last time. *Your time has come*, they said. *Go, be brave.*

I do not know where this voyage I have begun will end. I do not know which direction I will take. I dropped the package on a park bench and started walking.

K. S. Maniam

Haunting the Tiger

The old man had trouble dying. The peace he had hoped for was disturbed by dreams. Some of these dreams took on the sharp edges of a nightmare and kept sleep away. They distorted his thinking so that he muttered to himself, "You've to be mindless to be mindful." And because he had been looking at the land outside his window, he thought, "You've to be landless to be landfull."

The late evenings, with the light fading, were the worst for then his ears filled with clamouring voices and his mind with vivid pictures from the past. His mind emptied itself of all that he himself had gathered through the years and left him naked, skinned. He chuckled, lying on his wooden bed, and said to himself, "This is the falling out of from the skin I knew of long ago." He had experienced this just after his mother died, when he was about eight. It was not a sense of loss his mother's death brought but a loss of the self. The person he had known himself to be suddenly died.

At that other occasion, as he went through the wedding rituals, he had felt worse. He saw no meaning at all in having toe-rings put on, arms plastered with sandalwood paste and at his feet a pot continually crackling with seeds, salt, barks and sticks. The young woman sitting beside him wasn't brought any nearer to him: she was a strangeness he had to give himself up for, to know. He had to, he had told himself, actually jump out of his skin and be refashioned to fit into the life with her.

Just then his wife came hobbling in, a cracked bowl of porridge in her hands, and said, "Must eat for the body's strength." Thin, almost only bones and silvery hair sitting on top, she danced out and disappeared into that thick miasma, his new consciousness. "Is this death at last?" he thought. "Is this why the body goes cold and stiff only afterwards?"

But death would not come easily. Instead there came to him, in the stillness of deep night, like creation stories, heard or read, the land that resided within sleep memory. Wasn't it Brahma, when woken from his slumbers, who created the universe for men to sport in? The land that came to him now came before the remigration of peoples to their original countries, the great war and harsh, sun-reflecting buildings.

On the mindscape that lay now between life and death, confused and murky, there rose a fresh, green land. Seeds popped, transparent thin stems reached out of the ground; the surface cracked and thick tree trunks heaved themselves through the resinous soil. Grass matted the slopes, lallang speared the bushes and creepers wove themselves into the green canopy. The country steamed and settled; the jungles screamed with lives and shook with dangers.

The young Muthu, now holding down a job and a house with a discontented family, often goes into one of these jungles at night. He doesn't go far, remaining always within safe distance of the town where he lives. At first, he merely wanders around, then hearing snorts and *belukar* startled into shivers, he decides to take up wild boar hunting. "What better way to know the country than to hunt down a beast that knows it well?" he thinks. Of late, he has been forced into thought by his disgruntled parents: they want to return to the country from which they came. "They can give up this land for a life they've known," he thinks. "But what do I have to give up?"

This fills him with a new purpose and takes him out to the jungle almost every other night. He passes a hut with a smooth, swept-out compound; children chase one another. The mother is watering the plants; the father sits watching the boys and girls play, childish amusement on his own face. Muthu nods at him briefly, his new possession, a gun, resting on his shoulder. The man gives him a smile which together with the gun puts him in expectation of a fulfilling discovery.

He has been some nights in the jungle fringe, beyond Zulkifli's hut, the gun ready, his shoulders squared. Nothing happens. The snorting and the shaking of the plants have mysteriously ceased. "Maybe I make too much noise," he thinks and becomes so quiet, stealthy, that his own breath sounds like another man's.

Then one moonlit night he surprises himself and the boar that is rooting at a clump of wild yams. The boar has dug with its trotters and revealed black-and-red earth; it has just tusked the pinkish tuber and hunches down to its meal. Muthu stands for a while, gun aimed at the animal, then sees the moonlight-washed broad leaves and hears the river not far away wending its way to the sea, and shoots. The boar turns, bewilderment on its mug, and falls, its blood splattering the heart-shaped leaves and the spongy ground. For some time Muthu doesn't move, then busies himself with the task of carrying the carcass back to the town.

At another time, a boar, outgrowing its surprise, hurtles towards him, a bulk of menace which he sidesteps and brings down with a single shot. The flash of the gun and the flash of the boar's tusk strike into each other over ground indisputably Muthu's. That kill he doesn't take home, burying the recently muscle-tensed body beside the river.

After that every time he points his gun at a boar, his skin tightens on his arms and face but the heart-shaped leaves are no more bathed in blood. Muthu sits against a tree and broods, the gun beside him useless against the silence of impenetrability.

His house in town is a long, rectangular building, zinc-roofed, and the heat travelling down makes him restless. The oblong hall is unrelieved except for a massive, old cupboard and his mother's *kolams* on the dark cement floor. These cabala-like designs in white, looped in upon themselves, drive him into further fury. Though he has stayed away from the jungle for a few days, he now picks up his gun and stumbles out of the house, passing his father reclining in a canvas chair.

"There's nothing there," his father says. "I was mistaken. There's nothing."

Muthu has gone past Zulkifli's hut but the words still echo in his ears. Turning over the words in his mind, Muthu almost passes the man without seeing him.

"You won't see anything there with eyes like this," Zulkifli says, laughing.

He has some strange plants and barks in his hand and a small bundle of rattan on his shoulder.

"Must be careful there," he says, seeing Muthu silent.

"Come with me," Muthu says impulsively, remembering the silence that had made him lonely.

"Can't hunt boars," Zulkifli says. "Only when they come to destroy our crops."

"Some other kind of hunting?"

Zulkifli's smile is there again but he neither accepts nor refuses.

"Already long time from the family," he says and heads towards his house.

That night, Muthu goes beyond his usual haunt. Envying Zulkifli's comfortable smile, he thinks, "He won't go as far as I can." As he advances, the path he has used trails away; he sees signs of man where he has got lost. A broken branch hangs down, the leaves a decayed, darkened cluster. The stump of a sawed-off young tree stares at him like a compass left behind by a strayed man for the use of others.

"I can't get lost," he tells himself as he steps over the line of familiarity. Immediately, his mental restlessness goes and the body's lethargy disappears. He is as if made anew. His father's words and Zulkifli's assured ease do not touch him. He has now entered the land of his sleep-dream; he is now ready to confront and bring into his sight those abundant slopes and fearful recesses.

He sets off, without the need for a choice, in some arbitrary direction. As he moves, bushes and plants part at his insistence but not without putting a sting or a scratch on him. These rouse or cut into his manliness and he treads on with clear-headed confidence. He moves tirelessly, as if time does not matter, when he comes back, puzzled, to where he started. There is the anthill, which he had mentally marked as a signpost, but the conical top has been knocked off and lies crumbled at the base.

Muthu is surprised to see no ants swarm about in alarm; he approaches and peers into the lately-made small cavern. With the torchlight he never fails to carry, he sees a dark, rustling mass beneath the lip of the opening. He shines the torch on the levelled anthill earth. If he had not been trained to pick out faint sounds and slight disordering of plants by his boar-hunting nights, he would have missed the barely visible pug mark on the dislodged soil.

Muthu is excited and afraid. As he stands there near the partially destroyed anthill he feels he is not alone. "But what can be so big and yet so gentle?" he thinks. It comes to him suddenly that it can only be a tiger. He will not move and so attract attention to himself but he knows too that he cannot stand there forever. As he withdraws cautiously and reaches the tree stump he feels he is being watched by amused and yet fierce eyes.

The old Muthu stirred on the plank bed and thought, "I shouldn't have gone back. Certainly not with that man from the hut. Brought him too much trouble. We went away from each other before knowing one another."

Muthu, though fascinated, is unable to go beyond Zulkifli's house. His mind runs with colours and stripes and he is fearful of the thing he will finally see; yet this is what he feels he has waited for and will not miss. But he will not go alone; he must have a companion.

His father has laughed at him. "Just a play thing, what you talk about. Be a real man and make up your mind." The others of his own age have wives and children and must care for them.

"Food, clothes and shelter! That's all they're about," Muthu thinks as his feet take him beyond boar-hunting territory. His father's jeering face comes down to him with the words, "Come back with us and I'll marry you to a girl who'll make you feel like a man!"

He is going to prove himself a man tonight for he does not look at Zulkifli's house as he passes it. He goes straight to the compass tree stump and crosses over into the silence he dreads but must face. Back at the disturbed anthill, he wonders if his obsessive preoccupation with the tiger has not distorted his vision: the pug mark is larger and more deeply pressed. He decides to show he is not afraid by breaking into the now threat-thick silence.

He now has a direction to follow which he holds on to as he does his gun. Putting every thing he passes into his mind, he draws himself into the fearful silence. But, strangely, after what seems an eternity, the silence is replaced by a loud conspiracy of exclusion. His ears pick up an infinitesimal flutter of wings; his eyes catch dark, hurtling shapes that wrench themselves out of the stillness. His torchlight is useless against the numerous bright green orbs — fireflies? — that advance upon him. He breaks into a run and cuts himself free from this web of scheming. But as he reaches, once more, the anthill he realizes blood has been drawn from his arms and legs.

The old Muthu struggled with the anger his younger self had felt long ago. "This isn't going to help me die," he thought. "Must have been anger that took me to Zulkifli." He lay on his side and made out in the approaching dawn the thin mound of a body that was his wife, under the white coverlet.

As he looked, he remembered the other shrouded figure he had sat beside after his parents left for India. He had decided to marry the young girl he had seen in a nearby estate without bothering to think what marriage meant. The shock he had experienced the first night they came together only emphasized his sense of inadequacy. He ignored the innocence and the unbounded mysteries that lay hidden behind the sari-veiled figure and took her that he recognized as a woman, violently, and made her a citizen of the dark country he would never know.

The Young Muthu is transformed: he lies awake most of the nights. In the dark, he can feel the striped, shallow scars where he has been scratched and cut. But he sees himself as torn and mangled inside. He is infuriated and restless, thinking an invisible thing can so frighten him. Full of schemes he goes the next day past the tree stump but is unable to break through the repetitive circles he makes, feeling all the while the inexorable eyes on him.

Zulkifli, who has been observing him, invites him to the house one evening. They are awkward with each other but Muthu is attentive and anxious. Their conversation ripples this way and that while the light in their eyes swirls about in the hidden inner crannies.

"You've found the thing you want to hunt," Zulkifli says at last.

"You know?"

"My forefathers had the same look in their eyes," Zulkifli says. "My father told me."

"But you?" Muthu says.

"Deep inside. No need to show it so loudly to the world," Zulkifli says, smiling. "And you've lost the way."

"You know so much," Muthu says.

"Centuries of living here," Zulkifli says. "We'll go together one day."

Muthu's sleep is filled with dreams. And they are always the same: he finds himself miraculously changed into a chameleon. His tapering, curled tail is hooked onto the branch of a huge tree. His eyes, encircled by lids that never close, look at the danger below but he is also excited by the leap he will have to make. His tail unclasps and as he hurtles through the changing hues of the foliage and sees the red, dark earth rush up at him, he screams, "I'll possess! I'll possess!"

He wakes up trying to wipe out the words but the dream continues into his wakefulness. He sees himself still as the chameleon, now landed on the ground matted with leaves, and the blood pulsing through veins carried beyond the centuries.

When Muthu and Zulkifli meet again, they work calmly but also feverishly, preparing themselves for the trek into tiger-land. Both are covered with an intensity as visible as the serenity of an ancient Buddha statue. And like that spiritual seeker, they leave home and family behind, at least for a few days, in search of the abstract, the satisfying.

They reach Muthu's boar-hunting grounds and he shows Zulkifli the compass tree stump. Shaking his head, Zulkifli strikes out in the opposite direction, Muthu hurrying after him. Sure-footed and *parang* in his hand, Zulkifli slashes creepers and interfering branches out of his way only when necessary. Muthu follows him, silent, wondering if the man knows what he is doing.

Then, suddenly, there is no time to wonder for the rhythm of their tread overtakes everything else. It is unlike any walking they have done before. Their legs and bodies, enchanted, move effortlessly; their minds are not their own. They are a motion — physical and mental — that comes from outside them. They are the quiver in the leaves, the flow of sap in the stems, the gentle opening out of petals in the dark, purple flowers. They look at each other and their faces are two sides of the same awe.

"We should have turned back," the old Muthu thought, sitting up on the hard bed, "before we became peoples. Peoples? Yes, I wanted to become somebody. And he? Show me he was somebody."

He turned, lay on his side and looked further in.

Though they have been walking steadily, they are unable to keep up the pace. The silence bears down upon them in their recognition of each other. But they cannot, any longer, accept the bodiless and mindless activity that they have become. Muthu begins to feel the weight of the gun on his shoulder, and Zulkifli the *parang* at his waist. They want to break into speech so as to banish the silence.

They recover themselves sufficiently to remember the purpose with which they had set out.

"Will we see the tiger soon?" Muthu says.

"We've come deep enough," Zulkifli says. "I've to be your ears and eyes."

"Just show it to me," Muthu says, sensing some anxiety in the other man.

"What will you do?"

"Shoot it," Muthu says.

"The tiger I'm going to show you can't be shot," Zulkifli says with deep conviction.

"I'll see it and possess it!"

"Nobody can possess it," Zulkifli says.

They have now gone beyond the massive, complex silence of the jungle and into their ordinariness. Though tensed, they enjoy the tussle of wills between themselves. The bristling readiness to combat each other keeps away, momentarily, the fear that has crept into them. For now they feel that the strength to discover and the strength to reveal are inadequate.

Nevertheless they will not let go of what they know in the flesh and in the mind. Muthu's flesh and mind crave: they would know where they are and for what purpose. Zulkifli has known it all: how to take Muthu into the knowledge that resides within him?

Now a strange thing happens. The land they have been walking on does not yield to their advance. The swing their bodies had not a while back is not even a memory now. The ground is hard, the slopes too steep; plants and bushes slash at them with unexpected cruelty. They look at each other, wondering.

"We can't continue this way," says Zulkifli.

"How then?" Muthu says.

"This hasn't happened before," Zulkifli says. "The land is going away from us. Maybe we're offending the tiger."

"We haven't seen it yet," Muthu says.

"It's here all around us," Zulkifli says.

"I've to see it clearly," says Muthu. "Face to face."

"The tiger roamed this land before man's mind learned to remember," Zulkifli says. "Its stripes are everywhere."

"Then take me where I can see them," Muthu says.

"Not with the gun," Zulkifli says. "You must leave it behind."

"If it attacks us?"

"Not in the way you're thinking," Zulkifli says.

"I'll possess the tiger by surprising it," Muthu says, leaning the gun against a tree.

"I thought it was a mistake at that time," the old Muthu told himself as he turned round on the planks. Dawn was a glow of revealing light across the window. He pulled himself up against the wooden wall. His gaze fell on his sleeping wife. The coverlet had come off and he saw a body pillaged, not fleshed out, by time. "Why did I let time take over," he thought as he struggled down to her and pulled the sheet over the fetal form. "What would she have become," he thought, lapsing into the irrational, "if I had added life to life?"

Back at the hard planks, he once more turned to seek out what he had not seen in the past. "Perhaps that what I've missed will release me into death," he thought.

Freed from the gun, Muthu feels as if the skin would peel from his body but he is also strangely light and buoyant. Zulkifli, too, lays aside his *parang*, and the thing that has held him back leaves him.

"There's more to do," Zulkifli says as once more they fall into motion.

They enter into the deeper thickness of the jungle but though they feel the fearful eyes upon them, they see nothing. Zulkifli halts and stands there thinking. As Muthu watches him, Zulkifli seems to blend into the landscape. "I'm the chameleon!" Muthu protests within himself. He is more than determined now to wrest the sight of the tiger out of the man.

"I know what's wrong," Zulkifli says. "There's something foreign to the tiger's nose. He won't show himself until the smells are gone."

Zulkifli fixes Muthu with a surveying stare. Muthu becomes nervous.

"What smells?" he says.

"Mind and body smells," Zulkifli says.

Muthu is offended and turns away from him.

"Not in the way you can't go near a person," Zulkifli says confronting Muthu. "The clothes you wear, the thoughts you think. Where do they come from?"

"They're just clothes and ideas," Muthu says.

"They must fit into the place where the tiger lives."

"Why must they fit in?" Muthu says. "I only want to break out from my father's hold on me."

"So you brought a purpose with you?" Zulkifli says. "And a way of thinking. How can you get into the tiger's stripes and spirit?"

"I can make the leap," Muthu says, thinking of the chameleon.

"I didn't make that leap," the old Muthu muttered as he sat up in bed. "Zul — that's what I called him later — tried to make me. He wanted me to think myself like a tiger, to feel myself like one. I refused. Still Zul took me through to the tiger's abode, which was everywhere."

By daylight the old man had slumped into exhaustion. He lay, watching, with unsurpassed calm, the fever spread from his legs, up his loins, through to his head. His wife, who had woken and prepared coffee, came and touched him.

"Your body is burning," she said.

"Yes, burning," he said and refused the coffee.

Through the fever, he sees himself beside Zulkifli, the time in between destroyed, locked into the struggle of wills. Not between wills, as the young Muthu realizes, but between his will and Zulkifli's willingness. In spite of himself, Muthu follows Zulkifli deeper into the interior. Zulkifli is talking but in Muthu's ears, it is an incessant chant, flowing with the energy of a timeless spirit.

Already, he feels he is beside himself; a nameless fear takes hold of him. He wants to run but restrains himself. The thickness around them increases and they stand still in the centre of it all. Zulkifli does not speak but his whole being is watchful.

A booming growl reaches them and almost immediately the sound dissipates into innumerable animal and insect cries and whines. Branches and leaves shiver and perhaps through a trick of the moonlight filtering in, Muthu sees the jungle close in on him in orange bands and black stripes. His skin begins to burn; he feels his clothes are no more there on his body. The light scars the land put on him, some months back, are opening up. He is flowing out towards the stripes, helplessly, when with a cry of anguish, he wills his consciousness into action.

The old man became delirious so that his wife had to wipe him with a damp cloth at intervals. He rambled on all the time as if speech was beyond his control and the body not in his keeping.

"Where's my body? Can't feel it. May be jumped out of its skin . . . There you are. Just a shape. Too dark now to see. Always standing, waiting. Not being yourself. What being yourself?. . . Long time ago, this young girl. A face with many destinies written on it. I didn't want to know. Too frightened. Afraid I would fall into a dark, deep hole. Took the only thing that could be touched. The body . . . Yes, like taking Zul's smile. Not the other things he had in him. Running away from those stripes. Too deep, too invisible. How to enter so deep in? Give up what I was . . . I was nothing. Am nothing . . . Accepting his smile, there was no need to understand. Now beyond understanding . . . Buying this house, land, becoming big man. Nothing in all these things. Only violence. Taking is violence . . . Just wanted the thing I could see, touch and be sure. What to be sure? I can't die. How can I die? The mind isn't full to be emptied. The body isn't there for the blood to go cold . . . This is the dying. Having not lived, this is the dying . . ."

Raymond Pillai

The Celebration

The sky all around had a lurid glow as cane fires lit up the December evening. It was the close of the crushing season and those who had not finished harvesting their cane redoubled their efforts while the more fortunate ones rested from their labours. The Gounden household was one of the lucky ones. With good weather, enough cane trucks and a hard-working cane gang, they had managed to move out all their cane. Now they took their ease in the cool of the evening and chatted idly over their bowls of yaqona.

"We've had a good crop this year, amma," Rama said to his mother. "Twelve hundred tons at the very least. And the final payment on last year's crop was a good one too. I think we can kill a goat for Christmas and celebrate. Nothing very big, mind you. Just a small affair for the family members only."

Rama's mother was taken aback. "It isn't a year yet since your father died," she said indignantly. "What will people think?"

"People will always think the worst of others. But we have nothing to fear. We said all the necessary prayers after appa's death. And the *kriyakaram* was a big one. We killed three goats, didn't we? Nobody can say we didn't observe the period of mourning correctly."

"It's the first Christmas since he died," his mother persisted.

"Look, amma, it happened ten months ago. You can't go on mourning him forever. You have to stop some time."

"Ramu, is there ever a time when we stop remembering completely? There are some things which are not easily forgotten, because they have become part of us. Since your father and I were married, forty years have passed. That's a long time."

Too long, thought Rama. He had never got on well with his father. "It's different for you, amma. I don't have to remember him."

"I know you never liked your father, but that's no reason to forget him now. True, he used to treat you harshly at times. But there was a reason for it. Your father wanted you to grow up into a strong, honest man. That's why he brought you up so firmly. And not just you only. We all felt the weight of his hand at one time or another. But we've all benefited. We are wealthy. We are respected in the whole district. And we are still a united family. So many families quarrel and break up after the father dies. But has that happened to us? And why hasn't it happened to us? Because your father showed us the right way. Even though he is no longer alive, his spirit is still with us, keeping us united and happy."

Rama had listened patiently to his mother's homily. After all, she had earned the right to her illusions. But he could not check himself any longer. "If his spirit is still with us, then I say we should celebrate Christmas the way he would have celebrated it — with feasting and drinking. He always enjoyed life. You know that well enough. He wouldn't miss his meat and whisky for anything. I'm sure he wouldn't want us to sit around like fools just because he wasn't alive to share the occasion with us."

"I'm sure your father would be filled with sorrow to see you making merry so soon after his death. Wait a little longer, and then you can have as much feasting and drinking as you want."

"But how much longer amma? We didn't do anything for Easter or Diwali. How long are we going to continue as if we were corpses ourselves? I say we should kill one goat at least for Christmas. And people can say what they like. I don't give a damn!"

Rama had his way in the end. He was the eldest son after all. But his decision was strongly resented. When he brought home the Christmas goat, the family showed not the slightest interest and this made Rama very sore. At the very least they could have asked him what the goat had cost.

The Christmas celebrations proved to be a dispiriting affair. With the exception of Logesan, who was the youngest and who dared not cross his brother, the others found reasons for not attending. The two sisters said they were unable to travel. Their damn fool husbands must have got them pregnant again, thought Rama. Govinda had to go and see his ailing mother-in-law. A likely story! That mother-in-law of Govinda's was strong as an ox and twice as stupid. Gopal gave the same reason as the year before — he was afraid somebody would set fire to his cane if he left his farm. All feeble excuses! Well, let them stay away if they liked, fumed Rama. If they wanted to be stubborn, that was their own affair, but he wasn't going to let them spoil his pleasure.

The goat was slaughtered early on Christmas morning. In the past, Rama's father would have conducted the job personally, wearying everybody with his imperious commands. Today that privilege was Rama's. He took charge of the operation as if born to the task and gave orders with the aplomb of a veteran.

Logesan held the goat down by the legs while Rama forced a drink of water into the goat's mouth — the final kindness. Then a deft stroke of the knife sliced through the animal's throat, releasing a jet of hot blood.

"Look how you're holding that basin, you ass!" Rama shouted at his son, Anand. "You'll let the whole stuff spill on the ground."

Anand did his best to hold the basin steady as the blood gushed into it erratically. The animal's eyes dilated in terror, its body heaving in spasms of agony. Uncomprehending, crazed with pain, it struggled to raise its head and look at his tormentors, but Rama's firm grip on its muzzle held it prisoner. Hot, tortured blasts of air snorted through its labouring nostrils. Its body arched in agonized convulsions. Desperately it fought to regain its feet, but the combined weight of the two men brutally quelled all resistance. The spasms slowly ceased as its life ebbed out. It sagged and went limp, defeated.

The basin was almost full — frothing, dark, sinister. The flow of blood dwindled to a trickle. Judging the right moment expertly, Rama motioned to Anand to remove the basin. It was not a second too soon as a stream of undigested food spurted from the severed gullet. Rama twisted the head round and sawed through the spinal cord. The goat convulsed once more, then subsided. The deed was done.

Rama stood up and flicked the sweat away from his forehead with the back of his hand. "He's a big bugger, isn't he?" he said. "Over a hundred pounds in my estimation."

Logesan murmured assent but Anand said nothing. Anand was sickened by the slaughter, more so because it was quite unnecessary. Young as he was, he was still perceptive enough to see that the goat was only a sacrifice to his father's ego.

Rama was not pleased with Anand's squeamishness. "Look at this boy of mine. He is nearly old enough to have hair on his chin, but he's frightened of a little blood."

Anand was stung. "It's not the blood. It's the pain that we give the animal when we kill it."

"Nonsense!" said Rama. "It doesn't feel a thing. It gets such a shock that it doesn't know what's happening to it. Look at that goat there. See how peacefully it lies. Do you think it feels anything? Not one bit. It's gone. Finished."

There was indeed something peaceful about the way it lay there, looking calm and composed even though its head was missing. Flies started buzzing round the neck of the carcass, and as the blood on the grass began to thicken and grow dark, the violent scene of a few minutes before seemed more remote and less reprehensible.

The goat yielded fifty-five pounds of meat, which should have pleased Rama, but he was still furious because the whole family was not present. "They should have come," he complained to his mother. "We always used to celebrate Christmas in a big way. It was fun for everybody. But this year they think they can have more fun by themselves in their own homes. Our neighbours must be laughing at us. They know we killed such a big goat, and now there's no one to eat it. Well then, if nobody wants it, I'll eat it all by myself."

"All this is your own doing, Ramu," said his mother. "You had no patience. You could not wait for even one year to show that you are the big man of the house now. I kept telling you, but you are too big now to listen to an old woman like me."

"Amma, that's not true. I just wanted to enjoy Christmas."

"Since when have you become a Christian, Ramu, that you must celebrate Christmas?"

"Haven't we always celebrated Christmas? Christmas is not a religious thing. It's only a public holiday. It's a time for feasting and merry-making."

"All right, then. You go ahead with your feasting and see how much you enjoy it."

"I will enjoy it!" he said defiantly. "Shanti!" he roared at his wife. "Why isn't the fried meat ready yet?"

"I'm just doing it now. I have only two hands, you know."

"Your tongue seems to be working more than your hands nowadays. Hurry up with that meat."

A few minutes later his wife brought in a bowl of chopped meat and liver mixed with fat and blood. It was done just the way he liked it, with plenty of chillies. In a separate saucer lay the goat's testicles, lightly fried in oil and neatly quartered. When Rama's father had been alive, the first meat was always reserved for him. No one might eat until he had tasted first and pronounced himself satisfied. It was almost a seignorial right, confirming him in his place of honour as head of the house. Now the old man was no more. His mantle had fallen upon Rama's shoulders, and with it all the prerogatives. "Ah, it's a long time since I've had such tasty meat," said Rama with exaggerated relish. In truth he was disappointed to find the meat a little tough, but he was not going to let his chagrin show. "Here, Anand," he called to his son. "Take some of this meat."

Anand shuffled to the table reluctantly and put a few spoonfuls of fried blood into his cupped hand.

"Have some of this too," said Rama, pointing to the saucer.

"I never eat that," said Anand hastily. The thought of eating goat's testicles repelled him.

"Go on, it's good stuff."

"I never eat it," repeated Anand dully.

"Well, you are going to eat some today, my boy."

"Why are you forcing him?" Anand's mother intervened. "He says he doesn't want it."

"Stop mollycoddling the boy. He's going to do what I tell him. Here, eat this." Rama picked up a piece from the saucer and thrust it at Anand.

Anand took the proffered morsel. With a tremendous effort of will he bit into it and tried to swallow, but the spongy texture and somewhat ammoniacal tang of the flesh made him retch. He rushed out to the drain which ran past the kitchen window and vomited until he was exhausted.

"See what you have done to the boy!" cried Anand's mother. "Why are you being so stubborn?"

"He's just enjoying his Christmas Day," said Rama's mother bitterly. "He just wants to show that he's the big man of the house. And he has proved it by bullying his son."

"Stop it!" shouted Rama. "I've had enough of you people!" With a violent motion of the hand he swept the meat bowl off the table and stamped out of the house.

His wife looked sadly at the meat strewn over the floor. She had prepared it so painstakingly, the way her husband liked it, and he had flung it aside to be trampled underfoot. Tears of exasperation welled up in her eyes.

"It's no use crying, Shanti," her mother-in-law said to her. "Men never change. In forty years of married life I never managed to change the ways of Ramu's father. And I don't think you'll ever be able to alter Ramu either. He's too much like his father. Make the most of your happy moments, and pray that the hard times are few. That's the only way to endure a lifetime together."

Shanti made no reply. There was practical wisdom in the old woman's words, but hardly a grain of comfort. Still, there was no point in lingering over her troubles. She brushed back her tears as if nothing had happened. Then she bent down and began picking up the pieces of meat one by one.

Farida Karodia

Crossmatch

Sushila Makanji sat on the step of the veranda at her parents' home in Lenasia, an Indian township just outside Johannesburg. On her lap, face down, lay the script for a stage play *Love Under the Banyan Tree*. Sushi found the story fascinating; a tour de force of emotional torment. From the moment she read the script there was a powerful connection with the main character. It was as if the role of the young wife, trapped in a loveless marriage, had been created specifically for her, and she was eager to get back to London to audition for the part. She leaned back against the veranda wall, tilting her face to the sun, imagining what it would be like to be forced into marrying someone she despised.

Through the window, Sushi caught a glimpse of her mother and her sister Indira, who was six months pregnant with her second child.

Although Indira was making a valiant effort to disguise it, Sushi had sensed a sadness about her that she had not detected on her previous visit. She had sensed this change in her sister almost immediately, but their mother, around her all the time, seemed to suspect nothing. Indira had always been good at hiding her emotions. They were so different, the two girls, both in looks and in temperament: Indira the pretty child with the endearing shyness; Sushi the wilful one, disconcertingly frank. She had large intelligent eyes and a bold gaze which could fix with such intensity that it was difficult to be anything but honest with her.

Paradoxically these unsettling traits were what made her such a desirable actress, because in her five years in theatre she'd never once been without work. Her success had not changed her. She was still dogged, intractable and tactless, a born cynic, and her earlier rebelliousness had merely intensified with age.

When her mother asked her why she always went out of her way to be rude to family friends who visited, Sushi said, "I have no time for all this insincerity. I know what they think and say about me."

"They all like you, darling. They think you're fabulous," her mother had said. "You mustn't be rude."

"Bullshit!" said Sushi.

Her mother had gazed at her in astonishment, the language totally unexpected, even from Sushi.

"Those are the people who would chase me home. They thought I was a bad influence on their daughters because I smoked and swore."

"You smoked?" her mother asked, aghast.

"We all smoked, but I was the one who took the rap."

Sushi had an uncanny knack for getting into trouble. Her secrets were always the first ones to be discovered, no matter how hard she tried to conceal them, like the photograph Indira had found the previous night, of her and Kevin in an embrace. Kevin was shirtless, the matted hair of his chest crushed against the spandex of her gym suit, the two of them pressed so close they seemed to be joined at the hips. "Look at it," Indira had said, "you guys are practically doing it for the camera."

"Oh come off it. We're just kissing. Some idiot took the picture."

"Some kiss. There'll be hell to play if Ma or Papa see this." Sushi could imagine the furor. The mere thought of her living with a man, let alone an Englishman, would drive her parents crazy. She took the picture from Indira and tucked it away under the newspaper-lining in the bottom drawer of her bureau, confident it was safely hidden.

"Please don't even mention Kevin or this photograph again. Walls have ears and if Ma ever gets wind of this picture and has the slightest suspicion that something is going on, she won't let go until she drags the truth out of us."

"God, Sushi . . . If they ever find out . . ."

But Sushi cut her short. "Find out what?" she demanded. "The only way they'll find out anything is if you tell them."

She tried to dismiss the conversation and Indira's warning, but of course her sister was right. It wasn't so much the fear of discovery which constrained her, but the energy required to deal with the firestorm which would result from such discovery. She was exhausted, emotionally burnt out from her last role. She had reluctantly agreed to visit her parents, in the hope that the time away from her work would restore the passion drained during all those nightly performances. The thought alone of a scene with her mother was exhausting.

She closed her eyes and turned her face to the sun, soaking in the warming rays. She missed London . . . missed Kevin and the comfort of his arms. The ripple of anticipation which accompanied thoughts of him roused her. She opened her eyes, leaned forward and gathered her damp hair, tying it in a knot on the top of her head.

Her mother watched as Sushi tied her hair back. She feared that Sushi had grown apart from them and that it was too late to bridge the gap. Sushi knew that her mother worried about her. She had no idea where her mother got the idea from that everyone in London lived a debauched lifestyle.

Thoughts of Sushi in London preoccupied Mrs. Makanji. Even though she tried not to dwell on it, it crept into her every waking thought. Sometimes, at night, the anxiety awakened her and she would lie in the darkness thinking about it. It was difficult for her to watch her youngest daughter drifting beyond her sphere of influence. Even more difficult was the possibility that Sushi might have abandoned her Hindu traditions.

What to do? she wondered. The question repeated itself over and over again, like a mantra echoing through her thoughts. What to do? What to do?

She turned to Indira. "We should never have let her stay in London. Just look at her. Who dresses like that, eh?" Mrs. Makanji inclined her head to where Sushi sat on the veranda.

Sushi, dressed in black leggings and a brief top, was absorbed in thought.

"Slacks are okay. I wear slacks too," Mrs. Makanji said. "But what is that she's wearing? Those tight, tight pants? You can see the shape of everything. Has she no shame to be seen in public like that?"

"It's the fashion in London, Ma," Indira said.

"Those people in London are all Mangparas! It would be much better for her to be wearing decent clothes, nice dresses, so she can look decent like a nice Hindu girl should. Why don't you take her to the Sandton Shopping Centre?"

"She doesn't want to go shopping with me," Indira said.

"She'll go. She'll go. Just talk to her. If she doesn't want to buy dresses let her get a couple of salwar-kameez or sari, or dress slacks at the Plaza in Fordsburg. Anything but what she is wearing now," Mrs. Makanji said, her lips curling contemptuously. "I'll phone my friend Shantiben. She'll pick out some good stuff for her."

"Forget it, Ma. You're dreaming. Sushi will never do it. Why don't *you* take her?"

Mrs. Makanji shook her head. "You know how stubborn she can be with me. Whatever I say, it's the opposite of what she will do."

The expense of such shopping trips was of little concern to Mrs. Makanji, who spent quite lavishly. The old argument of Sushi's that she was saving them thousands of rands in wedding costs, just didn't wash with her parents. By local standards her family was well-off. In the days of rampant apartheid, when there had been no choice about where they could live, her parents had built their dream home here in Lenasia. It was at a time when Lenasia was designated a residential area for Indians.

"What do they care?" her father had asked, referring to the Group Areas Board. "They are going to implement their policies of Separate Development whether we like it or not. So why fight it?"

Mr. Makanji had grown tired of the uncertainty. He had wanted to provide a decent home for his wife and his family, and so had moved before the evictions began.

"I had to give up the ghost," he explained with a wan smile, when asked why he had been amongst the first to move.

Sushi and her father often discussed the changing face of the country. It was apparent to Sushi that considerable transformation had taken place since her last visit. And in the new liberal atmosphere many people who had made their money quickly had moved out of the townships into affluent white areas. Places like Sandton, Houghton and Rivonia had become neighbourhoods of choice for those non-whites who could afford to live there. Admitted to these hallowed neighbourhoods, the new rich sported all the trappings of their wealth. Electronic gates swung open to admit their brand new Mercedes-Benzs and BMWs.

But for the Makanjis this was home. Despite the fact that the crime rate had increased in Lenasia lately, Mr. Makanji was quite content to stay where he was. There had been some incidents. Some break-ins. And once a woman had been murdered only a few blocks from where they lived.

Sushi observed her mother from under lowered eyelids. Her mother was still very youthful. She was tall with a good figure and there was a certain elegance about her that Sushi admired. She also admired the way her father lavished attention on her mother. He was thoughtful of her. Whenever he went on his business trips to India and Taiwan, he always brought back exquisite gifts for her, seeking out the finest silk saris money could buy.

Mr. Makanji considered himself fortunate to have found a woman like her and hoped that Sushi would turn out to be more like her mother. Sushi was his favourite even though she was stubborn and wilful, and not at all like Indira who had never given them a day's trouble. Sushi was always stirring the trouble-pot.

Now that Sushi was home for a visit, her mother was preoccupied again with finding a good *match* for her. Mr. Makanji had reminded his wife that they had not been successful before, but Mrs. Makanji was adamant that this time would be different. He was not so sure. They had already arranged three meetings, none of which had turned out well. Sushila had been rude and indifferent towards the boys and their families. It was embarrassing for Mr. Makanji, who had known the families of two of the three boys for a long time.

"What kind of parents do you think we'd be, if we made no attempt to find someone for her?" Mrs. Makanji demanded, when her husband remarked that Sushi would only frustrate all their attempts. "You have to put your foot down, Arun. You're her father. She has to obey you."

"When has that ever happened?" Mr. Makanji asked with a grimace.

"We have lost her, Arun," Mrs. Makanji despaired. "We have lost her. I can't bear the thought of her going back to London to work on that stage." She spat out the word *stage* as though it were an obscenity. "What kind of a life is that for an Indian girl from a good home?" she demanded.

Mr. Makanji was at a loss and shook his head. It was obviously too late to forbid her from continuing this kind of work. They had made a mistake by giving into her pleas to stay in London after she graduated from college. She was only supposed to stay for a few months, but the few months dragged into years. He was sorry now that they hadn't insisted she come home at once after getting her B.A. degree.

When she didn't come home right away, and they had heard she was working as an actress, Mr. Makanji had gone to London immediately to see what was happening. He was horrified. "A B.A. degree to do this?" he demanded.

"Papa please, just for a little while?" she pleaded.

At first he was adamant, but she put up a tearful scene and he didn't have the heart to see her so miserable. He returned home without her, and he and his wife worried themselves sick about their youngest daughter.

One day she sent them a copy of a review in *The Guardian*. Mrs. Makanji hid it in a drawer, but couldn't help thinking about the nice things they had said about her daughter. Eventually, after showing it to a few friends and receiving a favourable reaction, she took the review out of the drawer and left it where it could be seen by everyone.

All her grey hair, she often complained, was due to Sushi, and she was as convinced as ever that the only solution to all their problems was to get her married.

Mrs. Makanji had heard that Dilip Vasant was in town visiting his family. He was a Chemical Engineer, teaching at Stanford. The boy sounded like an answer to their prayers.

Mr. Makanji did not know the Vasants very well but he was acquainted with Mr. Vasant whom he had met at a few social gatherings. Now, pressed by his wife, Mr. Makanji made enquiries.

Sushi entered the front room, wearing her tights and the scandalous little top, even shorter than the choli blouse worn under a sari. Sushi became aware of her mother's disapproving gaze.

"Are you talking about me again, Ma?" she asked, winking at her sister.

Mrs. Makanji threw up her hands and rolled her eyes.

Indira grinned. "Think we have nothing better to do than to sit around gossiping about you?"

"Come sit here," Mrs. Makanji said, patting the seat next to her, but Sushi ignored her mother's invitation.

"I see you've hired two more security guards," she said.

"You know your Papa," Mrs. Makanji replied.

This was so typical of her father, Sushi thought. Her mother didn't have to do a thing. He took care of everything. Others envied her mother, but it was not a life that Sushi would have wanted for herself. Her mother only had to speak once, to voice a thought, or a desire, and her father would respond. Her mother had a safety-deposit box full of jewellery, diamond rings and gold necklaces to attest to his generosity. She had all that jewellery and couldn't show it off. Even the ring with the enormous diamond had to be locked away. Instead, she wore a piece of coloured glass on her finger — a trinket made in Taiwan.

Mrs. Makanji complained bitterly about the exploding crime rate. Nothing was sacred any more, not even the gold chains around your neck. Thugs just walked by and yanked them right off. If they came off easily, you were lucky, otherwise they dragged you by the chain until they broke either the chain, or your neck.

She told Sushi that costume jewellery was preferred. Big pieces, so gaudy that it was obvious to any fool that they were worthless. Women flaunted them, wore them brazenly. No one was interested in stealing the junk. Sushi's father had cashed in on this trend; he'd seen it coming. Now his company sold tons of the junk jewellery, imported from India and Taiwan.

Mrs. Makanji sat on the sofa in the living room. The room had all the trappings of wealth. The TV and stereo were concealed behind a secret panel which opened with the flick of a switch. It was one added feature of security.

Since she could not display her wealth on her person, she had lavished it on her home. The furniture was leather; the carpets from Afghanistan and Iran. The pictures on the wall were of Hindu deities; prints of Krishna playing the flute with the gopies dancing around in their colourful skirts, pictures of Lakshmi and Ganesh — all in the best quality crystal frames which her husband had bought on one of his trips.

Sushi sat on the floor with her legs crossed, still wearing the clothes her mother found so offensive. She was applying the final coat of Scarlet Passion to her toenails, with as much care as an artist putting the finishing touches to a canvas.

Mrs. Makanji sat cross-legged on the sofa, her gold bracelets jangling as she gestured with her hands. Sushi surreptitiously watched as her mother's long elegant fingers fluttered and curled, jabbed and sparred in the air as she spoke. Her mother had been a dancer. One could see it in the graceful way she walked and moved.

In the background the sound of music seemed to rise into the dead spaces of the room. Sushi had put on a tape of ghazals by a popular Indian singer. She had brought many of her tapes from London. She was familiar with the words and sang along under her breath. Mrs. Makanji, drawn by the plaintive wail of the singer, stopped talking to listen. Better this, she had said to Indira, than the other unbearable loud pop music for which Sushi seemed to have such a passion.

"Sushi, I think you ought to wear a pale-blue sari on Sunday. What do you think, eh Indira?"

"I told you Ma, I'm not going to dress up for anyone. I'm not interested in this idiot from Blythe or wherever it is he comes from," Sushi said without looking up from her toenails.

"He's from California," her mother added.

"Just so you get your story straight, Ma . . . his brother is from Blythe, he's from Stanford," Indira said. "Both places are in California."

"Well, same thing. No difference," Mrs. Makanji said, tossing her head.

"Who cares!" Sushi cried, her gaze shifting from her mother to her sister. "How come you suddenly know so much about him, Indira? Have you been in on this, too?"

Indira chose not to respond. Sushi noticed that her sister was more subdued than usual. She had complained about the baby being too active and that she was constantly tired. Sushi had noticed how edgy she was and had assumed that it was because Ravi was away. Sushi finished painting her nails. She screwed the bottle shut, carefully got up and padded into the next room.

Indira exchanged glances with her mother.

"She has turned down every eligible young man. What is wrong with her? One of these days she'll be too old. Then what?" Mrs. Makanji asked. "You speak to her, Indira. She'll listen to you. This is a nice boy. He's an engineer, teaching at Stanford. Good looking, too, or so I've heard. He's just visiting with his parents. He's not going to be around forever. We have to get the two of them together for an introduction."

"You know you're just wasting your time," Indira said.

Mrs. Makanji called out to Sushi in the next room. "He's a nice fellow. You're making a mistake not wanting to meet him. He can have any girl he wants."

Sushi returned. "If he's such hot stuff, why isn't he married yet?"

"Perhaps he's fussy," Indira said.

Sushi went over to the stereo to change the tape. "Or perhaps there's something wrong with him. Have any of you considered that possibility?"

Mrs. Makanji threw up her hands in frustration. "Better that I would have had a dozen sons. Boys are much less trouble!"

Sushi laughed. "Ma, you're so quaint!"

"What does that mean?"

Sushi continued to laugh. Indira joined in despite her attempts at self-control.

"What does it mean, this being quaint?" Mrs. Makanji's glance darted from Sushi to Indira.

"It means, sweet Ma. Sweet," Indira said.

"A little old-fashioned, too," Sushi added.

Mrs. Makanji thought about what her daughters had said. Old-fashioned wasn't exactly the way she perceived herself.

"You should've asked for a snapshot, Ma," Indira said.

"I did. Mrs. Lalji, who is his mother's cousin, said she'd send me one. But I never got it."

"Likely story. He probably thought we'd figure out he looks like the rear end of a jackass."

Indira laughed so hard she almost lost control of her bladder. She struggled out of the chair and waddled over to the window, still laughing. She gazed out into the yard as she pressed her hands into her back. She was six months into her pregnancy and enormous. Most of their friends took one look at her shape and promptly declared, "Girl?" It was disconcerting because Ravi had set his heart on a boy. One girl was enough. Now he wanted a son to carry on the family business.

When Sushi left the room Mrs. Makanji turned to Indira, patting the seat beside her on the chesterfield. "Sit down, Indira. Are you all right?" she asked, leaning forward and gently lifting a strand of hair out of her daughter's face. "You don't look well."

"I'm fine, Ma."

"Listen, my darling, talk to your sister. One of these days she'll be too old and then no man will want her."

"She doesn't have to worry, Ma. She has a career . . ."

"What career?" Mrs. Makanji snorted. "What is acting? That's not a career!" She paused, her glance softening as she gazed at her daughter. "Why can she not be more like you? Look how happy you and Ravi are. We knew the instant we saw Ravi that he was the one for you."

Indira's glance flickered away. She just couldn't bring herself to tell her parents about the problems she and Ravi were having. Her mother gazed at her affectionately.

"And now the baby is coming too," Mrs. Makanji added. "Maybe this time it'll be a boy?"

Indira seemed to brace herself against her mother's words, and then slowly raised her head. "Boy or girl, it doesn't matter," she said.

"Of course not. We're so happy for you, Indira. We know how long you've waited for this pregnancy."

Indira nodded and smiled with a touch of wistfulness. "I know you are," she said, patting her mother's hand.

"I just wish you would speak to your sister. She has great affection for you and Ravi." Mrs. Makanji's hands fluttered to her lap as gracefully as a butterfly settling on a delicate plant. "Better we talk to her now, than have trouble when Dilip Vasant comes with his family on Sunday. Go please, Indira, my dear. See what you can do, eh?"

With a boost from her mother, Indira got up off the chesterfield, but did not go after her sister. She was in pain and uncomfortable. Her mother, however, didn't seem to notice.

"I don't know what to do with her any more. Stubborn! You will not believe how stubborn that girl is. I don't know where she gets such stubbornness," Mrs. Makanji said. "Your Papa is not like that."

Sushi heard this comment as she went upstairs to her room. She needed some quiet space to concentrate on the script, but there was obviously not going to be any peace and quiet until this whole issue of meeting this boy was over.

"God," Sushi muttered as she flung the script onto the bed. "I should've stayed in London."

At breakfast the next morning Sushi listened indifferently to the conversation at the table. Her father had left for his office already and her mother was making plans for Sunday. It was hard to believe that her parents had gone to so much trouble, they had even consulted an astrologer to fix an auspicious date and time for the meeting. But though Sushi might have found the situation amusing, her parents were proceeding in all earnestness.

"I know this time will be different, Sushi," her mother said. "I have a feeling about it."

Sushi exchanged glances with her sister, who smiled encouragingly. She wondered for a brief instant about the "boy," imagining that he was probably being subjected to the same pressures as she.

In the meantime, across town the Vasants had just finished their breakfast. Dilip was seated in an easy chair enjoying his second cup of tea while listening to a CD on the brand new stereo system. He seemed distracted and drew a hand through his hair in a characteristic gesture of frustration.

Mrs. Vasant watched her son. A robust, traditional Indian woman who always wore a sari, she sat cross-legged on the sofa. On her lap was a thali tray, with an assortment of relishes, chutneys and pickles. Mrs. Vasant seemed quite unperturbed by the loudness of the modern Indian music as she nimbly picked at the food on the tray.

Her son was thirty-six years old and still unmarried, a fact she feared might raise questions in the minds of others. She had prayed that he would return to stay but he was home only for a short visit. Her sari slipped off her shoulder. As she raised an arm to carry the food to her mouth, she revealed a too-tight bodice which exposed the upper rise of her breasts. Around her midriff, pinched, pale folds of skin were visible. Her hair hung loose to her waist.

Dilip got up and walked over to the stereo. He had the easy fluid grace of a dancer and although his face was pocked with acne scars, there was still something very attractive about him, something in the expressiveness of his eyes. But he was thirty-six and unmarried and try as she might, his mother could not get beyond that fact. She studied him as he leaned over the stereo and for the first time noticed that his hair had receded.

Mr. Vasant, seated in an easy chair, seemed preoccupied.

Mrs. Vasant paused in her eating to gaze fondly at Dilip. "I have told everyone about our son who is an engineer at Stanford in California, USA. But I wish you could stay here with us and not go back there," she said.

Dilip raised his head and smiled distractedly at his mother.

Mr. Vasant seemed to rouse himself from his thoughts. "Arunbhai Makanji has invited us on Sunday. It seems he has expressed great interest in meeting you. He's heard about you."

Dilip glanced up from where he was sorting through the CDs and shook his head. "There's a cricket game on Sunday. I promised some friends I'd go with them." He selected a CD and slid it into the player.

"Your father and I are very proud of you, son. You cannot refuse such an invitation," Mrs. Vasant said to Dilip, and turned her eyes on her husband in a mute appeal for help.

Mr. Vasant frowned his disapproval. "Forget cricket. On Sunday you will come with us."

Dilip felt his throat tighten. His parents tended to have this effect on him. Sometimes he felt as though he was going to choke, but he suppressed his feelings and turned away from them so they couldn't see his expression. He hated it when they made decisions without consulting him. But, above all, he hated the way they still treated him like a child. His visit had been nothing but an aggravation. First they criticized his taste in music, then it was the earring. To keep the peace he had removed the stud from his ear. Now they were putting the pressure on him to meet this girl. He opened his mouth to protest, but saw the look of eager anticipation on his mother's face and his anger dissipated. He wished that they didn't have so many unreasonable expectations about him, and that his mother didn't always give him this guilt trip. She had actually cried when she discovered he was eating meat. The underlying issue, he realized, was not only marriage, but also their desire to keep him at home.

"I wish you'd drop this idea. I've told you, I'm not interested in finding a bride," Dilip said returning to his chair.

"What makes you think we're finding a match for you?" Mrs. Vasant asked coyly.

"Because I know you."

His mother smiled. "I hear their daughter Sushila is very educated and very beautiful. You'll see. You'll change your mind once you meet her," she said.

"I'm not going to change my mind."

"Don't worry about liking her or not liking her, just come along so we can meet the family. If you don't like her it's okay," his mother said.

"Ma, please . . ."

"We will not utter one more word about it, dikra. See my lips are sealed." Mrs. Vasant put up her hand to silence any further discussion. Then she laughed and gave her son an affectionate glance. Dilip shook his head in resignation and smiled, tightly.

"Your brother phoned from Blythe this morning. He says you don't visit much anymore," Mr. Vasant said.

"I told you that I've been busy. I've had my hands full with my new job," Dilip replied.

"That's why you need a wife . . . to help you," said his mother.

"I don't need a wife. Now will you please drop the subject," Dilip snapped.

Mrs. Vasant's startled gaze sought her husband's. She sensed a new element. Something was wrong. "There is someone in your life already?" she said, turning the statement into a question.

Dilip got up abruptly, almost upsetting his cup of tea. He walked to the window and gazed out. He wondered how he could tell them. They would never understand. Never. He had to lie again. His whole life had become a lie. His parents waited. "There is someone at Stanford . . ." he said.

Mr. and Mrs. Vasant exchanged troubled glances.

"I was going to tell you about it," he muttered.

"Who is she?" Mrs. Vasant asked.

"Why have you not mentioned this before?" Mr. Vasant demanded, leaving his chair with startling agility.

"Who is she, my darling? What is her name?" his mother asked, her shrewd glance studying her son's face.

Dilip tried to remain calm. He had opened the sluice gates, now he had to control the flow.

"Well," his father said. "Why don't you answer your mother?"

Dilip regretted that he had given them an opening. They were obviously not going to let go of it. His mother was like a dog with a bone.

"Who is she, Dilip?" she asked.

"Where is she from?" his father asked.

Dilip felt the room closing in on him. "It's someone from California," he said, affecting nonchalance. The music ended and he went over to the audio system to change the compact disc, turning up the music a little more, to make conversation awkward.

"What is her family name?" His mother had to speak loud enough to be heard over the music.

Dilip mumbled something.

"Turn the volume down!" his father cried.

Dilip hesitated. He needed time to get his thoughts together. His father glared at him. His mother put her hand to her head.

Dilip turned down the volume. "Sorry," he said, smiling sheepishly. He glanced at his mother. Her arm was poised above the thali tray. He could feel the noose tightening.

"Ma, I'm going to tell you all about it, but not right now. Why don't we meet this lady on Sunday and we'll see . . . ?"

"We'll see what?" his father asked, still perturbed by the way Dilip was avoiding their questions.

For the moment, though, his mother was satisfied.

"Okay," she said. "It's a deal. No problem now, eh? We go to the Makanjis on Sunday."

Mr. Vasant watched his wife eating. "I wish you would stay here instead of going back to the USA. There'll be good prospects here for engineers. It'll be much easier to get a job at the university. They're going to need people and we have a responsibility to this country. We can't just run. We have to give something back to make it work."

"It's ironical, isn't it, Pop, that there was a time when blacks couldn't even enroll in engineering. It was one of the faculties closed to them because the government figured they would never be able to work as engineers in this country. Now here we are . . ." Dilip said with a sardonic shrug.

"So, what do you say? You don't need to rush back to California," Mr. Vasant persisted.

"My life is in California, Pop. Not here."

"I was hoping that someday the business could be passed on to my sons," Mr. Vasant said. "But now you have your engineering job and your brother has his motel in Blythe . . ." He paused, his expression pained. "Work, work, work, all my life and for what? Who will there be to take over the family business? I fought to stay here . . . I went to jail even," he said, shaking his head at the recollection. "I spent my life building this business, expanding it . . . and for what?" Mr. Vasant shook his head. His heart ached with disappointment and a tear gathered in the corner of one eye as he stared at the food tray on his wife's lap. "We'd better get to the shop," he said.

Dilip said he'd join them later. He didn't feel like going with them. He'd never imagined his visit home would be so stressful. It was as though he had been dropped into a fishbowl, everything he said or did was subject to scrutiny by his parents. In a matter of three weeks, his mother had somehow managed to reduce him to a twelve-year-old boy again. Although he hated it, resisted it, he was no match for his mother, who was an expert at manipulation. She'd had years of practice on his father. He was anxious to get back to Stanford and his life there. He had only been home for three weeks, but it already felt like months.

At home in Lenasia Sushi shared these sentiments. She glanced into the mirror and with a start saw her sister. "I didn't hear you come in," she said. She examined her image in the bedroom mirror, turning her head this way and that way, holding her hair up in a knot at the top of her head. "What do you think?" she asked. "You think I should cut it?" She turned to Indira. "I've been thinking of cutting it and maybe getting a perm. I'm so tired of the way I look."

"Don't be silly. You look wonderful. I like your hair the way it is," Indira said.

"You're so old-fashioned," Sushi retorted. "You're just like Ma."

Indira groaned. "I don't think so. But never mind me," she said. "What are you going to do when they find out that you're shacked up with an Englishman?"

Sushi shrugged. She gazed into the mirror and caught her sister's eye. "I don't know," she said to her sister's reflection.

"He's cute. I suppose you're being careful?" Indira said, with the same habit as her mother of turning a statement into a question, or vice versa.

"Oh come on, Indira! What do you think? I'm not that stupid!"

Indira grimaced and leaned back against the pillows. "This is the fourth boy they've invited," she said.

"I don't care. It's their problem. Anyway, I'm only humouring them. In another ten days I'll be out of here and all of this will be history." Sushi glanced at her sister who looked so forlorn. "You okay?" she asked, sitting beside her on the bed.

Indira nodded and was silent for a moment. She scowled at Sushi, her expression darkening with pent-up frustration. "Oh damn . . . No! I'm not all right! My back hurts. I'm exhausted. I don't sleep well. I eat like a pig and I throw up like a fucking sick dog!"

Startled, Sushi glanced at her sister — Indira's strongest expletive was usually "Shoot," which under extreme conditions could be translated into "Shit" — then she fell back on the bed, howling with laughter. "If Ma could hear you she'd have a fit!" Sushi said, amidst peals of laughter.

Indira started to laugh, holding onto her belly, shedding tears of mirth and pain.Finally she caught her breath. "God, I hate being like this," she said, dabbing at the tears with a crumpled tissue. "Look at me, only six months and I can't even get my shoes on by myself. I have to ask Ma or Anna. What am I going to be like when I'm eight or nine months?"

Sushi saw the sad look returning to her sister's eyes. "I think Ravi is a jerk. He doesn't know what a wonderful wife he has," she said. "I sure as hell would never put up with his crap. And where is he? . . . He's jetting around while you're struggling to function with this . . . this enormous belly." She put her hand on her sister's stomach and felt the baby move. "Why do you put up with it, Indira?"

Indira's glance slid away. She took a shuddering breath. "Ravi is away on business. It's not like he's deliberately staying away . . ."

"Bullshit! When are you going to stop covering up for him! He took off the moment you started your morning sickness! It's easier to send you gifts and make long-distance phone calls than to be here supporting you through this time. And what about those tests he wanted you to take?"

"How . . . ?"

"You wrote to me, remember? I read between the lines. I know you too well, sister."

Indira picked at the edge of the bedspread, twisting and untwisting the cloth around her finger. "I don't care about the sex of the child . . . but Ravi wants a son. When I refused to take the tests he went on a business trip to the UK and India." She paused, glancing away. "I used to go with him all the time you know, but now it's like he's punishing me because I refused to take the tests."

"The bastard . . ." Sushi muttered.

Indira raised her head, her expression disconsolate.

Sushi's glance softened. "Never mind, it'll all be over soon and whatever it is, it'll be adored by all. I'm glad you refused to have the tests," she said.

"I almost agreed," Indira confessed. "But I heard him telling his mother that if it was a girl he would try to persuade me to have an abortion in the States."

"Crafty bastard, he knew that if you came to London, he'd have to deal with me. Do Ma and Papa know about this?"

Indira shook her head and shut her eyes, too ashamed to look at her sister sitting cross-legged, looking for all the world like a vengeful Buddha.

"You're too soft. Too easy to manipulate, that's why everyone thinks you're such a good daughter."

Indira was silent, uncomfortable both physically and emotionally. She swung her legs off the bed, looking so miserable, so unhappy, that Sushi could only feel sorry for her. Indira had leaped directly into marriage. She had never had the opportunity to explore her potential; to see what she was capable of, or to determine her own worth.

Sushi got up and returned to the dresser. She caught her sister's eye in the mirror and quickly glanced away.

"Ma and Papa," Indira said, "are wondering why you've been turning all these men away. You should tell them something . . ." She knew her parents would persist. Things might have been different for her if she'd had the strength to stand up to them.

"You're right," Sushi said. "I'll talk to them. Isn't it incredible. I'm twenty-eight years old, I've walked in off the street and auditioned stone-cold for major roles, I've played to tough audiences, and yet here I am worrying about telling Ma and Papa that I'm living with a man."

"Yes, but this isn't just any man. It's an Englishman . . ."

Sushi grimaced wryly, picked up the brush and started to brush her hair again.

On Sunday Mr. and Mrs. Vasant and Dilip arrived at the Makanji house in Lenasia. Mrs. Vasant gazed around curiously. It was obvious the Makanjis were well-off. This, of course, was no surprise. She and her husband had made discreet enquiries about their hosts. She maintained that it was always good to be prepared, so no time was wasted fumbling around. In this case, everything seemed to indicate a good match.

Mr. Makanji and his wife welcomed them. The men shook hands. Mrs. Vasant put her hands together. "Namaste," she said. Her glance travelled around surreptitiously before she raised her head. In that brief instant she had made a mental note of the entire entrance hall and the living room.

Nita, dressed prettily in a dress of flounces and bows, shyly joined her grandmother in the entrance hall. Mrs. Makanji gently urged her forward to greet the visitors.

"Come inside please," Mrs. Makanji said, taking Mrs. Vasant's arm and escorting her to the smaller entertainment room, leaving the men in the care of Mr. Makanji who led them into the living room.

"You have a lovely home," Mrs. Vasant said.

Mrs. Makanji beamed. "Thank you," she said. "We'll sit over here and I'll bring my daughters to meet you. Go call your mother and Sushila," she said to Nita.

Nita hesitated, her grandmother waved her on and she hurried away to call her mother and her aunt.

Mrs. Vasant sat down. "She is a darling," she said.

"My daughter Indira's little girl," Mrs. Makanji replied proudly.

Mrs. Vasant smiled, glancing around the room at the pictures on the walls while she and Mrs. Makanji made polite conversation. Mrs. Vasant sat back in the sofa, but her legs were too short and dangled uncomfortably. She tried sliding forward, perching on the edge of her seat so that her feet touched the floor, but she was still uncomfortable. She would have loved to draw her legs up on the sofa, but she couldn't; it wouldn't be polite. She shimmied back in her seat, and reaching for a pillow, placed it behind her back.

Indira waddled in, looking pained and uncomfortable. She greeted Mrs. Vasant and sat down. Sushi sauntered in a few moments later, looking unconcerned. She had resisted the pressure from her mother to wear a sari. "Not on your life, Ma," she had said. "I'm not wearing a sari just to impress anyone. I'll wear one because I want to, and I don't want to wear a sari today."

Mrs. Makanji had wrung her hands, had put on a tearful perfor-mance, but Sushi was adamant.

"You're not going to wear any of the stuff you brought along with you . . . Are you?" Mrs. Makanji had asked, in a small pained voice.

"I'll wear slacks," Sushi tossed back casually.

Fearing something even more outrageous, Mrs. Makanji refrained from critical comment when she saw Sushi's white tight pants and long Nehru-style blouse.

Sushi greeted Mrs. Vasant, noting the woman had none of her mother's elegance. Mrs. Vasant was fat and squat. From her sister's expression, Indira knew that there was no hope for Dilip Vasant.

The older women took Indira and Sushi into the living room to introduce them to Mr. Vasant and Dilip. Sushi was extremely polite and Mrs. Makanji could find no fault with her behaviour, except that she was so cold and aloof. It was as though she was deliberately put-ting the boy off.

What is wrong with this girl? Mrs. Makanji asked herself as they sat down with the men. "The servant will bring some refreshments in a moment," she said to the others. Anna came in with a tray laden with cold drinks and snacks. "How's business, Chimanbhai?" Mr. Makanji asked Mr. Vasant.

"Not bad for me, but many of the shopkeepers in town are com-plaining. They say that the African vendors are ruining their business. They are opening stands everywhere. If there is a fruit shop, right in front of the fruit shop they will open a fruit stand. If there is a dress shop, right in front of that dress shop they will have a rack of dresses on the pavement, selling much cheaper than the shop because they don't have to pay any rent."

"Some people would admire such entrepreneurial spirit," Dilip said.

Mr. Vasant shrugged. "Depends on how you look at it. If you were one of the shopkeepers, you wouldn't be saying that."

"I wouldn't be downtown if you paid me to go there. Too many robberies lately," Mr. Makanji said.

Dilip laughed and shook his head. "It's a sign of the economic crisis here and elsewhere. People have to survive somehow. It's the same problem in the States."

"I hear you're an engineer there," Mr. Makanji said.

Dilip nodded, his gaze straying to Sushi, who had not as much as given him a second glance. Mr. Makanji noticed the glance and was hopeful.

"So you're a university teacher?" Mrs. Makanji said, turning the statement into a question.

"Yes. I'm teaching at Stanford."

"Are you thinking of coming back to South Africa?" Mr. Makanji asked.

Dilip glanced at his parents and shook his head.

"It was my question to him as well," Mr. Vasant said. "Just the other day I was saying, now that things had changed, it might be a good idea to come back home."

Sushi looked across at Dilip. She couldn't help feeling sorry for him as both sets of parents put him through the third-degree. She and Indira excused themselves and went to the kitchen. Neither of them were there when Nita sidled over to her grandmother holding the picture of her and Kevin which she had discovered in Sushi's drawer. Nita, fascinated with everything about her aunt, particularly enjoyed rummaging through her possessions and playing with her make-up. As usual she had been going through Sushi's bureau drawers when she found the photograph.

Nita quietly waited in adult company for the opportunity to show off the picture. She leaned up against her grandmother's lap, photo in her hand, waiting for a break in the conversation knowing her grandmother would be annoyed at her for interrupting.

"Nani, see this picture of Aunty Sushi," she said, the moment her grandmother paused to take a breath.

Distracted, her grandmother took the photograph from her, smiled indulgently and glanced at it. The picture was a blur without her glasses. She still held the picture in her hand as she gestured, while conversing, her gold bracelets clinking with every movement. Dolefully, Nita gazed at the two women, disappointed about being ignored by her grandmother who was merrily laughing at something Mrs. Vasant had said. Mrs. Vasant paused as she noticed the expression on Nita's face. Mrs. Makanji became aware of Nita still waiting beside her chair.

She glanced at the photograph again. "Later, darling. I'll look at the picture later. I don't have my glasses," she said, handing the photograph back to Nita. Sushi entered the room as Nita slipped away feeling slighted. She didn't notice the photograph in Nita's hand, or notice Nita pausing at the sideboard to put it in the drawer.

In the meantime Mrs. Vasant had observed the look Sushi had given Dilip as she entered the room and was relieved. The match would be an excellent one. The girl had a nice face and was respectful. She seemed like an obedient daughter, just the kind of girl Mrs. Vasant was hoping Dilip would meet. It would have been better, though, if she had worn a sari instead of those pants, she would have preferred a more traditional girl for Dilip, but at this stage she wasn't going to let minor details distract her.

Mrs. Makanji thought that everyone was getting along splendidly. Still, she held her breath. Even though Sushi seemed to be on her best behaviour, Mrs. Makanji wasn't prepared to trust her luck. Any moment now she expected her happiness-bubble to burst.

After dinner they sat talking again. Sushi had managed throughout dinner to avoid glancing at Mrs. Vasant who was eating with such uninhibited relish. Once or twice she had caught her mother's eye and her mother had shaken her head unobtrusively to discourage any comment from Sushi. Dilip had intercepted the exchange. Embarrassed, he had glanced away.

Later, Indira, Sushi and Dilip went out onto the veranda. Dilip and Sushi were a bit awkward with each other at first.

"When is your husband coming back?" Dilip asked Indira.

"In about two weeks," Indira said.

Sushi studied Dilip. He wasn't too bad, she reflected. Of the four men, or "boys" her parents had introduced her to, Dilip was the least offensive, but . . . his mother was definitely a different story.

They spoke for a while. Dilip asked her about her work in London. She asked him about his work at Stanford. He was easy to talk to. She was genuinely beginning to like him and felt relaxed and comfortable in his company. There was something non-threatening about him and she listened with great interest as he described his life in California. Indira, feeling left out of their common experiences and anecdotes, went inside.

"It's crazy isn't it," Dilip said to Sushi. "I'm glad you're not taking any of this seriously."

Sushi grinned. "They're just buzzing with excitement now," she said.

"Each time I come for a visit, we go through the same routine. That's why I don't get back that often," he said.

"I know what you mean," Sushi chuckled, imagining how their parents would probably be interpreting this exchange she was having with Dilip out on the veranda.

They sat outside, perched on the wall, talking as though they had been friends for years. Mrs. Makanji smiled, the brilliance of her smile spreading around the room until Mrs. Vasant felt it too, and smiled in return. Things were certainly going much better than either of them had hoped for.

Eventually Dilip and his parents left. There was no firm commitment from either family to meet again, but there was hope. Lots of hope. It was there in the smiles as the two families said goodbye to each other; it was in the sparkling air and in Mrs. Makanji's laughter which was so rich with undertones.

Mrs. Makanji was anxious to find out what Sushi thought about Dilip. *She* thought he was perfect, but knowing her daughter she didn't dare ask, in case Sushi turned him down out of contrariness. So Mrs. Makanji went to bed that night, bristling with questions and anxiety. She was so highly strung that Mr. Makanji had to sit up half the night, reassuring her.

"They were talking so much. Didn't you see?" Mr. Makanji said.

"But darling, you don't know her as I do," Mrs. Makanji said.

"Don't worry. She'll make up her mind."

"But when, Arun? When she's an old woman and no one will want to marry her?"

Mr. Makanji laughed.

"If only she would be as easy to please as Indira," Mrs. Makanji muttered.

"We have given her an education. We have taught her to think independently. Now we have to trust that she will make a good decision."

"If we had boys we might have had less problems," Mrs. Makanji grumbled.

Mr. Makanji smiled. He knew not to take her seriously.

"Look at Indira. I can see that something is wrong, but she is not telling me," Mrs. Makanji continued.

"She will tell us when she is ready. Only then can we help her," Mr. Makanji soothed. "For now we have to be satisfied and be thankful that we all have our good health."

In Sushi's room, Indira and Sushi were up, talking.

"He's not too bad, but I don't think I could take much of his mother!" Sushi said, laughing. "My God!" she cried, giving a mock shudder.

"She wasn't so bad . . ." Indira said.

"What!" Sushi cried. "I'd rather be dead . . ." she threw her hands up into the air with all the drama she could muster. Then she leaped onto the bed and bounced up and down with child-like exuberance.

"I'm surprised you're taking the meeting with Dilip so lightly." Indira was puzzled by her sister's lack of concern. She had expected her to be angry.

Sushi laughed. "He's very sweet and . . . he's also very gay."

"You're joking. Right?" Indira said.

Sushi shook her head. "No, I'm not."

"How do you know?"

"I have lots of gay friends in London."

"I can't believe it. Are you sure?"

"Of course, I'm sure. Why?"

"Well . . . Hindu boys . . . I mean . . ."

"Come off it, Indira . . . Why do you find it so hard to believe that a Hindu boy can be gay?"

"I don't know. I've just never known any."

Sushi smiled and shook her head in gentle reproach. "You're still very naive, you know."

Indira smiled. "I suppose so." She paused and met her sister's glance. "I'm going to miss you when you're gone," she said, suddenly serious again.

"If things here get really rough for you, come and spend some time with me," Sushi said, ". . . and bring Nita. You'll like Kevin. He's a lot of fun. And don't worry. We do have a spare bedroom." She reached for the light. "I'm going to miss you, too. Believe it or not, I'll probably miss Ma and Papa as well, but it's better to keep my distance from them. We get along much better that way."

Indira sighed and lay back. "God, I can't get him out of my mind," she said in the dark, the issue of Dilip and his being gay still troubling her.

"Who?"

"Dilip."

"Why?" Sushi asked.

"I can imagine what's it's going to be like when his parents find out."

Sushi was silent. She, too, had been thinking about it.

Mrs. Makanji sat up and turned on her light. "I can't sleep, Arun. I think I'll go make myself some warm milk." She got up and went to the kitchen.

She warmed some milk in the microwave. She usually kept a small box of sleeping powder in the sideboard drawer. It was an ayurvedic remedy for insomnia and the only things that helped her through those awful nights when she couldn't get to sleep.

Mrs. Makanji opened the drawer. Lying right on top was the picture of Sushi and Kevin in passionate embrace. She found her spare glasses in the other sideboard drawer and took the picture into the light. Stunned, she felt her knees weaken. Her hand flailed behind her for a chair and she sat down heavily. She studied the picture and then turned it over. On the back of the picture was the corny message — "To Sushi. My lips, my heart and all those important parts, love you forever! Kevin."

Her face was ashen.

"Sushi. Oh Sushi," she moaned, clasping her chest, writhing. "Such a curse! . . . Oh my God . . . Oh my God," she cried softly.

Sushi lay awake in the darkness, thinking about Dilip. It was going to be a shock to her parents when she told them the truth about him. She knew that somehow she was going to have to tell them about Kevin, too. But she wanted to ease into it, slowly. She wasn't quite sure how, yet. Sushi sighed wearily. She was too tired to deal with it now. There would be time enough tomorrow.

Michael Ondaatje

The Passions of Lalla

My Grandmother died in the blue arms of a jacaranda tree. She could read thunder.

She claimed to have been born outdoors, abruptly, during a picnic, though there is little evidence for this. Her father — who came from a subdued line of Keyts — had thrown caution to the winds and married a Dickman. The bloodline was considered eccentric (one Dickman had set herself on fire) and rumours about the family often percolated across Colombo in hushed tones. "People who married the Dickmans were afraid."

There is no information about Lalla growing up. Perhaps she was a shy child, for those who are magical break from silent structures after years of chrysalis. By the time she was twenty she was living in Colombo and tentatively engaged to Shelton de Saram — a very good looking and utterly selfish man. He desired the good life, and when Frieda Donhorst arrived from England "with a thin English varnish and the Donhorst chequebook" he promptly married her. Lalla was heartbroken. She went into fits of rage, threw herself on and pounded various beds belonging to her immediate family, and quickly married Willie Gratiaen — a champion cricketer — on the rebound.

Willie was also a broker, and being one of the first Ceylonese to work for the English firm of E. John and Co. brought them most of their local business. The married couple bought a large house called "Palm Lodge" in the heart of Colombo and here, in the three acres that came with the house, they began a dairy. The dairy was Willie's second attempt at raising livestock. Fond of eggs, he had decided earlier to import and raise a breed of black chicken from Australia. At great expense the prize Australorp eggs arrived by ship, ready for hatching, but Lalla accidentally cooked them all while preparing for a dinner party.

Shortly after Willie began the dairy he fell seriously ill. Lalla, unable to cope, would run into neighbours' homes, pound on their beds, and promise to become a Catholic if Willie recovered. He never did and Lalla was left to bring up their two children.

She was not yet thirty, and for the next few years her closest friend was her neighbour, Rene de Saram, who also ran a dairy. Rene's husband disliked Lalla and disliked his wife's chickens. Lalla and the chickens would wake him before dawn every morning, especially Lalla with her loud laughter filtering across the garden as she organized the milkers. One morning Rene woke to silence and, stepping into the garden, discovered her husband tying the beaks of all the chickens with little pieces of string, or in some cases with rubber bands. She protested, but he prevailed and soon they saw their chickens perform a dance of death, dying of exhaustion and hunger, a few managing to escape along Inner Flower Road, some kidnapped by a furious Lalla in the folds of her large brown dress and taken to Palm Lodge where she had them cooked. A year later the husband lapsed into total silence and the only sounds which could be heard from his quarters were barkings and later on the cluck of hens. It is believed he was the victim of someone's charm. For several weeks he clucked, barked and chirped, tearing his feather pillows into snowstorms, scratching at the expensive parquet floors, leaping from first-storey windows onto the lawn. After he shot himself, Rene was left at the age of thirty-two to bring up their children. So both Rene and Lalla, after years of excessive high living, were to have difficult times — surviving on their wits and character and beauty. Both widows became the focus of the attention of numerous bored husbands. Neither of them was to marry again.

Each had thirty-five cows. Milking began at four-thirty in the morning and by six their milkmen would be cycling all over town to deliver fresh milk to customers. Lalla and Rene took the law into their own hands whenever necessary. When one of their cows caught Rinderpest Fever — a disease which could make government officials close down a dairy for months — Rene took the army pistol which had already killed her husband and personally shot it dead. With Lalla's help she burnt it and buried it in her garden. The milk went out that morning as usual, the tin vessels clanking against the handlebars of several bicycles.

Lalla's head milkman at this time was named Brumphy, and when a Scot named McKay made a pass at a servant girl Brumphy stabbed him to death. By the time the police arrived Lalla had hidden him in one of her sheds, and when they came back a second time she had taken Brumphy over to a neighbour named Lillian Bevan. For some reason Mrs. Bevan approved of everything Lalla did. She was sick when Lalla stormed in to hide Brumphy under the bed whose counterpane had wide lace edges that came down to the floor. Lalla explained that it was only a minor crime; when the police came to the Bevan household and described the brutal stabbing in graphic detail Lillian was terrified as the murderer was just a few feet away from her. But she could never disappoint Lalla and kept quiet. The police watched the house for two days and Lillian dutifully halved her meals and passed a share under the bed. "I'm proud of you darling!" said Lalla when she eventually spirited Brumphy away to another location.

However, there was a hearing in court presided over by Judge E.W. Jayawardene — one of Lalla's favourite bridge partners. When she was called to give evidence she kept referring to him as "My Lord My God." E.W. was probably one of the ugliest men in Ceylon at the time. When he asked Lalla if Brumphy was good looking — trying humorously to suggest some motive for her protecting him — she replied, "Good looking? Who can say, My Lord My God, some people may find *you* good looking." She was thrown out of court while the gallery hooted with laughter and gave her a standing ovation. This dialogue is still in the judicial records in the Buller's Road Court Museum. In any case she continued to play bridge with E.W. Jayawardene and their sons would remain close friends.

Apart from rare appearances in court (sometimes to watch other friends give evidence), Lalla's day was carefully planned. She would be up at four with the milkers, oversee the dairy, look after the books and be finished by 9 A.M. The rest of the day would be given over to gallivanting — social calls, lunch parties, visits from admirers and bridge. She also brought up her two children. It was in the garden at Palm Lodge that my mother and Dorothy Clementi-Smith would practise their dances, quite often surrounded by cattle.

For years Palm Lodge attracted a constant group — first as children, then teenagers and then young adults. For most of her life children flocked to Lalla, for she was the most casual and irresponsible of chaperones, being far too busy with her own life to oversee them all. Behind Palm Lodge was a paddy field which separated her house from "Royden," where the Daniels lived. When there were complaints that hordes of children ran into Royden with muddy feet, Lalla bought ten pairs of stilts and taught them to walk across the paddy fields on these "boruka-kuls" or "lying legs." Lalla would say yes to any request if she was busy at bridge so they knew when to ask her for permission to do the most outrageous things. Every child had to be part of the group. She particularly objected to children being sent for extra tuition on Saturdays and would hire a Wallace Carriage and go searching for children like Peggy Peiris. She swept into the school at noon yelling "PEGGY!!!," fluttering down the halls in her long black clothes loose at the edges like a rooster dragging its tail, and Peggy's friends would lean over the bannisters and say, "Look, look, your mad aunt has arrived."

As these children grew older they discovered that Lalla had very little money. She would take groups out for meals and be refused service as she hadn't paid her previous bills. Everyone went with her anyway, though they could never be sure of eating. It was the same with adults. During one of her grand dinner parties she asked Lionel Wendt who was very shy to carve the meat. A big pot was placed in front of him. As he removed the lid a baby goat jumped out and skittered down the table. Lalla had been so involved with the joke — buying the kid that morning and finding a big enough pot — that she had forgotten about the real dinner and there was nothing to eat once the shock and laughter had subsided.

In the early years her two children, Noel and Doris, could hardly move without being used as part of Lalla's daily theatre. She was constantly dreaming up costumes for my mother to wear to fancy dress parties, which were the rage at the time. Because of Lalla, my mother won every fancy dress competition for three years while in her late teens. Lalla tended to go in for animals or sea creatures. The crowning achievement was my mother's appearance at the Galle Face Dance as a lobster — the outfit bright red and covered with crustaceans and claws which grew out of her shoulder blades and seemed to move of their own accord. The problem was that she could not sit down for the whole evening but had to walk or waltz stiffly from side to side with her various beaux who, although respecting the imagination behind the outfit, found her beautiful frame almost unapproachable. Who knows, this may have been Lalla's ulterior motive. For years my mother tended to be admired from a distance. On the ballroom floor she stood out in her animal or shellfish beauty but claws and caterpillar bulges tended to deflect suitors from thoughts of seduction. When couples paired off to walk along Galle Face Green under the moonlight it would, after all, be embarrassing to be seen escorting a lobster.

When my mother eventually announced her engagement to my father, Lalla turned to friends and said, "What do you *think*, darling, she's going to marry an Ondaatje . . . she's going to marry a *Tamil!*" Years later, when I sent my mother my first book of poems, she met my sister at the door with a shocked face and in exactly the same tone and phrasing said, "What do you *think*, Janet" (her hand holding her cheek to emphasize the tragedy), "Michael has become a *poet!*" Lalla continued to stress the Tamil element in my father's background, which pleased him enormously. For the wedding ceremony she had two marriage chairs decorated in a Hindu style and laughed all through the ceremony. The incident was, however, the beginning of a war with my father.

Eccentrics can be the most irritating people to live with. My mother, for instance, strangely, *never* spoke of Lalla to me. Lalla was loved most by people who saw her arriving from the distance like a storm. She did love children, or at least loved company of any kind — cows, adults, babies, dogs. She always had to be surrounded. But being "grabbed" or "contained" by anyone drove her mad. She would be compassionate to the character of children but tended to avoid holding them on her lap. And she could not abide having grandchildren hold her hands when she took them for walks. She would quickly divert them into the entrance of the frightening maze in the Nuwara Eliya Park and leave them there, lost, while she went off to steal flowers. She was always determined to be physically selfish. Into her sixties she would still complain of how she used to be "pinned down" to breast feed her son before she could leave for dances.

With children grown up and out of the way, Lalla busied herself with her sisters and brothers. "Dickie" seemed to be marrying constantly; after David Grenier drowned she married a de Vos, a Wombeck and then an Englishman. Lalla's brother Vere attempted to remain a bachelor all his life. When she was flirting with Catholicism she decided that Vere should marry her priest's sister — a woman who *had* planned on becoming a nun. The sister also had a dowry of thirty thousand rupees, and both Lalla and Vere were short of money at the time, for both enjoyed expensive drinking sessions. Lalla master-minded the marriage, even though the woman wasn't good looking and Vere liked good looking women. On the wedding night the bride prayed for half an hour beside the bed and then started singing hymns, so Vere departed, foregoing nuptial bliss, and for the rest of her life the poor woman had a sign above her door which read "Unloved. Unloved. Unloved." Lalla went to mass the following week, having eaten a huge meal. When refused mass she said, "Then I'll resign," and avoided the church for the rest of her life.

A good many of my relatives from this generation seem to have tormented the church sexually. Italian monks who became enam-oured of certain aunts would return to Italy to discard their robes and return to find the women already married. Jesuit fathers too were falling out of the church and into love with the de Sarams with the regularity of mangoes thudding onto dry lawns during a drought. Vere also became the concern of various religious groups that tried to save him. And during the last months of his life he was "held captive" by a group of Roman Catholic nuns in Galle so that no one knew where he was until the announcement of his death.

Vere was known as "a sweet drunk" and he and Lalla always drank together. While Lalla grew loud and cheerful, Vere became excessively courteous. Drink was hazardous for him, however, as he came to believe he escaped the laws of gravity while under the influ-ence. He kept trying to hang his hat on walls where there was no hook and often stepped out of boats to walk home. But drink qui-etened him except for these few excesses. His close friend, the lawyer Cox Sproule, was a different matter. Cox was charming when sober and brilliant when drunk. He would appear in court stumbling over chairs with a mind clear as a bell, winning cases under a judge who had pleaded with him just that morning not to appear in court in such a condition. He hated the English. Unlike Cox, Vere had no profession to focus whatever talents he had. He did try to become an auctioneer but being both shy and drunk he was a failure. The only job that came his way was supervising Italian prisoners during the war. Once a week he would ride to Colombo on his motorcycle, bringing as many bottles of alcohol as he could manage for his friends and his sister. He had encouraged the prisoners to set up a brewery, so that there was a distillery in every hut in the prison camp. He remained drunk with the prisoners for most of the war years. Even Cox Sproule joined him for six months when he was jailed for helping three German spies escape from the country.

What happened to Lalla's other brother, Evan, no one knows. But all through her life, when the children sent her money, Lalla would immediately forward it on to Evan. He was supposedly a thief and Lalla loved him. "Jesus died to save sinners," she said, "and I will die for Evan." Evan manages to escape family memory, appearing only now and then to offer blocs of votes to any friend running for public office by bringing along all his illegitimate children.

By the mid-thirties both Lalla's and Rene's dairies had been wiped out by Rinderpest. Both were drinking heavily and both were broke.

We now enter the phase when Lalla is best remembered. Her children were married and out of the way. Most of her social life had been based at Palm Lodge but now she had to sell the house, and she burst loose on the country and her friends like an ancient monarch who had lost all her possessions. She was free to move wherever she wished, to do whatever she wanted. She took thorough advantage of everyone and had bases all over the country. Her schemes for organizing parties and bridge games exaggerated themselves. She was full of the "passions," whether drunk or not. She had always loved flowers but in her last decade couldn't be bothered to grow them. Still, whenever she arrived on a visit she would be carrying an armful of flowers and announce, "Darling, I've just been to church and I've stolen some flowers for you. These are from Mrs. Abeysekare's, the lilies are from Mrs. Ratnayake's, the agapanthus is from Violet Meedeniya and the rest are from *your* garden." She stole flowers compulsively, even in the owner's presence. As she spoke with someone her straying left hand would pull up a prize rose along with the roots, all so that she could appreciate it for that one moment, gaze into it with complete pleasure, swallow its qualities whole and then hand the flower, discarding it, to the owner. She ravaged some of the best gardens in Colombo and Nuwara Eliya. For some years she was barred from the Hakgalle Public Gardens.

Property was there to be taken or given away. When she was rich she had given parties for all the poor children in the neighbourhood and handed out gifts. When she was poor she still organized them but now would go out to the Pettah market on the morning of the party and steal toys. All her life she had given away everything she owned to whoever wanted it and so now felt free to take whatever she wanted. She was a lyrical socialist. Having no home in her last years, she breezed into houses for weekends or even weeks, cheated at bridge with her closest friends, calling them "damn thieves," "bloody rogues." She only played cards for money and if faced with a difficult contract would throw down her hand, gather the others up and proclaim "the rest are mine." Everyone knew she was lying but it didn't matter. Once when my brother and two sisters who were very young were playing a game of "beggar-my-neighbour" on the porch, Lalla came to watch. She walked up and down beside them, seemingly very irritated. After ten minutes she could stand it no longer, opened her purse, gave them each two rupees and said, "Never, *never* play cards for love."

She was in her prime. During the war she opened up a boarding house in Nuwara Eliya with Muriel Potger, a chain smoker who did all the work while Lalla breezed through the rooms saying, "Muriel, for godsake, we can't breathe in this place!" — being more of a pest than a help. If she had to go out she would say, "I'll just freshen up" and disappear into her room for a stiff drink. If there was none she took a quick swig of eau de cologne to snap her awake. Old flames visited her constantly throughout her life. She refused to lose friends; even her first beau, Shelton de Saram, would arrive after breakfast to escort her for walks. His unfortunate wife, Frieda, would always telephone Lalla first and would spend most afternoons riding in her trap through the Cinnamon Gardens or the park searching for them.

Lalla's great claim to fame was that she was the first woman in Ceylon to have a mastectomy. It turned out to be unnecessary but she always claimed to support modern science, throwing herself into new causes. (Even in death her generosity exceeded the physically possible for she had donated her body to six hospitals). The false breast would never be still for long. She was an energetic person. It would crawl over to join its twin on the right hand side or sometimes appear on her back, "for dancing" she smirked. She called it her Wandering Jew and would yell at the grandchildren in the middle of a formal dinner to fetch her tit as she had forgotten to put it on. She kept losing the contraption to servants who were mystified by it as well as to the dog, Chindit, who would be found gnawing at the foam as if it were tender chicken. She went through four breasts in her lifetime. One she left on a branch of a tree in Hakgalle Gardens to dry out after a rainstorm, one flew off when she was riding behind Vere on his motorbike and the third she was very mysterious about, almost embarrassed though Lalla was never embarrassed. Most believed it had been forgotten after a romantic assignation in Trincomalee with a man who may or may not have been in the Cabinet.

Children tell little more than animals, said Kipling. When Lalla came to Bishop's College Girls School on Parents' Day and pissed behind bushes — or when in Nuwara Eliya she simply stood with her legs apart and urinated — my sisters were so embarrassed and ashamed they did not admit or speak of this to each other for over fifteen years. Lalla's son Noel was most appalled by her. She, however, was immensely proud of his success, and my Aunt Nedra recalls seeing Lalla sitting on a sack of rice in the fish market surrounded by workers and fishermen, with whom she was having one of her long daily chats, pointing to a picture of a bewigged judge in *The Daily News* and saying in Sinhalese that *this* was *her* son. But Lalla could never be just a mother; that seemed to be only one muscle in her chameleon nature, which had too many other things to reflect. And I am not sure what my mother's relationship was to her. Maybe they were too similar to even recognize much of a problem, both having huge compassionate hearts that never even considered revenge or small-mindedness, both howling and wheezing with laughter over the frailest joke, both carrying their own theatre on their backs. Lalla remained the centre of the world she moved through. She had been beautiful when young but most free after her husband died and her children grew up. There was some sense of divine right she felt she and everyone else had, even if she had to beg for it or steal it. This overbearing charmed flower.

In her last years she was searching for the great death. She never found, looking under leaves, the giant snake, the fang which would brush against the ankle like a whisper. A whole generation grew old or died around her. Prime Ministers fell off horses, a jellyfish slid down the throat of a famous swimmer. During the forties she moved with the rest of the country towards Independence and the 20th century. Her freedom accelerated. Her arms still flagged down strange cars for a lift to the Pettah market where she could trade gossip with her friends and place bets in the "bucket shops." She carried everything she really needed with her, and a friend meeting her once at a train station was appalled to be given as a gift a huge fish that Lalla had carried doubled up in her handbag.

She could be silent as a snake or flower. She loved the thunder; it spoke to her like a king. As if her mild dead husband had been transformed into a cosmic umpire, given the megaphone of nature. Sky noises and the abrupt light told her details of careers, incidental wisdom, allowing her to risk everything because the thunder would warn her along with the snake of lightning. She would stop the car and swim in the Mahaveli, serene among currents, still wearing her hat. Would step out of the river, dry in the sun for five minutes and climb back into the car among the shocked eyeballs of her companions, her huge handbag once more on her lap carrying four packs of cards, possibly a fish.

In August 1947, she received a small inheritance, called her brother Vere and they drove off to Nuwara Eliya on his motorcycle. She was 68 years old. These were to be her last days. The boarding house she had looked after during the war was empty and so they bought food and booze and moved in to play "Ajoutha" — a card game that normally takes at least eight hours. It was a game the Portuguese had taught the Sinhalese in the 15th century to keep them quiet and preoccupied while they invaded the country. Lalla opened the bottles of Rocklands Gin (the same brand that was destroying her son-in-law) and Vere prepared the Italian menus, which he had learned from his prisoners of war. In her earlier days in Nuwara Eliya, Lalla would have been up at dawn to walk through the park — inhabited at that hour only by nuns and monkeys — walk round the golf-course where gardeners would stagger under the weight of giant python-like hoses as they watered the greens. But now she slept till noon, and in the early evening rode up to Moon Plains, her arms spread out like a crucifix behind Vere.

Moon Plains. Drowned in blue and gold flowers whose names she had never bothered to learn, tugged by the wind, leaning in angles for miles and miles against the hills 5000 feet above sea level. They watched the exit of the sun and the sudden appearance of the moon half way up the sky. Those lovely accidental moons — a horn a chalice a thumbnail — and then they would climb onto the motorcycle, the 60-year-old brother and the 68-year-old sister, who was his best friend forever.

Riding back on August 13, 1947, they heard the wild thunder and she knew someone was going to die. Death, however, not to be read out there. She gazed and listened but there seemed to be no victim or parabola end beyond her. It rained hard during the last mile to the house and they went indoors to drink for the rest of the evening. The next day the rains continued and she refused Vere's offer of a ride knowing there would be death soon. "Cannot wreck this perfect body, Vere. The police will spend hours searching for my breast thinking it was lost in the crash." So they played two-handed Ajoutha and drank. But now she could not sleep at all, and they talked as they never had about husbands, lovers, his various possible marriages. She did not mention her readings of the thunder to Vere, who was now almost comatose on the bluebird print sofa. But she could not keep her eyes closed like him and at 5 A.M. on August 15,

1947, she wanted fresh air, needed to walk, a walk to Moon Plains, no motorcycle, no danger, and she stepped out towards the still dark night of almost dawn and straight into the floods.

For two days and nights they had been oblivious to the amount of destruction outside their home. The whole country was mauled by the rains that year. Ratmalana, Bentota, Chilaw, Anuradhapura, were all under water. The forty-foot-high Peredeniya Bridge had been swept away. In Nuwara Eliya, Galways's Land Bird Sanctuary and the Golf Course were ten feet under water. Snakes and fish from the lake swam into the windows of the Golf Club, into the bar and around the indoor badminton court. Fish were found captured in the badminton nets when the flood receded a week later. Lalla took one step off the front porch and was immediately hauled away by an arm of water, her handbag bursting open. 208 cards moved ahead of her like a disturbed nest as she was thrown downhill still comfortable and drunk, snagged for a few moments on the railings of the Good Shepherd Convent and then lifted away towards the town of Nuwara Eliya.

It was her last perfect journey. The new river in the street moved her right across the race course and park towards the bus station. As the light came up slowly she was being swirled fast, "floating" (as ever confident of surviving this too) alongside branches and leaves, the dawn starting to hit flamboyant trees as she slipped past them like a dark log, shoes lost, false breast lost. She was free as a fish, travelling faster than she had in years, fast as Vere's motorcycle, only now there was this *roar* around her. She overtook Jesus lizards that swam and ran in bursts over the water, she was surrounded by tired half-drowned fly-catchers screaming *tack tack tack tack*, frogmouths, nightjars forced to keep awake, brain-fever birds and their irritating ascending scales, snake eagles, scimitar-babblers, they rode the air around Lalla wishing to perch on her unable to alight on anything except what was moving.

What was moving was rushing flood. In the park she floated over the intricate fir tree hedges of the maze — which would always continue to terrify her grandchildren — its secret spread out naked as a skeleton for her. The symmetrical flower beds also began to receive the day's light and Lalla gazed down at them with wonder, moving as lazily as that long dark scarf which trailed off her neck brushing the branches and never catching. She would always wear silk, as she showed us, her grandchildren, would pull the scarf like a fluid through the ring removed from her finger, pulled sleepily through, as she moved now, awake to the new angle of her favourite trees, the Syzygium, the Araucaria Pine, over the now unnecessary iron gates of the park, and through the town of Nuwara Eliya itself and its shops and stalls where she had haggled for guavas, now six feet under water, windows smashed in by the weight of all this collected rain.

Drifting slower she tried to hold onto things. A bicycle hit her across the knees. She saw the dead body of a human. She began to see the drowned dogs of the town. Cattle. She saw men on roofs fighting with each other, looting, almost surprised by the quick dawn in the mountains revealing them, not even watching her magic ride, the alcohol still in her — serene and relaxed.

Below the main street of Nuwara Eliya the land drops suddenly and Lalla fell into deeper waters, past the houses of "Cranleigh" and "Ferncliff." They were homes she knew well, where she had played and argued over cards. The water here was rougher and she went under for longer and longer moments coming up with a gasp and then pulled down like bait, pulled under by something not comfortable any more, and then there was the great blue ahead of her, like a sheaf of blue wheat, like a large eye that peered towards her, and she hit it and was dead.

Rooplall Monar

Bahadur

This Bahadur couldn't read and write at all people say, but he gat more commonsense than most estate people who uses to wuk in the backdam from soon-soon morning until six o'clock in the evening, when cricket and night beetle does croak inside the cane field, by the beezie-beezie and the blacksage bush-corner.

And too besides, them ole people say that this Bahadur was damn independent. You couldn't dare eye-pass he or want fo push yuh finger in he face, else was real trouble. And he don't stand fo nonsense from them driver and overseer and backraman, never mind they been control the estate at that time. And beside, Bahadur was lil fussy chap. True-true, if he ain't feel to wuk one day he staying home, and the next day he get excuse in he sleeve long time to tell driver and overseer. So it come that them estate people does say Bahadur is a real sense man.

Well, it so happen that soon after Bahadur get married he start to think serious about building he future. He know that if he continue wukking in the Creole gang, then move to spray gang, then shovel gang, by the time he reach forty he body turn like packsawal mango. True, he might lose he manhood like one-two sugar worker and he still gon live in logie. And pardna, if you couldn't wuk Sunday to Sunday in the sugar estate, you on the brim of starvation. Tings always hard guava season. And though sugar had good price in Europe because of the war, in backdam money been still too small.

So one Wednesday night while he on he bed, Bahadur tell he wife Sumintra that he gon leff cane wuk and start fo hustle fish, because he ain't like the damn slavery going-on in the estate. And too beside he can't stem the blasted advantage them driver and overseer does take on them good-looking coolie and black woman who does wuk in the weeding gang.

"But is not all time fish does run, Bahadur," Sumintra say, and though she eye brighten up, she face serious.

"And is not fo all time people does keep they strength fo wuk in backdam. People is no engine," Bahadur say while he stroking Sumintra round face and she long hair, which run down till by she hip.

"But you can think up something better?" Sumintra ask. She want make sure they future build up step by step.

"Arite woman, gimme some time," Bahadur say. You see he didn't want fo displease Sumintra, he like she too bad. Is the first woman he had you know. So after they make a lil sweetness, he assure she that he gon think up some smart way fo earn he bread and live in better logie, or he name not Bahadur.

And he been thinking that whosoever get ranger wuk in the estate come damn independent. Ranger wuk get authority, and you does get lil bit privilege with Big Manager, and the work easy too. But only brave and trustful men like Sugrim and Mutton, who been serve estate faithfully like them backdam mule ever since them was small boys, could get that sort of job, so Bahadur couldn't dream of get ranger wuk until he prove heself faithfully. And too beside, Bahadur daddy or uncle is not a driver so they na able fo sweet-talk Big Manager to get Bahadur ranger wuk. But if one smart man wuk he brain good, he must get ranger wuk, Bahadur tell heself.

And day-in, day-out, while Bahadur still wukking in creole gang, he thinking-thinking. Some day when sun real hot and them creole boys and Bahadur sweating like donkey working in the thick-thick sugarcane, Bahadur does feel to curse the driver and walk off the job. But when he mind flash-back pon Sumintra he does clam up he mouth. True, he don't want Sumintra to feel he lazy and good-fo-nothing.

And one-two day when rainy season heavy, and sandfly, cap-cap and scorpion reigning like king in them cane field, and try fo suck out yuh blood while yuh throwing manure on them young cane-root, Bahadur does leggo some stinking mumma cuss and attempt o smash them cap-cap forthwith which does sting he. Then he does say kiss-me-rass, to hell with backdam wuk. But when he mind flash at Sumintra, he passion does cool down, and then he does strain he brain-nerve fo think up quick-quick how he could get one ranger wuk.

Then one morning when Bahadur wake up, he get one bright idea, but he ain't tell Sumintra, who been cooking on the chulaside in the rickety front-shading which been join the logie. And throughout the day while Bahadur wukking in the backdam, he shuffling the idea in he mind just like he shuffling card at wakenight. After dinner he decide fo work forthwith on the idea.

Round nine o'clock night time when he notice that moonlight come out, he tuck in one white flour-bag bed-sheet inside he shirt, which he dig out from the trunk in the bedroom unknown to Sumintra. Then he walk by Sumintra while she darning he shirt by one hand-lamp and say, "Gal, I now remember Das ole man want see me important tonight-tonight, so I gat fo go out."

Sumintra agree, but she advice he that he must be careful by Cabbage-Dam side, cause she hear that it does have one jumbie there that does frighten people.

"None jumbie ain't dead yet fo frighten me, gal," Bahadur say as he walk out.

When Bahadur pass Cabbage-Dam, and turn in the next dry mud-dam which running behind the sugar factory compound, he notice the dam clear. Is only the estate cowpen, surround partly by some fruit tree and beezie-beezie bush he seeing. This time the two ranger-watchman, Sugrim and Mutton, patrolling cowpen like security guard; one-two time they gaffing, then they smoking and laughing.

Good, Bahadur shake he head and say. Then Bahadur hide heself behind one cork tree which been growing aside the mud-dam don-key years now, while he studying the surrounding like one tief-man before he go fo tief. Twenty minutes later Bahadur tek out the sheet and throw it over he self. Now he does look like one judge-night peo-ple you does see on the road preaching. Only thing is that he face cover, though Bahadur make sure he seeing through the sheet. When he certain the mud-dam clear, and is only Sugrim and Mutton he see-ing around the cowpen, he step on the mud-dam from out the cork tree and start fo walk slow-slow toward the cowpen. This time he tip-toeing and stretching one-two time so he could look tall, while the breeze flapping the sheet flap flap flap . . .

Meanwhile Sugrim and Mutton bussing-down one gaff. True, they saying that since Head Ranger place them to watch cowpen one year now, they never see jumbie, although backdam people say too much jumbie does reign round this side. But that is chupidness they say. And if you hear how they boasting and bragging, eh-eh, you gon think they could strangle one lion if it materialize in front of them.

And Mutton start talk how some watchman is cockroach . . . they just frighten they own shadow, especially Ramdat. Sametime Sugrim raise he eye and it happen to drop on this thing in white, walking slowly toward the cowpen. Eh-eh, Sugrim puke. And he still watch-ing this thing as though he hypnotized. When Mutton notice that Sugrim ain't listening to he, he follow Sugrim eye and he too spot the white thing.

This time Bahadur done notice Sugrim and Mutton reaction, and he know that they frighten-frighten. So he start walk more slow, tip-toeing and stretching heself like Moongaza.

"Shit, dat is what?" Mutton ask while he getting cold sweat and he teeth knocking.

"That is no people. That is something strange," Sugrim talk while he mind reflect that some jumbie does look just like this, but he ain't tell Mutton.

Meanwhile Bahadur still walking slow, and when he about to reach the cowpen he leggo one screech like night owl. Then he chuckle and laugh in one big tone ha ha ha, and then he turn back.

"O Gawd, Mutton, is a Dutchman," Sugrim say. "And me hear Dutchman is bad-bad."

Soon as Mutton hear that he scramble he dinner bag and bolt to factory side, saying, "To hell wid cowpen. Me ain't want Dutchman kill me tonight."

And don't matter how much Sugrim saying, "Hold on, hold on, Mutton," Mutton ain't stopping. Eh-eh, he speeding more. Then sametime as Sugrim shout that Dutchman jumbie disappear, he hear the screech and see the white thing coming toward the cowpen again.

"O Gawd, this gat to be one Dutchman. Me ain't want dead tonight," Sugrim shout, and start fo gallop like jackass toward the factory, hollering, "Mutton, Mutton, wait, boy Mutton . . ."

When Bahadur see the rigmarole he want buss-down one laugh. He plan working exactly how he'd seen it. One hour later while he on the bed, and Sumintra sleeping and snoring as though she work whole day in the backdam, Bahadur start plan how he gon operate the next night.

Come morning, whole estate know one Dutchman jumbie been frightening Sugrim and Mutton, and they had was to run fo they life. And don't matter how much time Big Manager and Head Ranger telling Sugrim an Mutton that it ain't gat nothing name jumbie, that is only vision, still Sugrim and Mutton insist that they want keep watch somewhere else that night, and begging Head Ranger that he must place two other watchman by cowpen. At last Head Ranger agree, and decide to place Ram and Pooran by the cowpen.

All time when people talking bout this Dutchman jumbie, Bahadur cool like cucumber, though he laughing in he mind. And people been too occupy with this jumbie, so they ain't have time to notice Bahadur.

When night come, round nine o'clock Bahadur tell Sumintra he belly griping bad-bad, and he going to the latrine which been situate about twenty-five rod away from the logie.

"But careful of this Dutchman jumbie, you hear, man," Sumintra warn Bahadur as he left the logie.

"Me na frighten na jumbie, gal," Bahadur say.

This time moonlight bright like day and the place look silvery. When Bahadur certain the mud-dam clear he go behind the tree and throw the sheet over he self. Coupla minute after he walk slow-slow toward the cowpen, and he howling like dog does howl when they see jumbie.

And like Ram and Pooran been on the look out. True, when they spot the white thing they done know is the very Dutchman jumbie, and like it really mean to kill them the way it howling. So pardna, they ain't tek chance at all, they grab they dinner bag and scoot toward the sugar factory like athlete, screaming all the way. They ain't want this Dutchman jumbie ketch them at all. They always hearing them ole people say is yuh neck them jumbie does break first and yuh does die like fowlcock. And they ain't want to die this way because them ole people say that if is so yuh soul don't get prappa resting.

Meantime Bahadur head to he logie and walk in easy like cat, and when he certain Sumintra sleeping he take out the sheet and put it inside the drawer next the bed.

Next morning, news spread like wildfire. Big Manager and Big Ranger come worry. True, if they ain't place watchman by estate cowpen, certain-sure it have people like Black, Sumeer and Nizam bound to tief one-two young calf and bull, slaughter them and sell it quick-quick to them butcher in Good Hope befo' morning come. And Big

Manager know that if calf or bull short in estate, them overseer and manager gon be disgruntled because they like to eat they beef every Gawd day.

And don't matter how much trap Big Manager and Head Ranger been set, they never catch Black, Sumeer and Nizam red-handed. Estate people does say them boys does smell the rat. And you can't accuse them on suspicion. Eh-eh, you have to catch them. And them boys know the law. And too beside they slippery like ochro.

By afternoon time every watchman refuse point blank to keep watch by the cowpen. They say they ain't mind going back to wuk in backdam, which they argue is better than if you does dead by one Dutchman jumbie. And don't matter how tempting is the sweet-talk and pay increase coming from Big Manager mouth, still them ranger an watchman hold they end. At last Big Manager turn to Head Ranger Sambo.

"Take your deputy and pass the night there until we work out something," Big Manager say.

"Yes, Boss," Sambo reply. But in he mind he frighten, specially of this Dutch jumbie. But he gat to obey Big Manager else he might be sent back to backdam wuk, and he ain't want that. Head ranger wuk give Sambo authority, and too beside Sambo greasing palm with driver and overseer, plus he getting sweet-talk with women.

By afternoon time news spread that Big Ranger Sambo and Second Ranger Burt self going to watch cowpen, and they mean to put one end to this jumbie. All time Sambo and Burt beetie yapping like suction pump, but they acting brave-brave. By eight o'clock night time, whole estate done bolt up inside they logie, because they ain't want tengle with this jumbie. By nine o'clock Bahadur tell Sumintra he gat one message fo Khan and he must deliver it tonight-tonight. This time he done tuck in the white sheet inside he shirt long time since.

When Bahadur bank Cabbage Dam Turn and enter the dry mud-dam, he notice them two ranger in front the cowpen smoking, so he duck down by the parapet and throw the sheet over he self. Then he raise-up and start walk slow-slow toward the cowpen.

Soon as Sambo and Burt spot the white thing, big-big sweat start drop down they forehead blop blop, and by the time word come out from Sambo mouth, "You is who?" Bahadur screech like one night owl, then he laugh with one strange big sound . . . Eh-eh, Sambo and Burt skin come heavy and they inside come cold like ice while they heart beating bap bap bap like water pump. They done know this is a bad jumbie and they can't tek chance. So by the time the white thing turn back and laugh, Sambo and Burt crawl through the bush which grow round the cowpen, reach one dry mud-dam, then head straight to they logie more quick than one cat with dog on he tail.

Next day news spread like wildfire. This time Sambo and Burt sick in bed, and every hour they screaming out as though they seeing this Dutchman in front they eye. Soontime fear done strike the estate so bad that even during the day the backdam people stop walking by the cowpen, while three other strong man had to accompany Khan and Paul fo clean cowpen. And soon as cowpen done clean them men vanish.

Big Manager try whole day to get two watchman fo watch the cowpen, but everybody refusing. Now Big Manager in one prickle, especially when he think bout Black, Sumeer and Nizam. By one o'clock he detail one message to all field worker saying that which male worker willing to watch cowpen that night gon get extra money. But everybody refusing, don't matter how much them driver sweet-talk them.

Then Bahadur notify the gang driver that he, Bahadur, taking up the challenge.

"Bahadur? Ah-eh, one pinnie-winnie thing like he gon watch cowpen?" some people talk when the news break out.

"Bahadur gat fo be mad," other people say.

And in order to certain that Bahadur ain't get away from cowpen, some men set up sentry by Cabbage Dam unknowing to Bahadur. And as the night hour going from ten to eleven to twelve in the bright moonlight, them men by Cabbage Dam only seeing cowpen, but they ain't seeing the jumbie. Two hour later them get baffle and left. Next day was rigmarole in estate. People saying Sambo, Burt, Mutton and Sugrim ain't see any damn jumbie. And don't matter how much Mutton and Sugrim saying that they did, estate people believe they lying.

But when Big Manager ask some men at order-line to help keep watch at the cowpen they tremble lil-bit and say no no . . . So was Bahadur had to watch the cowpen again. Three night later when Big Manager and Second Manager check by cowpen at twelve o'clock midnight, Bahadur in position in front the cowpen brave like one tiger, and all the cattle safe.

"The only brave person we have in this damn superstitious estate is Bahadur," Big Manager tell Second Manager next morning by order-line. And from that day on, Bahadur was confirm as Head Ranger.

And one morning two-three week later when Bahadur and Sum-intra lying on they bed, and Bahadur stroking she smooth round face and she long hair which run down till she hip, he tell she how he get the Head Ranger job. She look at he real proud, while in she mind she saying that her man ain't going to lose he manhood like them other backdam worker what get shrivel up by hard-wuk and the sun. And she smile at he and they do they lil sweetness.

Salman Rushdie

The Courter

1

Certainly-Mary was the smallest woman Mixed-Up the hall porter had come across, dwarfs excepted, a tiny sixty-year-old Indian lady with her greying hair tied behind her head in a neat bun, hitching up her red-hemmed white sari in the front and negotiating the apartment block's front steps as if they were Alps. "No," he said aloud, furrowing his brow. What would be the right peaks. Ah, good, that was the name. "Ghats," he said proudly. Word from a schoolboy atlas long ago, when India felt as far away as Paradise. (Nowadays Paradise seemed even further away but India, and Hell, had come a good bit closer.) "Western Ghats, Eastern Ghats and now Kensington Ghats," he said, giggling. "Mountains."

She stopped in front of him in the oak-panelled lobby. "But ghats in India are also stairs," she said. "Yes yes certainly. For instance in Hindu holy city of Varanasi, where the Brahmins sit taking the pilgrims' money is called Dasashwamedh-ghat. Broad-broad stair-case down to River Ganga. O, most certainly! Also Manikarnika-ghat. They buy fire from a house with a tiger leaping from the roof — yes certainly, a statue tiger, coloured by Technicolor, what are you thinking? — and they bring it in a box to set fire to their loved ones' bodies. Funeral fires are of sandal. Photographs not allowed; no, cer-tainly not."

He began thinking of her as Certainly-Mary because she never said plain yes or no; always this O-yes-certainly or no-certainly-not. In the confused circumstances that had prevailed ever since his brain, his one sure thing, had let him down, he could hardly be certain of anything any more; so he was stunned by her sureness, first into nos-talgia, then envy, then attraction. And attraction was a thing so long forgotten that when the churning started he thought for a long time it must be the Chinese dumplings he had brought home from the High Street carry-out.

English was hard for Certainly-Mary, and this was a part of what drew damaged old Mixed-Up towards her. The letter p was a particular problem, often turning into an f or a c; when she proceeded through the lobby with a wheeled wicker shopping basket, she would say, "Going shocking," and when, on her return, he offered to help lift the basket up the front ghats, she would answer, "Yes, fleas." As the eleva-tor lifted her away, she called through the grille: "Oé, courter! Thank you, courter. O, yes, certainly." (In Hindi and Konkani, however, her p's knew their place.)

So: thanks to her unexpected, somehow stomach-churning magic, he was no longer porter, but courter. "Courter," he repeated to the mirror when she had gone. His breath made a little dwindling pic-ture of the word on the glass. "Courter courter caught." Okay. People called him many things, he did not mind. But this name, this courter, this he would try to be.

2

For years now I've been meaning to write down the story of Certainly-Mary, our ayah, the woman who did as much as my mother to raise my sisters and me, and her great adventure with her "courter" in London, where we all lived for a time in the early sixties in a block called Waverley House; but what with one thing and another I never got round to it.

Then recently I heard from Certainly-Mary after a longish silence. She wrote to say that she was ninety-one, had had a serious operation, and would I kindly send her some money, because she was embarrassed that her niece, with whom she was now living in the Kurla district of Bombay, was so badly out of pocket.

I sent the money, and soon afterwards received a pleasant letter from the niece, Stella, written in the same hand as the letter from "Aya" — as we had always called Mary, palindromically dropping the "h." Aya had been so touched, the niece wrote, that I remembered her after all these years. "I have been hearing the stories about you folks all my life," the letter went on, "and I think of you a little bit as family. Maybe you recall my mother, Mary's sister. She unfortunately passed on. Now it is I who write Mary's letters for her. We all wish you the best."

This message from an intimate stranger reached out to me in my enforced exile from the beloved country of my birth and moved me, stirring things that had been buried very deep. Of course it also made me feel guilty about having done so little for Mary over the years. For whatever reason, it has become more important than ever to set down the story I've been carrying around unwritten for so long, the story of Aya and the gentle man whom she renamed — with unintentional but prophetic overtones of romance — "the courter." I see now that it is not just their story, but ours, mine, as well.

3

His real name was Mecir: you were supposed to say Mishirsh because it had invisible accents on it in some Iron Curtain language in which the accents had to be invisible, my sister Durré said solemnly, in case somebody spied on them or rubbed them out or something. His first name also began with an m but it was so full of what we called Communist consonants, all those z's and c's and w's walled up together without vowels to give them breathing space, that I never even tried to learn it.

At first we thought of nicknaming him after a mischievous little comic-book character, Mr. Mxyztplk from the Fifth Dimension, who looked a bit like Elmer Fudd and used to make Superman's life hell until ole Supe could trick him into saying his name backwards, Klptzyxm, whereupon he disappeared back into the Fifth Dimension; but because we weren't too sure how to say Mxyztplk (not to mention Klptzyxm) we dropped that idea. "We'll just call you Mixed-Up," I told him in the end, to simplify life. "Mishter Mikshed-Up Mishirsh." I was fifteen then and bursting with unemployed cock and it meant I could say things like that right into people's faces, even people less accommodating than Mr. Mecir with his stroke.

What I remember most vividly are his pink rubber washing-up gloves, which he seemed never to remove, at least not until he came calling for Certainly-Mary . . . At any rate, when I insulted him, with my sisters Durré and Muneeza cackling in the lift, Mecir just grinned an empty good-natured grin, nodded, "You call me what you like, okay," and went back to buffing and polishing the brasswork. There was no point teasing him if he was going to be like that, so I got into the lift and all the way to the fourth floor we sang "I Can't Stop Loving You" at the top of our best Ray Charles voices, which were pretty awful. But we were wearing our dark glasses, so it didn't matter.

4

It was the summer of 1962, and school was out. My baby sister Scheherazade was just one year old. Durré was a beehived fourteen; Muneeza was ten, and already quite a handful. The three of us — or rather Durré and me, with Muneeza trying desperately and unsuccessfully to be included in our gang — would stand over Scheherazade's cot and sing to her. "No nursery rhymes," Durré had decreed, and so there were none, for though she was a year my junior she was a natural leader. The infant Scheherazade's lullabies were our cover versions of recent hits by Chubby Checker, Neil Sedaka, Elvis and Pat Boone.

"Why don't you come home, Speedy Gonzales?" we bellowed in sweet disharmony: but most of all, and with actions, we would jump down, turn around and pick a bale of cotton. We would have jumped down, turned around and picked those bales all day except that the Maharaja of B— in the flat below complained, and Aya Mary came in to plead with us to be quiet.

"Look, see, it's Jumble-Aya who's fallen for Mixed-Up," Durré shouted, and Mary blushed a truly immense blush. So naturally we segued right into a quick me-oh-my-oh; son of a gun, we had big fun. But then the baby began to yell, my father came in with his head down bull-fashion and steaming from both ears, and we needed all the good luck charms we could find.

I had been at boarding school in England for a year or so when Abba took the decision to bring the family over. Like all his decisions, it was neither explained to nor discussed with anyone, not even my mother. When they first arrived he rented two adjacent flats in a seedy Bayswater mansion block called Graham Court, which lurked furtively in a nothing street that crawled along the side of the ABC Queensway cinema towards the Porchester Baths. He commandeered one of these flats for himself and put my mother, three sisters and Aya in the other; also, on school holidays, me. England, where liquor was freely available, did little for my father's *bonhomie*, so in a way it was a relief to have a flat to ourselves.

Most nights he emptied a bottle of Johnnie Walker Red Label and a soda-siphon. My mother did not dare to go across to "his place" in the evenings. She said: "He makes faces at me."

Aya Mary took Abba his dinner and answered all his calls (if he wanted anything, he would phone us up and ask for it). I am not sure why Mary was spared his drunken rages. She said it was because she was nine years his senior, so she could tell him to show due respect.

After a few months, however, my father leased a three-bedroom fourth-floor apartment with a fancy address. This was Waverley House in Kensington Court, W8. Among its other residents were not one but two Indian Maharajas, the sporting Prince P— as well as the old B— who has already been mentioned. Now we were jammed in together, my parents and Baby Scare-zade (as her siblings had affectionately begun to call her) in the master bedroom, the three of us in a much smaller room, and Mary, I regret to admit, on a straw mat laid on the fitted carpet in the hall. The third bedroom became my father's office, where he made phone-calls and kept his *Encyclopaedia Britannica*, his *Reader's Digest*s, and (under lock and key) the television cabinet. We entered it at our peril. It was the Minotaur's lair.

One morning he was persuaded to drop in at the corner pharmacy and pick up some supplies for the baby. When he returned there was a hurt, schoolboyish look on his face that I had never seen before, and he was pressing his hand against his cheek.

"She hit me," he said plaintively.

"Hai! Allah-tobah! Darling!" cried my mother, fussing. "Who hit you? Are you injured? Show me, let me see."

"I did nothing," he said, standing there in the hall with the pharmacy bag in his other hand and a face as pink as Mecir's rubber gloves. "I just went in with your list. The girl seemed very helpful. I asked for baby compound, Johnson's powder, teething jelly, and she brought them out. Then I asked did she have any nipples, and she slapped my face."

My mother was appalled. "Just for that?" And Certainly-Mary backed her up. "What is this nonsense?" she wanted to know. "I have been in that chemist's shock, and they have plenty nickels, different sizes, all on view."

Durré and Muneeza could not contain themselves. They were rolling round on the floor, laughing and kicking their legs in the air.

"You both shut your face at once," my mother ordered. "A mad-woman has hit your father. Where is the comedy?"

"I don't believe it," Durré gasped. "You just went up to that girl and said," and here she fell apart again, stamping her feet and hold-ing her stomach, "*have you got any nipples?*'"

My father grew thunderous, empurpled. Durré controlled her-self. "But Abba," she said, at length, "here they call them teats."

Now my mother's and Mary's hands flew to their mouths, and even my father looked shocked. "But how shameless!" my mother said. "The same word as for what's on your bosoms?" She coloured, and stuck out her tongue for shame.

"These English," sighed Certainly-Mary. "But aren't they the limit? Certainly-yes; they are."

I remember this story with delight, because it was the only time I ever saw my father so discomfited, and the incident became legendary and the girl in the pharmacy was installed as the object of our great vener-ation. (Durré and I went in there just to take a look at her — she was a plain, short girl of about seventeen, with large, unavoidable breasts — but she caught us whispering and glared so fiercely that we fled.) And also because in the general hilarity I was able to conceal the shaming truth that I, who had been in England for so long, would have made the same mistake as Abba did.

It wasn't just Certainly-Mary and my parents who had trouble with the English language. My schoolfellows tittered when in my Bombay way I said "brought-up" for upbringing (as in "where was your brought-up?") and "thrice" for three times and "quarter-plate" for side-plate and "macaroni" for pasta in general. As for learning the difference between nipples and teats, I really hadn't had any opportunities to increase my word power in that area at all.

5

So I was a little jealous of Certainly-Mary when Mixed-Up came to call. He rang our bell, his body quivering with deference in an old suit grown too loose, the trousers tightly gathered by a belt; he had taken off his rubber gloves and there were roses in his hand. My father opened the door and gave him a withering look. Being a snob, Abba was not pleased that the flat lacked a separate service entrance, so that even a porter had to be treated as a member of the same universe as himself.

"Mary," Mixed-Up managed, licking his lips and pushing back his floppy white hair. "I, to see Miss Mary, come, am."

"Wait on," Abba said, and shut the door in his face.

Certainly-Mary spent all her afternoons off with old Mixed-Up from then on, even though that first date was not a complete success. He took her "up West" to show her the visitors' London she had never seen, but at the top of an up escalator at Piccadilly Circus, while Mecir was painfully enunciating the words on the posters she couldn't read — *Unzip a banana*, and *Idris when I's dri* — she got her sari stuck in the jaws of the machine, and as the escalator pulled at the garment it began to unwind. She was forced to spin round and round like a top, and screamed at the top of her voice, "O BAAP! BAAPU–RÉ! BAAP–RÉ–BAAP–RÉ–BAAP!" It was Mixed-Up who saved her by pushing the emergency stop button before the sari was completely unwound and she was exposed in her petticoat for all the world to see.

"O, courter!" she wept on his shoulder. "O, no more escaleater, courter, nevermore, surely not!"

My own amorous longings were aimed at Durré's best friend, a Polish girl called Rozalia, who had a holiday job at Faiman's shoe shop on Oxford Street. I pursued her pathetically throughout the holidays and, on and off, for the next two years. She would let me have lunch with her sometimes and buy her a Coke and a sandwich, and once she came with me to stand on the terraces at White Hart Lane to watch Jimmy Greaves's first game for the Spurs. "Come on you whoi-oites," we both shouted dutifully. "Come on you *Lily-whoites*." After that she even invited me into the back room at Faiman's, where she kissed me twice and let me touch her breast, but that was as far as I got.

And then there was my sort-of-cousin Chandni, whose mother's sister had married my mother's brother, though they had since split up. Chandni was eighteen months older than me, and so sexy it made you sick. She was training to be an Indian classical dancer, Odissi as well as Natyam, but in the meantime she dressed in tight black jeans and a clinging black polo-neck jumper and took me, now and then, to hang out at Bunjie's, where she knew most of the folk-music crowd that frequented the place, and where she answered to the name of Moonlight, which is what *chandni* means. I chain-smoked with the folkies and then went to the toilet to throw up.

Chandni was the stuff of obsessions. She was a teenage dream, the Moon River come to Earth like the Goddess Ganga, dolled up in slinky black. But for her I was just the young greenhorn cousin to whom she was being nice because he hadn't learned his way around.

She-E-rry, won't you come out tonight? yodelled the Four Seasons. I knew exactly how they felt. *Come, come, come out toni-yi-yight.* And while you're at it, love me do.

6

They went for walks in Kensington Gardens. "Pan," Mixed-Up said, pointing at a statue. "Los' boy. Nev' grew up." They went to Barkers and Pontings and Derry & Toms and picked out furniture and curtains for imaginary homes. They cruised supermarkets and chose little delicacies to eat. In Mecir's cramped lounge they sipped what he called "chimpanzee tea" and toasted crumpets in front of an electric bar fire.

Thanks to Mixed-Up, Mary was at last able to watch television. She liked children's programmes best, especially *The Flintstones*. Once, giggling at her daring, Mary confided to Mixed-Up that Fred and Wilma reminded her of her Sahib and Begum Sahiba upstairs; at which the courter, matching her audaciousness, pointed first at Certainly-Mary and then at himself, grinned a wide gappy smile and said, "Rubble."

Later, on the news, a vulpine Englishman with a thin moustache and mad eyes declaimed a warning about immigrants, and Certainly-Mary flapped her hand at the set: "Khali-pili bom marta," she objected, and then, for her host's benefit translated: "For nothing he is shouting shouting. Bad life! Switch it off."

They were often interrupted by the Maharajas of B— and P—, who came downstairs to escape their wives and ring other women from the call-box in the porter's room.

"Oh, baby, forget that guy," said sporty Prince P—, who seemed to spend all his days in tennis whites, and whose plump gold Rolex was almost lost in the thick hair on his arm. "I'll show you a better time than him, baby; step into my world."

The Maharaja of B— was older, uglier, more matter-of-fact. "Yes, bring all appliances. Room is booked in name of Mr. Douglas Home. Six forty-five to seven fifteen. You have printed rate card? Please. Also a two-foot ruler, must be wooden. Frilly apron, plus."

This is what has lasted in my memory of Waverley House, this seething mass of bad marriages, booze, philanderers and unfulfilled young lusts; of the Maharaja of P— roaring away towards London's

casinoland every night, in a red sports car with fitted blondes, and of
the Maharaja of B— skulking off to Kensington High Street wearing
dark glasses in the dark, and a coat with the collar turned up even
though it was high summer; and at the heart of our little universe
were Certainly-Mary and her courter, drinking chimpanzee tea and
singing along with the national anthem of Bedrock:

Flintstones! Meet the Flintstones!
They're the modern stone age family.

But they were not really like Barney and Betty Rubble at all. They
were formal, polite. They were . . . courtly. He courted her, and, like a
coy, ringleted ingénue with a fan, she inclined her head, and entertained his suit.

They're a page right out of his-to-ry.

7

I spent one half-term weekend in 1963 at the home in Beccles, Suf-
folk of Field Marshal Sir Charles Lutwidge-Dodgson, an old India
hand and a family friend who was supporting my application for
British citizenship. "The Dodo," as he was known, invited me down
by myself, saying he wanted to get to know me better.

He was a huge man whose skin had started hanging too loosely on
his face, a giant living in a tiny thatched cottage and forever bump-
ing his head. No wonder he was irascible at times; he was in Hell, a
Gulliver trapped in that rose-garden Lilliput of croquet hoops, church
bells, sepia photographs and old battle-trumpets.

The weekend was fitful and awkward until the Dodo asked if
I played chess. Slightly awestruck at the prospect of playing a Field
Marshal, I nodded; and ninety minutes later, to my amazement, won
the game.

I went into the kitchen, strutting somewhat, planning to boast a
little to the old soldier's long-time housekeeper, Mrs. Liddell. But as
soon as I entered she said: "Don't tell me. You never went and won?"

"Yes," I said, affecting nonchalance. "As a matter of fact, yes, I did."

"Gawd," said Mrs. Liddell. "Now there'll be hell to pay. You go back in there and ask him for another game, and this time make sure you lose."

I did as I was told, but was never invited to Beccles again.

Still, the defeat of the Dodo gave me new confidence at the chessboard, so when I returned to Waverley House after finishing my O levels, and was at once invited to play a game by Mixed-Up (Mary had told him about my victory in the Battle of Beccles with great pride and some hyperbole), I said: "Sure, I don't mind." How long could it take to thrash the old duffer, after all?

There followed a massacre royal. Mixed-Up did not just beat me; he had me for breakfast, over easy. I couldn't believe it — the canny opening, the fluency of his combination play, the force of his attacks, my own impossibly cramped, strangled positions — and asked for a second game. This time he tucked into me even more heartily. I sat broken in my chair at the end, close to tears. *Big girls don't cry*, I reminded myself, but the song went on playing in my head: *That's just an alibi.*

"Who are you?" I demanded, humiliation weighing down every syllable. "The devil in disguise?"

Mixed-Up gave his big, silly grin. "Grand Master," he said. "Long time. Before head."

"You're a Grand Master," I repeated, still in a daze. Then in a moment of horror I remembered that I had seen the name Mecir in books of classic games. "Nimzo-Indian," I said aloud. He beamed and nodded furiously.

"That Mecir?" I asked wonderingly.

"That," he said. There was saliva dribbling out of a corner of his sloppy old mouth. This ruined old man was in the books. He was in the books. And even with his mind turned to rubble he could still wipe the floor with me.

"Now play lady," he grinned. I didn't get it. "Mary lady," he said. "Yes yes certainly."

She was pouring tea, waiting for my answer. "Aya, you can't play," I said, bewildered.

"Learning, baba," she said. "What is it, na? Only a game."

And then she, too, beat me senseless, and with the black pieces, at that. It was not the greatest day of my life.

8

From *100 Most Instructive Chess Games* by Robert Reshevsky, 1961:

M. Mecir — M. Najdorf
Dallas 1950, Nimzo-Indian Defense

The attack of a tactician can be troublesome to meet — that of a strategist even more so. Whereas the tactician's threats may be unmistakable, the strategist confuses the issue by keeping things in abeyance. He threatens to threaten!

Take this game for instance: Mecir posts a Knight at Q6 to get a grip on the center. Then he establishes a passed Pawn on one wing to occupy his opponent on the Queen side. Finally he stirs up the position on the King side. What does the poor bewildered opponent do? How can he defend everything at once? Where will the blow fall?

Watch Mecir keep Najdorf on the run, as he shifts the attack from side to side!

Chess had become their private language. Old Mixed-Up, lost as he was for words, retained, on the chessboard, much of the articulacy and subtlety which had vanished from his speech. As Certainly-Mary gained in skill — and she had learned with astonishing speed, I thought bitterly, for someone who couldn't read or write or pronounce the letter p — she was better able to understand, and respond to, the wit of the reduced maestro with whom she had so unexpectedly forged a bond.

He taught her with great patience, showing-not-telling, repeating openings and combinations and endgame techniques over and over until she began to see the meaning in the patterns. When they played, he handicapped himself, he told her her best moves and demonstrated their consequences, drawing her, step by step, into the infinite possibilities of the game.

Such was their courtship. "It is like an adventure, baba," Mary once tried to explain to me. "It is like going with him to his country, you know? What a place, baap-ré! Beautiful and dangerous and funny and full of fuzzles. For me it is a big-big discovery. What to tell you? I go for the game. It is a wonder."

I understood, then, how far things had gone between them. Certainly-Mary had never married, and had made it clear to old Mixed-Up that it was too late to start any of that monkey business at her age. The courter was a widower, and had grown-up children somewhere, lost long ago behind the ever-higher walls of Eastern Europe. But in the game of chess they had found a form of flirtation, an endless renewal that precluded the possibility of boredom, a courtly wonderland of the ageing heart.

What would the Dodo have made of it all? No doubt it would have scandalized him to see chess, chess of all games, the great formalization of war, transformed into an art of love.

As for me: my defeats by Certainly-Mary and her courter ushered in further humiliations. Durré and Muneeza went down with the mumps, and so, finally, in spite of my mother's efforts to segregate us, did I. I lay terrified in bed while the doctor warned me not to stand up and move around if I could possibly help it. "If you do," he said, "your parents won't need to punish you. You will have punished yourself quite enough."

I spent the following few weeks tormented day and night by visions of grotesquely swollen testicles and a subsequent life of limp impotence — finished before I'd even started, it wasn't fair! — which were made much worse by my sisters' quick recovery and incessant gibes. But in the end I was lucky; the illness didn't spread to the deep South. "Think how happy your hundred and one girlfriends will be, bhai," sneered Durré, who knew all about my continued failures in the Rozalia and Chandni departments.

On the radio, people were always singing about the joys of being sixteen years old. I wondered where they were, all those boys and girls of my age having the time of their lives. Were they driving around America in Studebaker convertibles? They certainly weren't in my neighbourhood. London, W8 was Sam Cooke country that summer. *Another Saturday night . . .* There might be a mop-top love-song stuck at number one, but I was down with lonely Sam in the lower depths of the charts, how-I-wishing I had someone, etc., and generally feeling in a pretty goddamn dreadful way.

How I wish I had someone to talk to,
I'm in an awful way.

9

"Baba, come quick."

It was late at night when Aya Mary shook me awake. After many urgent hisses, she managed to drag me out of sleep and pull me, pyjama'ed and yawning, down the hall. On the landing outside our flat was Mixed-Up the courter, huddled up against a wall, weeping. He had a black eye and there was dried blood on his mouth.

"What happened?" I asked Mary, shocked.

"Men," wailed Mixed-Up. "Threaten. Beat."

He had been in his lounge earlier that evening when the sporting Maharaja of P— burst in to say, "If anybody comes looking for me, okay, any tough-guy type guys, okay, I am out, okay? Oh you tea. Don't let them go upstairs, okay? Big tip, okay?"

A short time later, the old Maharaja of B— also arrived in Mecir's lounge, looking distressed.

"Suno, listen on," said the Maharaja of B—. "You don't know where I am, samajh liya? Understood? Some low persons may inquire. You don't know. I am abroad, achha? On extended travels abroad. Do your job, porter. Handsome recompense."

Late at night two tough-guy types did indeed turn up. It seemed the hairy Prince P— had gambling debts. "Out," Mixed-Up grinned in his sweetest way. The tough-guy types nodded, slowly. They had long hair and thick lips like Mick Jagger's. "He's a busy gent. We should of made an appointment," said the first type to the second. "Didn't I tell you we should of called?"

"You did," agreed the second type. "Got to do these things right, you said, he's royalty. And you was right, my son, I put my hand up, I was dead wrong. I put my hand up to that."

"Let's leave our card," said the first type. "Then he'll know to expect us."

"Ideal," said the second type, and smashed his fist into old Mixed-Up's mouth. "You tell him," the second type said, and struck the old man in the eye. "When he's in. You mention it."

He had locked the front door after that; but much later, well after midnight, there was a hammering. Mixed-Up called out, "Who?"

"We are close friends of the Maharaja of B—" said a voice. "No, I tell a lie. Acquaintances."

"He calls upon a lady of our acquaintance," said a second voice. "To be precise."

"It is in that connection that we crave audience," said the first voice.

"Gone," said Mecir. "Jet plane. Gone."

There was a silence. Then the second voice said, "Can't be in the jet set if you never jump on a jet, eh? Biarritz, Monte, all of that."

"Be sure and let His Highness know," said the first voice, "that we eagerly await his return."

"With regard to our mutual friend," said the second voice. "Eagerly."

What does the poor bewildered opponent do? The words from the chess book popped unbidden into my head. *How can he defend everything at once? Where will the blow fall? Watch Mecir keep Najdorf on the run, as he shifts the attack from side to side!*

Mixed-Up returned to his lounge and on this occasion, even though there had been no use of force, he began to weep. After a time he took the elevator up to the fourth floor and whispered through our letter-box to Certainly-Mary sleeping on her mat.

"I didn't want to wake Sahib," Mary said. "You know his trouble, na? And Begum Sahiba is so tired at end of the day. So now you tell, baba, what to do?"

What did she expect me to come up with? I was sixteen years old. "Mixed-Up must call the police," I unoriginally offered.

"No, no, baba," said Certainly-Mary emphatically. "If the courter makes a scandal for Maharaja-log, then in the end it is the courter only who will be out on his ear."

I had no other ideas. I stood before them feeling like a fool, while they both turned upon me their frightened, supplicant eyes.

"Go to sleep," I said. "We'll think about it in the morning." *The first pair of thugs were tacticians*, I was thinking. *They were troublesome to meet. But the second pair were scarier; they were strategists. They threatened to threaten.*

Nothing happened in the morning, and the sky was clear. It was almost impossible to believe in fists, and menacing voices at the door. During the course of the day both Maharajas visited the porter's lounge and stuck five-pound notes in Mixed-Up's waistcoat pocket. "Held the fort, good man," said Prince P——, and the Maharaja of B—— echoed those sentiments: "Spot on. All handled now, achha? Problem over."

The three of us — Aya Mary, her courter and me — held a council of war that afternoon and decided that no further action was necessary. The hall porter was the front line in any such situation, I argued, and the front line had held. And now the risks were past. Assurances had been given. End of story.

"End of story," repeated Certainly-Mary doubtfully, but then, seeking to reassure Mecir, she brightened. "Correct," she said. "Most certainly! All-done, finis." She slapped her hands against each other for emphasis. She asked Mixed-Up if he wanted a game of chess; but for once the courter didn't want to play.

10

After that I was distracted, for a time, from the story of Mixed-Up and Certainly-Mary by violence nearer home.

My middle sister Muneeza, now eleven, was entering her delinquent phase a little early. She was the true inheritor of my father's black rage, and when she lost control it was terrible to behold. That summer she seemed to pick fights with my father on purpose; seemed prepared, at her young age, to test her strength against his. (I intervened in her rows with Abba only once, in the kitchen. She grabbed the kitchen scissors and flung them at me. They cut me on the thigh. After that I kept my distance.)

As I witnessed their wars I felt myself coming unstuck from the idea of family itself. I looked at my screaming sister and thought how brilliantly self-destructive she was, how triumphantly she was ruining her relations with the people she needed most.

And I looked at my choleric, face-pulling father and thought about British citizenship. My existing Indian passport permitted me to travel only to a very few countries, which were carefully listed on the second right-hand page. But I might soon have a British passport and then, by hook or by crook, I would get away from him. I would not have this face-pulling in my life.

At sixteen, you still think you can escape from your father. You aren't listening to his voice speaking through your mouth, you don't see how your gestures already mirror his; you don't see him in the way you hold your body, in the way you sign your name. You don't hear his whisper in your blood.

On the day I have to tell you about, my two-year-old sister Chhoti Scheherazade, Little Scare-zade, started crying as she often did during one of our family rows. Amma and Aya Mary loaded her into her push-chair and made a rapid getaway. They pushed her to Kensington Square and then sat on the grass, turned Scheherazade loose and made philosophical remarks while she tired herself out. Finally, she fell asleep, and they made their way home in the fading light of the evening. Outside Waverley House they were approached by two well-turned-out young men with Beatle haircuts and the buttoned-up, collarless jackets made popular by the band. The first of these young men asked my mother, very politely, if she might be the Maharani of B——.

"No," my mother answered, flattered.

"Oh, but you are, madam," said the second Beatle, equally politely. "For you are heading for Waverley House and that is the Maharaja's place of residence."

"No, no," my mother said, still blushing with pleasure. "We are a different Indian family."

"Quite so," the first Beatle nodded understandingly, and then, to my mother's great surprise, placed a finger alongside his nose, and winked. "Incognito, eh. Mum's the word."

"Now excuse us," my mother said, losing patience. "We are not the ladies you seek."

The second Beatle tapped a foot lightly against a wheel of the push-chair. "Your husband seeks ladies, madam, were you aware of that fact? Yes, he does. Most assiduously, may I add."

"Too assiduously," said the first Beatle, his face darkening.

"I tell you I am not the Maharani Begum," my mother said, growing suddenly alarmed. "Her business is not my business. Kindly let me pass."

The second Beatle stepped closer to her. She could feel his breath, which was minty. "One of the ladies he sought out was our ward, as you might say," he explained. "That would be the term. Under our protection, you follow. Us, therefore, being responsible for her welfare."

"Your husband," said the first Beatle, showing his teeth in a frightening way, and raising his voice one notch, "damaged the goods. Do you hear me, Queenie? He damaged the fucking goods."

"Mistaken identity, fleas," said Certainly-Mary. "Many Indian residents in Waverley House. We are decent ladies; *fleas*."

The second Beatle had taken out something from an inside pocket. A blade caught the light. "Fucking wogs," he said. "You fucking come over here, you don't fucking know how to fucking behave. Why don't you fucking fuck off to fucking Wogistan? Fuck your fucking wog arses. Now then," he added in a quiet voice, holding up the knife, "unbutton your blouses."

Just then a loud noise emanated from the doorway of Waverley House. The two women and the two men turned to look, and out came Mixed-Up, yelling at the top of his voice and windmilling his arms like a mad old loon.

"Hullo," said the Beatle with the knife, looking amused. "Who's this, then? Oh oh fucking seven?"

Mixed-Up was trying to speak, he was in a mighty agony of effort, but all that was coming out of his mouth was raw, unshaped noise. Scheherazade woke up and joined in. The two Beatles looked displeased. But then something happened inside old Mixed-Up; something popped, and in a great rush he gabbled, "Sirs sirs no sirs these not B— women sirs B— women upstairs on floor three sirs Maharaja of B— also sirs God's truth mother's grave swear."

It was the longest sentence he had spoken since the stroke that had broken his tongue long ago.

And what with his torrent and Scheherazade's squalls there were suddenly heads poking out from doorways, attention was being paid, and the two Beatles nodded gravely. "Honest mistake," the first of them said apologetically to my mother, and actually bowed from the waist. "Could happen to anyone," the knife-man added, ruefully. They turned and began to walk quickly away. As they passed Mecir, however, they paused. "I know you, though," said the knife-man. "'*Jet plane. Gone.*'" He made a short movement of the arm, and then Mixed-Up the courter was lying on the pavement with blood leaking from a wound in his stomach. "All okay now," he gasped, and passed out.

11

He was on the road to recovery by Christmas; my mother's letter to the landlords, in which she called him a "knight in shining armour," ensured that he was well looked after, and his job was kept open for him. He continued to live in his little ground-floor cubby-hole, while the hall porter's duties were carried out by shift-duty staff. "Nothing but the best for our very own hero," the landlords assured my mother in their reply.

The two Maharajas and their retinues had moved out before I came home for the Christmas holidays, so we had no further visits from the Beatles or the Rolling Stones. Certainly-Mary spent as much time as she could with Mecir; but it was the look of my old Aya that worried me more than poor Mixed-Up. She looked older, and powdery, as if she might crumble away at any moment into dust.

"We didn't want to worry you at school," my mother said. "She has been having heart trouble. Palpitations. Not all the time, but."

Mary's health problems had sobered up the whole family. Muneeza's tantrums had stopped, and even my father was making an effort. They had put up a Christmas tree in the sitting-room and decorated it with all sorts of baubles. It was so odd to see a Christmas tree at our place that I realized things must be fairly serious.

On Christmas Eve my mother suggested that Mary might like it if we all sang some carols. Amma had made song-sheets, six copies, by hand. When we did "O come, all ye faithful" I showed off by singing from memory in Latin. Everybody behaved perfectly. When Muneeza suggested that we should try "Swinging on a Star" or "I Wanna Hold Your Hand" instead of this boring stuff, she wasn't really being serious. So this is family life, I thought. This is it.

But we were only play-acting.

A few weeks earlier, at school, I'd come across an American boy, the star of the school's Rugby football team, crying in the Chapel cloisters. I asked him what the matter was and he told me that President

Kennedy had been assassinated. "I don't believe you," I said, but I could see that it was true. The football star sobbed and sobbed. I took his hand.

"When the President dies, the nation is orphaned," he eventually said, broken-heartedly parroting a piece of cracker-barrel wisdom he'd probably heard on Voice of America.

"I know how you feel," I lied. "My father just died, too."

Mary's heart trouble turned out to be a mystery; unpredictably, it came and went. She was subjected to all sorts of tests during the next six months, but each time the doctors ended up by shaking their heads: they couldn't find anything wrong with her. Physically, she was right as rain; except that there were these periods when her heart kicked and bucked in her chest like the wild horses in *The Misfits*, the ones whose roping and tying made Marilyn Monroe so mad.

Mecir went back to work in the spring, but his experience had knocked the stuffing out of him. He was slower to smile, duller of eye, more inward. Mary, too, had turned in upon herself. They still met for tea, crumpets and *The Flintstones*, but something was no longer quite right.

At the beginning of the summer Mary made an announcement.

"I know what is wrong with me," she told my parents, out of the blue. "I need to go home."

"But, Aya," my mother argued, "homesickness is not a real disease."

"God knows for what-all we came over to this country," Mary said. "But I can no longer stay. No. Certainly not." Her determination was absolute.

So it was England that was breaking her heart, breaking it by not being India. London was killing her, by not being Bombay. And Mixed-Up? I wondered. Was the courter killing her, too, because he was no longer himself? Or was it that her heart, roped by two different loves, was being pulled both East and West, whinnying and rearing, like those movie horses being yanked this way by Clark Gable and that way by Montgomery Clift, and she knew that to live she would have to choose?

"I must go," said Certainly-Mary. "Yes, certainly. *Bas*. Enough."

That summer, the summer of '64, I turned seventeen. Chandni went back to India. Durré's Polish friend Rozalia informed me over a sandwich in Oxford Street that she was getting engaged to a "real man," so I could forget about seeing her again, because this Zbigniew was the jealous type. Roy Orbison sang "It's Over" in my ears as I walked away to the Tube, but the truth was that nothing had really begun.

Certainly-Mary left us in mid-July. My father bought her a one-way ticket to Bombay, and that last morning was heavy with the pain of ending. When we took her bags down to the car, Mecir the hall porter was nowhere to be seen. Mary did not knock on the door of his lounge, but walked straight out through the freshly polished oak-panelled lobby, whose mirrors and brasses were sparkling brightly; she climbed into the back seat of our Ford Zodiac and sat there stiffly with her carry-on grip on her lap, staring straight ahead. I had known and loved her all my life. *Never mind your damned courter*, I wanted to shout at her, *what about me?*

As it happened, she was right about the homesickness. After her return to Bombay, she never had a day's heart trouble again; and, as the letter from her niece Stella confirmed, at ninety-one she was still going strong.

Soon after she left, my father told us he had decided to "shift location" to Pakistan. As usual, there were no discussions, no explanations, just the simple fiat. He gave up the lease on the flat in Waverley House at the end of the summer holidays, and they all went off to Karachi, while I went back to school.

I became a British citizen that year. I was one of the lucky ones, I guess, because in spite of that chess game I had the Dodo on my side. And the passport did, in many ways, set me free. It allowed me to come and go, to make choices that were not the ones my father would have wished. But I, too, have ropes around my neck, I have them to this day, pulling me this way and that, East and West, the nooses tightening, commanding, *choose, choose.*

I buck, I snort, I whinny, I rear, I kick. Ropes, I do not choose between you. Lassoes, lariats, I choose neither of you, and both. Do you hear? I refuse to choose.

A year or so after we moved out I was in the area and dropped in at Waverley House to see how the old courter was doing. Maybe, I thought, we could have a game of chess, and he could beat me to a pulp. The lobby was empty, so I knocked on the door of his little lounge. A stranger answered.

"Where's Mixed-Up?" I cried, taken by surprise. I apologized at once, embarrassed. "Mr. Mecir, I meant, the porter."

"I'm the porter, sir," the man said. "I don't know anything about any mix-up."

Rukhsana Ahmad

The Spell and the Ever-Changing Moon

Nisa looked around nervously as she walked along the dusty edge of the road on that suffocating July afternoon. She was in a part of Lahore which she did not know very well but all the landmarks her neighbour Apa Zarina had described had been appearing so far. She tugged at the burqa round her shoulders as if afraid of being recognized through its thin georgette veil and the black silky folds that cloaked her neat, compact little figure. It belonged to her unmarried friend Seema and had been borrowed specially for the occasion. It was the first time in her life that she had embarked on a mission aware that it wasn't "permitted." She was trembling a little with guilt and fear. Her breathing and heartbeat quickened as she approached the house.

Just as Zarina had said, it stood at the end of the *kutchi abaadi*. A small house, one of the few here which were brick built. Right outside its entrance was the lean-to of the motorbike repair shop which she was told to look out for. Two men sat there tinkering with motorbikes which looked too rusty and battered to be repaired. They looked up from their sweaty labour each time a woman went in or out of the green door of Talat's house.

Most of the women who came had their faces covered with shawls or dupattas and some, like Nisa, wore burqas. But occasionally the men succeeded in catching a glimpse of a young and fresh female face. In any case they weren't discouraged by the veils and cloaks. If the outline or gait indicated a youngish woman they did their best to draw attention by shouting a veiled obscenity or by humming a snatch of a film song.

The women had been trained for years to sidestep and ignore this kind of behaviour. So they all scurried past, hastening their footsteps just a little. Nisa, who was skilled in the same strategy, quickened her pace to reach the shelter of the house although she had been fearful of the ultimate step she was going to take. It was for her a house of Evil.

She stood looking around the bare courtyard for a second. In one corner was the usual outside tap in its sunken cemented square used for washing. Across the length of the courtyard hung the laundry drying at the remarkable speed which only the brilliant afternoon sun made possible. She hesitated for an instant and then walked into the small room beyond.

Her eyes were blinded by the sudden fragrant darkness of the room and she steadied herself against the door jamb as she stumbled over the stock of shoes near the door. Slipping off hers, Nisa sat down just inside the doorway. She gasped as her eyes began to see.

Talat sat on a low stage with two huge black snakes entwined round her body. She was dramatically good looking and very fashionable. Her large black eyes were highlighted by the blackest kohl and her small delicate mouth was painted a brilliant red, matching the nail varnish on her carefully manicured hands. Through her fine black lawn kurta was clearly outlined a shapely bosom and a slender waist. She was muttering to herself, eyes closed, body swaying rhythmically, whilst the women round her stared in hypnotized fascination.

Nisa's glance surveyed the room quickly. The sunlight had been shut out. In the dim lamplight she could make out crudely painted pictures of holy faces which she had never seen before. She remembered hearing about distant foreign lands where it was customary to paint portraits of saints, a practice she knew was definitely blasphemous, and she hastily touched her ears inwardly in a gesture of pardon. "*Tauba, tauba*," she sought forgiveness. In one corner burned scented candles emitting whitish clouds of smoke with a cloying sweet smell. On the mantelshelf stood a photo of Talat with her "guru" who looked remarkably young and healthy as he smiled down at her with his hand resting on her head in benediction.

The queue was moving slowly. People were leaving one by one as each managed to get a personal audience with Talat. There was the usual assortment of problems: mother-in-law or daughter-in-law ones, there were patients seeking cures for incurable diseases, the destitute looking for a better future. Whatever their problems, Talat gave them that hope they knew they did not have.

No one seemed to have come alone except Nisa. She trembled again. It would be her turn soon to speak to Talat. She wasn't sure even now what she would say or what she would ask for. She held her cheap plastic handbag in a fierce clutch under her left arm and in her right hand she held a brown paper bag containing the four eggs she had bought on her way up, according to Zarina's instructions. The sweat from her fingers had formed a damp, dark ring round the base of the paper bag. She wondered uncomfortably if it was going to give way.

As the crowd in the room thinned, Nisa found herself slowly moving nearer to the raised dais. Within half an hour she was face to face with Talat. Nisa looked up into the dark, warm, liquid eyes. Disconcerted by Talat's youthful appearance, she felt for an instant she had made a mistake. Talat's eyes smiled as if they'd read her thoughts.

"How can I help you, my daughter?" she asked, as if a little amused by this belated scepticism. Her manner and her address claimed for herself the supremacy and status which age automatically bestows on everyone in that world, a manner which seemed strangely inappropriate in someone who was perhaps only nineteen or twenty.

But Nisa was overwhelmed by the encouraging sympathy and affection in her voice and felt the tears welling up in her throat. She could only say, "It's my husband . . ." before she broke down into a fit of sobbing, aware that she was being stared at very curiously. This kind of desperation was always useful as it impressed other clients. Talat soothed her gently and tenderly.

"Hush, my daughter, have faith. I can help you." Her voice was reassuring. She eyed the bag in Nisa's hands and asked in a whisper, "Do you want me to do a *chowkie* for you?" Nisa could only nod an affirmative. Talat proceeded quickly to perform that ritual. She relieved Nisa of the eggs and placed them in a neat square on a small wooden stool. Nisa stopped crying as she watched in fascination. Talat's fingers moved dextrously as she placed a bowl beside the stool and then began to unwind the snakes from her body. She pulled both of them up to the eggs and closed her eyes, rocking forwards and backwards as if in a trance.

Nisa's body stiffened with fear as the snakes stood dangerously close to her for a few seconds, sniffing the eggs and then raising their heads in what looked like vicious contempt. There was absolute silence in the room as everyone watched. Talat came out of her trance and her assistant, a very plain woman of around thirty-five or so, helped her to capture the snakes and put them away in two large colourful wicker baskets.

The snakes slithered and hissed as if in protest, but were soon put away. While the other woman was covering the baskets with pieces of black cloth, Talat began to break the eggs one by one into the clay bowl. Nisa tried to watch her but felt compelled to watch the snakes.

Suddenly she heard Talat's voice cursing under her breath and looked fearfully down at the bowl. On top of the cracked eggs floated nails, blood and some strange, noxious and ugly greenish matter.

"Ah, my daughter," Talat exclaimed as she folded her hands and closed her eyes as if to seek help from above. Nisa shuddered and covered her face with both hands in shock and horror.

"You are deep in difficulties, I can see." Talat was shaking her head in concern. "You need the Art to help you. You can change the path of your man, you know. There is a way . . ."

The pitch of her voice had changed. Nisa was shivering visibly now. Talat had come out of her trance and leaned closer to Nisa. She whispered confidentially in her ears as the other women stared. Nisa had kept the lower half of her veil stretched across her face but the curious audience could see her anxious brown eyes widen with horror as they hung on Talat's face, drinking in her whispered words.

She felt dumbfounded and shaken. With her finger on the clasp of her handbag she looked at Talat's companion and began fumblingly, "What's the . . . the fee? What shall I . . . ?"

The woman glanced at Talat's face and replied gushingly, "Oh, there's no fee really, Bibi. But we do have to take some *nazars* for the snakes, you know. It's ten rupees for the *chowkie*, Bibi. And," she continued again quickly, "you know Talat Bibi has to draw a *chilla* many times to get her powers. That's very very hard work, Bibi. And you need *nazars* for the snakes, you know, Bibi. It's twenty-five rupees in all."

She was observing Nisa closely as she spoke, the changing expression in Nisa's eyes guiding her in her reckoning of the bill. Nisa pushed the greasy notes with clumsy and clammy fingers into the assistant's eager hands and stumbled to her feet hastily.

Outside, she tripped over the burning stones in the paved courtyard and then on the threshold of the green door. The two men looked up and jeered again but Nisa neither saw nor heard them. She was too preoccupied with those strange whispered words. She saw the bus approaching from the right direction and ran towards it, relieved at not having to wait in the blistering heat near that evil place.

In all her twenty-six years she had never been so shocked by what she had heard or seen. Neither the shock years ago, of seeing some pornographic pictures that a girl at school had found in her father's trunk; nor that other time when she had woken up in the middle of the night as the family slept on the rooftop and suddenly realized that the neighbours were actually "doing it" could compare. She had blushed into the pillow and covered her ears to block out the muffled sounds. The mental picture of Chachi Nuggo's massive breasts flashed in her mind and the thought of Chachaji on top of her embarrassed her even as she remembered it now, almost ten years later.

"It's indecent even to think of it," she reprimanded herself. Her mind returned again to the present and tried to grapple with what Talat had just told her.

"Women," she'd said, "are powerful beings. If you want your man to be utterly in your power all you have to do is to give him a drop of your own blood to drink." As Nisa stared at Talat, vaguely apprehensive, she elaborated her meaning. "Menstrual blood has great magical powers, you know. A man can never overcome the spell. He will become a slave to your will."

Nisa shuddered again as she remembered the words with horror and revulsion. The very thought seemed so impure to her, so unclean. She felt certain that the knowledge came from the devil. "I couldn't do such an awful thing, even to Hameed," she mused to herself, wondering longingly for a few seconds about how it would feel if Hameed was indeed a slave to her will. She tried determinedly to shake off the idea.

"Ammah was right," she thought. "Never to go to these weird places. They are truly evil . . . There can be no doubt about it."

She really regretted having gone to see Talat. If it hadn't been for Zarina she'd never have done it. "No one really believes in these things these days," she thought. "Yet Zarina's mother does look so much better now." The justification for the trip also rose from within her heart.

The debate continued in her mind all the way back through town on the bus. It was almost time for Asar prayers; the shadows had doubled in length, she noticed, as she got off near the Mini Market and walked round the shops to the row of poky little houses behind them.

Her footsteps quickened as she thought of the children being looked after by Zarina.

Her neighbour was full of questions but Nisa could not bring herself to repeat what Talat had told her. She just hedged round the questions and rushed off with her brood, saying she still had the dinner to cook.

She fed the older children and sat down to nurse the youngest of her two boys, Zafar. Her mind was still occupied by her afternoon's adventure. She now felt curiously subdued and guilty about it. Zarina had meant well. In fact Nisa often felt guilty even about the fact that her neighbours knew the problems she was having with her marriage.

Her mother had always stressed the dignity and value of reserve. "A good woman," she used to say, "knows how to keep the family's secrets. What's the use, anyway, of telling people seven doors away that your month's allowance hasn't quite stretched to the last four days this month? If possible you manage to survive without letting the world know."

Nisa felt that was indeed where she'd failed to act as a really good wife. Her neighbours on all three sides of her knew her dark secret. Her own family did not know. She was proud of that. Every time someone had come to visit her from her home town, Sialkot, she had kept up appearances quite well. But she hadn't been able to hide the truth from her neighbours.

Each night when Hameed got home, looking drunk and forbidding, she strengthened her resolve to keep out of his way and not to cause a row, but five nights out of ten she failed. He seemed to seek her out as if that was what he'd been waiting for all day. She wished sometimes that he could come home earlier so that the noise of his rowing would be less noticeable. At eleven the whole neighbourhood was quiet and each abusive mouthful he hurled at her could be heard at least three doors away. Sometimes there were flying plates and howling children, if they happened to wake up. A couple of times she had lost control herself and had begun to scream hysterically with fear.

Anyway she realized that it had got easier for her since the neighbours knew. Sometimes when the row was a really bad one Zarina would call out to ask if she was all right. The shame of that always got through to Hameed, even if he was really drunk, and it made him stop and go to bed grumbling about interfering busybody neighbours.

His anger and abuse was often followed by an overbearingly vicious assertion of his conjugal rights which Nisa never dared to deny him, and she believed she ought not to dare to deny him either. She never resisted him but she resented his heavy-handed impatience. She hated the stink of cheap home-brewed beer on his breath with all the moral weight of her mother's censure of drinking. And she missed the snatches of wooing from the early days of her marriage.

After the day's wearying labour, it was that physical humiliation borne in silence five nights out of ten which was consuming her. She loathed that physical submission to his will. It had to be done like the housework and the caring of the children. It was her part of the deal, her return for the housekeeping allowance. She didn't argue about that but she bitterly resented his drinking. Though she wouldn't dare argue with him, she was unable to conceal her disapproval. And her tight-lipped hostility aggravated his bad temper. He was riled by her strong sense of moral superiority into an even deeper viciousness. Sometimes this worked for her. He would be too angry to want her afterwards. Sometimes he would be too drunk to notice her aloofness or her lofty anger and he just pleased himself.

That evening as she lay on her charpoy in the courtyard staring at the clear night sky, a vision of Talat's face kept intruding into her thoughts. It was a picture of Talat which compelled her imagination. She saw her standing waist-deep in the shallower waters of the Ravi, dressed in black, eyes uplifted to the moon, invoking her powers. Power, the very thought of power, seemed so seductive to Nisa in her helpless situation. She had been adventurous that morning but she knew she couldn't be as brave as Talat, though she longed to have some control over her circumstances.

She jumped up as she heard Hameed's footsteps at the door. It was nearly eleven, his usual time. She quickly raised the simmering water on the stove to the boil and tipped the rice in. That night as Hameed launched into his usual nagging and complaining between each morsel of curried lentils and rice, Nisa felt her resolve to never think about magic weakening.

She wondered how much pain it took, how much courage, to pollute a man's cup of tea or glass of sherbet. She watched Hameed's lips pressed against the glass of water and shivered. Through her mind flashed a memory of her first-born Karim, newly arrived, lying across her belly, sticky and a little blood-stained. She had touched him unbelievingly . . . the sight of the drops of blood on the cord hadn't really worried her or repulsed her then. That was the clot of blood that had made him possible, given him life.

"What are you staring at?" Hameed snapped peevishly, and Nisa jumped to her feet again to clear up the plates. Somewhere in the recesses of her mind she had caught a glimpse of herself performing a grossly sacrilegious spell and that glimpse had unnerved her for a few seconds.

All her life she had seen the women around her observing the taboos as far as this area of their lives was concerned. Nisa herself had developed a deep sense of shame over the years through the secrecy and the avoidances. Now it was as though Talat had pulled out a vital brick at the base of that belief.

If it really had magical powers, why did women abhor it so, she wondered. She knew she was too simple to work out the answers but the question rose insistently within her heart each month when she menstruated. The abhorrence didn't make sense to her now that she thought about it. After all, they all knew enough about the physical aspect of menstruation. Wasn't there some mild relief when girls "started" or worry when they were "late"?

Seven months passed by with the creeping pace of a prison sentence. Each month she wondered if she would dare. Each month when the moon was full she remembered Talat's eyes, her face aglow in the moonlight, standing waist-deep in the waters of the Ravi, and each month the spell seemed less shocking. She thought about herself, her life and her body a great deal in those months. Each time she saw the moon she prayed for a better month, but things did not change. Except for her own attitude to her own body. That changed subtly.

Towards the end of the month, when the money began to run out on the twenty-fifth or thereabouts, a deep bitterness filled her heart. She had to turn to him again to ask him for more and have him spit in her face. They'd always been the worst nights of the month, when his anger had a sharper, more righteous edge to it. But now when that happened she resented him as deeply as he resented the increased expenses.

She had grown weary of her life. The skimping and the managing, the hard work and the violence and finally the humiliating abuse of her body. She began to refuse him. That was the way of wayward women, she'd been taught, but she no longer cared.

Hameed was nonplussed by her refusal, too surprised and hurt to argue or insist at first. But then she began to reject him more frequently and he had to react. Surprisingly, he did not take her forcibly, but became more violent in other ways. It was almost as if he was aware of her newly found veneration for her own body, and *had* to violate her in some other way.

For Nisa those refusals became a small triumph each time. The black eyes, the swollen lips or bruised face became more commonplace for her. Zarina's mother would shake her head sadly sometimes and say, "Oh, that man, Beti. God will reward you for your patience. What makes him so angry?"

For Nisa the bruises became an option she preferred to humiliating sex. She wasn't sure that she wanted rewards in heaven; she only wished she had to suffer less on earth.

That spring Zarina's mother became ill again. The doctor came but the old lady was not reassured. She kept talking of Talat and how well her remedy had worked the year before. Nisa came back from their house with her head full of memories of the day she had gone to see Talat.

Talat was no longer an evil practitioner of magic for her. She appeared in her memory as someone gentle and loving, a friend and a sympathizer, who cared for the underdog, for her. The knowledge that Talat had imparted to her of the strange sinful spell had given her a sense of strength. Nisa had changed from being a shivering, huddled creature into a calmer and pensive woman.

That evening was women's night out. Seema was getting married the next day. They were all getting together to assemble her clothes for her trousseau, ready to be shown to the in-laws the following day. Nisa had found the right moment to obtain Hameed's permission to attend. She went round early, dressed in glittering clothes, her best earrings swinging from her ears, Zafar in her arms and the older two trailing by her side.

The girls were in high spirits, the singing was buoyant and loud. Nisa tried hard to blend into the scene but her laughter was laboured. The same old familiar well-loved tunes were jarringly painful today. The lies they told of marital bliss, of loving husbands and contented days irritated her. Nisa looked round at the little house sadly and remembered her mother's house. She was pulled out of her nostalgia by the sound of Seema's aunt lecturing her on how to cope with her new life. Forbearance and forgiveness were the operative words. That too was all too familiar.

Nisa could restrain herself no longer. She suddenly erupted, "And how much exactly is she really supposed to endure, Chachi? How many tears does it take to make a home?" She asked quietly, "If Seema was really drowning in her own tears and being choked by her own screams, would you still not want her to look backwards at this house?"

Looking a little discomfited and annoyed, the aunt said, "Heaven forbid, an inauspicious question for tonight, isn't it?"

Other women around them showed an interest in the conversation. Most of them knew about Nisa. Suddenly Nisa felt an arm around her shoulders. It was Seema's mother. The pain beneath the question had communicated itself to her. "No mother could shut her doors behind her daughter forever. If Seema needed help, I would gladly let her in, of course."

Nisa smiled with difficulty and returned to the kitchen for another teapot. Zarina was assisting in the kitchen.

"You know what?" she chirped as she saw Nisa coming in. "I went today to Talat's house to get Ammah's medicine and I found to my great surprise that Talat and her family have disappeared."

"What do you mean?"

"Well, packed up and shot off into the night."

"And why?" Nisa's heart was throbbing.

"Well! The motorcycle mechanic said they had to flit because too many people kept returning to demand their money back. It seems she was a fraud."

Nisa was quiet as she walked the short distance back home with Zarina. The children were exhausted. She took their shoes off one by one and then went into the kitchen to cook the rice, still wondering about Talat. At times she could have sworn that she actually felt the power of the magic, the spell she carried within her body. Now she felt lost and bereft again. She kept hoping that the spell she knew about was genuine.

Hameed came in later and more drunk than usual. He attacked her more viciously than usual, taunting her about her finery and the earrings. Nisa, overwrought and frightened, got up hurriedly to leave the room but he pulled her by the arm. She lost her balance, stumbled and fell to the floor. Her head hit the corner of the wooden *chowkie* and began to bleed furiously. There was a terrible clang as enamelled mugs, plates and bowls rolled off the kitchen shelf. The noise shook Hameed. He pulled himself up and tried to help Nisa up.

But she was hysterical. "No! No! No!" she was screaming. "Don't touch me! Don't come near me. I'll kill you. I'll stab you. I'll poison you." Words poured out of her as fast as the blood sprang from her wound. She looked strange in her glittering clothes, blood-stained face and dishevelled hair.

Zarina was knocking on the door furiously. Hameed, bemused and shaken, let her in and went out again himself. At once Zarina took charge. She nursed Nisa's injuries, calmed her down and helped her to bed. The children had slept through the commotion.

The next morning when Nisa woke up everything was quite clear in her head. She knew what she had to do. She packed some things for herself and Zafar in a small steel trunk. The older children were at school. They walked up and came back with Zarina's children. She stood on a small stool near the wall and called Zarina to tell her.

"I'm going to my mother's house, Apa," she said. "I'm taking Zafar with me. I think they will not turn us away. If nothing else, I can wash dishes and cook. If Hameed cannot keep Safia and Karim let him dump them in Sialkot as well."

Zarina nodded tearfully and promised to keep an eye on them for her. For once she did not have the courage to persuade Nisa that she must endure and that he would change. She didn't know of a magic which worked. Nisa had seen a vision she could not forget, she'd felt a power she could not deny. As she turned away and walked out of the courtyard, clutching both Zafar and the silver trunk, her steps were laboriously slow but firm and determined.

Kirpal Singh

Jaspal

Jaspal always began his day by shitting. Shitting, he maintained, was man's most important bodily function. If one did not shit — or if one did not have a proper shit — one's mood for the rest of the day was spoiled. Furthermore, shitting meant getting rid of dirt, the dirt that had accumulated in one's system. It was absolutely necessary, said Jaspal, that we get rid of the dirt in our systems. Too much dirt blocks perception and rots the soul. Hence, all those golden rules surrounding one's morning ablutions — from the Hinduistic rituals to the unuttered Christian imperatives . . .

He had not quite learned how to seat himself on this modern toilet. So, unknown to his friends — but known to his wife who had a peculiar fascination with Jaspal's shitting — he still squatted on the toilet seat. A little uncomfortable, especially since he suffered immensely from constipation and had therefore to remain longer at his task than most, but it was the only way to a proper shit. Years spent in childhood habit had ensured that squatting was the only way to do it. Jaspal remembered the first time he actually shat. He had to take a changkol and go some distance away from his house (in those early days there was plenty of land and houses were spaciously located) and then dig for himself a suitable hole in the ground. This hole had to be about three to four feet deep and about a foot in diameter. Not that at his age — Jaspal was then six — he needed such a big hole to accommodate his shit, but from the start he had wanted to be an adult and so imitated the adults' shitting holes. Then he squatted himself over the hole — with legs spread apart — and did his business. After it was over, he washed his anus with the bucket of water he had brought (his elders, being good Sikhs, had impressed upon Jaspal the special need for keeping one's anus clean always) and then began to cover the hole with the earth just dug up. The whole process took roughly half an hour, so that he had ample time to contemplate on various matters important to a six-year-old . . .

So perhaps, he dared not explain this to his wife who always complained about his taking too long in the toilet — this was why he enjoyed constipating; it gave him time to think over serious matters affecting his life, now that he was a grown man of thirty-six.

And what a change the intervening thirty years had brought. A new city. A new nation. A brand new Singapore. He had witnessed it all. He had seen the swamp cleared and made into a new town. He had seen the cemetery exhumed and made into a lovers' park. He had seen the beach removed to build that piece of wonder — the new Airport. He had been part of the story. He was proud to have been the prime witness of this astonishing process of historical reshaping.

Thirty years had gone by since he was six. Even his primary school — he had attended Jalan Eunos School — had gone to make way for housing developments. Memories of primary school days brought back some odd assortment of mental images. A messenger sent to the young Malay girl in Five D with a black spot, requesting for that treasured island between her young breasts. That day of great pride when, having been made a prefect, he subjected that scoundrel Yong to pick up all the pieces of paper that littered the school field — even those on the other side where Jalan Daud's part of the field began — to teach Yong a good lesson, not to touch his little knot of hair. And that horrific experience of a near-murder . . .

From the start Jaspal had been made conscious of the fact that he was a Sikh. His parents had instilled in him the fundamental belief that he was very different from the Malays, Tamils, Seranees, Chinese and others of all description that lived in the same kampong. And what about Goondoo's people, he had asked. Oh, yes, they are Sikhs, his mother had replied, but not very good ones. We are good Sikhs, no one in our family has cropped. Look at Goondoo's family. His elder brother smokes non-stop, his mother's brother is totally cropped, his uncle married a Tamil woman. In our family, nothing of this sort happens. And you, being our only son, you Jaspal, must make sure never to bring disgrace to our family. We come from a proud race, even now the English sing our praises, and our ancestors will be grieved if you, or any of us, ever do anything to mark the family name. Being a Sikh, when one was six, meant being able to keep one's own anus clean, and being able to walk with pride with that little knot of hair on one's head.

Ah, yes, thought Jaspal now as he squatted over the toilet bowl, yes, that little knot of hair. The other boys and girls at school called it tonchet. And they would tease him. There was one other Sikh boy in the school but no one seemed to disturb him ever, thought Jaspal, because he came to school everyday with his father — and a typical Sikh father was a burly man, huge, the very nightmare of a young Malay or Chinese boy. Yes, the others would sing in unison:

Bengkali tonchet, motor-car punchet
Bengkali tonchet, motor-car punchet

One day, while playing basketball, he had his own back. Ah Kong, a young boy from the same kampong, was among the leaders of the groups of boys who shouted at Jaspal, Eh tonchet, why don't you catch the ball? Stupid tonchet — but before he could continue Jaspal had taken hold of him, pushed him against the bars supporting the net and was about to strangle him dead. Ahmad, the school gardener, who had come in the nick of time, gave Jaspal a tight slap and saved Ah Kong. A near murder, thought Jaspal now, but for Ahmad. Ahmad, that cheery, happy man, always smiling, now dead. Part of the story, too.

Many years afterwards, Jaspal and Kong were to sit at the Newton Food Stalls and laugh away the episode over a delicious plate of fried hokkien mee.

But laugh as they may at such episodes, there was the gnawing realization that their individual upbringing had not always trained them properly for the new Singapore — the Singapore of multiracial harmony. Ah Kong's father, for instance, had always made it a point never to sit next to an Indian in a bus. The Indians smell terrible, he said. So it was humiliating for Jaspal to notice Mr. Lim standing when the seat next to Jaspal was empty; even though Ah Kong's father knew that Jaspal was a friend of his son, he would not on principle sit down. Ah Kong's mother, on the other hand, objected strenuously to Jaspal's tonchet. Get rid of that hair, she said, and you will be siang sek. One of us. Why must you keep long hair? They always kept asking even after Jaspal had married Kong's sister, even after their first baby had been born . . .

Jaspal's marriage to Jenny had not flattered his parents at all. It was a disgrace, the old man said, an insult to the family tradition. Worse than Goondoo's family. Worse than cutting one's hair. Jaspal had argued and argued, tried to reason, but to no avail. Show me the Scriptures where it stated "Thou shalt not marry unto a Chinese virgin . . ." Of course it was irrational. As irrational as Jenny's father insisting that it was better for her to have died a virgin than marry a bengkali-kwi. How does one reason with such people?

Don't worry, Jenny's auntie (who herself had married an orang puteh — but orang putehs are more acceptable than bengkali-kwis) said, wait till the children come, everything is sure to be okay. Well, everything was not okay now that the children had come. Jenny's mother pampered the kids, thought they were such sweet and charming creatures, that they should grow up without little knots of hair on their heads. And, of course, Jenny agreed. Jaspal's mother was so overwhelmed she could not believe she was a grandmother. Oh God, thank you, thank you. This boy will grow to be handsome, smart, rich, a real good Sikh. You must bring him to the Temple every Sunday and teach him Punjabi. He will carry forward the family pride and heritage. Most of all he must never smoke, drink or cut his hair.

And in the meantime Jaspal had learned how to drink — smoking he gave a miss. Even the Prime Minister was against smoking. And the PM was right, smoking was bad; otherwise why did all cigarette packets in Australia carry the warning "Smoking is a health hazard"? But drinking was different.

Look at all those Sikhs with their big bellies, mum, Jaspal one day told his indignant mother, who are the pillars of the Sikh community, look at them — aren't they beer-bellies? Or, to be more accurate, whisky-bellies? Shut up, the mother said, you are not to talk like that. Education has spoiled you.

And so Jaspal had grown to be a man of thirty-six. He had a good job, enjoyed a certain amount of social respect, had even thought of going into politics — there was no Sikh MP in Singapore (there had been in Malaysia) — but Jenny restrained him. Politics is not good for marriage, she argued, it'll take you away from me and the kids. Look at Rangasamy, he is so busy seeing people he has no time to see his wife or even you these days. Okay, okay, I'll leave politics alone. One had to decide between withdrawal and commitment. Jaspal withdrew.

Thirty-six was a good age to be at. One had seen the absolute transformation of one's country into a bustling, modern, technological metropolis, one had got married, produced children, contributed to the community through volunteer work, upheld the family tradition by not cutting one's hair, helped in racial harmony by marrying outside the race, etc. Yes, Jaspal was quite a philosopher in his own way and he always philosophized when he shat every morning.

This morning Jenny had actually remarked, "Aren't you going to come out, Jas? You've been there nearly an hour, you'll be late for work!" Jaspal had not realized time had gone by so fast. Was shitting so profound that one lost track of time? Had it something to do with one's education? (My Jenny, Jenny, Jenny — shits — Jaspal had once made fun of his good wife à la Swift.) Or was it that he was growing old and so did not want too much activity — shifting those squatting legs from one position to another was an ordeal now. Ah, well, can't be sitting here all day, thought Jaspal, better get up and wash my anus.

And so Jaspal got rid of the dirt in his system.

"Make sure you wash with soap," Jenny yelled out.

M. G. Vassanji

In the Quiet of a Sunday Afternoon

Sunday afternoon languor descends over the street as usual. The day is hot but clear and a soft breeze blows bits of paper about. The street gradually empties of people and business comes to a halt. The last strains of Akashwani on the airwaves from India mingle with the smell of hot ghee, fried onions and saffron that wafts down from people's homes. Hussein, my father-in-law, sits on the bench and stares out through the doorway, as intently as though watching some action on the pavement. In his hands are the two halves of a ball, a soft bouncy red ball, the kind kids call flesh-ball, and he squeezes the two parts together.

A short while ago the ball fell from a roof three floors up, bounced a few times on the street and pavement and landed inside the store.

Hussein was upon it even before I realized it was there. Minutes later some boys came in, with a side of wood, their bat.

"Uncle, did you see a ball fall here somewhere?" they asked.

"Pigs!" yelled Hussein, jumping up from his seat in rage. "Do you want to hurt people? *How* many times do you have to be told . . . ?"

"We won't do it again, uncle," pleaded a boy.

"Pigs from hell! I will show you . . . devils!" He brought out a large knife and sliced the ball in two. A bit of rubber fell to the ground. "Here," said the old man, "take this —" They looked at what remained of their ball in his hands and ruefully left the shop.

The boys call him "German," because, he says, he can speak German. I've heard him say two things, "Mein Herr," and "Mein Gott," which I presume are German. He was still a youth when the Germans were here, and when he's in the mood he can spin quite a yarn about those times. We all have a name here. They think I don't know they call me "Black." Because I'm dark, almost an African. They have to give me a name, and what better name than something so obvious. Black. My wife is "Baby," the whole town calls her Baby, and you have to see the rolls of blubber hanging on her to see why. She was brought up on nothing but the purest butter, proclaims her mother proudly. "Our Baby was most dear to us," says Good Kulsum, whenever I need reminding of the good fortune that has come my way. How I landed in this situation is another story. I married to attain respectability, but right now I wonder if I've not had enough of it.

Now Baby and her mother sleep after the biriyani and I wait up, the shop half closed as usual. The quiet of the Sunday afternoon has always been mine — it is nice and pleasant in the shade and the town sleeps. I sit on the armchair and read the *Sunday Standard* column by column, and when I've finished and solved the puzzle set for children by Uncle Jim, and noted last week's winner, I have tea and wait for the woman to bring samosas. All this peace while they sleep and snore. But not today. Today German sits with me.

And the woman who brings samosas at four every Sunday will not come, today she catches the bus to go to her brother's town.

Her name is Zarina and she first came a few months ago and called out softly from outside, "Brother, do you want samosas for tea?"

I looked up from the paper and gave a good look at her and said, "Yes, I'll take a few." She came in, a small dark woman, her shallow basket covered with a newspaper. I fetched a plate from inside and she squatted and counted out five samosas and spooned out the chutney. I looked at those firm and large hips, the tight bodice, and I felt my blood thicken, a tightening in my limbs. Oh, how long since I had a good woman before my days of respectability began. What blubber I have to manipulate just to father a child. Her face was smooth and round, her hair long and wavy, tied at the back. What misfortune befell you, woman, that you are reduced to ferrying samosas, I thought. I looked into those dark shiny eyes and I touched her arm as I gave her the shilling.

She pulled it back and her eyes flared. "Aren't you ashamed, brother? Just because I am a widow and I come unaccompanied doesn't mean that I am a loose woman! My boy is asleep and I didn't have the heart to wake him up."

"Forgive me, sister," I said. "I was not myself."

She prepared to go. "Baby is asleep?"

"Yes. They're all resting."

The following Sunday she brought her son, and every Sunday thereafter. He would sit on the doorstep, watching the empty street, and she would sit inside on the bench. Her husband had been a coal seller and had died suddenly of a fever. She had only recently rented a room in the old house across the street and lived with Roshan. This Roshan has a certain reputation for her free ways. In any case, Zarina made a living selling snacks which she prepared and her son Amin helped to bear from place to place. Amin was ten years old or so and a quiet sickly fellow, surprisingly fair, for the coal seller wasn't very fair either. I would look at him sitting on the step and wonder, How long before he takes to the streets, before he starts stealing and pimping . . .

It turned out so that whenever we were out of bread in the morning, I crossed the street for fresh vitumbua. The door was always kept ajar there for customers, and I would walk inside into the dark and narrow corridor, at the end of which she sat beside the fire. There were three rooms on the left which I passed, closed with curtains. Zarina's face glowed like the coals and there would be a film of sweat on her face. The air was rich with a sweet smell of frying and the ceiling was covered with soot. She sat on a low stool, her hair undone and wavy, the hem of her frock tucked in front of her. The dough would be ready by her side, yellow and yeasty, which she would pour with a ladle into the small woks in front of her. Then she would prod the contents and turn them with a long skewer until they were raised like little tummies, brown and crisp, sizzling in the oil, almost filling the woks.

Baby loves vitumbua and she could eat two at a time. I would watch as Zarina brought them out one by one, and Amin would get the first lot to take away and sell. When he was gone I would await my share. Roshan would bring tea, and the two women would start to kid me. "You left Baby's side early today!" Once Roshan caught my eye at the door as I was leaving and said: "You know, if you find it difficult at home, you can always come here!" There was suggestion in those eyes and a wickedness in that smile that could give your heart a flutter. At the far end of the corridor the flames glowed yellow and blue, the little tummies sizzled, and Zarina watched us, one hand on a skewer. Without a word I stepped outside into the brilliant morning sunshine.

German's suspicions were aroused perhaps when he saw me give a shilling to the boy.

"Eh, Amin!" I called out one afternoon as he emerged with a few others from behind the store. He came in and stood in front of me, eyes shining and mouth open. "What were you doing back there?"

"Why? Playing."

"Don't take me for a fool! I too was your age once — shall I report to your mother?"

He knew I had him, but gave one more try. "Tell me, then, what was I doing?"

"Smoking! And shall I also tell you what? Why, look at you — all bones you are and you want to burn your insides smoking cigarettes! Play cricket, play football —"

"We don't have a ball!"

I still don't know what exactly it was that made me do it. "Here," I said, "take this — buy one and stay out of mischief." I gave him a shilling.

It was at this point that German shuffled in.

"You know, bapa," I told him, a little guiltily, "it's a pity there is no playing ground around here. The school is too far and at the Khalsa ground the caretaker chases them away. Boys need room to play."

"They are pigs, all of them." He made for the bench and picked up the measuring rod.

I thought this was too much. "Why, what have they done to you?" I asked, a little sharply.

But the man refused the challenge. "I said they are all pigs," he said simply, and with that we stared silently in front of us. Good Kulsum was out and at the back we could hear Baby commanding the servant in her thick husky voice. It was dull and hot outside, few customers came in, and you wondered how long the lull would last. A little later, towards evening, things picked up. Baby puffed in and Good Kulsum stepped in exhausted from her rounds. German stood up and went out for a stroll and I was glad to see the back of him. Customer traffic picked up. Kulsum sang hymns in her grating tone-less voice, counting beads from the bench, Baby served the customers and I gave out change and helped with wrapping. Baby is good with customers. She walks them in from the door, chatting amiably with them, and sees that they walk out with at least a good feeling if not something more.

That night she was angry and hurt.

"One whole shilling to someone we hardly know!" She looked at me reproachfully as she applied a generous layer of butter on a thick slice of bread, spread jam over it and handed it to me. Good Kulsum looked mournfully at me as she poured me my tea, and German smirked, slurping over his bread over which he had poured his tea.

"We should be charitable to our neighbours," I said in defence. "We should do things for each other." At which Baby and Kulsum remained silent, and the old man let out a series of muffled grunts through his skull, until I was forced to murmur, "Watch it, bapa, the bread does not get into your brain." And Kulsum looked more mournful than ever.

One morning he shuffled in as I sat kidding with the two women, sipping tea and watching the vitumbua frying in their woks.

"Indeed," he muttered, "one also gets tea while one waits!"

"Oh yes, bapa," I said, "have a seat, have a seat. Roshan, bring my father-in-law a chair!" You would have thought I owned the place.

"I have no intention of sitting," said the man testily. "I have a home. If it takes this long to cook vitumbua here, we can go elsewhere."

The two women eyed each other. "Go," Zarina then said. The old man stood watching the fire.

"You are the daughter of Jamal Meghji," he said at length.

"Yes," said Zarina.

German loudly cleared his throat as if he were about to spit on the floor, then shuffled off to the door, stuck his head out and spat.

"I knew your father," he said when he returned. "What town was he from?"

"Mbinga," she answered.

"I know that! Where in India?"

"I don't know. In Cutch or Gujarat somewhere."

"Mudra," he said, nodding at me. "I remember when he came to Africa."

She said nothing.

"Third class family," he told me, as we came out with our basket of vitumbua. "You know how he made his money?"

"They were rich, then?"

"He bought stolen goods. Flour and sugar. Then he sold it back. To the Germans. In one year, when the Great War in Europe began, he made all his money. And at the end of the war he lost it."

"How?"

"Ah!" His mood changed as we approached the shop, and he waved away my question. "But remember," he said, "third class family."

That night after supper he told the story. The table lay uncleared and we all sat around, waiting for someone to start something. First he burped, and then he asked his question, which is his way of starting a story.

"How did Jamal Meghji lose his wealth, Kulsa?"

"I don't know, it was all so long ago," Good Kulsum murmured.

"Listen, then." He looked at me. "In the year 1916 a rumour went around that the Germans were losing the Great War, in Europe and even here. And with that rumour went another little rumour that the German soldiers were going around looting the businesses. People started hiding their cash and their jewellery, burying it and stuffing mattresses. Some other time I'll tell you what I did. This is what Jamal Meghji did. He had a lot of cash, ten thousand rupees, it was said. Even for Europeans that was a lot of money.

"Outside his house was a large tree, from which hung six, seven beehives. In those days this was the custom among Africans. People kept beehives. And according to the custom, you did not go near other people's beehives. You could not touch them, no. So Jamal Meghji hid his money in beehives. And there it was as safe as it could be. He could go to sleep in peace.

"The Germans were losing the war. Some months later some German troops camped about five, six miles from the village. One day early in the morning a few German soldiers set out in search of food. And when they saw the beehives hanging from the trees, they pointed their rifles at them and shot them down. Jamal Meghji's beehives came down with all his wealth in them. In this way the woman's father died a pauper."

On Sunday evenings we walk to the seashore. Always in the same order, Good Kulsum in the lead, then Baby talking loudly over her shoulder at me just behind her, and German bringing up the rear.

And when the girls in pretty new dresses we pass on the road pull aside and giggle at our procession Baby gives them a good piece of her mind.

"What are you laughing at? — Khi-khi-khi . . . ? They think they are so beautiful. Look at the teeth of that one! She scares me, she does!"

At the seashore we drink coconut water, the old man buys peanuts, and we stroll for a while watching kids playing in the sand, boats bobbing up and down on the water, steamers coming into or leaving the harbour. We wave at the passengers when they wave at us and we wonder from what world beyond they could be coming, what country the ship's flag represents. The Goan church starts to fill up and we troop slowly home.

In that same order I was brought home after the wedding, a prize. The taxi we took from the railway station deposited us on the road outside the shop. Kulsum got out of the front seat, and Baby beside me on one side and German on the other opened their doors. Already a small group of bystanders had gathered and people came to stand at the doors of their shops pretending to be casual. The old man was haggling with the driver and Kulsum was at the door when Baby and I walked in. The servant brought the trunks behind us. Good Kulsum never misses such a chance. A shower of rice fell upon us at the doorstep as she greeted us in the traditional way, cracked her knuckles against our heads for luck, and pushed sweets into our mouths. The African girls who had gathered to watch smiled with pleasure and shyness, saying, "Mr. Bridegroom!" "May this union be blessed with long life and many children," Kulsum crooned with pleasure, as the bride and groom stepped on and cracked the clay saucers for more good luck. "God give you a long and contented life together." Then she sobbed. By this time German had arrived and angrily shooed the girls away.

I was an orphan half-caste when I married, mother black. I was brought up by an Indian family, half servant and half son, and the night following the arrival of Good Kulsum and German with their proposal, I was told to take it.

The other day Amin walked into the store.

"Uncle, Roshan says she wants to talk to you."

"What, now? What is it?" I asked a little anxiously. This Roshan is a little disconcerting.

"She says now, if possible."

"Alright. Go. Tell her I'm coming."

I told Baby to come and wait in the shop, and I crossed the road to find out what Roshan wanted. A most unusual request, this, but for her perhaps not so. I entered the dark corridor. The first room on my left was her sitting room and parlour. At the end of the corridor the fires were cold, but the broken-backed chair on which I sometimes sat was there. Inside the room, I sat on an old sofa with faded embroidered flower patterns, whose legs had been cut. A cup of tea duly came my way and Amin was dispatched to buy something. Roshan sat across from me at her dressing table and I realized that I was sitting there like one of her customers.

"You wanted to discuss something?" I began.

"Yes, I have something to tell you. You must have heard that Zarina is going to live with her brother in Mbinga."

"No, I haven't heard. What happened? Can't she make it here?"

"No, it is difficult. And the boy is giving her a hard time. He needs a father. A man he can fear and respect."

"Yes, yes. His uncle will be good for him." I felt a little uncomfortable. Behind her a faint light poured in through a small window almost blotted with dust. She was slurping tea. "She is a good and clever woman," I ventured warily. But you, I said in my mind, are the equal of ten ordinary men.

"If you were a bachelor, you would marry her, I know!" And she laughed merrily, her cup tinkled against the saucer. "Why don't you take her for your second wife?"

"This is no time for joking, Roshan," I answered severely. She had me positively flustered.

"I am not joking, brother. You like her and the other day you touched her in your shop. You should marry her! Go with her!"

I spoke gravely. "I don't need a second wife, Roshan. I have Baby, and I am satisfied."

"Ho! Who says? Why don't you have children then, tell me! You like this woman and you touched her. And she is good and fertile, I tell you. Good and fertile! And she works hard, as hard as your Baby. You know what they are saying about you? They say you are hen-pecked. 'Like her son,' they say. 'Follows her like a tail, wherever she goes. No stuff! Hides in her armpits!'"

When I've had enough I've had enough. I got up. "Who says this?" I asked. "Let them say it to my face. Let them dare to say it to my face! Just once, I tell you! Do you hear me? Tell them to say it to my face!" I told her what I thought of them, whoever they were, and I left.

Behind the rooms in the courtyard the servant irons the clothes I've decided to take with me. They include the shirts and trousers I brought with me and the wedding suit which was a gift from my guardian, nothing that I received from here. Behind me stashed away inside a shelf is a wad of money that I've surely contributed to earning and which they could easily earn at month's end. These two things, the clothes and the money, I would like to take with me in a small wooden trunk I bought for this purpose from a hawker. Soon Baby and Kulsum will get up and prepare for the Sunday walk to the seashore. It has to be soon. But German sits there like an old dog who's smelt something. He sits patiently on the bench, with the knife in one hand and one half of the sliced ball in the other. If I go, it will have to be with the clothes on my body and the few shillings jingling in my pocket.

Rohinton Mistry

The Collectors

1

When Dr. Burjor Mody was transferred from Mysore to assume the principalship of the Bombay Veterinary College he moved into Firozsha Baag with his wife and son Pesi. They occupied the vacant flat on the third floor of C Block, next to the Bulsara family.

Dr. Mody did not know it then, but he would be seeing a lot of Jehangir, the Bulsara boy; the boy who sat silent and brooding every evening watching the others at play, and called *chaarikhao* by them — quite unfairly, since he never tattled or told tales — (Dr. Mody would call him, affectionately, the observer of C Block). And Dr. Mody did not know this, either, at the time of moving that Jehangir

Bulsara's visits at ten A.M. every Sunday would become a source of profound joy for himself. Or that just when he would think he had found someone to share his hobby with, someone to mitigate the perpetual disappointment about his son Pesi, he would lose his precious Spanish dancing-lady stamp and renounce Jehangir's friendship both in quick succession. And then two years later, he himself would — but *that* is never knowable.

Soon after moving in, Dr. Burjor Mody became the pride of the Parsis in C Block. C Block, like the rest of Firozsha Baag, had a surfeit of low-paid bank clerks and bookkeepers, and the arrival of Dr. Mody permitted them to feel a little better about themselves. More importantly, in A Block lived a prominent priest, and B Block boasted a chartered accountant. Now C Block had a voice in Baag matters as important as the others did.

While C Block went about its routine business, confirming and authenticating the sturdiness of the object of their pride, the doctor's big-boned son Pesi established himself as leader of the rowdier elements among the Baag's ten-to-sixteen population. For Pesi, too, it was routine business; he was following a course he had mapped out for himself ever since the family began moving from city to city on the whims and megrims of his father's employer, the government.

To account for Pesi's success was the fact of his brutish strength. But he was also the practitioner of a number of minor talents which appealed to the crowd where he would be leader. The one no doubt complemented the other, the talents serving to dissemble the brutish qualifier of strength, and the brutish strength encouraging the crowd to perceive the appeal of his talents.

Hawking, for instance, was one of them. Pesi could summon up prodigious quantities of phlegm at will, accompanied by sounds such as the boys had seldom heard except in accomplished adults: deep, throaty, rasping resonating rolls which culminated in a pthoo, with the impressive trophy landing in the dust at their feet, its size leaving them all slightly envious. Pesi could also break wind that sounded like questions, exclamations, fragments of the chromatic scale and clarion calls, while the others sniffed and discussed the merits of pungency versus tonality. This ability earned him the appellation of Pesi *paad-maroo*, and he wore the sobriquet with pride.

Perhaps his single most important talent was his ability to improvise. The peculiarities of a locale were the raw material for his inventions. In Firozsha Baag, behind the three buildings, or blocks, as they were called, were spacious yards shared by all three blocks. These yards planted in Pesi's fecund mind the seed from which grew a new game: stoning-the-cats.

Till the arrival of the Mody family the yards were home for stray and happy felines, well fed on scraps and leftovers disgorged regularly as clockwork, after mealtimes, by the three blocks. The ground floors were the only ones who refrained. They voiced their protests in a periodic cycle of reasoning, pleading and screaming of obscenities, because the garbage collected outside their windows where the cats took up permanent residency, miaowing, feasting and caterwauling day and night. If the cascade of food was more than the cats could devour, the remainder fell to the fortune of the rats. Finally, flies and insects buzzed and hovered over the dregs, little pools of pulses and curries fermenting and frothing till the *kuchrawalli* came next morning and swept it all away.

The backyards of Firozsha Baag constituted its squalid underbelly. And this would be the scenario for stoning-the-cats, Pesi decided. But there was one hitch: the backyards were off limits to the boys. The only way in was through the *kuchrawalli*'s little shack standing beyond A Block, where her huge ferocious dog, tied to the gate, kept the boys at bay. So Pesi decreed that the boys gather at the rear windows of their homes, preferably at a time of day when the adults were scarce, with the fathers away at work and the mothers not yet finished with their afternoon naps. Each boy brought a pile of small stones and took turns, chucking three stones each. The game could just as easily have been stoning-the-rats; but stoned rats quietly walked away to safety, whereas the yowls of cats provided primal satisfaction and verified direct hits: no yowl, no point.

The game added to Pesi's popularity — he called it a howling success. But the parents (except the ground floor) complained to Dr.

Mody about his son instigating their children to torment poor dumb and helpless creatures. For a veterinarian's son to harass animals was shameful, they said.

As might be supposed, Pesi was the despair of his parents. Over the years Dr. Mody had become inured to the initial embarrassment in each new place they moved to. The routine was familiar: first, a spate of complaints from indignant parents claiming their sons *bugree nay dhoor thai gaya* — were corrupted to become useless as dust; next, the protestations giving way to sympathy when the neighbours saw that Pesi was the worm in the Modys' mango.

And so it was in Firozsha Baag. After the furor about stoning-the-cats had died down, the people of the Baag liked Dr. Mody more than ever. He earned their respect for the initiative he took in Baag matters, dealing with the management for things like broken lifts, leaking water tanks, crumbling plaster and faulty wiring. It was at his urging that the massive iron gate, set in the stone wall which ran all around the buildings, compound and backyards, was repaired, and a watch-man installed to stop beggars and riff-raff. (And although Dr. Mody would be dead by the time of the *Shiv Sena* riots, the tenants would remember him for the gate which would keep out the rampaging mobs.) When the Bombay Municipality tried to appropriate a section of Baag property for its road-widening scheme, Dr. Mody was in the forefront of the battle, winning a compromise whereby the Baag only lost half the proposed area. But the Baag's esteem did nothing to lighten the despair for Pesi that hung around the doctor.

At the birth of his son, Dr. Mody had deliberated long and hard about the naming. Peshotan, in the Persian epic *Shah-Nameh*, was the brother of the great Asfandyar, and a noble general, lover of art and learning and man of wise counsel. Dr. Mody had decided his son would play the violin, acquire the best from the cultures of East and West, thrill to the words of Tagore and Shakespeare, appreciate Mozart and Indian ragas; and one day, at the proper moment, he would introduce him to his dearest activity, stamp-collecting.

But the years passed in their own way. Fate denied fruition to all of Dr. Mody's plans; and when he talked about stamps, Pesi laughed and mocked his beloved hobby. This was the point at which, hurt and confused, he surrendered his son to whatever destiny was in store. A perpetual grief entered to occupy the void left behind after the aspirations for his son were evicted.

The weight of grief was heaviest around Dr. Mody when he returned from work in the evenings. As the car turned into the compound he usually saw Pesi before Pesi saw him, in scenes which made him despair, scenes in which his son was abusing someone, fighting or making lewd gestures.

But Dr. Mody was careful not to make a public spectacle of his despair. While the car made its way sluggishly over the uneven flagstones of the compound, the boys would stand back and wave him through. With his droll comments and jovial countenance he was welcome to disrupt their play, unlike two other car-owners of Firozsha Baag: the priest in A Block and the chartered accountant in B who habitually berated, from inside their vehicles, the sons of bank clerks and bookkeepers for blocking the driveway with their games. Their well-worn curses had become so predictable and ineffective that sometimes the boys chanted gleefully, in unison with their nemeses: "Worse than *saala* animals!" or "*junglee* dogs-cats have more sense!" or "you *sataans* ever have any lesson-*paani* to do or not!"

There was one boy who always stayed apart from his peers — the Bulsara boy, from the family next door to the Modys. Jehangir sat on the stone steps every evening while the gentle land breezes, drying and cooling the sweaty skins of the boys at play, blew out to sea. He sat alone through the long dusk, a source of discomfiture to the others. They resented his melancholy, watching presence.

Dr. Mody noticed Jehangir, too, on the stone steps of C Block, the delicate boy with the build much too slight for his age. Next to a hulk like Pesi he was diminutive, but things other than size underlined his frail looks: he had slender hands, and forearms with fine downy hair. And while facial fuzz was incipient in most boys of his age (and Pesi was positively hirsute), Jehangir's chin and upper lip were smooth as a young woman's. But it pleased Dr. Mody to see him evening after evening. The quiet contemplation of the boy on the steps and the noise and activity of the others at play came together in the kind of balance that Dr. Mody was always looking for and was quick to appreciate.

Jehangir, in his turn, observed the burly Dr. Mody closely as he walked past him each evening. When he approached the steps after parking his car, Jehangir would say *"Sahibji"* in greeting and smile wanly. He saw that despite Dr. Mody's constant jocularity there was something painfully empty about his eyes. He noticed the peculiar way he scratched the greyish-red patches of psoriasis on his elbows, both elbows simultaneously, by folding his arms across his chest. Sometimes Jehangir would arise from the stone steps and the two would go up together to the third floor. Dr. Mody asked him once, "You don't like playing with the other boys? You just sit and watch them?" The boy shook his head and blushed, and Dr. Mody did not bring up the matter after that.

Gradually, a friendship of sorts grew between the two. Jehangir touched a chord inside the doctor which had lain silent for much too long. Now affection for the boy developed and started to linger around the region hitherto occupied by grief bearing Pesi's name.

2

One evening, while Jehangir sat on the stone steps waiting for Dr. Mody's car to arrive, Pesi was organizing a game of *naargolio*. He divided the boys into two teams, then discovered he was one short. He beckoned to Jehangir, who said he did not want to play. Scowling, Pesi handed the ball to one of the others and walked over to him. He grabbed his collar with both hands, jerking him to his feet. *"Arré choosya!"* he yelled, "want a pasting?" and began dragging him by the collar to where the boys had piled up the seven flat stones for *naargolio*.

At that instant, Dr. Mody's car turned into the compound, and he spied his son in one of those scenes which could provoke despair. But today the despair was swept aside by rage when he saw that Pesi's victim was the gentle and quiet Jehangir Bulsara. He left the car in the middle of the compound with the motor running. Anger glinted in his eyes. He kicked over the pile of seven flat stones as he walked blindly towards Pesi who, having seen his father, had released Jehangir. He had been caught by his father often enough to know that it was best to stand and wait. Jehangir, meanwhile, tried to keep back the tears.

Dr. Mody stopped before his son and slapped him hard, once on each cheek, with the front and back of his right hand. He waited, as if debating whether that was enough, then put his arm around Jehangir and led him to the car.

He drove to his parking spot. By now, Jehangir had control of his tears, and they walked to the steps of C Block. The lift was out of order. They climbed the stairs to the third floor and knocked. He waited with Jehangir.

Jehangir's mother came to the door. "*Sahibji*, Dr. Mody," she said, a short, middle-aged woman, very prim, whose hair was always in a bun. Never without a *mathoobanoo*, she could do wonderful things with that square of fine white cloth which was tied and knotted to sit like a cap on her head, snugly packeting the bun. In the evenings, after the household chores were done, she removed the *mathoobanoo* and wore it in a more conventional manner, like a scarf.

"*Sahibji*," she said, then noticed her son's tear-stained face. "*Arré*, Jehangoo, what happened, who made you cry?" Her hand flew automatically to the *mathoobanoo*, tugging and adjusting it as she did whenever she was concerned or agitated.

To save the boy embarrassment, Dr. Mody intervened: "Go, wash your face while I talk to your mother." Jehangir went inside, and Dr. Mody told her briefly about what had happened. "Why does he not play with the other boys?" he asked finally.

"Dr. Mody, what to say. The boy never wants even to go out. *Khoedai salaamat raakhé*, wants to sit at home all the time and read story books. Even this little time in the evening he goes because I force him and tell him he will not grow tall without fresh air. Every week he brings new-new story books from school. First, school library would allow only one book per week. But he went to Father Gonzalves who is in charge of library and got special permission for two books. God knows why he gave it."

"But reading is good, Mrs. Bulsara."

"I know, I know, but a mania like this, all the time?"

"Some boys are outdoor types, some are indoor types. You shouldn't worry about Jehangir, he is a very good boy. Look at my Pesi, now there is a case for worry," he said, meaning to reassure her.

"No, no. You mustn't say that. Be patient, *Khoedai* is great," said Mrs. Bulsara, consoling him instead. Jehangir returned, his eyes slightly red but dry. While washing his face he had wet a lock of his hair which hung down over his forehead.

"Ah, here comes my indoor champion," smiled Dr. Mody, and patted Jehangir's shoulder, brushing back the lock of hair. Jehangir did not understand, but grinned anyway; the doctor's joviality was infectious. Dr. Mody turned again to the mother. "Send him to my house on Sunday at ten o'clock. We will have a little talk."

After Dr. Mody left, Jehangir's mother told him how lucky he was that someone as important and learned as Burjor Uncle was taking an interest in him. Privately, she hoped he would encourage the boy towards a more all-rounded approach to life and to the things other boys did. And when Sunday came she sent Jehangir off to Dr. Mody's promptly at ten.

Dr. Mody was taking his bath, and Mrs. Mody opened the door. She was a dour-faced woman, spare and lean — the opposite of her husband in appearance and disposition, yet retaining some quality from long ago which suggested that it had not always been so. Jehangir had never crossed her path save when she was exchanging civilities with his mother, while making purchases out by the stairs from the vegetablewalla or fruitwalla.

Not expecting Jehangir's visit, Mrs. Mody stood blocking the doorway and said: "Yes?" Meaning, what nuisance now?

"Burjor Uncle asked me to come at ten o'clock."

"Asked you to come at ten o'clock? What for?"

"He just said to come at ten o'clock."

Grudgingly, Mrs. Mody stepped aside. "Come in then. Sit down there." And she indicated the specific chair she wanted him to occupy, muttering something about a *baap* who had time for strangers' children but not for his own son.

Jehangir sat in what must have been the most uncomfortable chair in the room. This was his first time inside the Modys' flat, and he looked around with curiosity. But his gaze was quickly restricted to the area of the floor directly in front of him when he realized that he was the object of Mrs. Mody's watchfulness.

Minutes ticked by under her vigilant eye. Jehangir was grateful when Dr. Mody emerged from the bedroom. Being Sunday, he had eschewed his usual khaki half-pants for loose and comfortable white pyjamas. His *sudra* hung out over it, and he strode vigorously, feet encased in a huge pair of *sapaat*. He smiled at Jehangir, who happily noted the crow's-feet appearing at the corners of his eyes. He was ushered into Dr. Mody's room, and man and boy both seemed glad to escape the surveillance of the woman.

The chairs were more comfortable in Dr. Mody's room. They sat at his desk and Dr. Mody opened a drawer to take out a large book.

"This was the first stamp album I ever had," said Dr. Mody. "It was given to me by my Nusserwanji Uncle when I was your age. All the pages were empty." He began turning them. They were covered with stamps, each a feast of colour and design. He talked as he turned the pages, and Jehangir watched and listened, glancing at the stamps flying past, at Dr. Mody's face, then at the stamps again.

Dr. Mody spoke not in his usual booming, jovial tones but softly, in a low voice charged with inspiration. The stamps whizzed by, and his speech was gently underscored by the rustle of the heavily laden pages that seemed to turn of their own volition in the quiet room. (Jehangir would remember this peculiar rustle when one day, older, he'd stand alone in this very room, silent now forever, and turn the pages of Nusserwanji Uncle's album.) Jehangir watched and listened.

It was as though a mask had descended over Dr. Mody, a faraway look upon his face, and a shining in the eyes which heretofore Jehangir had only seen sad with despair or glinting with anger or just plain and empty, belying his constant drollery. Jehangir watched, and listened to the euphonious voice hinting at wondrous things and promises and dreams.

The album on the desk, able to produce such changes in Dr. Mody, now worked its magic through him upon the boy. Jehangir, watching and listening, fascinated, tried to read the names of the countries at the top of the pages as they sped by: Antigua . . . Australia . . . Belgium . . . Bhutan . . . Bulgaria . . . and on through to Malta and Mauritius . . . Romania and Russia . . . Togo and Tonga . . . and a final blur through which he caught Yugoslavia and Zanzibar.

"Can I see it again?" he asked, and Dr. Mody handed the album to him.

"So what do you think? Do you want to be a collector?"

Jehangir nodded eagerly and Dr. Mody laughed. "When Nusserwanji Uncle showed me his collection I felt just like that. I'll tell your mother what to buy for you to get you started. Bring it here next Sunday, same time."

And next Sunday Jehangir was ready at nine. But he waited by his door with a Stamp Album For Beginners and a packet of 100 Assorted Stamps — All Countries. Going too early would mean sitting under the baleful eyes of Mrs. Mody.

Ten o'clock struck and the clock's tenth bong was echoed by the Modys' doorchimes. Mrs. Mody was expecting him this time and did not block the doorway. Wordlessly, she beckoned him in. Burjor Uncle was ready, too, and came out almost immediately to rescue him from her arena.

"Let's see what you've got there," he said when they were in his room. They removed the cellophane wrapper, and while they worked Dr. Mody enjoyed himself as much as the boy. His deepest wish appeared to be coming true: he had at last found someone to share his hobby with. He could not have hoped for a finer neophyte than

Jehangir. His young recruit was so quick to learn how to identify and sort stamps by countries, learn the different currencies, spot watermarks. Already he was skilfully folding and moistening the little hinges and mounting the stamps as neatly as the teacher.

When it was almost time to leave, Jehangir asked if he could examine again Nusserwanji Uncle's album, the one he had seen last Sunday. But Burjor Uncle led him instead to a cupboard in the corner of the room. "Since you enjoy looking at my stamps, let me show you what I have here." He unlocked its doors.

Each of the cupboard's four shelves was piled with biscuit tins and sweet tins: round, oval, rectangular, square. It puzzled Jehangir: all this bore the unmistakable stamp of the worthless hoardings of senility, and did not seem at all like Burjor Uncle. But Burjor Uncle reached out for a box at random and showed him inside. It was chock-full of stamps! Jehangir's mouth fell open. Then he gaped at the shelves, and Burjor Uncle laughed. "Yes, all these tins are full of stamps. And that big cardboard box at the bottom contains six new albums, all empty."

Jehangir quickly tried to assign a number in his mind to the stamps in the containers of Maghanlal Biscuitwalla and Lokmanji Mithaiwalla, to all of the stamps in the round tins and the oval tins, the square ones and the oblong ones. He failed.

Once again Dr. Mody laughed at the boy's wonderment. "A lot of stamps. And they took me a lot of years to collect. Of course, I am lucky I have many contacts in foreign countries. Because of my job, I meet the experts from abroad who are invited by the Indian Government. When I tell them about my hobby they send me stamps from their countries. But no time to sort them, so I pack them in boxes. One day, after I retire, I will spend all my time with my stamps." He paused, and shut the cupboard doors. "So what you have to do now is start making lots of friends, tell them about your hobby. If they also collect, you can exchange duplicates with them. If they don't, you can still ask them for all the envelopes they may be throwing away with stamps on them. You do something for them, they will do something for you. Your collection will grow depending on how smart you are."

He hesitated, and opened the cupboard again. Then he changed his mind and shut it — it wasn't yet time for the Spanish dancing-lady stamp.

3

On the pavement outside St. Xavier's Boys School, not far from the ornate iron gates, stood two variety stalls. They were the stalls of *Patla Babu* and *Jhaaria Babu*. Their real names were never known. Nor was known the exact source of the schoolboy inspiration that named them thus, many years ago, after their respective thinness and fatness.

Before the schoolboys arrived in the morning, the two would unpack their cases and set up the displays, beating the beggars to the choice positions. Occasionally, there were disputes if someone's space was violated. The beggars did not harbour great hopes for alms from schoolboys but they stood there, nonetheless, like mute lessons in realism and the harshness of life. Their patience was rewarded when they raided the dustbins after breaks and lunches.

At the end of the school day the pavement community packed up. The beggars shuffled off into the approaching dark, *Patla Babu* went home with his cases, and *Jhaaria Babu* slept near the school gate under a large tree to whose trunk he chained his boxes during the night.

The two sold a variety of nondescript objects and comestibles, uninteresting to any save the eyes and stomachs of schoolboys: *supari*, A-1 chewing gum (which, in a most ungumlike manner, would, after a while, dissolve in one's mouth), *jeeragoli*, marbles, tops, *aampapud* during the mango season, pens, Camel Ink, pencils, rulers and stamps in little cellophane packets.

Patla Babu and *Jhaaria Babu* lost some of their goods regularly due to theft. This was inevitable when doing business outside a large school like St. Xavier's, with a population as varied as its was. The loss was an operating expense stoically accepted, like the success or failure of the monsoons, and they never complained to the school authorities or held it against the boys. Besides, business was good despite the losses: insignificant items like a packet of *jeeragoli* worth ten paise, or a marble of the kind that sold three for five paise. More often than not, the stealing went on for the excitement of it, out of bravado or on a dare. It was called "flicking" and was done without any malice towards *Patla* and *Jhaaria*.

Foremost among the flickers was a boy in Jehangir's class called Eric D'Souza. A tall, lanky fellow who had been suspended a couple of times, he had had to repeat the year on two occasions, and held out the promise of more repetitions. Eric also had the reputation of doing things inside his half-pants under cover of his desk. In a class of fifty boys it was easy to go unobserved by the teacher, and only his immediate neighbours could see the ecstasy on his face and the vigorous back and forth movement of his hand. When he grinned at them they looked away, pretending not to have noticed anything.

Jehangir sat far from Eric and knew of his habits only by hearsay. He was oblivious to Eric's eye which had been on him for quite a while. In fact, Eric found Jehangir's delicate hands and fingers, his smooth legs and thighs very desirable. In class he gazed for hours, longingly, at the girlish face, curly hair, long eyelashes.

Jehangir and Eric finally got acquainted one day when the class filed out for games period. Eric had been made to kneel down by the door for coming late and disturbing the class, and Jehangir found himself next to him as he stood in line. From his kneeling position Eric observed the smooth thighs emerging from the half-pants (half-pants was the school uniform requirement), winked at him and, unhindered by his underwear, inserted a pencil up the pant leg. He tickled Jehangir's genitals seductively with the eraser end, expertly, then withdrew it. Jehangir feigned a giggle, too shocked to say anything. The line started to move for the playground.

Shortly after this incident, Eric approached Jehangir during break-time. He had heard that Jehangir was desperate to acquire stamps.

"*Arré* man, I can get you stamps, whatever kind you want," he said.

Jehangir stopped. He had been slightly confused ever since the pass with the pencil; Eric frightened him a little with his curious habits and forbidden knowledge. But it had not been easy to accumulate stamps. Sundays with Burjor Uncle continued to be as fascinating as the first. He wished he had new stamps to show — the stasis of his collection might be misinterpreted as lack of interest. He asked Eric: "Ya? You want to exchange?"

"No *yaar*, I don't collect. But I'll get them for you. As a favour, man."

"Ya? What kind do you have?"

"I don't have, man. Come on with me to *Patla* and *Jhaaria*, just show me which ones you want. I'll flick them for you."

Jehangir hesitated. Eric put his arm around him: "C'mon man, what you scared for, I'll flick. You just show me and go away." Jehangir pictured the stamps on display in cellophane wrappers: how well they would add to his collection. He imagined album pages bare no more but covered with exquisite stamps, each one mounted carefully and correctly, with a hinge, as Burjor Uncle had showed him to.

They went outside, Eric's arm still around him. Crowds of schoolboys were gathered around the two stalls. A multitude of groping, exploring hands handled the merchandise and browsed absorbedly, a multitude that was a prerequisite for flicking to begin. Jehangir showed Eric the individually wrapped stamps he wanted and moved away. In a few minutes Eric joined him triumphantly.

"Got them?"

"Ya ya. But come inside. He could be watching man."

Jehangir was thrilled. Eric asked, "You want more or what?"

"Sure," said Jehangir.

"But not today. On Friday. If you do me a favour in visual period on Thursday."

Jehangir's pulse speeded slightly — visual period, with its darkened hall and projector, and the intimacy created by the teacher's policing abilities temporarily suspended. He remembered Eric's pencil. The cellophane-wrapped stamp packets rustled and crackled in his hand. And there was the promise of more. There had been nothing unpleasant about the pencil. In fact it had felt quite, well, exciting. He agreed to Eric's proposal.

On Thursday, the class lined up to go to the Visual Hall. Eric stood behind Jehangir to ensure their seats would be together.

When the room was dark he put his hand on Jehangir's thigh and began caressing it. He took Jehangir's hand and placed it on his crotch. It lay there inert. Impatient, he whispered, "Do it, man, c'mon!" But Jehangir's lacklustre stroking was highly unsatisfactory. Eric arrested the hand, reached inside his pants and said, "OK, hold it tight and rub it like this." He encircled Jehangir's hand with his to show him how. When Jehangir had attained the right pressure and speed he released his own hand to lean back and sigh contentedly. Shortly, Jehangir felt a warm stickiness fill his palm and fingers, and the hardness he held in his hand grew flaccid.

Eric shook off the hand. Jehangir wiped his palm with his hanky. Eric borrowed the hanky to wipe himself. "Want me to do it for you?" he asked. But Jehangir declined. He was thinking of his hanky. The odour was interesting, not unpleasant at all, but he would have to find some way of cleaning it before his mother found it.

The following day, Eric presented him with more stamps. Next Thursday's assignation was also fixed.

And on Sunday Jehangir went to see Dr. Mody at ten o'clock. The wife let him in, muttering something under her breath about being bothered by inconsiderate people on the one day that the family could be together.

Dr. Mody's delight at the new stamps fulfilled Jehangir's every expectation: "Wonderful, wonderful! Where did you get them all? No, no, forget it, don't tell me. You will think I'm trying to learn your tricks. I already have enough stamps to keep me busy in my retirement. Ha! ha!"

After the new stamps had been examined and sorted Dr. Mody said, "Today, as a reward for your enterprise, I'm going to show you a stamp you've never seen before." From the cupboard of biscuit and sweet tins he took a small satin-covered box of the type in which rings or bracelets are kept. He opened it and, without removing the stamp from inside, placed it on the desk.

The stamp said España Correos at the bottom and its denomination was noted in the top left corner: 3 PTAS. The face of the stamp featured a flamenco dancer in the most exquisite detail and colour. But it was something in the woman's countenance, a look, an ineffable sparkle he saw in her eyes, which so captivated Jehangir.

Wordlessly, he studied the stamp. Dr. Mody waited restlessly as the seconds ticked by. He kept fidgeting till the little satin-covered box was shut and back in his hands, then said, "So you like the Spanish dancing-lady. Everyone who sees it likes it. Even my wife who is not interested in stamp-collecting thought it was beautiful. When I retire I can spend more time with the Spanish dancing-lady. And all my other stamps." He relaxed once the stamp was locked again in the cupboard.

Jehangir left, carrying that vision of the Spanish dancer in his head. He tried to imagine the stamp inhabiting the pages of his album, to greet him every time he opened it, with the wonderful sparkle in her eyes. He shut the door behind him and immediately, as though to obliterate his covetous fantasy, loud voices rose inside the flat.

He heard Mrs. Mody's, shrill in argument, and the doctor's, beseeching her not to yell lest the neighbours would hear. Pesi's name was mentioned several times in the quarrel that ensued, and accusations of neglect, and something about the terrible affliction on a son of an unloving father. The voices followed Jehangir as he hurried past the inquiring eyes of his mother, till he reached the bedroom at the other end of the flat and shut the door.

When the school week started, Jehangir found himself looking forward to Thursday. His pulse was racing with excitement when visual period came. To save his hanky this time he kept some paper at hand.

Eric did not have to provide much guidance. Jehangir discovered he could control Eric's reactions with variations in speed, pressure, and grip. When it was over and Eric offered to do it to him, he did not refuse.

The weeks sped by and Jehangir's collection continued to grow, visual period by visual period. Eric's and his masturbatory partnership was whispered about in class, earning the pair the title of *moothya-maroo*. He accompanied Eric on the flicking forays, helping to swell the milling crowd and add to the browsing hands. Then he grew bolder, studied Eric's methods, and flicked a few stamps himself.

But this smooth course of stamp-collecting was about to end. *Patla Babu* and *Jhaaria Babu* broke their long tradition of silence and complained to the school. Unlike marbles and *supari*, it was not a question of a few paise a day. When Eric and Jehangir struck, their haul could be totalled in rupees reaching double digits; the loss was serious enough to make the *Babus* worry about their survival.

The school assigned the case to the head prefect to investigate. He was an ambitious boy, always snooping around, and was also a member of the school debating team and the Road Safety Patrol. Shortly after the complaint was made he marched into Jehangir's class one afternoon just after lunch break, before the teacher returned, and made what sounded very much like one of his debating speeches: "Two boys in this class have been stealing stamps from *Patla Babu* and *Jhaaria Babu* for the past several weeks. You may ask: who are those boys? No need for names. They know who they are and I know who they are, and I am asking them to return the stamps to me tomorrow. There will be no punishment if this is done. The *Babus* just want their stamps back. But if the missing stamps are not returned, the names will be reported to the principal and to the police. It is up to the two boys."

Jehangir tried hard to appear normal. He was racked with trepidation, and looked to the unperturbed Eric for guidance. But Eric ignored him. The head prefect left amidst mock applause from the class.

After school, Eric turned surly. Gone was the tender, cajoling manner he reserved for Jehangir, and he said nastily: "You better bring back all those fucking stamps tomorrow." Jehangir, of course, agreed. There was no trouble with the prefect or the school after the stamps were returned.

But Jehangir's collection shrunk pitiably overnight. He slept badly the entire week, worried about explaining to Burjor Uncle the sudden disappearance of the bulk of his collection. His mother assumed the dark rings around his eyes were due to too much reading and not enough fresh air. The thought of stamps or of *Patla Babu* or *Jhaaria Babu* brought an emptiness to his stomach and a bitter taste to his mouth. A general sense of ill-being took possession of him.

He went to see Burjor Uncle on Sunday, leaving behind his stamp album. Mrs. Mody opened the door and turned away silently. She appeared to be in a black rage, which exacerbated Jehangir's own feelings of guilt and shame.

He explained to Burjor Uncle that he had not bothered to bring his album because he had acquired no new stamps since last Sunday, and also, he was not well and would not stay for long.

Dr. Mody was concerned about the boy, so nervous and uneasy; he put it down to his feeling unwell. They looked at some stamps Dr. Mody had received last week from his colleagues abroad. Then Jehangir said he'd better leave.

"But you *must* see the Spanish dancing-lady before you go. Maybe she will help you feel better. Ha! ha!" and Dr. Mody rose to go to the cupboard for the stamp. Its viewing at the end of each Sunday's session had acquired the significance of an esoteric ritual.

From the next room Mrs. Mody screeched: "Burjorji! Come here at once!" He made a wry face at Jehangir and hurried out.

In the next room, all the vehemence of Mrs. Mody's black rage of that morning poured out upon Dr. Mody: "It has reached the limit now! No time for your own son and Sunday after Sunday sitting with some stranger! What does he have that your own son does not? Are you a *baap* or what? No wonder Pesi has become this way! How can I blame the boy when his own *baap* takes no interest . . ."

"Shh! The boy is in the next room! What do you want, that all the neighbours hear your screaming?"

"I don't care! Let them hear! You think they don't know already? You think you are . . ."

Mrs. Bulsara next door listened intently. Suddenly, she realized that Jehangir was in there. Listening from one's own house was one thing — hearing a quarrel from inside the quarrellers' house was another. It made feigning ignorance very difficult.

She rang the Modys' doorbell and waited, adjusting her *math-oobanoo*. Dr. Mody came to the door.

"Burjorji, forgive me for disturbing your stamping and collecting work with Jehangir. But I must take him away. Guests have arrived unexpectedly. Jehangir must go to the Irani, we need cold drinks."

"That's okay, he can come next Sunday." Then added, "He *must* come next Sunday," and noted with satisfaction the frustrated turning away of Mrs. Mody who waited out of sight of the doorway. "Jehangir! Your mother is calling."

Jehangir was relieved at being rescued from the turbulent waters of the Mody household. They left without further conversation, his mother tugging in embarrassment at the knots of her *mathoobanoo*.

As a result of this unfortunate outburst, a period of awkwardness between the women was unavoidable. Mrs. Mody, though far from garrulous, had never let her domestic sorrows and disappointments interfere with the civilities of neighbourly relations, which she respected and observed at all times. Now for the first time since the arrival of the Modys in Firozsha Baag these civilities experienced a hiatus.

When the *muchhiwalla* arrived next morning instead of striking a joint deal with him as they usually did, Mrs. Mody waited till Mrs. Bulsara had finished. She stationed an eye at her peephole as he emphasized the freshness of his catch. "Look *bai*, it is *saféd paani*," he said, holding out the pomfret and squeezing it near the gills till white fluid oozed out. After Mrs. Bulsara had paid and gone, Mrs. Mody emerged, while the former took her turn at the peephole. And so it went for a few days till the awkwardness had run its course and things returned to normal.

But not so for Jehangir; on Sunday, he once again had to leave behind his sadly depleted album. To add to his uneasiness, Mrs. Mody invited him in with a greeting of "Come *bawa* come," and there was something malignant about her smile.

Dr. Mody sat at his desk, shoulders sagging his hands dangling over the arms of the chair. The desk was bare — not a single stamp anywhere in sight, and the cupboard in the corner locked. The absence of his habitual, comfortable clutter made the room cold and cheerless. He was in low spirits; instead of the crow's-feet at the corners of his eyes were lines of distress and dejection.

"No album again?"

"No. Haven't got any new stamps yet," Jehangir smiled nervously.

Dr. Mody scratched the psoriasis on his elbows. He watched Jehangir carefully as he spoke. "Something very bad has happened to the Spanish dancing-lady stamp. Look," and he displayed the satin-covered box minus its treasure. "It is missing." Half-fearfully, he looked at Jehangir, afraid he would see what he did not want to. But it was inevitable. His last sentence evoked the head prefect's thundering debating-style speech of a few days ago, and the ugliness of the entire episode revisited Jehangir's features — a final ignominious postscript to Dr. Mody's loss and disillusion.

Dr. Mody shut the box. The boy's reaction, his silence, the absence of his album, confirmed his worst suspicions. More humiliatingly, it seemed his wife was right. With great sadness he rose from his chair. "I have to leave now, something urgent at the College." They parted without a word about next Sunday.

Jehangir never went back. He thought for a few days about the missing stamp and wondered what could have happened to it. Burjor Uncle was too careful to have misplaced it; besides, he never removed it from its special box. And the box was still there. But he did not resent him for concluding he had stolen it. His guilt about *Patla Babu* and *Jhaaria Babu*, about Eric and the stamps was so intense, and the punishment deriving from it so inconsequential, almost non-existent, that he did not mind this undeserved blame. In fact, it served to equilibrate his scales of justice.

His mother questioned him the first few Sundays he stayed home. Feeble excuses about homework, and Burjor Uncle not having new stamps, and it being boring to look at the same stuff every Sunday did not satisfy her. She finally attributed his abnegation of stamps to sensitivity and a regard for the unfortunate state of the Modys' domestic affairs. It pleased her that her son was capable of such concern. She did not press him after that.

4

Pesi was no longer to be seen in Firozsha Baag. His absence brought relief to most of the parents at first, and then curiosity. Gradually, it became known that he had been sent away to a boarding-school in Poona.

The boys of the Baag continued to play their games in the compound. For better or worse, the spark was lacking that lent unpredictability to those languid coastal evenings of Bombay; evenings which could so easily trap the unwary, adult or child, within a circle of lassitude and depression in which time hung heavy and suffocating.

Jehangir no longer sat on the stone steps of C Block in the evenings. He found it difficult to confront Dr. Mody day after day. Besides, the boys he used to watch at play suspected some kind of connection between Pesi's being sent away to boarding-school, Jehangir's former friendship with Dr. Mody, and the emerging of Dr. Mody's constant sorrow and despair (which he had tried so hard to keep private all along and had succeeded, but was now visible for all to see). And the boys resented Jehangir for whatever his part was in it — they bore him open antagonism.

Dr. Mody was no more the jovial figure the boys had grown to love. When his car turned into the compound in the evenings, he still waved, but no crow's-feet appeared at his eyes, no smile, no jokes.

Two years passed since the Mody family's arrival in Firozsha Baag.

In school, Jehangir was as isolated as in the Baag. Most of his effeminateness had, of late, transformed into vigorous signs of impending manhood. Eric D'Souza had been expelled for attempting to sodomize a junior boy. Jehangir had not been involved in this affair, but most of his classmates related it to the furtive activities of their callow days and the stamp-flicking. *Patla Babu* and *Jhaaria Babu* had disappeared from the pavement outside St. Xavier's. The Bombay police, in a misinterpretation of the nation's mandate: *garibi hatao* — eradicate poverty, conducted periodic round-ups of pavement dwellers, sweeping into their vans beggars and street-vendors, cripples and alcoholics, the homeless and the hungry, and dumped them somewhere outside the city limits; when the human detritus made its way back into the city, another clean-up was scheduled. *Patla* and *Jhaaria* were snared in one of these raids, and never found their way back. Eyewitnesses said their stalls were smashed up and *Patla Babu* received a *lathi* across his forehead for trying to salvage some of his inventory. They were not seen again.

Two years passed since Jehangir's visits to Dr. Mody had ceased.

It was getting close to the time for another transfer for Dr. Mody. When the inevitable orders were received, he went to Ahmedabad to make arrangements. Mrs. Mody was to join her husband after a few days. Pesi was still in boarding-school, and would stay there.

So when news arrived from Ahmedabad of Dr. Mody's death of heart failure, Mrs. Mody was alone in the flat. She went next door with the telegram and broke down.

The Bulsaras helped with all the arrangements. The body was brought to Bombay by car for a proper Parsi funeral. Pesi came from Poona for the funeral, then went back to boarding-school.

The events were talked about for days afterwards, the stories spreading first in C Block, then through A and B. Commiseration for Mrs. Mody was general. The ordeal of the body during the two-day car journey from Ahmedabad was particularly horrifying and was discussed endlessly. Embalming was not allowed according to Parsi rituals, and the body in the trunk, although packed with ice, had started to smell horribly in the heat of the Deccan Plateau which the car had had to traverse. Some hinted that this torment suffered by Dr. Mody's earthly remains was the Almighty's punishment for neglecting his duties as a father and making Mrs. Mody so unhappy. Poor Dr. Mody, they said, who never went a day without a bath and talcum powder in life, to undergo this in death. Someone even had, on good authority, a count of the number of eau de cologne bottles used by Mrs. Mody and the three occupants of the car over the course of the journey — it was the only way they could draw breath, through cologne-watered handkerchiefs. And it was also said that ever after, these four could never tolerate eau de cologne — opening a bottle was like opening the car trunk with Dr. Mody's decomposing corpse.

A year after the funeral, Mrs. Mody was still living in Firozsha Baag. Time and grief had softened her looks, and she was no longer the harsh and dour-faced woman Jehangir had seen during his first Sunday visit. She had decided to make the flat her permanent home now, and the trustees of the Baag granted her request "in view of the unfortunate circumstances."

There were some protests about this, particularly from those whose sons or daughters had been postponing marriages and families till flats became available. But the majority, out of respect for Dr. Mody's memory, agreed with the trustees' decision. Pesi continued to attend boarding-school.

One day, shortly after her application had been approved by the trustees, Mrs. Mody visited Mrs. Bulsara. They sat and talked of old times, when they had first moved in, and about how pleased Dr. Mody had been to live in a Parsi colony like Firozsha Baag after years of travelling, and then the disagreements she had had with her husband over Pesi and Pesi's future; tears came to her eyes, and also to Mrs. Bulsara's, who tugged at a corner of her *mathoobanoo* to reach it to her eyes and dry them. Mrs. Mody confessed how she had hated Jehangir's Sunday visits although he was such a fine boy, because she was worried about the way poor Burjorji was neglecting Pesi: "But he could not help it. That was the way he was. Sometimes he would wish *Khoedai* had given him a daughter instead of a son. Pesi disappointed him in everything in all his plans, and . . ." and here she burst into uncontrollable sobs.

Finally, after her tears subsided she asked, "Is Jehangir home?" He wasn't. "Would you ask him to come and see me this Sunday? At ten? Tell him I won't keep him long."

Jehangir was a bit apprehensive when his mother gave him the message. He couldn't imagine why Mrs. Mody would want to see him.

On Sunday, as he prepared to go next door, he was reminded of the Sundays with Dr. Mody, the kindly man who had befriended him, opened up a new world for him, and then repudiated him for something he had not done. He remembered the way he would scratch the greyish-red patches of psoriasis on his elbows. He could still picture the sorrow on his face as, with the utmost reluctance, he had made his decision to end the friendship. Jehangir had not blamed Dr. Mody then, and he still did not; he knew how overwhelmingly the evidence had been against him, and how much that stamp had meant to Dr. Mody.

Mrs. Mody led him in by his arm: "Will you drink something?"

"No, thank you."

"Not feeling shy, are you? You always were shy." She asked him about his studies and what subjects he was taking in high school. She told him a little about Pesi, who was still in boarding-school and had twice repeated the same standard. She sighed. "I asked you to come today because there is something I wanted to give you. Something of Burjor Uncle's. I thought about it for many days. Pesi is not interested, and I don't know anything about it. Will you take his collection?"

"The album in his drawer?" asked Jehangir, a little surprised.

"Everything. The album, all the boxes, everything in the cupboard. I know you will use it well. Burjor would have done the same."

Jehangir was speechless. He had stopped collecting stamps, and they no longer held the fascination they once did. Nonetheless, he was familiar with the size of the collection, and the sheer magnitude of what he was now being offered had its effect. He remembered the awe with which he had looked inside the cupboard the first time its doors had been opened before him. So many sweet tins, cardboard boxes, biscuit tins . . .

"You will take it? As a favour to me, yes?" she asked a second time, and Jehangir nodded. "You have some time today? Whenever you like, just take it." He said he would ask his mother and come back.

There was a huge, old iron trunk which lay under Jehangir's bed. It was dented in several places and the lid would not shut properly. Undisturbed for years, it had rusted peacefully beneath the bed. His mother agreed that the rags it held could be thrown away and the stamps temporarily stored in it till Jehangir organized them into albums. He emptied the trunk, wiped it out, lined it with brown paper and went next door to bring back the stamps.

Several trips later, Dr. Mody's cupboard stood empty. Jehangir looked around the room in which he had once spent so many happy hours. The desk was in exactly the same position, and the two chairs. He turned to go, almost forgetting and went back to the desk. Yes, there it was in the drawer, Dr. Mody's first album, given him by his Nusserwanji Uncle.

He started to turn the heavily laden pages. They rustled in a peculiar way — what was it about that sound? Then he remembered: that first Sunday, and he could almost hear Dr. Mody again, the soft inspired tones speaking of promises and dreams, quite different from his usual booming jovial voice, and that faraway look in his eyes which had once glinted with rage when Pesi had tried to bully him . . .

Mrs. Mody came into the room. He shut the album, startled: "This is the last lot." He stopped to thank her but she interrupted: "No, no. What is the thank-you for? You are doing a favour to me by taking it, you are helping me to do what Burjor would like." She took his arm. "I wanted to tell you. From the collection one stamp is missing. With the picture of the dancing-lady."

"I know!" said Jehangir. "That's the one Burjor Uncle lost and thought that I . . ."

Mrs. Mody squeezed his arm which she was still holding and he fell silent. She spoke softly, but without guilt: "He did not lose it. I destroyed it." Then her eyes went moist as she watched the disbelief on his face. She wanted to say more, to explain, but could not, and clung to his arm. Finally, her voice quavering pitiably, she managed to say, "Forgive an old lady," and patted his cheek. Jehangir left in silence, suddenly feeling very ashamed.

Over the next few days, he tried to impose some order on that greatly chaotic mass of stamps. He was hoping that sooner or later his interest in philately would be rekindled. But that did not happen; the task remained futile and dry and boring. The meaningless squares of paper refused to come to life as they used to for Dr. Mody in his room every Sunday at ten o'clock. Jehangir shut the trunk and pushed it back under his bed where it had lain untroubled for so many years.

From time to time his mother reminded him about the stamps: "Do something Jehangoo, do something with them." He said he would when he felt like it and had the time; he wasn't interested for now.

Then, after several months, he pulled out the trunk again from under his bed. Mrs. Bulsara watched eagerly from a distance, not daring to interrupt with any kind of advice or encouragement: her Jehangoo was at that difficult age, she knew, when boys automatically did the exact reverse of what their parents said.

But the night before, Jehangir's sleep had been disturbed by a faint and peculiar rustling sound seeming to come from inside the trunk. His reasons for dragging it out into daylight soon became apparent to Mrs. Bulsara.

The lid was thrown back to reveal clusters of cockroaches. They tried to scuttle to safety, and he killed a few with his slipper. His mother ran up now, adding a few blows of her own *chappal*, as the creatures began quickly to disperse. Some ran under the bed into hard-to-reach corners; others sought out the trunk's deeper recesses.

A cursory examination showed that besides cockroaches, the trunk was also infested with white ants. All the albums had been ravaged. Most of the stamps which had not been destroyed outright were damaged in one way or another. They bore haphazard perforations and brown stains of the type associated with insects and household pests.

Jehangir picked up an album at random and opened it. Almost immediately, the pages started to fall to pieces in his hands. He remembered what Dr. Mody used to say: "This is my retirement hobby. I will spend my retirement with my stamps." He allowed the tattered remains of Burjor Uncle's beloved pastime to drop back slowly into the trunk.

He crouched beside the dented, rusted metal, curious that he felt no loss or pain. Why, he wondered. If anything, there was a slight sense of relief. He let his hands stray through the contents, through worthless paper scraps, through shreds of the work of so many Sunday mornings, stopping now and then to regard with detachment the bizarre patterns created by the mandibles of the insects who had feasted night after night under his bed, while he slept.

With an almost imperceptible shrug, he arose and closed the lid. It was doubtful if anything of value remained in the trunk.

Hanif Kureishi

We're Not Jews

Azhar's mother led him to the front of the lower deck, sat him down with his satchel, hurried back to retrieve her shopping, and took her place beside him. As the bus pulled away Azhar spotted Big Billy and his son Little Billy racing alongside, yelling and waving at the driver. Azhar closed his eyes and hoped it was moving too rapidly for them to get on. But they not only flung themselves onto the platform, they charged up the almost empty vehicle hooting and panting as if they were on a fairground ride. They settled directly across the aisle from where they could stare at Azhar and his mother.

At this his mother made to rise. So did Big Billy. Little Billy sprang up. They would follow her and Azhar. With a sigh she sank back down. The conductor came, holding the arm of his ticket machine.

He knew the Billys, and had a laugh with them. He let them ride for nothing.

Mother's grey perfumed glove took some pennies from her purse. She handed them to Azhar who held them up as she had shown him.

"One and a half to the Three Kings," he said.

"Please," whispered Mother, making a sign of exasperation.

"Please," he repeated.

The conductor passed over the tickets and went away.

"Hold onto them tightly," said Mother. "In case the inspector gets on."

Big Billy said, "Look, he's a big boy."

"Big boy," echoed Little Billy.

"So grown up he has to run to teacher," said Big Billy.

"Cry baby!" trumpeted Little Billy.

Mother was looking straight ahead, through the window. Her voice was almost normal, but subdued. "Pity we didn't have time to get to the library. Still, there's tomorrow. Are you still the best reader in the class?" She nudged him. "Are you?"

"S'pose so," he mumbled.

Every evening after school Mother took him to the tiny library nearby where he exchanged the previous day's books. Tonight, though, there hadn't been time. She didn't want Father asking why they were late. She wouldn't want him to know they had been in to complain.

Big Billy had been called to the headmistress's stuffy room and been sharply informed — so she told Mother — that she took a "dim view." Mother was glad. She had objected to Little Billy bullying her boy. Azhar had had Little Billy sitting behind him in class. For weeks Little Billy had called him names and clipped him round the head with his ruler. Now some of the other boys, mates of Little Billy, had also started to pick on Azhar.

"I eat nuts!"

Big Billy was hooting like an orang-utan, jumping up and down and scratching himself under the arms — one of the things Little

Billy had been castigated for. But it didn't restrain his father. His face looked horrible.

Big Billy lived a few doors away from them. Mother had known him and his family since she was a child. They had shared the same air-raid shelter during the war. Big Billy had been a Ted and still wore a drape coat and his hair in a sculpted quiff. He had black bitten-down fingernails and a smear of grease across his forehead. He was known as Motorbike Bill because he repeatedly built and rebuilt his Triumph. "Triumph of the Bill," Father liked to murmur as they passed. Sometimes numerous lumps of metal stood on rags around the skeleton of the bike, and in the late evening Big Billy revved up the machine while his record player balanced on the windowsill repeatedly blared out a 45 called "Rave On." Then everyone knew Big Billy was preparing for the annual bank holiday run to the coast. Mother and the other neighbours were forced to shut their windows to exclude the noise and fumes.

Mother had begun to notice not only Azhar's dejection but also his exhausted and dishevelled appearance on his return from school. He looked as if he'd been flung into a hedge and rolled in a puddle — which he had. Unburdening with difficulty, he confessed the abuse the boys gave him, Little Billy in particular.

At first Mother appeared amused by such pranks. She was surprised that Azhar took it so hard. He should ignore the childish remarks: a lot of children were cruel. Yet he couldn't make out what it was with him that made people say such things, or why, after so many contented hours at home with his mother, such violence had entered his world.

Mother had taken Azhar's hand and instructed him to reply, "Little Billy, you're common — common as muck!'

Azhar held onto the words and repeated them continuously to himself. Next day, in a corner with his enemy's taunts going at him, he closed his eyes and hollered them out. "Muck, muck, muck — common as muck you!"

Little Billy was as perplexed as Azhar by the epithet. Like magic it shut his mouth. But the next day Little Billy came back with the renewed might of names new to Azhar: sambo, wog, little coon. Azhar returned to his mother for more words but they had run out.

Big Billy was saying across the bus, "Common! Why don't you say it out loud to me face, eh? Won't say it, eh?"

"Nah," said Little Billy. "Won't!"

"But we ain't as common as a slut who marries a darkie."

"Darkie, darkie," Little Billy repeated. "Monkey, monkey!"

Mother's look didn't deviate. But, perhaps anxious that her shaking would upset Azhar, she pulled her hand from his and pointed at a shop.

"Look."

"What?" said Azhar, distracted by Little Billy murmuring his name.

The instant Azhar turned his head, Big Billy called, "Hey! Why don't you look at us, little lady?"

She twisted round and waved at the conductor standing on his platform. But a passenger got on and the conductor followed him upstairs. The few other passengers, sitting like statues, were unaware or unconcerned.

Mother turned back. Azhar had never seen her like this, ashen, with wet eyes, her body stiff as a tree. Azhar sensed what an effort she was making to keep still. When she wept at home she threw herself on the bed, shook convulsively and thumped the pillow. Now all that moved was a bulb of snot shivering on the end of her nose. She sniffed determinedly, before opening her bag and extracting the scented handkerchief with which she usually wiped Azhar's face, or, screwing up a corner, dislodged any stray eyelashes around his eye. She blew her nose vigorously but he heard a sob.

Now she knew what went on and how it felt. How he wished he'd said nothing and protected her, for Big Billy was using her name: "Yvonne, Yvonne, hey, Yvonne, didn't I give you a good time that time?"

"Evie, a good time, right?" sang Little Billy.

Big Billy smirked. "Thing is," he said, holding his nose, "there's a smell on this bus."

"Pooh!"

"How many of them are there living in that flat, all squashed together like, and stinkin' the road out, eatin' curry and rice!"

There was no doubt that their flat was jammed. Grandpop, a retired doctor, slept in one bedroom, Azhar, his sister and parents in another, and two uncles in the living room. All day big pans of Indian food simmered in the kitchen so people could eat when they wanted. The kitchen wallpaper bubbled and cracked and hung down like ancient scrolls. But Mother always denied that they were "like that." She refused to allow the word "immigrant" to be used about Father, since in her eyes it applied only to illiterate tiny men with downcast eyes and mismatched clothes.

Mother's lips were moving but her throat must have been dry: no words came, until she managed to say, "We're not Jews."

There was a silence. This gave Big Billy an opportunity. "What you say?" He cupped his ear and his long dark sideburn. With his other hand he cuffed Little Billy, who had begun hissing. "Speak up. Hey, tart, we can't hear you!"

Mother repeated the remark but could make her voice no louder.

Azhar wasn't sure what she meant. In his confusion he recalled a recent conversation about South Africa, where his best friend's family had just emigrated. Azhar had asked why, if they were to go somewhere — and there had been such talk — they too couldn't choose Cape Town. Painfully she replied that there the people with white skins were cruel to the black and brown people who were considered inferior and were forbidden to go where the whites went. The coloureds had separate entrances and were prohibited from sitting with the whites.

This peculiar fact of living history, vertiginously irrational and not taught in his school, struck his head like a hammer and echoed through his dreams night after night. How could such a thing be possible? What did it mean? How then should he act?

"Nah," said Big Billy. "You no Yid, Yvonne. You us. But worse. Goin' with the Paki."

All the while Little Billy was hissing and twisting his head in imitation of a spastic.

Azhar had heard his father say that there had been "gassing" not long ago. Neighbour had slaughtered neighbour, and such evil hadn't died. Father would poke his finger at his wife, son and baby daughter, and state, "We're in the front line!"

These conversations were often a prelude to his announcing that they were going "home" to Pakistan. There they wouldn't have these problems. At this point Azhar's mother would become uneasy. How could she go "home" when she was at home already? Hot weather made her swelter; spicy food upset her stomach; being surrounded by people who didn't speak English made her feel lonely. As it was, Azhar's grandfather and uncle chattered away in Urdu, and when Uncle Asif's wife had been in the country, she had, without prompting, walked several paces behind them in the street. Not wanting to side with either camp, Mother had had to position herself, with Azhar, somewhere in the middle of this curious procession as it made its way to the shops.

Not that the idea of "home" didn't trouble Father. He himself had never been there. His family had lived in China and India; but since he'd left, the remainder of his family had moved, along with hundreds of thousands of others, to Pakistan. How could he know if the new country would suit him, or if he could succeed there? While Mother wailed, he would smack his hand against his forehead and cry, "Oh God, I am trying to think in all directions at the same time!"

He had taken to parading about the flat in Wellington boots with a net curtain over his head, swinging his portable typewriter and saying he expected to be called to Vietnam as a war correspondent, and was preparing for jungle combat.

It made them laugh. For two years Father had been working as a packer in a factory that manufactured shoe polish. It was hard physical labour, which drained and infuriated him. He loved books and wanted to write them. He got up at five every morning; at night he wrote for as long as he could keep his eyes open. Even as they ate he scribbled over the backs of envelopes, rejection slips and factory stationery, trying to sell articles to magazines and newspapers. At the same time he was studying for a correspondence course on "How To

Be A Published Author." The sound of his frenetic typing drummed into their heads like gunfire. They were forbidden to complain. Father was determined to make money from the articles on sport, politics and literature which he posted off most days, each accompanied by a letter that began, "Dear Sir, Please find enclosed . . ."

But Father didn't have a sure grasp of the English language which was his, but not entirely, being "Bombay variety, mish and mash." Their neighbour, a retired schoolteacher, was kind enough to correct Father's spelling and grammar, suggesting that he sometimes used "the right words in the wrong place, and vice versa." His pieces were regularly returned in the self-addressed stamped envelope that the *Writers' and Artists' Yearbook* advised. Lately, when they plopped through the letter-box, Father didn't open them, but tore them up, stamped on the pieces and swore in Urdu, cursing the English who, he was convinced, were barring him. Or were they? Mother once suggested he was doing something wrong and should study something more profitable. But this didn't get a good response.

In the morning now Mother sent Azhar out to intercept the postman and collect the returned manuscripts. The envelopes and parcels were concealed around the garden like an alcoholic's bottles, behind the dustbins, in the bike shed, even under buckets, where, mouldering in secret, they sustained hope and kept away disaster.

At every stop Azhar hoped someone might get on who would discourage or arrest the Billys. But no one did, and as they moved forward the bus emptied. Little Billy took to jumping up and twanging the bell, at which the conductor only laughed.

Then Azhar saw that Little Billy had taken a marble from his pocket, and, standing with his arm back, was preparing to fling it. When Big Billy noticed this even his eyes widened. He reached for Billy's wrist. But the marble was released: it cracked into the window between Azhar and his mother's head, chipping the glass.

She was screaming. "Stop it, stop it! Won't anyone help! We'll be murdered!"

The noise she made came from hell or eternity. Little Billy blanched and shifted closer to his father; they went quiet.

Azhar got out of his seat to fight them but the conductor blocked his way.

Their familiar stop was ahead. Before the bus braked Mother was up, clutching her bags; she gave Azhar two carriers to hold, and nudged him towards the platform. As he went past he wasn't going to look at the Billys, but he did give them the eye, straight on, stare to stare, so he could see them and not be so afraid. They could hate him but he would know them. But if he couldn't fight them, what could he do with his anger?

They stumbled off and didn't need to check if the crêpe-soled Billys were behind, for they were already calling out, though not as loud as before.

As they approached the top of their street the retired teacher who assisted Father came out of his house, wearing a three-piece suit and trilby hat and leading his Scottie. He looked over his garden, picked up a scrap of paper which had blown over the fence, and sniffed the evening air. Azhar wanted to laugh: he resembled a phantom; in a deranged world the normal appeared the most bizarre. Mother immediately pulled Azhar towards his gate.

Their neighbour raised his hat and said in a friendly way, "How's it all going?"

At first Azhar didn't understand what his mother was talking about. But it was Father she was referring to. "They send them back, his writings, every day, and he gets so angry . . . so angry . . . Can't you help him?"

"I do help him, where I can," he replied.

"Make him stop, then!"

She choked into her handkerchief and shook her head when he asked what the matter was.

The Billys hesitated a moment and then passed on silently. Azhar watched them go. It was all right, for now. But tomorrow Azhar would be for it, and the next day, and the next. No mother could prevent it.

"He's a good little chap," the teacher was saying, of Father.

"But will he get anywhere?"

"Perhaps," he said. "Perhaps. But he may be a touch —" Azhar stood on tiptoe to listen. "Over hopeful. Over hopeful."

"Yes," she said, biting her lip.

"Tell him to read more Gibbon and Macaulay," he said. "That should set him straight."

"Right."

"Are you feeling better?"

"Yes, yes," Mother insisted.

He said, concerned, "Let me walk you back."

"That's all right, thank you."

Instead of going home, mother and son went in the opposite direction. They passed a bomb site and left the road for a narrow path. When they could no longer feel anything firm beneath their feet, they crossed a nearby rutted muddy playing field in the dark. The strong wind, buffeting them sideways, nearly had them tangled in the slimy nets of a soccer goal. He had no idea she knew this place.

At last they halted outside a dismal shed, the public toilet, rife with spiders and insects, where he and his friends often played. He looked up but couldn't see her face. She pushed the door and stepped across the wet floor. When he hesitated she tugged him into the stall with her. She wasn't going to let him go now. He dug into the wall with his penknife and practised holding his breath until she finished, and wiped herself on the scratchy paper. Then she sat there with her eyes closed, as if she were saying a prayer. His teeth were clicking; ghosts whispered in his ears; outside there were footsteps; dead fingers seemed to be clutching at him.

For a long time she examined herself in the mirror, powdering her face, replacing her lipstick and combing her hair. There were no human voices, only rain on the metal roof, which dripped through onto their heads.

"Mum," he cried.

"Don't you whine!"

He wanted his tea. He couldn't wait to get away. Her eyes were scorching his face in the yellow light. He knew she wanted to tell him not to mention any of this. Recognizing at last that it wasn't necessary, she suddenly dragged him by his arm, as if it had been his fault they were held up, and hurried him home without another word.

The flat was lighted and warm. Father, having worked the early shift, was home. Mother went into the kitchen and Azhar helped her unpack the shopping. She was trying to be normal, but the very effort betrayed her, and she didn't kiss Father as she usually did.

Now, beside Grandpop and Uncle Asif, Father was listening to the cricket commentary on the big radio, which had an illuminated panel printed with the names of cities they could never pick up, Brussels, Stockholm, Hilversum, Berlin, Budapest. Father's typewriter, with its curled paper tongue, sat on the table surrounded by empty beer bottles.

"Come, boy."

Azhar ran to his father who poured some beer into a glass for him, mixing it with lemonade.

The men were smoking pipes, peering into the ashy bowls, tapping them on the table, poking them with pipe cleaners, and relighting them. They were talking loudly in Urdu or Punjabi, using some English words but gesticulating and slapping one another in a way English people never did. Then one of them would suddenly leap up, clapping his hands and shouting, "Yes — out — out!"

Azhar was accustomed to being with his family while grasping only fragments of what they said. He endeavoured to decipher the gist of it, laughing, as he always did, when the men laughed, and silently moving his lips without knowing what the words meant, whirling, all the while, in incomprehension.

Romesh Gunesekera

Captives

Sunset is a good time to arrive in this part of the world, but I had expected them much earlier: tea-time was what the agent had said when the booking was first made.

Hearing the car turn in, I quickly dried myself. Nimal, my boy, would see them in, but I wanted to be there to welcome them: they were my first guests. While buttoning up my shirt I peeped out of my window. The man, a tall narrow Englishman, unfolded himself from the car. The dickey boot sprang open, and I heard the thump of baggage. Where the heck is that boy Nimal?

I would have been down straightaway but my zip got stuck and I had to pry the thing loose with a screwdriver. By then Nimal had turned up; I heard his squeaky voice. Somebody, I suppose Mr.

Horniman, rang the bell on the reception desk and Nimal called for me. "Sir! Sir!" he shouted out, "The party is here!"

When I got downstairs I found Mr. Horniman leafing through the register. The lady, Mrs. Horniman, had collapsed on the green armchair. She was staring at my flowers: lovely white lilies I had specially arranged for the visitors. Only then I saw how obscene the yellow stamens looked sticking out the way they did. But what's to be done? I hurried towards them and stuck my hand out. "Good Evening, Good Evening!" I said.

They must have been driving all afternoon, down the hill road from Kandy through Matale and on. The lady looked exhausted, encrusted in a thin mud shell of sweat and dust. She had slipped her sandals off and was rubbing her ankle. Bits of red lacquer had chipped off her toe-nails. She needed a bath.

"Welcome. Please welcome. You must be Mr. and Mrs. Horniman. We were expecting you."

Mr. Horniman said they would like a good room.

I told him I had prepared the Blue Suite. "It is perfect Sir," I nodded in the lady's direction, "for the honeymoons." They were coming to me on the second week of their tour around the island; newly wed, I thought. Nimal picked up the suitcase with both hands and wobbled walking on the outer edges of his bare feet.

The Blue Suite is set apart in its own wing. There are two rooms and a bathroom. In the bedroom I have put a wonderful old four-poster bed with a lace canopy.

The lady was impressed. "My goodness, this is the real thing." The other room has cane furniture and opens on to a private patio. The garden beyond was deserted. The trees at the end of it were in shadow, and up in the sky Venus gleamed, nice and early.

I stepped into the bathroom and opened the sink taps. The pipes hissed and coughed and water spluttered out. I tested it. "Look, Madam, hot water!"

She was seated on the bed examining the bedspread. It was made of a special white lace. It came from up country, I was going to tell her. But I could see she was waiting for me to leave. She kept fiddling with her buttons, undoing the top ones on her blouse and making her bracelets go jingle-jangle.

I said there were many mosquitoes around and advised they kept the nets drawn across the windows. I switched on the fan and explained how the knob had to be turned backwards, anti-clockwise, because it had been installed upside down. "But it works very well, Sir, no problem." Then I also showed how the door to the patio and the garden opened. I asked if they would like some tea, but they said not for the moment. So I left them.

As I walked slowly back to my room upstairs I heard her laugh: a sound mounting over all the other sounds outside. How good it was to hear some happiness in this place.

When I first came there was nothing here. I mean it was a palace all right, a real *maligawa*, but a ruin not a hotel. I told my boss I would need at least six months to get the *maligawa* on the map. We were not far from Sigiriya and I believed, when the tourist trade picked up, there would be room for another hotel in the area. I was immediately appointed manager.

As it was getting dark I called Nimal and told him to light the brazier for the smoke and then make sure the corridor lights were on for our guests. We need to fumigate the place every evening. I have a special fumigation recipe from my grandmother who used to burn the leaves of the nutmeg tree, mixed with *dummula* resin, to keep away the insects at night. I found a nutmeg tree in the garden here when I came, and so every evening Nimal carries a smoking brazier of my special mix around the palace to ward off the insects. Fumigating.

"Now, Sir?" he asked.

"Of course now," I said.

About ten minutes later I heard the hiss of the incense on hot coals. Nimal came rushing into the room carrying the small black pan, like a sorcerer's apprentice with smoke billowing out behind him. He did the front swiftly, tracing the perimeter of each room, before heading back towards the bedrooms. I heard him knock on the blue door. There was no immediate answer. He must have caught them at an awkward moment, but he stayed with the pan hissing like a cobra. Then I heard Mr. Horniman call out and Nimal reply, "Mosquito smoke." He was let in; I thought for a moment that perhaps I should have taken the brazier myself.

After that I got the table set in the dining-room and went to check that the kitchen was ready to take the orders for dinner. I like to have everything planned and ready.

About an hour later I heard them come out of the bedroom. I was sitting at my desk in the lounge reading the newspaper. I have positioned the desk so that I can see all the main approaches to the centre of the *maligawa*. They came along the open walkway where I had the lights on for them. He held her by the arm and steered her, his head lowered next to hers, past the big olden-day moonstone I had set into the floor. I thought of the deer you sometimes see taking their first steps into a clearing, looking for food. The air out there was thick with insects and they ducked trying to avoid the flying ants and our huge moths that were banging against my pearl-glass lampshades; they hurried towards the lounge.

"Good evening," I said, and ushered them in. Mrs. Horniman wore a loose caftan which she drew closer to her. It was like a long large shirt and allowed the warm night air in right next to her bare skin.

They had both bathed and gave an impression of freshness, but I could tell from the way her shoulders drooped that she was tired. She had her hair plaited at the back and her face looked tender; the lips a little swollen. I found it difficult to take my eyes off her.

"We wondered about some dinner . . ." Mr. Horniman said.

I led them to the far end of the room and threw open the dining-room doors like a conjuror.

They both looked around the room. "Is there no one else eating?"

"No, Madam," I said. "Tonight the whole *maligawa* is yours!" I seated them at the table. "Now, something to drink first?"

Mr. Horniman reached for his shoulder-bag. "We have a bottle here, if that is OK?"

We do have beer, liquor, gin — everything, but guests are permitted to bring their own special drinks if they so wish. We have no wines, and no proper Scotch whisky yet.

"Do you perhaps have some soda then?"

I immediately snapped my fingers for my waiter. Jinadasa came with a white towel in his hands. He peered at me and I told him to bring glasses and soda. Meanwhile she touched a silver fork with her finger. Since they were our only guests I had asked Jinadasa to put our best cutlery out. That was done fine but he had used the heavy white china from our everyday set for the side-plates! Fortunately though he had got the napkins folded beautifully into lotus flowers.

While they were having their drinks I retired to the other room.

"Do you like it then?" I heard him ask as I left.

"The hotel's a bit empty but . . ."

"Not like the beach? Beruwela."

I could see them on the beach. She would have a turquoise swim-suit. Her round throat dazzling as she turned her face up, away from the spray of the surf. The water would shatter like glass in the hot light. I wanted to say to them, you should see the east coast. Trinco. Beautiful white sand, and you can walk for miles into the sea. But they couldn't go now, not with the war up there.

Then the damn lights went out. The whole place plunged into darkness. The cacophony outside increased tenfold: the shrieks of night birds, the roar of the jungle. I heard her call out timidly to her husband, "Where are you?"

I made my way out to the back with my torch and shouted out for Nimal or Jinadasa. The bloody generator had conked out. Why did it have to happen this night, with our first guests here? There was a big commotion outside. Nimal was shouting. I told him to get the tool kit while I got an oil-lamp from the kitchen and took it in to the dining-room. I found them still seated at the table. I set the lamp down. It was smoking a bit but it made the skin of her hand glow against his arm.

"Sorry, sorry. I'm so sorry about this," I said. "The electricity has gone off. Some rascal has busted the generator. Excuse me. I'm very sorry."

He told me not to worry. "But will we have something to eat?"

"Oh yes, certainly," I said. "Electricity doesn't matter. Our *koki*, our cook, likes to use wood fire anyway. Anything you like." I turned to her. "Madam, dinner by candle-light. Like in Paris!"

"You have a menu?"

The menu was not yet available. "Please say what you would like," I said. "Rice and curry? Soup? *Bistake*? Macaroni cheese?"

"What?"

"Sir?" Our *bistake* is very good. I took the initiative and recommended it. "The *bistake* maybe? Actually it is *val ura* — wild pig. Very, good. Some hunters brought it." You have to take the initiative sometimes.

Mrs. Horniman said "fine. Let's have that."

"Very good, Madam," I said, and melted back into the darkness. But I could hear them . . .

"Wild boar beefsteak?"

"It's wild pig, not quite the same thing."

"Isn't it just the sow?"

She laughed. "I think it's just the one of the litter that got away. *Lost* more than wild. A roaming piglet."

They sounded quite cheerful; not put out by the adversities of the night. I suppose it is because they have each other, and therefore nothing to fear even here in the middle of nowhere. But I expected them to feel a little apprehensive: a big empty *maligawa* like this takes some getting used to. Outside I could hear the jungle flex and move. The jungle grass growing. Leaves unfurling. Things slithering around, searching, circling, fornicating. In between there was the terrible sound of metal on metal.

I went and gave the *bistake* order to *koki* and then went out to see how the repairs were going.

In that noisy darkness, with the oil-lamp flickering, Mr. Horniman still looked calm. So far from home, waiting for food and for light, and yet seeming to understand that nothing could matter very much. The waiting didn't matter. There was nowhere to rush to. Nothing particular to do. Only to sit and pass the time. Only to sit and watch our tropical night shadows loom across his wife's face.

When the food was ready I sent Nimal in with the trolley. I put metal lids over the dishes: the grey steaks — *val ura* in coconut sauce — a plate of thickly sliced bread, fried bitter-gourd and sliced tomato and cucumber. The boy served them, carefully scooping out the sauce with a wooden spoon.

"Not bad, eh?" Mr. Horniman said brightly.

Jinadasa got the generator going just as Mr. Horniman was mopping up the last of his sauce with bread.

I went in to them as soon as the bulbs brightened. "The lights are on," I said.

"Very good," Mr. Horniman said. It was already nine-thirty. He looked at his wife. I could see she too was thinking of their bodies nestling in a bed of jungle moonlight.

"The *bistake* was good?" I asked. I wanted to know whether we were getting things right. It is best to know early so that you can rectify any shortcomings and keep your guests happy. I was most relieved when they complimented the food. I said I was very glad to be of service and offered them wood-apple for dessert. Then I asked them about the next day. Would they want to climb Sigiriya — the rock fortress?

Mr. Horniman nodded firmly. "Yes, tomorrow we want to see it."

I said I would arrange everything. Nimal could take them in the morning.

"No, no, we can go on our own."

"Sir, believe me it would be better for Nimal to guide you."

"Isn't there a road straight from here, and then a path to the top?"

I wanted them to have a proper guide. I explained that Nimal would take them right to the top of the rock, and to the throne, and then bring them back in time for lunch.

Mrs. Horniman interrupted to agree that the boy should lead them.

"But I wanted to explore. And why can't we do it alone? Always guides. You can't do anything in this country without guides."

"Anything? Come on, don't be silly," she laughed. "Anyway I like that Nimal. He's sweet."

Mr. Horniman frowned, but eventually agreed. "What time should we go then?"

I suggested they have an early breakfast and set off by seven in the morning. They would be back by eleven or eleven-thirty then, before the midday sun.

"Is that long enough to see everything?"

"Sir," I said in my gravest voice, "you could spend your whole life there and it won't be long enough. But for tomorrow it is best to try and be back before midday. It gets very hot in our country, you know."

"But we want to see the frescoes and also the ruins."

"No problem. You will see enough. Kassyapa, the king who built the fortress, spent eighteen years there but, you know, I think maybe he would have been happier with a three-hour visit!"

"Kassyapa?" For the first time she looked at me as if I had something really interesting to say. I felt my heart quicken and tried hard not to let it show. I wanted to impress her. To keep cool. The best thing to do was talk I thought. Talk, talk, talk.

I asked whether she knew the story? How Kassyapa built the fortress? Our famous lion-rock?

She shook her head, faintly amused I think by my nervousness. I was so excited by her attention. I pressed my tongue hard against my teeth until it hurt.

"We've heard about the frescoes."

"But do you know what *he* was trying to do?" I asked.

They both shook their heads.

Films have been made about Sigiriya and dozens of books written with all kinds of different theories. I have seen none, and read none, but I told them what I thought had happened.

Kassyapa was a prince whose father was a good sort of man, but a fool. He was getting old and so he decided to give his kingdom over to his proper son, Mogallana. Kassyapa, who was a bastard — illegit-imate — was going to get nothing. But Kassyapa was an ambitious man with a lust for power and wealth. So he killed his father. They say he had him walled up alive in the mud of his famous water tank. At least according to the ancient chronicles. The brother fled to India swearing that he would one day avenge the killing and regain his rightful kingdom.

Kassyapa decided to make the rock Sigiriya his capital: an impen-etrable fortress that would be the centre of the universe. He set out to be the god of his kingdom and planned Sigiriya as a pathway to heaven. Mount Kailasa, the ancient holy mountain, they say was created, or re-created, here.

They say that every bit of Sigiriya has been constructed according to this grand design to match it to the holy mountain. I can believe that. Without some such belief in what you are doing, how can any-one stay here in this wilderness?

When Kassyapa's brother came back from India with his enormous army, eighteen years later, Kassyapa came down from his citadel to fight on the plains. That's why he lost. Now, I ask myself: why did he come down to fight, if all his life he was building a fortress to pro-tect himself? They say it was because he was so full of remorse he wanted to lose. Or that his evil deeds had so poisoned his mind that he couldn't think straight. But he couldn't have created the beauty of the place if he was so poisoned, could he? Could such a bad and wicked man create such beauty?

"You mean the frescoes?" Mr. Horniman asked. "We've seen pho-tographs. They are very beautiful."

"I mean everything. In this God-forsaken place he created a real magic. The frescoes, the palace, the gardens. Could he have done all of that and still been the terrible man they say he was? A parricide?"

"But he was not the man who did it, was he? Not the painter him-self? He was only the king. Like kings everywhere." She breathed deeply. Seeing her flesh suddenly move as she spoke startled me. Then she said, "But you are right Mr. Udaweera. History is not a simple matter."

Mr. Horniman looked at his watch. "Perhaps you can tell us more about it after we've seen the place tomorrow. But it's late now, especially if we are to start at seven."

I had kept them up much too long, but I felt they needed to know where they were, and where they were going. I bade them goodnight and watched them return to their room. To them it seemed my *maligawa* was just another night-stop — a steamy bed — in a passionate itinerary. But could they not feel something about this place?

I locked up my desk and did my late night stroll to make sure everything was in order before going to bed. Outside their door I stopped for a moment then quickly walked on. I could see the sweat running down between their legs; stains like balloons ruining my brand new sheets.

Then a truck stopped on the main road. There were voices chanting, *raban* drums. I thought of my two guests, how they would have tensed up; holding each other, listening, imagining the worst: witchcraft, demons, bandits. The sound rose to a crescendo, then the truck moved on. The chanting and the drums receded. Ordinary jungle sounds returned to fill the night, but the intrusion lingered in the air.

The next morning I felt sluggish, puffed with sleep. My limbs ached. I suppose I had been worried about how things would go with them. I knew practically nothing about them and yet they seemed somehow indispensable to the hotel and to me. It was part of knowing that they had been there all night, partaking in the pleasures of a palace that was my *maligawa*, knowing that they relied on me for keeping them safe in their love-making, for ensuring their day went according to plan. Our destinies seemed intertwined.

After their two days at the *maligawa* they'd return to Colombo. Another week and they would be back in England. A garden with apple blossom and thyme and lavender. A kitchen with a fridge that didn't need mending. It was unreal. Across the lawn I saw Mr. Horniman open the door and come out on to his patio. He yawned and stretched out, letting his maroon robe slip open. A tiny squirrel appeared on the ground in front of him. The black stripes on its back bunched as it crouched. It was nervous. Afraid of the big expanse it had suddenly found, the vast stretch of grass and gravel. Then suddenly it saw something and bounded off in a fast straight line.

Mr. Horniman went in to wake his wife.

I could see her through the window on the bed with the white cotton sheet bunched under her. She looked up at him, uncoiling.

Then Nimal came across the lawn with a tea-tray tinkling in his outstretched arms. He put it down and knocked on the outside door. Mr. Horniman came out on to the patio again. Nimal stood there looking at Mr. Horniman — at his satin robe and the fair hair trapping the sun on his legs — as if he'd never seen anyone like him before.

"Goodbye, I'll call you when we are ready," I heard Mr. Horniman say eventually. Nimal waited a few minutes staring at the door chewing his lower lip. I decided then I should go with them too, up Sigiriya.

I met them after they had finished their breakfast and asked whether they had been comfortable. "I hope the truck last night didn't worry you too much."

They shook their heads. "What was it?" she asked. She had a slightly dreamy look, as if she were thinking of something mysterious.

"Pilgrims," I said. "You get pilgrims going this way. They hire a truck or something for the village and travel through the night."

"Did they stop here for rest?"

I explained that for some people the trance induced by these rituals is a kind of rest. It is time taken out of a hard and weary life. I wanted to support her.

"All that shouting!" Mr. Horniman said, and got up to go.

When I suggested I would take them to the rock myself in my Jeep, Mr. Horniman's narrow pointed head sank down. His mouth was tight. "Sure, why not?" he said grimly. "Bring the whole hotel."

But she looked relieved, and asked whether I was sure I could spare the time.

I nodded happily and went to get the Jeep ready.

We drove right up to the foot of the rock and I parked under a tree. From there Nimal led the way, striking out in his grubby shorts, barefoot, with a stick in his hand. He used it to flick twigs and pebbles out of the way. Mr. Horniman followed him like a slow giant — he was twice the boy's height. She walked a little bit behind, watching the other two.

I caught up with her. The first part of the climb was gentle. Ahead of us Nimal chucked a stone at a green partridge sitting solemnly on a branch. He missed. Mr. Horniman clicked his tongue like a father.

The lower reaches of the hill were wreathed in jungle scrub, clumps of dense undergrowth; and the earth was pitted with small ravines. Above us the granite loomed.

"Are there animals here?" Mr. Horniman asked fingering his camera.

Nimal looked up at him with a serious face. He was wide-eyed. "Yes boss. Many animals. Monkeys, deer, tigers." He gestured at the trees. "Maybe in there, not easy to see. Dangerous at night-time. Elephants!"

Mr. Horniman immediately searched the path for dung and footprints and checked the edge of the forest. But there was nothing. Only the tall dry grass, the thick bush and tangled trees. An army could hide there and he wouldn't know.

The hill gave way to a big black bone of a rock to which the earth, like flesh, clung in red strands. The stone sucked the heat out of the sky and radiated it back, stronger almost than the sun itself. I showed them the bathing ponds that had been built and explained the ingenious hydro-system, or at least what I understood of it. The two of them didn't say very much. They listened but seemed to be preoccupied with their own thoughts. I explained about the famous Mirror Wall they had seen from a distance. How it had stayed polished like a mirror for one thousand five hundred years. I told them about the graffiti etched on it through the ages, verses of lust and love for the women in the frescoes. And I told them to take care to be quiet because of the wasps in the big brown hives guarding the rock.

"Oh God!" she said fanning herself with a map. But when we came to the frescoes my two guests were completely overawed. Such delicate larger-than-life figures in the rock gazing out at the sky and the world and each other. Their golden skin almost turned the plaster into flesh. Long noses flaring out over large sensual lips. Pale amber eyes. Breasts heaving out of stone, the nipples lifting the thin transparent unbearable veils. Deep and perfect navels curving in.

I watched the other two take everything in inch by inch. Mr. Horniman was peering through his view-finder trying to get it all in; he started shifting from side to side on a tiny ledge. "What do you think?" I asked.

"Wonderful!" She touched my arm. I felt it burn. "They are beautiful."

Mr. Horniman was clicking the apertures, whirring, snapping. "Fucking shadows! If only the fucking sun moved."

"So why did this king of yours have these painted here?" She stayed near me, ignoring her husband.

"I don't know. For his pleasure?"

She laughed and her laugh seemed to echo, perhaps just inside my head. Her fingers were wet. "Here?"

"Some people say it was just the guards, an artist among the guards. But others say these are *apsaras*, divine angels. That hundreds were painted all over the rock face."

Her windswept face pinched into a mouth of purple lips made her look more and more like an *apsara*: exquisitely alive. She ran a thick tongue over her lips rejuvenating them. I could feel her breath.

When he had finished photographing, Mr. Horniman said, "Should we go on?"

We climbed back down the open stairway to the start of the mirror wall. She let her fingers brush it, feeling the roughness of the words scratched in the plaster. We followed the bulge of the rock, sheltered by its overhang, and crossed an open walkway to the carved stone lion paws above. The carved claw alone was taller than Mr. Horniman.

"It's huge," she said.

I said that was why it was called the lion rock. Only the paws remained but originally the lion would have been colossal. Kassyapa's enemies would fear it from miles away.

From the paws it was a steep climb up the rock face through the lion to reach the summit. You had to scramble up footholds cut directly into the rock. Nimal and Mr. Horniman started climbing, but she suddenly turned away.

"I think I'll stay here," she said. "You go on," she told her husband.

I said I would stay with her, but my voice felt awkward when I spoke.

"Fine. Do that," he said, and disappeared.

When we stepped back from the lion it felt as though the jungle unrolled like a carpet in front of us. The clearing, a small rust-red plateau, extended about fifty yards. At the edge was a cliff and then a drop of several hundred feet down to the plains below. Below us the jungle spread towards the ocean unfurling in a continuous green spray to meet the surf beyond the horizon. We were higher than anything else in sight except for the granite dome behind us. We sat in the shade of a tree and gazed out at the huge sky. There was no sound except for the wind. The babble of the jungle was flattened by the sun. Occasionally a hawk, or a kite, would flap its wings and stir the air.

She took off the thin cotton jacket she was wearing. It was hot, the air was hot and thick in my mouth; I wanted to say something to her.

"You will go back today?" I asked.

"Yes," she replied. "We have one more stop and then back to Colombo. On Friday we fly back."

"To London?"

She turned and looked at me and nodded. "Yes, another world."

"You have a house in London?"

She said she lived in a flat, an apartment. "It will be funny going back there, to be living alone again, after all this."

I puzzled over what she said and then slowly realized that perhaps they were not husband and wife after all. "This is not your honeymoon?"

She smiled at me. She didn't say anything. I wanted to ask her what they were doing here? How long had she known him? Did she have to go back? Everything inside me was racing. On that plateau alone with her I felt, for a moment, anything was possible. Kassyapa made this place his heaven. Surely that counts for something.

I looked down at her feet. She wore a pair of light blue canvas shoes. The thin material changed shape as she bunched her toes and the black and white ribbed elastic on either side of each shoe stretched in turn. She didn't have socks and her ankles and legs a third of the way up to her knees were bare. Her skin was a dusty gold. Her trousers which stopped short on her legs were tight round her calves. Each leg had a short slit at the bottom of the outside seam and a black button doing nothing. She was sitting with her legs apart, her elbows on her knees, cupping her face in her hands. She had undone her hair and it fell about her bare shoulders in wisps. It had curled into rings where it was wet from her sweat. I saw her arms were freckled. Small tufts of hair hung underneath in the triangles she made with her arms and her body. I could see the sky framed there, blue and warm.

I wanted her to understand that I was not a base or vulgar man. In my original plans for the *maligawa* I had included a large rectangular bathing pool made of stone, grey stone, with moss and lichen on its sides. The water would be like ink, dark with algae. I wanted big lily pads to hold the surface still, and pink lotuses sipping on top. I would have liked to have taken her there, to drink and feel the cool water, but we never built it. I wanted to touch her.

I wished I could remember how the pilgrim poets spoke their love. *The open lips, round cheeks . . . geese lifting their big wings . . . long still eyes and swans drunk with juice of heaven . . . fountains of flowers.*

> *Their lips once kissed warm flowers,*
> *until flesh paint glazed them captive*
> *in the chalk fingers of a king's rock.*

> *Their long eyes now light a private court*
> *impalpable as their rounded breasts,*
> *while hot dry climbers make signs of love.*

I want to but know I cannot match
the rhythm behind those curves, barely feel
the pulse that beats a lifetime at a time.

It is the rock I envy most of all,
that ruined rock that holds you
and still remains the bed of your being.

Could she imagine what I was talking about? I felt she might as well have been in the rock herself, and I a mendicant climbing a pointless stairway through a lion's wet loins, groping for hope.

When Mr. Horniman appeared from between the lion's paws he looked hot and flushed but pleased for having done what he set out to do. He wiped his hands on his trousers as he walked towards us.

"You saw the top?" I asked, quickly. "Nimal showed you?"

He nodded. "Yes. Excellent." He adjusted his camera strap. "How are we doing for time? Are we late?"

I said no, his timing was perfect.

"Where's the boy?" she asked from behind me.

"He's coming, I was faster coming downhill."

"You must be thirsty," I said. "In this heat you must drink. I brought some cool drinks in the Jeep."

I got up and led the way back down the hill. I, like everyone else, left behind my confusions smeared on the walls of the rock. My legs felt damp.

When we got down to the Jeep I got Nimal to open the cream soda I had brought in the ice-box. Mr. Horniman drank with great gusto, looking hard at me.

Then we clambered into the vehicle. The two of them squeezed into the back. "Where's Nimal?" she asked.

"Don't you worry."

Nimal jumped on to the trailer knob at the back and clung to the spare wheel. We bounced down the hill raising a cloud of red dust, scattering partridges off the road.

At the hotel I left them to their lunch and went and had a cold beer on my own at the back. The heat was stultifying. My head turned to stone. I slept in my chair for more than an hour and woke up only when Mr, Horniman called out to tell me they were going. He wanted to settle up.

He took out a wad of notes and peeled off a number of them. He said, "Keep the change."

I didn't count the money.

She was already at the car looking towards the rock. I called out, "Goodbye!" and a few seconds later they had gone completely out of sight.

I was staring at the place where the car had been when Nimal appeared with a bundle of soiled sheets in his hands. He lifted them up to show me. I told him we had to change them every day; that's what you do when you run a hotel. You have to.

Aamer Hussein

Karima

Listen, brother, she says, you can read Urdu, can't you? I'd like you to read this for me. This picture here, what do the words under it say? The man in it, you know, yes, Naeem, he went from Dhaka to Karachi after the troubles and he's one of our Biharis, his parents were in a camp and look at him now, such a big star and he sings so beautifully too. I've seen him on television and I always listen to his cassettes. He's coming to Wembley? No, I don't think I could. No, it's just that he looks like my Shahzad.

(Karima. She used to work in the food shop opposite. I'd go there late in the evening, tired of thinking or writing, for a pack of cigarettes. I don't know how it began but one night we talked and soon she started coming up to get her letters written. Sometimes to someone in Karachi or Pindi, or sometimes, rarely, to addresses in Dhaka. Her messages were always the same. I'm well, working hard, sorry I can't send more money this time, I can't come home, not this year, how is Bachu? He must have grown so big by now. She didn't have an address, so all mail should be sent to her care of us. And then, at the end, she'd ask for news of Shahzad.)

— Shahzad was my son, she says, born when I was still a child. His father was called Badshah. He was hardly older than me. Born in the old country though, in Patna, before they came away — his parents and mine — when the country was divided by the strong ones. I was born in Dhaka. I always knew my Badshah, always knew that I'd marry him. His parents had a shop that sold provisions, but he was a mechanic. Already working hard when I married him, looking after his mother and younger brother too. He'd sold his father's business and put the money to good use, to set up on his own. We lived quite well. I didn't have to work, though so many women around me did, and some of our neighbours envied me. In the evenings I'd put on a bright fresh cotton sari and white or red flowers in my hair. Sometimes he'd take me in a rickshaw to the cinema. They'd tease me — unkindly, at times — when my man wasn't around, calling us the royal family because of our good food and our happy faces. In our community no one lived beyond their means but we looked as though we did. And when my son was born I called him Shahzad because I thought a king should have a prince for a son, because I wanted to turn their taunts into blessings, because I wanted him to have a hundred times our luck. His father wanted us to go to Karachi. That's where the real rewards could be had. That was where he should have gone in the first place, he said — that's where they spoke our language, that was the real Pakistan. Those Banglas, he said he couldn't really understand them. We always spoke Urdu at home. He could read and write it, too. But I couldn't really understand him. Perhaps I was too young. And I was born in Dhaka, it was the only place I'd ever known, I could speak Bangla like my own tongue. The people, too, they seemed like my own. But these were matters for men and the old people, who remembered the old country, remembered something better, and told us of what they'd had to sacrifice to bring us to this new land, where we could follow our beliefs in peace, live our lives in peace. But what peace? My boy was two when the trouble came. Perhaps my husband shouldn't have loved his country so much. Because suddenly East Pakistan wasn't going to be his country any more. It was changing names.

(Karima. One of those ageless women with figure and features carved from ebony. When she loosened her hair it looked like a black stormwind. She spoke the rapid Bihari Urdu of Dhaka but over the years I knew her it acquired an even more pronounced Bengali intonation and a strong overlay of English words. How old must she be now? Was she thirty-three when she first came to see us, all those years ago, when we helped her with her papers, when her man slapped her, and all those other times when life became too much for her? Well, almost — life will never be too much for Karima. I changed addresses and stopped thinking about her, life doesn't take me her way all that often. Anti-Muslim tracts, the BJP, sectarianism and fundamentalism, desolation over the Gulf War — the computerization of my writing, failure to read Foucault, distaste for Derrida and deconstruction — and yet again my stories hadn't earned me the fare home. No time to spare, to write letters for Karima. Maya would see her at the shelter sometimes, she'd bring her man to the community centre twice a year on Eid, and helped out with the creche when she wasn't working in their shop till midnight. But then Maya left the shelter for a job in the media and life doesn't take her that way all that often.

Karima. She used to talk so freely she'd shock me sometimes. But there are things she wouldn't talk about. I've seen too much, she'd say, and fall into silence.)

— Brother, don't ask me to tell you about the camp, she says, how can you expect me to remember anything about it? Crowding, filth, hunger, people complaining. We'd lost everything. Later I went out with the other women to sell things in the city — pencils, feathers, whatever we could lay hands on — while our men found work in factories, did the jobs that men in that rich city would never do. They called us refugees. But how could we be? If the only home we'd ever known had cast us away because we were suddenly foreigners, how come we were foreigners here, too, in Pakistan, the country where we were supposed to belong? Homeless here, homeless there. Sometimes the shit-stink of those camps still fills my nostrils and I think of it as the smell of fear.

— Long live Pakistan. He was still shouting those words as he lay dying, my man. Those last terrible days in Dhaka. My boy was two years old. First the Punjabi soldiers had come in from across the sea and begun to pillage around the edges of the city, so people said, and people said that Bengalis and Biharis alike should run for their skins. There were stories of massacres — of students, peasants, passers-by. But Badshah said the soldiers were our friends and they'd come to rescue us from those marauding Banglas. And then even the neighbours began to turn on us. They'd always loved me. I was young and pretty, shared food with them and didn't really mind their teasing. Because I often wore yellow they said I looked like springtime and called me Basanti. But now they'd changed their faces. Dirty Biharis, they said, go home or we'll get you. That day a group of them, so big, all men, turned up. Some of them were the sons of women we knew. Get out, get out, go to your murdering Punjabi masters, they shouted. But we're not harming any one, this is our home, said my man in Bangla. So say Joy Bangla, Joy Mukti Bahini, one of them said — Victory to Bangladesh and its liberation army. Another one had seen me, cowering in my thin night sari with the screeching boy in my arms, and he came toward me. Badshah went mad. Out, you Bangla traitors, he said in Urdu. He had a broken bottle in his hand. This is Pakistan. Pakistan Zindabad. I'll live and die in Pakistan. Then die, said the one who'd been ready to attack me, and he set my man on fire. I swear he did. The stench of burning flesh still fills my nostrils. I saw my Badshah burn, still screaming, Long live Pakistan. He told me to run. At least I think it must have been him. Because those bastards, too, they let me go, and one of them said, in Urdu, Take your child and run. And I did. Through the flames of houses dying, past burning bodies, beneath the stars of the sky veiled in the smoke of shame, amid brothers tearing out each other's throats, I ran. To where God took me. He must have been weeping. Or perhaps He had just turned His face away, who can blame Him if this is what His children do?

— What I remember next is being on that boat to Pakistan. With my mother-in-law and husband's brother. Memories of the camp are blurred, but the city beside it was dry and cold at night, grey instead of green like green, moist Dhaka where the sun warms your skin even in winter. Those feelings, fire and ice, those my bones remember. Of course I never knew then that my destiny lay in cold cities. All I thought of was my grief, survival, and when I began to regain my senses I thought about my child's future. That's why, when Rahim, my husband's brother, began to look at me with longing in his eyes, I too began to turn toward him. The women around me — so many of them knew more about men than I did, they'd tie their saris tight when they went into the market place, and wink and smile at customers — the women around me told me I could do much worse by myself and Shahzad than a man who was related to my son by blood. He was younger than me, at least three years. I remember his calf-eyes, his scabby knees and his dirty feet when I first came to his mother's house as a bride. Even then he'd bring me gifts of jasmine buds and guavas. Now, in our new homeland, I saw him for the first time as a man. We'd seen too much, our eyes had changed. Grown old. And after all, how old was I, barely twenty-one? My man dead, my boy barely speaking, with only my untrained hands to help me live? And young blood has its needs, too, you know, sister, and Rahim my husband's brother was handsome. But I never would forget my Badshah.

— So I married again. Of course my mother-in-law wasn't happy, but at first I thought that my moment of happiness had brought the sorrow of her son's death back to her. I thought that having her grandson with her would console her and once again, in a new city, we'd bring back to her a family and some fragment of a new life, however fragile. For we were in Karachi now, a city bigger than I'd ever imagined, with tall tower blocks and smelly camels and the salt stale smell of the nearby sea rushing, gushing into our nostrils. My husband's brother, now my husband, took me to the sea once, by Clifton, you could ride tin horses on the pier and men in Punjabi clothes sold salted peanuts in their shells and blond children pulled at their mothers' skirts. I was happy for an hour but then I started weeping. I don't know whether it was because I missed Badshah who used to take me for walks and on pleasure-trips, or because the big heavy men around us reminded me of the Punjabi soldiers I'd seen in Dhaka, or because among all these strange people I suddenly felt strange, and foreign, and poor. We were small and thin and dark and the Urdu we spoke was alien to the people around us, we could scarcely make them understand us, even though we thought we were speaking their language and we understood them quite well. Bengali log, they called us, but we were Bihari and Pakistani, we thought, even if we'd never seen Bihar and we were new in Pakistan. And I was pregnant with Rahim's child, too, and a heavy belly makes me weep. I don't know why, but I knew that I'd have a boy. When my second son was born his father called him Habib but in my heart I called him Badshah after his dead uncle who should have been his father, and when his grandmother began to call him Bachu I often wondered whether we shared a secret name for him, knowing that our lost one had sent us a sign.

— Rahim started work as a chauffeur in a big house in Defence and as soon as I could get Bachu away from my breast I began to work in the same house, nannying, ironing, stitching and looking after the mistress's needs. That went on for years. My mother-in-law was cruel to me, but most of all she was cruel to my older boy. She'd go into rages and shout at him, blaming him for all sorts of things. Her worst outbursts were when she'd accuse him of having brought ill-fortune to the family and sucking out his father's life. As if she'd forgotten that he was two when his father died and it was the big men on top who'd united and divided countries and set brothers against each other to tear out each other's throats and their sisters' wombs.

Even today our relatives write to us from Bangladesh, begging us to send them money, begging us to send for them, to bring them to Karachi, to Dubai, to London — anywhere. And Lord, your floods and storms, they respect no one, but love us poor best of all.

— New days of misery had come upon us. Rahim's exhaustion, his sense of not living up to his brother's dreams, his disappointment in the new country where we lived beneath a stairway in two small rooms and shared an outside latrine with other servants from the compound, all served to turn him against the child that was not his son, who reminded him, perhaps, of his older brother, who was one more mouth to feed, clothe and send to school. I'd insisted that Shahzad like his father should learn how to read and write, have a profession, at least live up to his father's memory that way, even if he couldn't go beyond what my dead man had done. We'd always been told that this was the land of money and opportunities, but Rahim felt we only had enough for one child, and that child had to be his son. I felt that Bachu was being taken away from me. I worked all day and the child was looked after by his grandmother. Maji, too, like Rahim, seemed to save all her love for Bachu. She wouldn't feed him when he came back from school, encouraging him to go up to the kitchen of the big house instead to beg the cook for scraps. So I became even more protective of Shahzad, keeping everything for him, my money and my love.

— The boil burst open one day when the children in the big house had a party. They sent for Shahzad, and Maji too went up with Bachu, to keep an eye on the children. Rahim was meant to help serving the fried savouries and sticky cakes and pink pastries while I was in the house, looking after the needs of the fancy ladies. I found out later that Saima, the little miss whose birthday it was, had turned on a big tape-recorder and got all her guests dancing to pop music. At some point she'd called to Shahzad and asked him to dance. Bachu came running to me on his fat legs, telling me to come out and see what was happening up there. I went out, into the garden, where the sun was just setting. Surrounded by a circle of clapping, cheering children, Shahzad was wiggling, twisting, his feet rose and fell, the music had him in thrall. Look at your beloved, said his grandmother. Dancing like a whore, like a eunuch. The boy had told me he wanted to be a star, like those men on television in bright jackets or the heroes in the movies with a song and a swinging step for every occasion, but I'd never listened to him, thinking of his words as a child's rambling dreams.

I grabbed him by the ear and pulled him down to our room. Down there I thrashed him while Maji watched exulting, it was the first time I'd ever hit him, but as I did I swear that I felt that the hand that struck was not mine but his uncle's, and as I flagged Maji came up for her turn and I slapped her as well with the back of my hand. When Rahim drove the Sahib home from his club that night he found us all crying and screaming, and without asking what had happened he gave Shahzad another few slaps and Bachu a smack, too, for good measure. The next day, early, Shahzad was gone, and it was weeks before we had news of him. He'd found a job skivvying for some mechanic. He was twelve years old.

(I picked up a book about the failure of Punjab's Green Revolution from a friend's place on Sunday afternoon, and read about the Sikh farmers and how their discontent derived not from religious differences but landlessness and dispossession. Three days later the book's author was on the box, supporting Malaysia's Mahathir in his diatribe against the North's exploitation of the South while screen images flung Filipino forms, scavenging in muck heaps, at our faces. The rule of Pepsi-cola capitalism. The Earth Summit is nigh. Anger's lava boils on both sides. The rich masters of destinies trade insults on behalf of the deprived. The Third World, convenient category, the forfeit. And I was trying to write about homelessness. Doing my research, my intellectual fieldwork. On public platforms, or private white paper in poetry or prose, we trace our trajectories of exile and expatriation, claim landless negativity as the writer's preserve and sing homelessness as the eternal ineradicable condition of the human soul. Celebrate the gap between our raw material and our present situation. With pride we assume the mantle of the dispossessed. What lies, what postures. So long since I've even thought about it. I wanted to write something about the Sikh farmers, but I'd been away too long. The smell of a subjective landscape gone. Irreducibles reduced to beckoning banalities. No grants or awards around for homesickness these days. Plan to save the price of a plane ticket "home" dissolves in the foggy business of living. You shouldn't even think of "home," it's out of intellectual fashion. Illiterate voices fight the vagaries of a language too remote to contain them. Polemic is out, the gentle weave of "fiction" veils the pain that mustn't be spoken. Too loud, aggressive or sentimental, simply over the top. This ain't no story, brother, you're overmining the documentary vein, it's journalism, a tract.

I watched the stub-end of a documentary about Green Revolution Technology in the Punjab, watched a Bihari farmer, one of the "Bhaiyyas," economic refugees migrating to work in the Punjab these days. They don't have their own land in Bihar though they have the skill to till the soil for others, and the money they send back helps the people at home. The Bhaiyya's tones and mangled verbs brought back the sound of Karima. Who used to bring me her letters and her questions and her stories. Bear witness to her, I wrote that night, in foreign words that she wouldn't understand.)

— It wasn't too bad in those first days in London, brother, she says. My salary was being paid in rupees back at home, and a secret part of it went to Shahzad. He'd promised he'd come home, continue his schooling. It was only for a short time. The mistress's son had some strange problem, he couldn't walk or speak properly, and she'd brought him here for treatment. One or two years, and then I'd go back home. The work load, if anything, was lighter than in Karachi. I slept in the children's room and could watch two, three Hindi videos in one day. The food was good. In the afternoon I took the children to the park, the boy in his push-chair, and I found some other women there. Some of them talked about being like prisoners, how hard their employers made life for them. One or two of them were Bangla. There was also the halal butcher down the road, he was Bangla too, and he told me about the women and men who would come here on one pretext or another and just disappear, into an underworld of sweatshops, restaurants, groceries, earn their living in pounds and send more money home than they'd ever imagined. A hard life, but worth it in the end. It didn't impress me much, then, but what I thought was that somehow I could bring Shahzad here, even if I had to go back he could stay, someone like the Bangla butcher could do with an able-bodied lad like him. He kept on asking me to come and work a few hours in his shop, he said a clever woman would be a help and I could have done with the extra foreign cash, but when I tried to talk to the mistress she wouldn't hear of it and thought I was being ungrateful.

— When I'd been here six months the mistress said my visa was up, I had to go home. I said: Sister, if my salary is too much for you to pay you can send me out to work at the neighbours', you know they could do with an extra hand, or I could do a few hours at the butcher's, maybe Saturday or Sunday. But, Karima, she says, I'm going back myself, you know little Baba's so much healthier now, and it's getting cold, and your husband wants you home, you've got your ten-year-old son to think of and your mother-in-law's getting old and very sick. But my other boy, sister, I said, you know I've been sending him money to go to school — She cut in. Karima, she said, there was an accident . . . your boy . . . a van . . . Rahim . . . When? I said. My feet had turned to sunken rocks. The sockets of my eyes were on fire. Oh . . . six weeks, a month, I think? There didn't seem to be any point . . . Saheb said your people thought it would be better if I didn't tell you, after all you'd find out soon enough at home, and I told him to advance Rahim some money . . . for the . . . you know, the prayers and all . . .

— I kept quiet. What could I say? The stench of burning flesh, the shit-smell of the camps, the faces of marauders and the scared eyes of the ones who ran, flowed before my eyes. They lived in me. I waited a day. Then I asked for fifteen pounds and an afternoon's leave to buy things for my husband's brother — yes, that's what I called him and the mistress didn't even notice — and my little boy. I left all my things in the flat, took the key with me, and I ran. I walked slowly, proudly, but I ran. The open market was Dhaka on fire, and if I didn't move calmly one side or the other would get me. I made my way to the butcher's shop. His eyes had told me the whole story. I knew I'd have to pay in some way the price of my stay, just a hiding place to start with. At first I was terrified that the mistress would set the immigration people on me because I'd unthinkingly walked away with her key, wanting to go there later to get my stuff, but of course I soon gave up that plan, and no one came after me. Later? I still tremble. That's another story.

— I've been with the butcher seven years now. I stay here alone when he goes to Bangladesh. What if someone recognized me and realized I couldn't be his wife? And how would he explain a strange Bihari wife from London, and what is there for me now in Dhaka? And how could I go with a Bangla man to the city that killed Badshah? But here, we're all the same, Bihari or Bangla. He's only hit me once, when he caught me taking more money from the till than he thought I should for Bachu, because I still send money to the people in Karachi, and always add a little for Shahzad because no one ever wrote from there to tell me that he'd gone. But of course I can't let them have my address — after all, who knows? — Rahim may still remember that he has a wife and somehow turn up here to find me. But maybe the money I send has made him forgive me, if there is anything to forgive. In the end, it's between me and my God. Of course I still think of Bachu, but he never really was mine to start with, and perhaps he's best off with his father. Life isn't any easier here for us, people stare and curse at you on the streets and threaten you in your shop late at night. And the hours are so long. This isn't a good home for our young, when you really think about it.

— When the butcher hit me I packed my stuff and walked off to a place that some Bangla women had told me about, run by women for other women. Some of them spoke Urdu. I stayed there a few days, then I called the butcher from a coinbox and told him where to meet me. When I admitted he was coming to get me from the post office down the road all the women said I was crazy to go back with him, but I explained to them that I'd told him, If you ever hit me again I'll cut you to pieces with your own carving knife, and if you don't pay me my proper share of the takings I'll report you for every petty crime under the sun. My words hadn't really been that hard, but I'd said enough to put the fear of God in him, and I think he wanted in his way to keep me happy.

— I hate these winters, especially when the butcher's away. Letters from my people are rare, and sometimes I wonder if the money I send there ever gets to them. I long for news of Bachu. I have a photograph of him which Maji sent in some moment of pity, but my greatest regret is that in my haste I forgot to pick up my photographs of Shahzad. After I lost him I've stopped feeling anything for Pakistan. Some nights I dream of him, talking to me, telling me he didn't really die, that he lives in the television now and sings there. That's why I collect every picture I can of the singer Naeem and paste it in my album. He's slim and strong, his eyes are like rain-clouds, and his skin shines like copper in the sun. I know that's how my boy would have looked if he'd grown to be a man, because that's what his father was like, and Shahzad was just like my Badshah.

Shani Mootoo

Out on Main Street

1

Janet and me? We does go Main Street to see pretty pretty sari and
bangle, and to eat we belly full a burfi and gulub jamoon, but we
doh go too often because, yuh see, is dem sweets self what does give
people like we a presupposition for untameable hip and thigh.

Another reason we shy to frequent dere is dat we is watered-down
Indians — we ain't good grade A Indians. We skin brown, is true,
but we doh even think 'bout India unless something happen over
dere and it come on de news. Mih family remain Hindu ever since
mih ancestors leave India behind, but nowadays dey doh believe in
praying unless things real bad, because, as mih father always singing,
like if is a mantra: "Do good and good will be bestowed unto you."

So he is a veritable saint cause he always doing good by his women friends and dey chilren. I sure some a dem must be mih half sister and brother, oui!

Mostly, back home, we is kitchen Indians: some kind a Indian food every day, at least once a day, but we doh get cardamom and other fancy spice down dere so de food not spicy like Indian food I eat in restaurants up here. But it have one thing we doh make joke 'bout down dere: we like we meethai and sweetrice too much, and it remain overly authentic, like de day Naana and Naani step off de boat in Port of Spain harbour over a hundred and sixty years ago. Check out dese hips here nah, dey is pure sugar and condensed milk, pure sweetness!

But Janet family different. In de ole days when Canadian missionaries land in Trinidad dey used to make a bee-line straight for Indians from down South. And Janet great grandparents is one a de first South families dat exchange over from Indian to Presbyterian. Dat was a long time ago.

When Janet born, she father, one Mr. John Mahase, insist on asking de Reverend MacDougal from Trace Settlement Church, a left-over from de Canadian Mission, to name de baby girl. De good Reverend choose de name Constance cause dat was his mother name. But de mother a de child, Mrs. Savitri Mahase, wanted to name de child sheself. Ever since Savitri was a lil girl she like de yellow hair, fair skin and pretty pretty clothes Janet and John used to wear in de primary school reader — since she lil she want to change she name from Savitri to Janet but she own father get vex and say how Savitri was his mother name and how she will insult his mother if she gone and change it. So Savitri get she own way once by marrying this fella name John, and she do a encore, by calling she daughter Janet, even doh husband John upset for days at she for insulting de good Reverend by throwing out de name a de Reverend mother.

So dat is how my girlfriend, a darkskin Indian girl with thick black hair (pretty fuh so!) get a name like Janet.

She come from a long line a Presbyterian school teacher, head-master and headmistress. Savitri still teaching from de same Janet and John reader in a primary school in San Fernando, and John, getting more and more obtuse in his ole age, is headmaster more dan twenty years now in Princes Town Boys' Presbyterian High School. Everybody back home know dat family good good. Dat is why Janet leave in two twos. Soon as A Level finish she pack up and take off like a jet plane so she could live without people only shoo-shooing behind she back . . . "But A A! Yuh ain't hear de goods 'bout John Mahase daughter, gyul? How yuh mean yuh ain't hear? Is a big thing! Everybody talking 'bout she. Hear dis, nah! Yuh ever see she wear a dress? Yes! Doh look at mih so. Yuh reading mih right!"

Is only recentish I realize Mahase is a Hindu last name. In de ole days every Mahase in de country turn Presbyterian and now de name doh have no association with Hindu or Indian whatsoever. I used to think of it as a Presbyterian Church name until some days ago when we meet a Hindu fella fresh from India name Yogdesh Mahase who never even hear of Presbyterian.

De other day I ask Janet what she know 'bout Divali. She say, "It's the Hindu festival of lights, isn't it?" like a line straight out a dictionary. Yuh think she know anything 'bout how lord Rama get himself exile in a forest for fourteen years, and how when it come time for him to go back home his followers light up a pathway to help him make his way out, and dat is what Divali lights is all about? All Janet know is 'bout going for drive in de country to see light, and she could remember looking forward, around Divali time, to the lil brown paper-bag packages full a burfi and parasad that she father Hindu students used to bring for him.

One time in a Indian restaurant she ask for parasad for dessert. Well! Since den I never go back in dat restaurant, I embarrass fuh so!

I used to think I was a Hindu *par excellence* until I come up here and see real flesh and blood Indian from India. Up here, I learning 'bout all kind a custom and food and music and clothes dat we never see or hear 'bout in good ole Trinidad. Is de next best thing to going to India, in truth, oui! But Indian store clerk on Main Street doh have no patience with us, specially when we talking English to dem. Yuh ask dem a question in English and dey insist on giving de answer in

Hindi or Punjabi or Urdu or Gujarati. How I suppose to know de difference even! And den dey look at yuh disdainful disdainful — like yuh disloyal, like yuh is a traitor.

But yuh know, it have one other reason I real reluctant to go Main Street. Yuh see, Janet pretty fuh so! And I doh like de way men does look at she, as if because she wearing jeans and T-shirt and high-heel shoe and make-up and have long hair loose and flying about like she is a walking-talking shampoo ad, dat she easy. And de women always looking at she beady eye, like she loose and going to thief dey man. Dat kind a thing always make me want to put mih arm round she waist like, she is my woman, take yuh eyes off she! and shock de false teeth right out dey mouth. And den is a whole other story when dey see me with mih crew cut and mih blue jeans tuck inside mih jim-boots. Walking next to Janet, who so femme dat she redundant, tend to make me look like a gender dey forget to classify. Before going Main Street I does parade in front de mirror practicing a jiggly-wiggly kind a walk. But if I ain't walking like a strong-man monkey I doh exactly feel right and I always revert back to mih true colours. De men dem does look at me like if dey is exactly what I need a taste of to cure me good and proper. I could see dey eyes watching Janet and me, dey face growing dark as dey imagining all kind a situation and position. And de women dem embarrass fuh so to watch me in mih eye, like dey fraid I will jump up and try to kiss dem, or make pass at dem. Yuh know, sometimes I wonder if I ain't mad enough to do it just for a little bacchanal, nah!

Going for a outing with mih Janet on Main Street ain't easy! If only it wasn't for burfi and gulub jamoon! If only I had a learned how to cook dem kind a thing before I leave home and come up here to live!

2

In large deep-orange Sanskrit-style letters, de sign on de saffron-colour awning above de door read "Kush Valley Sweets." Underneath in smaller red letters it had "Desserts fit For The Gods." It was a corner building. The front and side was one big glass wall. Inside was big. Big like a gymnasium. Yuh could see in through de brown tint windows: dark brown plastic chair, and brown table, each one de length of a door, line up stiff and straight in row after row like if is a school room.

Before entering de restaurant I ask Janet to wait one minute outside with me while I rumfle up mih memory, pulling out all de sweet names I know from home, besides burfi and gulub jamoon: meethai, jilebi, sweetrice (but dey call dat kheer up here) and ladhoo. By now, of course, mih mouth watering fuh so! When I feel confident enough dat I wouldn't make a fool a mih Brown self by asking what dis one name? and what dat one name? we went in de restaurant. In two twos all de spice in de place take a flying leap in our direction and give us one big welcome hug up, tight fuh so! Since den dey take up permanent residence in de jacket I wear dat day!

Mostly it had women customers sitting at de tables, chatting and laughing, eating sweets and sipping masala tea. De only men in de place was de waiters, and all six waiters was men. I figure dat dey was brothers, not too hard to conclude, because all a dem had de same full round chin, round as if de chin stretch tight over a ping-pong ball, and dey had de same big roving eyes. I know better dan to think dey was mere waiters in de employ of a owner who chook up in a office in de back. I sure dat dat was dey own family business, dey stomach proudly preceeding dem and dey shoulders throw back in de confidence of dey ownership.

It ain't dat I paranoid, yuh understand, but from de moment we enter de fellas dem get over-animated, even armorously agitated. Janet again! All six pair a eyes land up on she, following she every move and body part. Dat in itself is something dat does madden me, oui! but also a kind a irrational envy have a tendency to manifest in me. It was like I didn't exist. Sometimes it could be a real problem going out with a good-looker, yes! While I ain't remotely interested in having a squeak of a flirtation with a man, it doh hurt a ego to have a man notice yuh once in a very long while. But with Janet at mih side, I doh have de chance of a penny shave-ice in de hot sun. I tuck mih elbows in as close to mih sides as I could so I wouldn't look like a strong man next to she, and over to de l-o-n-g glass case jam up with sweets I jiggle and wiggle in mih best imitation a some a dem gay fellas dat I see downtown Vancouver, de ones who more femme dan even Janet. I tell she not to pay de brothers no attention, because if any a dem flirt with she I could start a fight right dere and den. And I didn't feel to mess up mih crew cut in a fight.

De case had sweets in every nuance of colour in a rainbow. Sweets I never before see and doh know de names of. But dat was alright because I wasn't going to order dose ones anyway.

Since before we leave home Janet have she mind set on a nice thick syrupy curl a jilebi and a piece a plain burfi so I order dose for she and den I ask de waiter-fella, resplendent with thick thick bright-yellow gold chain and ID bracelet, for a stick a meethai for mihself. I stand up waiting by de glass case for it but de waiter/owner lean up on de back wall behind de counter watching me like he ain't hear me. So I say loud enough for him, and every body else in de room to hear, "I would like to have one piece a meethai please," and den he smile and lift up his hands, palms open-out motioning across de vast expanse a glass case, and he say, "Your choice! Whichever you want, Miss." But he still lean up against de back wall grinning. So I stick mih head out and up like a turtle and say louder, and slowly, "One piece a meethai — dis one!" and I point sharp to de stick a flour mix with ghee, deep fry and den roll up in sugar. He say, "That is koorma, Miss. One piece only?"

Mih voice drop low all by itself. "Oh ho! Yes, one piece. Where I come from we does call dat meethai." And den I add, but only loud enough for Janet to hear, "And mih name ain't 'Miss.'"

He open his palms out and indicate de entire panorama a sweets and he say, "These are all meethai, Miss. Meethai is Sweets. Where are you from?"

I ignore his question and to show him I undaunted, I point to a round pink ball and say, "I'll have one a dese sugarcakes too please." He start grinning broad broad like if he half-pitying, half-laughing at dis Indian-in-skin-colour-only, and den he tell me, "That is called chum-chum, Miss." I snap back at him, "Yeh, well back home we does call dat sugarcake, Mr. Chum-chum."

At de table Janet say, "You know, Pud [Pud, short for Pudding; is dat she does call me when she feeling close to me, or sorry for me], it's true that we call that 'meethai' back home. Just like how we call 'siu mai' 'tim sam.' As if 'dim sum' is just one little piece a food. What did he call that sweet again?"

"Cultural bastards, Janet, cultural bastards. Dat is what we is. Yuh know, one time a fella from India who living up here call me a bastardized Indian because I didn't know Hindi. And now look at dis, nah! De thing is: all a we in Trinidad is cultural bastards, Janet, all a we. *Toutes bagailles!* Chinese people, Black people, White people. Syrian. Lebanese. I looking forward to de day I find out dat place inside me where I am nothing else but Trinidadian, whatever dat could turn out to be."

I take a bite a de chum-chum, de texture was like grind-up coconut but it had no coconut, not even a hint a coconut taste in it. De thing was juicy with sweet rose water oozing out a it. De rose water perfume enter mih nose and get trap in mih cranium. Ah drink two cup a masala tea and a lassi and still de rose water perfume was on mih tongue like if I had a overdosed on Butchart Gardens.

Suddenly de door a de restaurant spring open wide with a strong force and two big burly fellas stumble in, almost rolling over on to de ground. Dey get up, eyes red and slow and dey skin burning pink with booze. Dey straighten up so much to overcompensate for falling forward, dat dey find deyself leaning backward. Everybody stop talking and was watching dem. De guy in front put his hand up to his forehead and take a deep Walter Raleigh bow, bringing de hand down to his waist in a rolling circular movement. Out loud he greet everybody with "Alarm o salay koom." A part a me wanted to bust out laughing. Another part make mih jaw drop open in disbelief. De calm in de place get rumfle up. De two fellas dem, feeling chupid now because nobody reply to dey greeting, gone up to de counter to

Chum-chum trying to make a little conversation with him. De same booze-pink alarm-o-salay-koom-fella say to Chum-chum, "Hey, howaryah?"

Chum-chum give a lil nod and de fella carry right on, "Are you Sikh?"

Chum-chum brothers converge near de counter, busying dey-selves in de vicinity. Chum-chum look at his brothers kind a quizzi-cal, and he touch his cheek and feel his forehead with de back a his palm. He say, "No, I think I am fine, thank you. But I am sorry if I look sick, Sir."

De burly fella confuse now, so he try again.

"Where are you from?"

Chum-chum say, "Fiji, Sir."

"Oh! Fiji, eh! Lotsa palm trees and beautiful women, eh! Is it true that you guys can have more than one wife?"

De exchange make mih blood rise up in a boiling froth. De restau-rant suddenly get a gruff quietness 'bout it except for a woman I hear whispering angrily to another woman at de table behind us, "I hate this! I just hate it! I can't stand to see our men humiliated by them, right in front of us. He should refuse to serve them, he should throw them out. Who on earth do they think they are? The awful fools!" And de friend whisper back, "If he throws them out all of us will suffer in the long run."

I could discern de hair on de back a de neck a Chum-chum broth-ers standing up, annoyed, and at de same time de brothers look like dey was shrinking in stature. Chum-chum get serious, and he politely say, "What can I get for you?"

Pinko get de message and he point to a few items in de case and say, "One of each, to go please."

Holding de white take-out box in one hand he extend de other to Chum-chum and say, "How do you say 'Excuse me, I'm sorry' in Fiji?"

Chum-chum shake his head and say, "It's okay. Have a good day."

Pinko insist, "No, tell me please. I think I just behaved badly, and I want to apologize. How do you say 'I'm sorry' in Fiji?"

Chum-chum say, "Your apology is accepted. Everything is okay." And he discreetly turn away to serve a person who had just entered de restaurant. De fellas take de hint dat was broad like daylight, and back out de restaurant like two little mouse.

Everybody was feeling sorry for Chum-chum and Brothers. One a dem come up to de table across from us to take a order from a woman with a giraffe-long neck who say, "Brother, we mustn't accept how these people think they can treat us. You men really put up with too many insults and abuse over here. I really felt for you."

Another woman gone up to de counter to converse with Chum-chum in she language. She reach out and touch his hand, sympathy-like. Chum-chum hold the one hand in his two and make a verbose speech to her as she nod she head in agreement generously. To italicize her support, she buy a take-out box a two burfi, or rather, dat's what I think dey was.

De door a de restaurant open again, and a bevy of Indian-looking women saunter in, dress up to weaken a person's decorum. De Miss Universe pageant traipse across de room to a table. Chum-chum and Brothers start smoothing dey hair hack, and pushing de front a dey shirts neatly into dey pants. One brother take out a pack a Dentyne from his shirt pocket and pop one in his mouth. One take out a comb from his back pocket and smooth down his hair. All a dem den converge on dat single table to take orders. Dey begin to behave like young pups in mating season. Only, de women dem wasn't impress by all this tra-la-la at all and ignore dem except to make dey order, straight to de point. Well, it look like Brothers' egos were having a rough day and dey start roving 'bout de room, dey egos and de crotch a dey pants leading far in front dem. One brother gone over to Giraffebai to see if she want anything more. He call she "dear" and put his hand on she back. Giraffebai straighten she back in surprise and reply in a not-too-friendly way. When he gone to write up de bill she see me looking at she and she say to me, "Whoever does he think he is! Calling me dear and touching me like that! Why do these men always think that they have permission to touch whatever and wherever they want! And you can't make a fuss about it in public, because it is exactly what those people out there want to hear about so that they can say how sexist and uncivilized our culture is."

I shake mih head in understanding and say, "Yeah. I know. Yuh right!"

De atmosphere in de room take a hairpin turn, and it was man aggressing on woman, woman warding off a herd a man who just had dey pride publicly cut up a couple a times in just a few minutes.

One brother walk over to Janet and me and he stand up facing me with his hands clasp in front a his crotch, like if he protecting it. Stiff stiff, looking at me, he say, "Will that be all?"

Mih crew cut start to tingle, so I put on mih femmest smile and say, "Yes, that's it, thank you. Just the bill please." De smart-ass turn to face Janet and he remove his hands from in front a his crotch and slip his thumbs inside his pants like a cowboy 'bout to do a square dance. He smile, looking down at her attentive fuh so, and he say, "Can I do anything for you?"

I didn't give Janet time fuh his intent to even register before I bulldoze in mih most un-femmest manner, "She have everything she need, man, thank you. The bill please." Yuh think he hear me? It was like I was talking to thin air. He remain smiling at Janet, but she, looking at me, not at him, say, "You heard her. The bill please."

Before he could even leave de table proper, I start mih tirade. "But A A! Yuh see dat? Yuh could believe dat! De effing so-and-so! One minute yuh feel sorry fuh dem and next minute dey harassing de heck out a you. Janet, he crazy to mess with my woman, yes!" Janet get vex with me and say I overreacting, and is not fuh me to be vex, but fuh she to be vex. Is she he insult, and she could take good enough care a sheself.

I tell she I don't know why she don't cut off all dat long hair, and stop wearing lipstick and eyeliner. Well, who tell me to say dat! She get real vex and say dat nobody will tell she how to dress and how not to dress, not me and not any man. Well I could see de potential dat dis fight had coming, and when Janet get fighting vex, watch out! It hard to get a word in edgewise, yes! And she does bring up incidents from years back dat have no bearing on de current situation. So I draw back quick quick but she don't waste time; she was already off to a good start. It was best to leave right dere and den.

Just when I stand up to leave, de doors dem open up and in walk Sandy and Lise, coming for dey weekly hit a Indian sweets. Well, with Sandy and Lise is a dead giveaway dat dey not dressing fuh any man, it have no place in dey life fuh man-vibes, and dat in fact dey have a blatant penchant fuh women. Soon as dey enter de room yuh could see de brothers and de couple men customers dat had come in minutes before stare dem down from head to Birkenstocks, dey eyes bulging with disgust. And de women in de room start shoo-shooing, and putting dey hand in front dey mouth to stop dey surprise, and false teeth, too, from falling out. Sandy and Lise spot us instantly and dey call out to us, shameless, loud and affectionate. Dey leap over to us, eager to hug up and kiss like if dey hadn't seen us for years, but it was really only since two nights aback when we went out to dey favourite Indian restaurant for dinner. I figure dat de display was a genuine happiness to be seen wit us in dat place. While we stand up dere chatting, Sandy insist on rubbing she hand up and down Janet back — wit friendly intent, mind you, and same time Lise have she arm round Sandy waist. Well, all cover get blown. If it was even remotely possible dat I wasn't noticeable before, now Janet and I were over-exposed. We could a easily suffer from hypothermia, specially since it suddenly get cold cold in dere. We say goodbye, not soon enough, and as we were leaving I turn to acknowledge Giraffebai, but instead a any recognition of our buddiness against de fresh brothers, I get a face dat look like it was in de presence of a very foul smell.

De good thing, doh, is dat Janet had become so incensed 'bout how we get scorned, dat she forgot I tell she to cut she hair and to ease up on de make-up, and so I get save from hearing 'bout how I too jealous, and how much I inhibit she, and how she would prefer if I would grow *my* hair, and wear lipstick and put on a dress sometimes. I so glad, oui! dat I didn't have to go through hearing how I too demanding a she, like de time, she say, I prevent she from seeing a ole boyfriend when he was in town for a couple hours *en route* to live in Australia with his new bride (because, she say, I was jealous dat ten years ago dey sleep together.) Well, look at mih crosses, nah! Like if I really so possessive and jealous!

So tell me, what yuh think 'bout dis nah, girl?

Ginu Kamani

Just Between Indians

"I wouldn't go in there if I were you," Sahil warned softly. He was dressed in white linen pants and a dark silk shirt, comfortably sprawled on the couch of green and yellow brocade. His eyes sloped down at the corners, adding to his relaxed look. Daya was instantly irritated by his tone. She stopped by the closed kitchen door and looked around the room as though searching out the person he might be addressing. She then turned to look at him.

"Are you talking to me?" she asked with mock surprise. "I just wanted something to drink."

"My father's on the phone with your parents. We could be part of the same family soon. You wouldn't want to jeopardize it." Sahil's eyes were twinkling. Daya looked at him as though seeing him for the first time. He was about five foot seven in his early-to-mid-twenties. He looked quite at ease and wore a studied expression of amusement.

"Could you stop smirking long enough to explain yourself?"

Sahil sat up and smiled cheerfully.

"There's nothing to explain, really. My brother took one look at you and decided you'd do. He's looking for a wife."

Daya had arrived on the airport shuttle over an hour earlier. She was on spring break from a hard junior year in college, and had come to New York to explore the city. It was her first visit as an adult to the home of her father's old friend Rohit Patel. Rohit Uncle had insisted that Daya stay at his house when he found out that she was coming East. She would have preferred any place other than the home of conservative Indian immigrants, but her parents had pressured her, saying that Rohit owed them a favour, and in any case, she didn't have the money for a hotel.

When she'd arrived, her fears were confirmed. Rohit greeted Daya in his megaphone voice and thumped her painfully on the shoulder, rubbing his palm up and down her back until she shrugged him off. Daya asked if Veena, Rohit's wife, was still at work. Rohit informed her, "No, Daya, Auntie Veena is away in India for a few more days." Daya's heart sank. She couldn't believe her bad luck. Veena, a big boisterous woman, was as full of humour and affection as her husband was full of bullying censure. Daya had been hoping for Veena's laughing presence; instead, Rohit was playing host to some relatives from London: his widowed brother Subhash, and Subhash's two grown sons, Ranjan and Sahil.

Daya stood in the front room of the house paralyzed with dismay. One by one the men came up to her. Sahil shook her hand firmly and regarded her with interest. Ranjan offered an awkward wave and stepped back hastily. Subhash patted her on the head like a child. Rohit beamed through the introductions, his hand once again vigorously massaging Daya's back. Finally he let go and Daya rushed up the stairs to her assigned room. Rohit's voice boomed behind her.

"The last time I saw you, you were an ugly duckling! Lucky for you, you've changed."

Daya cursed herself for listening to her parents. She was incensed at the prospect of spending a whole week with this gang of Indian men. *I might as well get back on the plane for home.* She emptied her duffel bag onto the bed and tossed her clothes into the chest of drawers. She kicked the bag under the bed and threw herself onto the mattress. With a wry smile she remembered her mother's goodbye at the airport.

"Learn to relax around people. You get so bad-tempered sometimes. What will Rohit Uncle think if you're badly behaved? Just smile, be friendly and make the most of it. It's not asking a lot; after all, this is just between Indians."

In high school, Daya had denounced her ties to Indian men. She resolved to stay away from them completely. Growing up, she had idolized her two older brothers. As children, the three of them had been inseparable. But as the boys entered high school, one behind the other, they turned against their adoring sister, labelling her "just a stupid girl." The summer she turned fourteen, she begged her brothers to let her join them on a camping trip with four of their Indian friends. After much tearful pleading on her part, they finally agreed, and Daya was elated. They would be going far into the woods, miles away from anywhere. Daya imagined a real adventure in the wild.

The camping trip turned out to be a nightmare. For four of the longest days of her young life, Daya was teased mercilessly. The boys were obsessed with flicking up her dress and shouting "Peep show! Peep show!" To add to the fun, Kishore would hold his sister tightly against him and tickle her, while Krishna reached down her back to snap her bra. Daya returned home, humiliated. She refused to speak to anyone about what had happened. Her brothers tried to joke with her and cheer her up when they saw how withdrawn she had become, but Daya refused to be comforted, and smouldered behind a wall of silence. The following week, the parents of her brothers' friends sent inquiries about Daya's future availability for marriage. Daya was horrified. She went wild with rage. Her parents tried to calm her with assurances that, naturally, marriage was out of the question until Daya reached eighteen. But it was clear to Daya that her mother's assurances only thinly disguised her delight at having received these early proposals.

From then on, in her own house, Daya felt afraid. She knew it was only a matter of time before she would be betrayed.

Sahil stood up as Daya flushed with anger.

"So your dad's on the phone with my parents. Does he think I'm for sale?" she demanded. "We've never even met before!"

She turned toward the kitchen.

"Wait!" He darted after her, but it was too late. Daya jerked open the kitchen door and marched in. She looked around. The phone was resting in its cradle. Ranjan and Subhash were seated at a sunny table at the far corner of the spacious kitchen, eating sandwiches. Father and son looked up and smiled as Daya cautiously crossed the length of the kitchen.

"Can we offer you a snack?" asked Ranjan in his soft English accent. He held up a plate of sandwiches for her inspection. "Dinner won't be served until much later."

"Uh . . . no. Actually, I . . . I wanted something to drink," stammered Daya, and wrenched open the refrigerator door. She stood there gasping, the waves of cold air chilling her to the bone. Her mind raced furiously, trying to make sense of the situation.

She slammed shut the refrigerator door and walked over to the table.

Ranjan pulled out a chair for her at the table and grimaced. "I know, there's nothing worth drinking in the fridge. I've told Uncle to buy juice or something . . ."

Daya sat down, pulled her chair forward and leaned her elbows on the table. "Did I hear you talking to my parents a little while ago?"

Ranjan blushed and cleared his throat.

"I didn't realize we were speaking that loudly . . ." he began.

"Well, thanks for taking the initiative and informing them that I've arrived safely." She paused, waiting for Ranjan's reply. Ranjan nibbled at his sandwich and said nothing. Subhash gently pushed his chair back, excused himself and went to wash his plate in the sink.

"I mean, that is what you told them, right?" Daya continued. She rubbed her sweating palms against her thighs. "You were making sure that my parents wouldn't worry about me, *right*?"

Ranjan winced at her loud voice and nodded vigorously. "Oh yes, of course. Absolutely! And . . . and . . . they send all their love, and they'll call you later tonight when the rates are lower."

"And did they pass on any messages from my *boyfriend*?" she barked.

Ranjan shook his head. "Oh no. Not at all. Perhaps later, when they talk to you in person?" He grabbed another sandwich and sank his teeth into it. The kitchen door swung shut as Subhash exited.

Daya exhaled loudly, feeling the blood pounding in her throat. She looked out over the garden to steady herself a little. The neat lawn reminded her of her parents' yard. Her family was all together for the week; all, that is, except Daya. Right at that moment, they were probably lounging around in deck chairs, playing endless rounds of cards. Her brothers would be mercilessly teasing their pretty new wives and her parents would be attempting to join in the fun.

Daya had disliked her sisters-in-law on sight. They resembled human sponges, ready to absorb all their husbands' demands as well as the commands of their mother-in-law. The weddings were agony for Daya, as she was continually scrutinized and remarked on as an "eligible girl." And immediately after marriage, her new sisters-in-law turned their attention to rectifying the unmarried plight of their dear Daya.

Within months, Daya cut off all contact with her brothers and made sure her visits home never coincided with theirs.

Ranjan darted uneasy glances at her. She turned to him in exasperation. He had a high forehead and curly black hair, high cheekbones

and a straight nose. He looked anywhere from twenty-five to thirty
years old.

"Your brother tells me you want to marry. Why?" demanded Daya.
"Why don't you just pay a prostitute?"

Ranjan stared unhappily at his empty plate.

"That's cruel," he replied softly. "I was actually engaged for quite a
while. I loved her. But . . . she changed her mind. Terrible mess, actually. So I'm . . . I'm forced to look again."

Ranjan gave a quick pained smile, then once again pushed the
plate of sandwiches toward Daya. "Won't you have one? They're quite
good."

Daya picked up a sandwich and lifted the top slice of bread. There
were slices of cucumber and tomato and a thick layer of butter.
Uptight vegetarians. "What are you guys doing here in New York?"

"Dad's thinking of moving to New York, so we've all come for a
look-see."

Daya gave a short laugh. "You men go everywhere together?"

Ranjan smiled. "You've heard of a two-in-one? Well, we're a . . . a
three-in-one." Ranjan waited for Daya to smile at his joke, but she
just stared at him.

"It's a joke . . ." he offered lamely.

Daya grimaced and wiped her mouth. "I have just one thing to
say. I won't have you doing things behind my back, okay? If you have
anything to say to my parents, you better tell me first. Got that?"

She stood up to leave but Ranjan lifted his hand to stop her.

"So . . . so . . . are you here on holiday?" he stuttered. "Because I am
too. Maybe we could go do . . . see . . . eat something together? My
treat of course!" Ranjan ended in a rush.

Daya giggled at the thought of going out to dinner with Ranjan.
Ranjan took her laughter as assent and relaxed somewhat. He quickly
wiped the sweat from his forehead.

"I know you eat meat and fish," he continued quickly, "and I
don't mind. We could go to the Victoria Palace. Have you been there?
It's very fancy, you'll be impressed . . . er . . . I mean, you'll really like
it. I hope you don't mind terribly but I've already booked us a table

there for lunch tomorrow since reservations are so hard to come by . . ."

"You what!" Daya gasped. "How dare you, you . . ." she stopped herself and stood up, then backed away, with one final warning. "Keep your distance, okay, and we'll get along fine."

"So my brother's incompetent with women. So what's new? Come to think of it, most men are." Sahil philosophized in his best BBC accent. He was reclining on the couch once more. Daya was on her way back upstairs, but she stopped, turned, took a deep breath and approached the couch.

"Well since you seem to know so much, professor, why don't you try to educate him a bit?"

Sahil spread his hands. "I'm here, aren't I? I'm watching out for him. What more can a brother do?" he laughed. "Ranjan really does believe that Dad can get him any woman he wants. And the trouble is, Dad believes it too!" He grinned from ear to ear and snapped his fingers. "It's a ma-ma-ma-ma *man's world* out there!"

Daya felt a smile trying to escape her lips. "That's not funny. I would never have come here had I known that this house was a pick-up joint for Indian men. This is supposed to be my vacation. I should get out of here."

Yet even as she voiced her desire, Daya knew she couldn't leave. Her parents would be furious and certainly refuse to pay a hotel bill.

"If you'd rather stay somewhere else," offered Sahil, "I have many friends in New York. Women. I'm sure they would understand the situation perfectly. None of them are *Indian*, as you might guess."

Daya couldn't help smiling at this last comment.

"Ah," said Sahil with delight. "You're beginning to trust me. Your face really lights up when you smile. I can read you like a book."

Daya clenched her fists in renewed irritation. "Would you please quit with the personal comments? It's really insulting to be checked out like a slab of meat."

"Oh, please! Now you're confusing me with my sexually repressed brother! You'll know jolly well when I'm 'checking you out.'" Sahil bounced off the couch and turned to face the French windows that overlooked the garden.

Daya was astonished at his outburst. What a joke! Each Patel with a bigger ego than the other.

Sahil turned to Daya with a sheepish smile. "I'm sorry, that was out of turn. I'm being insensitive and making a bigger mess of all of this . . ."

"It's a friggin' circus," Daya jeered.

Sahil nodded solemnly and launched into another apology. "I'm sorry, it appears that everyone here is rather worked up. All it takes is for one attractive Indian woman to walk in the door and the next thing you know . . ."

Ranjan peered around the kitchen door, then stepped cautiously into the living room. Daya moved away in disgust. Sahil quickly stepped in front of her and motioned for his brother to back off. Ranjan's face crumpled in confusion.

"Let's get out of here," Daya whispered loudly to Sahil, "before Romeo whips out the engagement ring."

Sahil tried to keep up with Daya as she walked furiously around the block.

"So, you and your brother have nothing in common."

"Not a thing."

"You have the same parents, you've lived together all your lives and yet you're utterly unconnected."

"Exactly. Those who know us well wonder what in god's name we're doing in the same family."

"Well?"

"Frankly, I've learned a lot by hanging around with my graceless brother. He makes the mistakes and I clean up after him. It works out well."

Daya puzzled over Sahil's words. *He's pulling my leg.*

"You think I'm joking," Sahil said, "Ranjan really is my lucky charm. In cleaning up after him, I've done my most interesting work and met the most interesting people. Like you."

"Oh I get it!" she cried. "You and your brother do a Jekyll and Hyde routine where he humiliates women and you step in to comfort the poor victims. Right?"

"You've got quite the talent for sarcasm."

"Why did you tell me, anyway? This whole business of your brother looking for a wife. He's such a klutz that I might never have found out, never have gotten insulted, and enjoyed my spring break after all."

"Well, frankly, I like you and couldn't bear to see my brother treat you like some senseless object."

Daya slowed her pace to take in his unexpected words.

"You're *not* by any chance interested in him, are you?" Sahil asked cautiously.

She looked at him in horror. "Are you kidding? No way! Your brother is petrified; I can barely see his face under all that angst. He hates himself. He'd be terrible in bed. I could never be attracted to a man like that."

"I see," Sahil nodded solemnly. "So you *are* as experienced as you look."

"Yes, and not with *Indian* men, either. They could drive a woman to her grave."

Sahil frowned at Daya's words, struggling with some remembered pain. "I . . . uh . . . I wouldn't *exactly* call myself 'Indian.' We were raised everywhere: Africa, Australia, Singapore, Canada, England . . . I've set foot on every continent."

"I'd rather be dead than involve myself with an Indian man!" Daya continued as though she hadn't heard him.

Sahil frowned again and walked in silence for a while. He resumed in an uncertain tone. "Funny you should mention graves, or perhaps you already knew? It's my mother's death anniversary tomorrow. That's probably why Ranjan is acting like such an arsehole. It's the same every year; he turns into a complete wreck."

Daya flushed with shock and came to a stop. "No, of course I didn't know. How could I know? I don't know anything about your family. We've never even met before. And tomorrow's her . . . oh god!

Is that why your brother wants me to go for . . . ?" Daya stopped herself from finishing the question.

"What?" asked Sahil.

"No, nothing. Never mind."

They walked around the block once again, past the sprawling suburban mansions. Daya looked at Sahil from the corner of her eye. He was just taller than her. His body was stocky, and from what she could see, his chest was covered with curly black hair. He walked gracefully and confidently with his shoulders thrown back. Daya suddenly realized that the Indian men she knew walked very differently, with stiff jerky strides, slouched over or with their chests and stomachs bouncing. He turned to her and smiled.

"You keep looking at me. Do I remind you of someone?" he asked.

Daya shook her head vigorously and exclaimed, "No, I would say definitely not!"

Amused, he looked at her with a warm expression. He looked directly into her eyes and she found herself imagining that she could forget he was Indian.

"Is your boyfriend American?"

"Am I required to answer that?"

Sahil walked in silence for a moment, then sighed. "I was just wondering. I can frequently predict all sorts of things about Indian women. I've, sort of, been observing them all my life. It's a sort of . . . *hobby* of mine, a bit like solving complex puzzles."

"So *you* must have an Indian girlfriend."

"No, actually. Never have," he replied matter-of-factly. "But there's always hope, don't you think?"

Daya stared at Sahil, stared right through him. *Never had one. He's like me.* She felt a sudden tightness in her chest and closed her eyes. She reached back and pressed her neck. Immediately Sahil moved behind her and she felt his warm fingers on her shoulder, pressing down on the knots of tension.

"What's wrong?" he asked gently. "Are you tired? Would you like to sit down?" Sahil walked around to face her, and Daya opened her eyes. Daya noticed Sahil's eyes clearly for the first time. They were amber, like cats' eyes, covered by thick curled lashes. His gaze was steady, quizzical, concerned.

She shivered. Her teeth were suddenly chattering in the cool evening breeze. She stepped back and hugged herself. "You can't disguise the way you look," she laughed. "You're definitely Indian."

Sahil inclined his head and gave a low bow. "I will take that as a challenge. I shall do my very best to prove you wrong."

"Daya, what can I offer you? We have Coke and other soft drinks in the fridge, or perhaps you'll take tea or coffee?"

Rohit was playing the genial host, bounding around the kitchen, setting out the Tandoori restaurant food he had brought home. Daya and Sahil sat next to each other at the table, with Ranjan across from them. Subhash sat at the foot of the table, and Rohit's place was, of course, at the head.

"Uh . . . actually, I'd like a drink please. Gin and tonic, if you have it."

Rohit opened his eyes wide in mock alarm and wagged his finger at Daya.

"You naughty girl! You're lucky that Auntie Veena is away because she would be very angry right now. A proper young lady like you shouldn't drink. Lucky for you, I am broad-minded. But keep in mind that liquor is expensive."

Rohit opened the liquor cabinet and pulled out the bottle of gin. Daya silently mimicked Rohit's wagging finger and shook it around the table. Ranjan blushed and looked down at his plate. Subhash cleared his throat loudly and adjusted the napkin in his lap. Sahil looked pointedly at the ceiling. Rohit placed the gin and tonic in front of Daya. All the men were drinking water.

"So tell me," Rohit snickered as he sat down, "does alcohol make you tipsy?" Rohit turned to Ranjan with a broad smile and winked at him.

Daya felt the anger rising in her throat, and was just opening her mouth for a quick retort when she felt Sahil's cautioning hand on her elbow. She exhaled slowly and pressed her lips shut.

Rohit leaned forward with a leer. "Drink up, drink up!" he boomed. "We are all waiting for you!"

"Shall we get started?" Sahil interrupted politely. He lifted the pan of curried peas and potatoes and ladled some onto his plate and Daya's. Subhash took the pan next and looked at Daya as she sipped her drink.

"So, young lady, are you thinking about marriage? I'm sure your parents have received many offers."

Rohit grunted with pleasure as he chewed a mouthful of chapati. "It's essential for our boys to meet girls from good families." Rohit wagged his finger again. "It will help them get sensible sooner. When I heard you were coming to New York, I told Subhash to bring his boys right away."

Daya coughed in surprise. She glared at Subhash and Rohit in turn, then set her glass down firmly. Sahil cautioned her again by shaking his head. "I will marry if and when I want to," she said deliberately, "and my parents will have *no say* in it. I don't need Indians meddling in my private life."

"Ah," Subhash nodded. "A modern girl. And how do you propose to find a man on your own?"

Daya narrowed her eyes and sneered, "By kidnapping and raping him, how else?" She cut into her samosa with an exaggerated swing of the knife, then licked the blade clean.

Sahil burst out laughing. Ranjan pushed the food around his plate in embarrassment and the two older men shook their heads grimly. "My god!" cried Rohit. "Quite a sense of humour you have there, young lady!"

Daya gulped down her drink and looked questioningly at Sahil. *Do something!* her eyes challenged him. Sahil shook his head in disbelief and looked away. His foot tapped nervously.

"American-style romance is not for you, my dear," Subhash continued. "You won't like it. These Americans get you undressed, then drop you just like *that!*" Subhash snapped his fingers. "Once an Indian girl's reputation is destroyed, that's the end of her."

"And this kissing thing!" bellowed Rohit. "My god, I hope you're not one of these junglees who likes spit and slobber and stuffing someone's dirty tongue in your mouth. *Chheee!*"

"And then, too, you have to put dangerous chemicals in your body so you don't get pregnant or diseased while you're fooling around. Naturally all of that harms the unborn babies."

"And you, young lady," Rohit pointed vigorously at Daya, "you definitely need to have a baby to round out your sharp edges."

Daya's dropped fork clattered loudly on her plate. She slumped forward in her chair. She felt her throat tightening with rage. *Enjoy yourself . . . smile . . . it's just between Indians.* Her mother's parting words echoed deafeningly in her ears.

"Perhaps you shouldn't talk about her like she's not in the room," Sahil cautioned the older men.

Rohit waved aside Sahil's comment. "What's the problem?" he demanded. "In my day, the women used to eat in a separate room. We could talk about whatever we wanted. If she's such a modern girl, let her deal with it. She's too proud to be one of us!"

"So, tell me again what you're doing hanging around with this family?"

Dinner was finally over. Rohit, Subhash and Ranjan had hurried down to the basement to watch sports on the giant screen TV, leaving Daya and Sahil to clear the table.

"On days like this," Sahil replied bitterly, "I really don't know. All three of them should be shot, or castrated, or both."

They stood side by side at the sink. Daya rinsed the plates and handed them to Sahil to place in the dishwasher.

"They're completely fucked up," she said gloomily. "It's really depressing." She pushed the hair out of her eyes. She couldn't handle another meal like this one. She wanted to talk to her parents, but as per their warning, she had to wait for them to call her. Long-distance phone bills were a touchy subject with her parents and their friends.

Sahil wiped his hands on his pants and turned Daya toward him.

"They really hurt you, didn't they? I'm so sorry. I felt like an utter fool sitting there, politely attempting to steer the conversation away."

She shrugged nonchalantly, but her grim face betrayed the pain she felt. "It's only normal. Indian men are like that."

He gently touched her arm. "Don't take it in," he murmured. "Don't let it get to you."

Daya turned back to the dishes in the sink. "I don't need your pity! I'm sure you've never been attacked like this."

"Mmmm. I thought we had joined forces. But here you are dismissing me once again."

Daya rinsed the plates in silence, then turned off the tap. "I've done quite well for myself, thank you, simply by staying away from Indians. No other men seem to have a stake in humiliating me in this way."

"I understand," Sahil nodded. "But I don't like you lumping me with them. I would never humiliate you the way they do. I've suffered at my uncle's hands before."

"And still you come back for more?"

He shrugged and pursed his lips. "Funny thing, this relationship with Uncle. It's because Rohit and Veena have no children of their own. You know how it is."

She shook her head. "No, actually, I don't. Why don't you tell me?"

Sahil thought for a moment. "Ever since my mother died, Rohit and Veena have been our real family. Rohit is a bit out of control; sadistic, even. He can't help it. But he did save our lives."

"You're going to inherit a packet of money, right?" Daya crossed her arms on her chest.

"What?" He was caught off guard. "Oh! Er . . . some, I'm sure."

"So that's why you put up with Unk."

Sahil's jaw tightened. She knew she had hit a nerve.

"Must be nice being an Indian son. Everyone wants you like you're going out of style!" Daya snapped her fingers and walked out of the kitchen.

"Now Sahil, you're in charge of the burglar alarm. Don't forget to turn it on before going to bed. Good night."

Daya lay on her bed in the dark, listening to Rohit's instructions in the hallway below. She heard him climb the stairs to his bedroom and shut the door. She heard Ranjan leave the bathroom in the hallway. He slowly walked over to Daya's closed door. She could feel him hesitating outside. The floor boards squeaked with his every move. He might even have raised a hand to knock, but then he turned around and walked back to the room he was sharing with Subhash. He shut his door.

Gathering courage, Daya thought idly, staring at the ceiling. Her parents had not called. Risking their wrath she had tried their number; but there was no answer. *Probably out to a lavish family dinner, celebrating the double pregnancies of their young brides or something.*

It was up to Daya. Should she take up Sahil's offer and go stay with his friends? Or should she stay in the house and go on the attack against the men? She had visions of grabbing Ranjan by his crotch and forcing him to his knees, while his father and uncle pleaded for his life. She imagined grabbing Sahil in the same way and suddenly felt hot. She pushed the image out of her mind.

Daya was incensed that Rohit had ordered his nephews to fly to New York. But what really made her burn was the realization that her parents must have given their blessings to this matchmaking. She had been unleashed into exactly the kind of situation she feared most. She had been preparing for this betrayal for years, and now the moment was upon her.

Choosing her own boyfriends had not sent a strong enough signal to her parents. They apparently could not let go of the fantasy that their daughter needed an Indian man. And a nephew of Rohit, their old friend! A coup, no less. They would be delirious with excitement if she reported back to her parents that the matchmaking had worked. Overnight, their attitude toward her would change, become more generous, more respectful, more relaxed. Her mother would hover around her, laughing, joking, confiding in her as she prepared

Daya for being a wife. *You're lucky*, she might say. *You don't have to deal with a mother-in-law in this case.* Or, *Rohit and Veena are wealthy. They will buy you everything, starting with your very own house!* And perhaps even, *Make sure and use birth control so that you can finish your studies in peace. Don't have any children until you're ready to, otherwise it will be the end.* On and on went the imagined dialogues in her head. Fantasizing intimate moments with her mother was something Daya could do for hours. Finally, she sat up and massaged her tense shoulders. *I need to look at this differently*, she cautioned herself. *Because I know I'm not about to get married.*

The thought of another gin and tonic felt good. She put on her clothes and shoes. She hoped Rohit didn't lock the liquor cabinet at night the way her parents did. She walked noiselessly down the stairs to the kitchen. The kitchen door was closed, the same way it had been earlier that day. What a nightmare of a day it had been. She pulled angrily on the door. It swung open silently. She walked right to the liquor cabinet and, with the help of the pale moonlight, located the bottle of gin. She opened the refrigerator and pulled out a bottle of tonic water and a tray of ice. In the vegetable bin she found half a lime.

She quickly poured her drink over the ice, squeezed in the lime and sucked on her wet fingers. She shut the refrigerator door, and walked towards the kitchen table, sipping on her drink. She stopped short, the hair rising on her arms. Her throat tightened with the now familiar anger.

"You've come to join me." Sahil's warm voice floated over to Daya.

Sahil's legs were stretched out on the tabletop and his hands were tucked behind his head. His silk shirt was open to the waist and his sleeves rolled up almost to his shoulders.

"Sorry," Daya said coldly. "I didn't know you were in here."

She stood for a moment, undecided. Should she take her drink up to the room? The room was like a prison. Better just to stay and talk to him. In the light of the moon, the hair on Sahil's chest glinted silver.

"You're catching a moon tan?" she asked dryly as she sat down.

"The truth is, I'm always warm in this house," he grinned. "*Hot*, actually."

She sipped on her drink then pushed the glass across the table to Sahil. "Have a sip," she offered. "Cool yourself down."

He drank out of the glass, then pressed its cool surface against his forehead.

"Do you come here often?"

"Third time this year."

"All because your dad wants to move to New York?"

Sahil looked up in surprise, then smiled knowingly. "Is that what Ranjan's been telling you? We have no intention of moving here. It's just that Rohit has been very active in searching out a wife for Ranjan."

"Just for Ranjan? What about you?"

"Ranjan's older, so he goes first."

"Yeah, but after he's found one, you'll want one too. That's how brothers are."

Sahil nodded noncommittally.

"So," Daya snorted. "I'm the third guinea pig this year?"

Sahil tapped on the table with his fingertips. "You really mustn't be Indian. You seem to have nothing but contempt for family obligations."

"It's only fitting," she murmured, "since Indian families show little more than contempt for their daughters."

She took a gulp of her drink. "Were you sitting here thinking about your mother?"

He took the glass from her hands and looked into the liquid. He ran his finger dejectedly around the rim of the glass. Daya sensed an overwhelming sadness in him and felt sorry.

"You don't have to answer that," she murmured.

"Actually, I was. It happened twenty years ago, you know, in this house."

"What!" Daya started in her chair. "Here? In this house?"

He nodded. "Right here."

She felt her stomach muscles knotting with shock. "I don't understand why no one's ever told me about this."

"Oh, they never talk about it. Ever."

Sahil paused.

"My mother killed herself when I was six. I was at the supermarket with Veena. Rohit was at work. Dad was in Africa."

Daya forced her eyes to stay open, forced her ears to listen. "She had planned to take Ranjan with her, to heaven, according to him. She didn't want *me*, again according to him. At the last minute, Ranjan ran from her bedroom. She had already swallowed all the pills. She called for him but he wouldn't go to her. She called for him again and again, but you see, Ranjan refused to go without . . ." his voice broke. He swallowed and coughed. "He . . . wouldn't . . . go . . . without . . . me. He's alive today because of . . . of me."

Daya watched as Sahil locked and unlocked his fingers in quick jerking movements. In the darkness his hands rose and subsided like netted birds. Slowly, she placed her hand on top of his. He exhaled loudly and squeezed her hand gratefully. "Quite frankly, Ranjan has never recovered. He's still afraid . . . he doesn't trust women . . . he has nightmares that any wife of his . . ." He shook his head sadly.

"Oh no! Why is he insisting on getting married, then?"

Sahil chuckled, despite himself. "He's thirty years old. He's never been with a woman. He's right on the edge!"

Daya pressed her lips together grimly. "I was right the first time. Someone should get him to a prostitute."

He patted her hand and pulled away. "My brother won't find Mum in a whorehouse." He tucked his hands back behind his head.

"I'm sorry," she mumbled. "I feel so stupid. I wish I'd known earlier. I feel bad about the way I treated your brother . . . I . . . I'm sure I would have been more sensitive if I'd known . . ."

Sahil flashed her a wry smile. "But I've enjoyed every minute of your headstrong company. You're . . . you're so *committed* to life."

She felt the hair rise alarmingly on the back of her neck. "Is that . . ." she began hesitantly. "Is that what you're trying to determine? Which women might kill themselves?"

He looked at her blankly. His breathing slowed. His forehead shone with perspiration. He licked his dry lips, and wiped the sweat off his face. "I suppose I am," he admitted finally. "I've never framed it quite like that before." He struggled for a moment before adding, "But I know you're right."

"And this has only to do with *Indian* women?"

He nodded, brows knit with pain. The conversation was over.

The kitchen clock rang loudly. Daya looked up. It was four A.M. She stood up from the table. Immediately Sahil got to his feet and came around. She knew instinctively what he would do next, and the anticipation of his touch carried her forward into Sahil's embrace.

They walked side by side up the stairs. At the door to her room, they embraced once more. Daya stepped into her room and shut the door quietly. She slid under the covers and sank into sleep.

"So how many other eligible girls have slept in my bed?"

"A few, but we've changed the sheets since then!"

Daya and Ranjan sat at a corner table in the dimly lit Victoria Palace. The restaurant was furnished like a Victorian doll house, with ruffled curtains on the windows, candy-stripe wallpaper and pink and white chairs with high backs. The waiters wore formal tails and high-collared shirts. The menu consisted entirely of meat dishes. Ranjan had insisted that she order a filet mignon or at least a rack of lamb. Ranjan meanwhile had ordered only a baked potato and a salad for himself. She found the situation extremely funny, and Ranjan was relaxed because Daya was having a good time.

Daya had awoken late that morning with the clear knowledge that she should accept Ranjan's invitation to lunch. She had dressed and descended the stairs, and much to her relief, Ranjan was the only one around. He was in the kitchen, and got up hurriedly when Daya walked in. Ranjan was sure that she would shout at him again. He almost burst into tears when instead Daya said she'd be happy to have lunch with him. But there was one condition, she had informed him: they had to speak honestly about themselves.

"Why are you so sure you want to marry an Indian woman? Are they somehow better than other women?" Daya popped another piece of red meat into her mouth, savouring the tenderness.

"I think so," Ranjan answered. "And anyway," he blushed visibly and concentrated on his salad, "they're the most beautiful women in the world."

"You think?" she asked with surprise. "Funny. I feel the same way. Those big dark eyes and lips . . ."

"You're extremely attractive," Ranjan interrupted quickly. "And rather intelligent. I saw that at once."

Daya smiled kindly and touched his hand.

"I'm not the one for you," she stated. "Don't waste your time."

Ranjan nodded silently and picked at his salad.

"Do you like my brother?" he asked, still looking at his plate.

She sighed and wondered how to answer.

"Your brother isn't looking for a wife. It . . . makes things a little easier between us."

Ranjan pushed the lettuce around his plate.

"He's stolen every girl I've been interested in. Once they meet him, they won't have anything to do with me. It's not fair."

Daya frowned impatiently.

"That doesn't sound like your brother. Where are these girls? What happened to them?"

"I don't know. He doesn't tell me anything. All I know is that he slept with Rachna, my . . . my . . . the girl I was engaged to."

Oh no, she groaned to herself. *More intrigue. These two are obsessed with each other.*

"Why are you telling me this?" Daya asked in irritation. "She obviously never loved you."

"She didn't love Sahil either," Ranjan cried bitterly. "But she slept with him and not me!"

Daya felt a headache coming on. She was still exhausted from the previous night. The steak sat heavily in her stomach. She suddenly wanted to lie down.

"Let's go," she said tiredly, pushing her plate away. "I feel terrible. I need a rest."

"Won't you finish your steak?" Ranjan blurted in a panic. "You don't have to waste good food on my account."

When Daya opened her eyes, it was dark outside. She was surprised. Her watch read 10:40 P.M. She had slept right through dinner! *Well, no big loss*, she thought, *the boys can manage their soap opera without me.* She smelled the armpit of her T-shirt. The sour smell reminded her immediately of her lunch with Ranjan. She sat up and reached for her jeans in the dark.

"You're awake." Sahil's soft voice floated up through the darkness.

Daya jumped off the bed in fright, clutching her pants to her body.

"What are you doing here?" she hissed. "*Why* are you here?" As her eyes adjusted, she saw Sahil was sitting on the floor by the dresser. "How long have you been sitting there?"

"Not long," Sahil smiled. "I didn't want to go to bed without seeing you. There's been a change in our plan and we're leaving early in the morning."

"Oh?" Daya quickly pulled on her jeans and shirt and sat on the bed. "Where are you going?"

"Home. To London."

"Why so suddenly?" Daya asked, irritated. "Is there a girl waiting for Ranjan?"

Sahil chuckled and stood up. "There could be, for all I know. We have relatives coming in from India. From my mother's side. We haven't seen them in years."

"You're looking forward to meeting them?" Daya asked with disbelief.

"I am, actually. They've always spoiled us rotten. My gran's a brilliant cook, and full of funny stories."

"About your mother?" Daya interjected.

"Yes, but so much more. She's as solid as a rock."

Daya looked at the ceiling, struggling with a sense of sadness.

"I'll miss you," she said finally. Sahil squatted at the foot of the bed.

"I was just thinking the same thing," he murmured. "I feel happy with you. Light. Something's opened up in me." Sahil ran a finger between Daya's toes and her foot jerked back.

"You're ticklish?" Sahil grinned.

"Very," Daya whispered hoarsely. She stopped herself from adding, *Except when I'm aroused.*

Daya and Sahil looked at each other. Sahil's jaw was tense. His amber eyes shone eerily like a cat's eyes in the moonlight. Daya swallowed hard. Her chest was so tight it hurt.

"Aren't your relatives wondering where you are?" Daya drew her legs under her and leaned back.

"Even if they knew, they would never come in here."

"Why? Are they all afraid of you?"

Sahil opened his palms to her and motioned for her to extend her legs. "No, that's not it," he replied. Daya unfolded her legs and wiggled her toes. Sahil caught hold of them and pulled her down the bed. He cradled one foot in his palms and put his mouth on her small toe. The intensity of his touch shot through Daya like a spark. She gripped the side of the mattress. Sahil switched to the next toe and Daya bit her lip to keep from crying out. She willed her body to relax, willed the surface tickling to move deeper, down, down into her belly where it flared and burned slowly.

She lay quieter, allowing Sahil's tongue to stroke her feet, arousing her. Her face felt hot, as though she had just sneezed. *Even if it's just once*, she said to herself, *I want him.*

Daya unbuttoned her jeans and pulled her T-shirt over her head. Sahil carefully eased her jeans and underpants off her body. He kissed her ankle and licked up the side of one leg, all the way up inside her thigh and then back down the other until he was at her toes again. Daya felt her body shivering in response. She watched Sahil licking and massaging her feet. His head was bent over in deep concentration. Daya wiggled her toes and Sahil looked up.

"Hi," she greeted him softly, her voice thick with arousal.

Sahil threw off his clothes and climbed over Daya. His entire body was covered with the thick soft hair that covered his chest. Daya pulled Sahil to her and they embraced in a long luxurious hug.

"It's so good to be holding you at last," Sahil whispered, running his fingers through her hair. "I've been sitting on an erection for an hour!" he laughed. "I tried talking to it, but it knew better."

Daya reached down with her hand. Sahil dug his face into her neck and bit her earlobe. Daya struggled out of his grasp and pinned his arms back against the headboard. She straddled him and sucked hard on his left nipple, feeling it stiffen. His body spasmed as she ran the edge of her teeth across the rigid flesh.

"Christ," he sighed happily. "You're a tigress."

"And you," she teased, "are not Indian."

Sahil pulled her face up to his and kissed her. He buried his mouth in her armpit and she pressed him hard against her to keep from crying out.

"You smell so good," he whispered between strokes of his tongue. "I want to taste you, put my mouth on you."

He slid down the bed. She guided his hand between her legs, then his head. He tasted her flesh with long strokes of his tongue. She closed her legs around his head.

"Has anyone told you what you taste like?" he asked, raising his head to look at her.

Daya smiled at him lazily.

"Tuna fish?" she asked jokingly.

Sahil shook his head vehemently.

"The cream inside a freshly cut lady finger," he corrected her solemnly. Daya gaped at him.

"Lady finger? You mean, okra?" She shook with silent laughter. "A vegetarian right down to the sex!"

Daya awoke with a start. Dawn was just breaking. She could hear footsteps on the staircase, and then below in the front room. She remembered that the London Patels were leaving that morning. She remembered her time with Sahil. The events of the previous night rushed through her head. She relived their tenderness together over and over in her mind. She felt exhausted and alive. Sahil had told her before leaving that she need not wake up to say goodbye in the morning. It would be awkward to exchange mere formalities after being so intimate together. She heard the car start, heard the car doors open and shut, and then the car drive away.

Daya looked out at the rising sun. It felt like the sun was setting already, the end of a long day. It was time to go back to sleep, to get some rest. She wondered if there was another pillow in the room. She looked around. There was a wardrobe next to the chest of drawers into which she had thrown her clothes. She climbed out of bed and pulled on the door of the wardrobe. It wouldn't open. *Great*, she thought. *Like good Indians, the Patels keep all their cupboards locked.* She pulled again on the door. This time the door opened a crack.

She pried the door open with her nails. The hinges moaned as she pushed each door to its limit. Folded neatly and hung on thick steel hangers were dozens of saris. She ran her fingers along the folds. She could tell immediately from the designs that the saris were dated: they were chiffons with loud multicoloured geometrical designs. Late '60s or early '70s. She smiled. Veena Auntie must have saved all her old saris, loath to throw them out. Daya's mother was the same way, with piles of saris that she refused to wear but was unwilling to give away. At the end of the row of saris hung a dozen or so sari blouses of different colours. Daya disliked saris, but loved the blouses for the midriffs they so wonderfully bared. She pulled out a green silk blouse and held it against her. It looked like it might fit. She imagined Sahil's fingers slowly undoing each hook that ran down the front of the blouse. She wanted to feel the soft material against her flesh. She pulled the blouse off the hanger. Was Veena really that thin in those days? A label sewn onto the inside of the blouse caught her eye. Similar white labels were sewn into every one of her mother's blouses. They had all been stitched in India.

Daya read the label, Manjuri S. Patel. Manjuri? She wondered who that could be . . . S. The middle initial stood for the husband's first name in the full name of a married Indian woman. S . . . could be S for Subhash . . .

Daya threw the blouse onto the bed. *It can't be! It can't be.* She looked around her at the walls of the bedroom. There were water stains on the ceiling. There were cobwebs in the corner. The windowsills were caked with dust.

Suddenly Sahil's words hit her in the face.

"They would never come in here."

Daya flung open the door and leaped out of the room before she realized she was naked. She stepped back into the room and grabbed her clothes off the floor. Her hands were shaking. Her legs got stuck in the jeans. She pulled them on with sheer force. Her arms were sweating. They got stuck in the sleeves of her T-shirt and she pulled the shirt roughly over her head. She ran into Rohit's bedroom, picked up the phone, and asked the operator to call her home collect. Her mother answered. The operator asked if she would accept the charges.

"I'm sorry but Daya is not home right now!"

Daya listened to her mother's vigorous denial to the operator. This was the arranged system to signal she wanted her parents to call back. Daya hung up the phone and waited. She looked around Rohit's room. The neatness of the room made her want to throw things about, empty the cupboards and dresser onto the floor, splash perfume and aftershave on the walls. A minute passed and the phone remained silent.

Mother! fumed Daya. *For god's sake take this seriously and call now. Not after you finish your conversation, not after you finish your cooking. Now!*

Another minute passed.

Betrayed again and again. Lies everywhere. Who was to blame?

The phone rang. Daya snatched it off the cradle furiously.

"Why the hell must you take so long to return my call? First of all you promised to call the day I arrived. Today is the third day. What excuse could you possibly have? You have no sense of time once your darling sons arrive in the house. I could have been killed by now!"

There was silence on the other end. Daya couldn't believe her mother's callousness.

"Do I mean so little to you? Did you have any thoughts for my feelings when you set me up with these morbid nephews of Rohit's? What in hell was going through your mind? Do you have any idea what sickos the two brothers are? Answer me, mother! I have a right to know." Daya fought back the tears of rage that choked her throat.

"Daya, sweetheart, is that you?" Her mother's voice sounded strange, differently pitched, very far away. "It's me, Auntie Veena, calling from Bombay. What is going on? What have those two naughty boys done now?" Daya pulled the receiver away from her ear.

Oh no; Veena! Not now. Where were you when I needed you?

"Daya!" Veena cried urgently. "Speak to me. Are you all right? Did they hurt you? Isn't your uncle around? Talk to him, darling, tell him everything. He loves you like a father. Daya, answer me!"

Daya felt the tears burning her face. *Why? Why in his mother's deathbed?*

"Sweetheart, those two boys are basically good at heart. They would never do anything to hurt you. Whatever happened, happened. Let it be now, let it go. I'm sorry I called when you were expecting your mother, but I'm sure she would say exactly what I'm telling you. You're young still, you have your whole life ahead of you. Forget it ever happened. Daya, are you there?"

She held her hand over her eyes and shook her head slowly.

"It's okay if you can't talk now, darling. I'll be home in two days. Uncle and I will take you out for a nice dinner, and then you can tell us everything . . ."

Daya put the phone down. Immediately it rang again. She walked into her bedroom, snatched up all her clothes and stuffed them into her bag. She walked down the stairs and out of the house. Daya checked her pocket for change. It would be a dollar or so to get to Manhattan. She should have gone the first day, should have gone and done what she came to do, instead of getting caught up with the men. When she arrived at the bus stop, a bus was pulling up. She asked the driver if he went down Museum Mile and he nodded.

Daya stared out of the window, concentrating on every shop name, every road sign, every hoarding. The intimacies of the night before tumbled through her head. She combed the images one by one to locate even a single dishonest touch, look or action. They had held each other for so long, in so many different ways. Not once had he pulled away from her. Not once had his loving attention flagged.

"Here's where the museums start, miss!" the bus driver called cheerfully to Daya. She sprang out of her seat and hurried off the bus.

Museum Mile on Fifth Avenue. Not a soul on the streets. She had hoped to encounter crowds of people, had envisioned losing herself in the rushing bodies of New Yorkers. She walked quickly. She would tire herself out.

How many women had been condemned to that bed? Daya felt numb with grief. She waited for the familiar anger to rise through her once again, but the memories of the previous night were still locked in her groin, glowing like coals. The warmth in her body moved upward and outward, comforting her. She felt his gentle hands on her face. And it was then that she understood. He'd had to do it. In some strange way, it had broken the spell that hung over him.

She walked past a hot dog vendor. He had big drooping eyes, chubby jowls and a bushy moustache. He looked Greek. He caught her eye and waved enthusiastically. His gaze was inquiring. Two blocks down he was there again. "You are Greek?" he shouted, arms in the air. "Come, come!"

Daya walked on.

"Armenian? Turkish? Palestinian?" he called frantically. She ducked into a museum.

The security guard at the museum addressed her before she had even crossed the gate. "I am from Guyana. You are also from Guyana?"

"No!" Daya snapped at the guard and rushed in.

"Trinidad? Jamaica? Fiji?" he called after her. "I'm sure I know you!"

Daya didn't know what museum she had walked into. There were old oil paintings in heavy gold frames. They were portraits of pale people, with faces brightly lit; the rest of their bodies were in darkness. The faces were expressionless and looked like they had been painted off cadavers. She decided to leave through a side exit, to avoid another encounter with the security guard.

As she pushed open the door, the hot dog vendor was right there again. He opened his hands wide and pleaded with her. "You are Lebanese? Egyptian? Iraqi? Come, come, I feed you!"

She frowned at him and turned away. The hot dog vendor followed at a trot, and walked alongside her. "Very nice!" he smiled, framing Daya's face in the air. "Woman," he added emphatically, "where you from?"

Daya stopped and scowled at him.

"Isn't it *obvious* that I'm Indian?"

The hot dog vendor clapped his hands.

"Ah, Indian!" he repeated with delight. "India! Most beautiful woman in India. Most wonderful woman in India. I see movies. Happy, happy, dancing, singing!" The Greek sprang from leg to leg and snapped his fingers in the air.

"Every man love Indian woman! Whole world love Indian woman!"

Daya took a long look at the singing shaking jowls and the merry twinkling eyes. She started laughing. This man was insane. Stark raving mad.

The Greek danced toward her, then away from her, then whirled around and around, encircling her. She watched the man through tired eyes. She drew in deep gulps of the warm spring air.

"Beautiful, beautiful Indian woman! Happy, happy Indian woman!" The Greek danced on, lost in his hymns of praise.

Daya watched him shout out his joy.

This is what I came for, this is what brought me here.

When he finally stopped, she clapped for him. He came up to her and saluted her, bowing low to the ground. Daya shook his hand. "Thanks for the reminder," she said softly.

The Greek smiled at her, not understanding. He snapped his fingers and leapt in the air one last time, then retreated to his hot dog stand. Daya waved to the Greek, but his back was turned to her as he resumed pushing his cart down the street.

So many years of anger, Daya mused, *and this man sees only beauty in my face.* She looked at her reflection in the window of the museum. Her smiling eyes shone back at her, gleaming with a mischievous light.

Shyam Selvadurai

Pigs Can't Fly

Besides Christmas and other festive occasions, spend-the-days were the days most looked forward to by all of us, cousins, aunts and uncles.

For the adults a spend-the-day was the one Sunday of the month they were free of their progeny. The eagerness with which they anticipated these days could be seen in the way Amma woke my brother, my sister and me extra early when they came. Unlike on school days, when Amma allowed us to dawdle a little, we were hurried through our morning preparations. Then, after a quick breakfast, we would be driven to the house of our grandparents.

The first thing that met our eyes on entering our grandparents' house, after we carefully wiped our feet on the doormat, would be the dark corridor running the length of it, on one side of which were the bedrooms and on the other the drawing and dining rooms. This corridor, with its old photographs on both walls and its ceiling so high that our footsteps echoed, scared me a little. The drawing room into which we would be ushered to pay our respects to our grandparents was also dark and smelt like old clothes that had been locked away in a suitcase for a long time. There my grandparents Ammachi and Appachi sat, enthroned in big reclining chairs. Appachi usually looked up from his paper and said vaguely, "Ah, hello, hello," before going back behind it, but Ammachi always called us to her with the beckoning movement of her middle and index fingers. With our legs trembling slightly, we would go to her, the thought of the big canes she kept behind her tall clothes almariah strongly imprinted upon our minds. She would grip our faces in her plump hands, and one by one kiss us wetly on both cheeks and say, "God has blessed me with fifteen grandchildren who will look after me in my old age." She smelt of stale coconut oil, and the diamond mukkuthi in her nose always pressed painfully against my cheek.

When the aunts and uncles eventually drove away, waving gaily at us children from car windows, we waved back at the retreating cars with not even a pretense of sorrow. For one glorious day a month we were free of parental control and the ever-watchful eyes and tale-bearing tongues of the house servants.

We were not, alas, completely abandoned, as we would have so liked to have been. Ammachi and Janaki were supposedly in charge. Janaki, cursed with the task of having to cook for fifteen extra people, had little time for supervision and actually preferred to have nothing to do with us at all. If called upon to come and settle a dispute, she would rush out, her hands red from grinding curry paste, and box the ears of the first person who happened to be in her path. We had learned that Janaki was to be appealed to only in the most dire emergencies. The one we understood, by tacit agreement, never to appeal to was Ammachi. Like the earth-goddess in the folktales, she was not to be disturbed from her tranquillity. To do so would have been the cause of a catastrophic earthquake.

In order to minimize interference by either Ammachi or Janaki, we had developed and refined a system of handling conflict and settling disputes ourselves. Two things formed the framework of this system: territoriality and leadership.

Territorially, the area around my grandparents' house was divided into two. The front garden, the road and the field that lay in front of the house belonged to the boys, although included in their group was my female cousin Meena. In this territory, two factions struggled for power, one led by Meena, the other by my brother, Varuna, who, because of a prevailing habit, had been renamed Diggy-Nose and then simply Diggy.

The second territory was called "the girls'," included in which, however, was myself, a boy. It was to this territory of "the girls," confined to the back garden and the kitchen porch, that I seemed to have gravitated naturally, my earliest memories of those spend-the-days always belonging in the back garden of my grandparents' home. The pleasure the boys had standing for hours on a cricket field under the sweltering sun, watching the batsmen run from crease to crease, was incomprehensible to me.

For me, the primary attraction of the girls' territory was the potential for the free play of fantasy. Because of the force of my imagination, I was selected as leader. Whatever the game, be it the imitation of adult domestic functions or the enactment of some well-loved fairy story, it was I who discovered some new way to enliven it, some new twist to the plot of a familiar tale. Led by me, the girl cousins would conduct a raid on my grandparents' dirty-clothes basket, discovering in this odorous treasure trove saris, blouses, sheets, curtains with which we invented costumes to complement our voyages of imagination.

The reward for my leadership was that I always got to play the main part in the fantasy. If it was cooking-cooking we were playing, I was the chef, if it was Cinderella or Thumbelina, I was the much-beleaguered heroine of these tales.

Of all our varied and fascinating games, bride-bride was my favourite. In it I was able to combine many elements of the other games I loved, and with time bride-bride, which had taken a few hours to play initially, became an event that spread out over the whole day and was planned for weeks in advance. For me the culmination of this game, and my ultimate moment of joy, was when I put on the clothes of the bride. In the late afternoon, usually after tea, I, along with the older girl cousins, would enter Janaki's room. From my sling-bag I would bring out my most prized possession, an old white sari, slightly yellow with age, its border torn and missing most of its sequins. The dressing of the bride would now begin, and then, by the transfiguration I saw taking place in Janaki's cracked full-length mirror — by the sari being wrapped around my body, the veil being pinned to my head, the rouge put on my cheeks, lipstick on my lips, kohl around my eyes — I was able to leave the constraints of my self and ascend into another, more brilliant, more beautiful self, a self to whom this day was dedicated, and around whom the world, represented by my cousins putting flowers in my hair, draping the palu, seemed to revolve. It was a self magnified, like the goddesses of the Sinhalese and Tamil cinema, larger than life; and like them, like the Malini Fonsekas and the Geetha Kumarasinghes, I was an icon, a graceful, benevolent, perfect being upon whom the adoring eyes of the world rested.

Those spend-the-days, the remembered innocence of childhood, are now coloured in the hues of the twilight sky. It is a picture made even more sentimental by the loss of all that was associated with them. By all of us having to leave Sri Lanka years later because of communal violence and forge a new home for ourselves in Canada.

Yet those Sundays, when I was seven, marked the beginning of my exile from the world I loved. Like a ship that leaves a port for the vast expanse of sea, those much-looked-forward-to days took me away from the safe harbour of childhood towards the precarious waters of adult life.

The visits at my grandparents' began to change with the return from abroad of Kanthi Aunty, Cyril Uncle, and their daughter, Tanuja, whom we quickly renamed "Her Fatness," in that cruelly direct way children have.

At first we had no difficulty with the newcomer in our midst. In fact we found her quite willing to accept that, by reason of her recent arrival, she must necessarily begin at the bottom.

In the hierarchy of bride-bride, the person with the least importance, less even than the priest and the pageboys, was the groom. It was a role we considered stiff and boring, that held no attraction for any of us. Indeed, if we could have dispensed with that role altogether we would have, but alas it was an unfortunate feature of the marriage ceremony. My younger sister, Sonali, with her patient good nature, but also sensing that I might have a mutiny on my hands if I asked anyone else to play that role, always donned the long pants and tattered jacket, borrowed from my grandfather's clothes chest. It was now deemed fitting that Her Fatness should take over the role and thus leave Sonali free to wrap a bedsheet around her body, in the manner of a sari, and wear araliya flowers in her hair like the other bridesmaids.

For two spend-the-days, Her Fatness accepted her role without a murmur and played it with all the skilled unobtrusiveness of a bit player. The third spend-the-day, however, everything changed. That day turned out to be my grandmother's birthday. Instead of dropping the children off and driving away as usual, the aunts and uncles stayed on for lunch, a slight note of peevish displeasure in their voices.

We had been late, because etiquette (or rather my father) demanded that Amma wear a sari for the grand occasion of her mother-in-law's sixtieth birthday. Amma's tardiness and her insistence on getting her palu to fall to exactly above her knees drove us all to distraction (especially Diggy, who quite rightly feared that in his absence Meena would try to persuade the better members of his team to defect to her side). Even I, who usually loved the ritual of watching Amma get dressed, stood in her doorway with the others and fretfully asked if she was ever going to be ready.

When we finally did arrive at Ramanaygam Road, everyone else had been there almost an hour. We were ushered into the drawing room by Amma to kiss Ammachi and present her with her gift, the three of us clutching the present. All the uncles and aunts were seated.

Her Fatness stood in between Kanthi Aunty's knees, next to Ammachi. When she saw us, she gave me an accusing, hostile look and pressed farther between her mother's legs. Kanthi Aunty turned away from her discussion with Mala Aunty, and, seeing me, she smiled and said in a tone that was as heavily sweetened as undiluted rose syrup, "So, what is this I hear, aah? Nobody will play with my little daughter."

I looked at her and then at Her Fatness, shocked by the lie. All my senses were alert.

Kanthi Aunty wagged her finger at me and said in a playful, chiding tone, "Now, now, Arjie, you must be nice to my little daughter. After all, she's just come from abroad and everything." Fortunately, I was prevented from having to answer. It was my turn to present my cheek to Ammachi, and, for the first time, I did so willingly, preferring the prick of the diamond mukkuthi to Kanthi Aunty's honeyed admonition.

Kanthi Aunty was the fourth oldest in my father's family. First there was my father, then Ravi Uncle, Mala Aunty, Kanthi Aunty, Babu Uncle, Seelan Uncle and finally Radha Aunty, who was much younger than the others and was away, studying in America. Kanthi Aunty was tall and bony, and we liked her the least, in spite of the fact that she would pat our heads affectionately whenever we walked past or greeted her. We sensed that beneath her benevolence lurked a seething anger, tempered by guile, that could have deadly consequences if unleashed in our direction. I had heard Amma say to her sister, Neliya Aunty, that Poor Kanthi was bitter because of the humiliations she had suffered abroad. "After all, darling, what a thing, forced to work as a servant in a whitey's house to make ends meet."

Once Ammachi had opened the present, a large silver serving tray, and thanked us for it (and insisted on kissing us once again), my brother, my sister and I were finally allowed to leave the room. Her Fatness had already disappeared. I hurried out the front door and ran around the side of the house.

When I reached the back garden I found the girl cousins squatting on the porch in a circle. They were so absorbed in what was happening in the centre that none of them even heard my greeting.

Lakshmi finally became aware of my presence and beckoned me over excitedly. I reached the circle, and the cause of her excitement became clear. In the middle, in front of Her Fatness, sat a long-legged doll with shiny gold hair. Her dress was like that of a fairy queen, the gauze skirt sprinkled with tiny silver stars. Next to her sat her male counterpart, dressed in a pale-blue suit. I stared in wonder at the marvellous dolls. For us cousins, who had grown up under a government that strictly limited all foreign imports, such toys were unimaginable. Her Fatness turned to the other cousins and asked them if they wanted to hold the dolls for a moment. They nodded eagerly, and the dolls passed from hand to hand. I moved closer to get a better look. My gaze involuntarily rested on Her Fatness, and she gave me a smug look. Immediately her scheme became evident to me. It was with these dolls that my cousin from abroad hoped to seduce the other cousins away from me.

Unfortunately for her, she had underestimated the power of bride-bride. When the other cousins had all looked at the dolls, they bestirred themselves and, without so much as a backward glance, hurried down the steps to prepare for the marriage ceremony. As I followed them, I looked triumphantly at Her Fatness, who sat on the porch, clasping her beautiful dolls to her chest.

When lunch was over, my grandparents retired to their room for a nap. The other adults settled in the drawing room to read the newspaper or doze off in the huge armchairs. We, the bride-to-be and the bridesmaids, retired to Janaki's room for the long-awaited ritual of dressing the bride.

We were soon disturbed, however, by the sound of booming laughter. At first we ignored it, but when it persisted, getting louder and more drawn out, my sister, Sonali, went to the door and looked out. Her slight gasp brought us all out onto the porch. There the groom strutted, up and down, head thrown back, stomach stuck out. She sported a huge bristly moustache (torn out of the broom) and a cigarette (of rolled paper and talcum powder), which she held between her fingers and puffed on vigorously. The younger cousins, instead of getting dressed and putting the final touches to the altar, sat along the edge of the porch and watched with great amusement.

"Aha, me hearties!" the groom cried on seeing us. She opened her hands expansively. "Bring me my fair maiden, for I must be off to my castle before the sun settest."

We looked at the groom, aghast at the change in her behaviour. She sauntered towards us, then stopped in front of me, winked expansively, and, with her hand under my chin, tilted back my head.

"Ahh!" she exclaimed. "A bonny lass, a bonny lass indeed."

"Stop it!" I cried, and slapped her hand. "The groom is not supposed to make a noise."

"Why not?" Her Fatness replied angrily, dropping her hearty voice and accent. "Why can't the groom make a noise?"

"Because."

"Because of what?"

"Because the game is called bride-bride, not groom-groom."

Her Fatness seized her moustache and flung it to the ground dramatically. "Well, I don't want to be the groom anymore. I want to be the bride."

We stared at her in disbelief, amazed by her impudent challenge to my position.

"You can't," I finally said.

"Why not?" Her Fatness demanded. "Why should you always be the bride? Why can't someone else have a chance too?"

"Because . . ." Sonali said, joining in. "Because Arjie is the bestest bride of all."

"But he's not even a girl," Her Fatness said, closing in on the lameness of Sonali's argument. "A bride is a girl, not a boy." She looked around at the other cousins and then at me. "A boy cannot be the bride," she said with deep conviction. "A girl must be the bride."

I stared at her, defenceless in the face of her logic.

Fortunately, Sonali, loyal to me as always, came to my rescue. She stepped in between us and said to Her Fatness, "If you can't play properly, go away. We don't need you."

"Yes!" Lakshmi, another of my supporters, cried.

The other cousins, emboldened by Sonali's fearlessness, murmured in agreement.

Her Fatness looked at all of us for a moment and then her gaze rested on me.

"You're a pansy," she said, her lips curling in disgust.

We looked at her blankly.

"A faggot," she said, her voice rising against our uncomprehending stares.

"A sissy!" she shouted in desperation.

It was clear by this time that these were insults.

"Give me that jacket," Sonali said. She stepped up to Her Fatness and began to pull at it. "We don't like you anymore."

"Yes!" Lakshmi cried. "Go away, you fatty-boom-boom!"

This was an insult we all understood, and we burst out laughing. Someone even began to chant, "Hey fatty-boom-boom. Hey fatty-boom-boom."

Her Fatness pulled off her coat and trousers. "I hate you all," she cried. "I wish you were all dead." She flung the groom's clothes on the ground, stalked out of the back garden, and went around the side of the house.

We returned to our bridal preparations, chuckling to ourselves over the new nickname we had found for our cousin.

When the bride was finally dressed, Lakshmi, the maid of honour, went out of Janaki's room to make sure that everything was in place. Then she gave the signal and the priest and choirboys began to sing, with a certain want of harmony and correct lyrics, "The voice that breathed on Eeeden, the first and glorious day. . . ." Solemnly, I made my way down the steps towards the altar that had been set up at one end of the back garden. When I reached the altar, however, I heard the kitchen door open. I turned to see Her Fatness with Kanthi Aunty. The discordant singing died out.

Kanthi Aunty's benevolent smile had completely disappeared and her eyes were narrowed with anger.

"Who's calling my daughter fatty?" Kanthi Aunty said. She came to the edge of the porch.

We stared at her, no one daring to own up.

Her gaze fell on me and her eyes widened for a moment. Then a smile spread across her face.

"What's this?" she said, the honey seeping back into her voice. She came down a few steps and crooked her finger at me. I looked down at my feet and refused to go to her.

"Come here, come here," she said.

Unable to disobey her command any longer, I went to her. She looked me up and down for a moment, and then gingerly, as if she were examining raw meat at the market, turned me around.

"What's this you're playing?" she asked.

"It's bride-bride, Aunty," Sonali said.

"Bride-bride," she murmured.

Her hand closed on my arm in a tight grip.

"Come with me," she said.

I resisted, but her grip tightened, her nails digging into my elbow. She pulled me up the porch steps and towards the kitchen door.

"No," I cried. "No, I don't want to."

Something about the look in her eyes terrified me so much I did the unthinkable and I hit out at her. This made her hold my arm even more firmly. She dragged me through the kitchen, past Janaki, who looked up, curious, and into the corridor and towards the drawing room. I felt a heaviness begin to build in my stomach. Instinctively I knew that Kanthi Aunty had something terrible in mind.

As we entered the drawing room, Kanthi Aunty cried out, her voice brimming over with laughter, "See what I found!"

The other aunts and uncles looked up from their papers or bestirred themselves from their sleep. They gazed at me in amazement as if I had suddenly made myself visible, like a spirit. I glanced at them and then at Amma's face. Seeing her expression, I felt my dread deepen. I lowered my eyes. The sari suddenly felt suffocating around my body, and the hairpins that held the veil in place pricked at my scalp.

Then the silence was broken by the booming laugh of Cyril Uncle, Kanthi Aunty's husband. As if she had been hit, Amma swung around in his direction. The other aunts and uncles began to laugh too, and I watched as Amma looked from one to the other like a trapped animal. Her gaze finally came to rest on my father, and for the first time I noticed that he was the only one not laughing. Seeing the way he kept his eyes fixed on his paper, I felt the heaviness in my stomach begin to push its way up my throat.

"Ey, Chelva," Cyril Uncle cried out jovially to my father, "looks like you have a funny one here."

My father pretended he had not heard and, with an inclination of his head, indicated to Amma to get rid of me.

She waved her hand in my direction and I picked up the edges of my veil and fled to the back of the house.

That evening, on the way home, both my parents kept their eyes averted from me. Amma glanced at my father occasionally, but he refused to meet her gaze. Sonali, sensing my unease, held my hand tightly in hers.

Later, I heard my parents fighting in their room.

"How long has this been going on?" my father demanded.

"I don't know," Amma cried defensively. "It was as new to me as it was to you."

"You should have known. You should have kept an eye on him."

"What should I have done? Stood over him while he was playing?"

"If he turns out funny like that Rankotwera boy, if he turns out to be the laughingstock of Colombo, it'll be your fault," my father said in a tone of finality. "You always spoil him and encourage all his nonsense."

"What do I encourage?" Amma demanded.

"You are the one who allows him to come in here while you're dressing and play with your jewellery."

Amma was silent in the face of the truth.

Of the three of us, I alone was allowed to enter Amma's bedroom and watch her get dressed for special occasions. It was an experience I considered almost religious, for, even though I adored the goddesses of the local cinema, Amma was the final statement in female beauty for me.

When I knew Amma was getting dressed for a special occasion, I always positioned myself outside her door. Once she had put on her underskirt and blouse, she would ring for our servant, Anula, to bring her sari, and then, while taking it from her, hold the door open so I could go in as well. Entering that room was, for me, a greater boon than that granted by any god to a mortal. There were two reasons for this. The first was the jewellery box which lay open on the dressing table. With a joy akin to ecstasy, I would lean over and gaze inside, the faint smell of perfume rising out of the box each time I picked up a piece of jewellery and held it against my nose or ears or throat. The second was the pleasure of watching Amma drape her sari, watching her shake open the yards of material, which, like a Chinese banner caught by the wind, would linger in the air for a moment before drifting gently to the floor; watching her pick up one end of it, tuck it into the waistband of her skirt, make the pleats, and then with a flick of her wrists invert the pleats and tuck them into her waistband; and finally watching her drape the palu across her breasts and pin it into place with a brooch.

When Amma was finished, she would check to make sure that the back of the sari had not risen up with the pinning of the palu, then move back and look at herself in the mirror. Standing next to her or seated on the edge of the bed, I, too, would look at her reflection in the mirror, and, with the contented sigh of an artist who has finally captured the exact effect he wants, I would say, "You should have been a film star, Amma."

"A film star?" she would cry and lightly smack the side my head. "What kind of a low-class-type person do you think I am?"

One day, about a week after the incident at my grandparents', I positioned myself outside my parents' bedroom door. When Anula arrived with the sari, Amma took it and quickly shut the door. I waited patiently, thinking Amma had not yet put on her blouse and skirt, but the door never opened. Finally, perplexed that Amma had forgotten, I knocked timidly on the door. She did not answer, but

I could hear her moving around inside. I knocked a little louder and called out "Amma" through the keyhole. Still no response, and I was about to call her name again when she replied gruffly, "Go away. Can't you see I am busy?"

I stared disbelievingly at the door. Inside I could hear the rustle of the sari as it brushed along the floor. I lifted my hand to knock again when suddenly I remembered the quarrel I had heard on the night of that last spend-the-day. My hand fell limply by my side.

I crept away quietly to my bedroom, sat down on the edge of my bed, and stared at my feet for a long time. It was clear to me that I had done something wrong, but what it was I couldn't comprehend. I thought of what my father had said about turning out "funny." The word "funny" as I understood it meant either humorous or strange, as in the expression "That's funny." Neither of these fitted the sense in which my father had used the word, for there had been a hint of disgust in his tone.

Later, Amma came out of her room and called Anula to give her instructions for the evening. As I listened to the sound of her voice, I realized that something had changed forever between us.

A little while after my parents had left for their dinner party, Sonali came looking for me. Seeing my downcast expression, she sat next to me, and, though unaware of anything that had passed, slipped her hand in mine. I pushed it away roughly, afraid that if I let her squeeze my hand I would start to cry.

The next morning Amma and I were like two people who had had a terrible fight the night before. I found it hard to look her in the eye and she seemed in an unusually gay mood.

The following spend-the-day, when Amma came to awaken us, I was already seated in bed and folding my bride-bride sari. Something in her expression however, made me hurriedly return the sari to the bag.

"What's that?" she said, coming towards me, her hand out-stretched. After a moment I gave her the bag. She glanced at its contents briefly. "Get up, it's spend-the-day," she said. Then, with the bag in her hand, she went to the window and looked out into the driveway. The seriousness of her expression, as if I had done something so awful that even the usual punishment of a caning would not suffice, frightened me.

I was brushing my teeth after breakfast when Anula came to the bathroom door, peered inside, and said with a sort of grim pleasure, "Missie wants to talk to you in her room." Seeing the alarm in my face, she nodded and said sagely, "Up to some kind of mischief as usual. Good-for-nothing child."

My brother, Diggy, was standing in the doorway of our parents' room, one foot scratching impatiently against the other. Amma was putting on her lipstick. My father had already gone for his Sunday squash game, and, as usual, she would pick him up after she had dropped us off at our grandparents'.

Amma looked up from the mirror, saw me, and indicated with her tube of lipstick for both of us to come inside and sit down on the edge of the bed. Diggy gave me a baleful look, as if it were my fault that Amma was taking such a long time to get ready. He followed me into the room, his slippers dragging along the floor.

Finally Amma closed her lipstick, pressed her lips together to even out the colour, then turned to us.

"Okay, mister," she said to Diggy, "I am going to tell you something, and this is an order."

We watched her carefully.

"I want you to include your younger brother on your cricket team."

Diggy and I looked at her in shocked silence, then he cried, "Ah! Come on, Amma!"

And I, too, cried out, "I don't want to play with them. I hate cricket!"

"I don't care what you want," Amma said. "It's good for you."

"Arjie's useless," Diggy said. "We'll never win if he's on our team."

Amma held up her hand to silence us. "That's an order," she said.

"Why?" I asked, ignoring her gesture. "Why do I have to play with the boys?"

"Why?" Amma said. "Because the sky is so high and pigs can't fly, that's why."

"Please, Amma! Please!" I held out my arms to her.

Amma turned away quickly, picked up her handbag from the dressing table, and said, almost to herself, "If the child turns out wrong, it's the mother they always blame, never the father." She clicked the handbag shut.

I put my head in my hands and began to cry. "Please, Amma, please," I said through my sobs.

She continued to face the window.

I flung myself on the bed with a wail of anguish. I waited for her to come to me as she always did when I cried, waited for her to take me in her arms, rest my head against her breasts, and say in her special voice, "What's this, now? Who's the little man who's crying?"

But she didn't heed my weeping any more than she had heeded my cries when I knocked on her door.

Finally I stopped crying and rolled over on my back. Diggy had left the room. Amma turned to me, now that I had become quiet, and said cheerfully, "You'll have a good time, just wait and see."

"Why can't I play with the girls?" I replied.

"You can't, that's all."

"But why?"

She shifted uneasily.

"You're a big boy now. And big boys must play with other boys."

"That's stupid."

"It doesn't matter," she said. "Life is full of stupid things and sometimes we just have to do them."

"I won't," I said defiantly. "I won't play with the boys."

Her face reddened with anger. She reached down, caught me by the shoulders, and shook me hard. Then she turned away and ran her hand through her hair. I watched her, gloating. I had broken her cheerful facade, forced her to show how much it pained her to do what she was doing, how little she actually believed in the justness of her actions.

After a moment she turned back to me and said in an almost pleading tone, "You'll have a good time."

I looked at her and said, "No, I won't."

Her back straightened. She crossed to the door and stopped. Without looking at me she said stiffly, "The car leaves in five minutes. If you're not in it by then, watch out."

I lay back on the bed and gazed at the mosquito net swinging gently in the breeze. In my mind's eye, I saw the day that stretched ahead of me. At the thought of having to waste the most precious day of the month in that field in front of my grandparents' house, the hot sun beating on my head, the perspiration running down the sides of my face, I felt a sense of despair begin to take hold of me. The picture of what would take place in the back garden became clear. I saw Her Fatness seizing my place as leader of the girls, claiming for herself the rituals I had so carefully invented and planned. I saw her standing in front of Janaki's mirror as the other girls fixed her hair, pinned her veil, and draped her sari. The thought was terrible. Something had to be done. I could not give up that easily, could not let Her Fatness, whose sneaking to Kanthi Aunty had forced me into the position I was now in, so easily take my place. But what could I do?

As if in answer, an object that rested just at the periphery of my vision claimed my attention. I turned my head slightly and saw my sling-bag. Then a thought came to me. I reached out, picked up the bag, and hugged it close to my chest. Without the sari in that bag, it was impossible for the girls to play bride-bride. I thought of Her Fatness with triumph. What would she drape around her body? A bedsheet like the bridesmaids? No! Without me and my sari she would not be able to play bride-bride properly.

There was, I realized, an obstacle that had to be overcome first. I would have to get out of playing cricket. Amma had laid down an order, and I knew Diggy well enough to know that, in spite of all his boldness, he would never dare to disobey an order from Amma.

I heard the car start up, and its sound reminded me of another problem that I had not considered. How was I going to smuggle the sari into the car? Amma would be waiting in the car for me, and if I arrived with the sling-bag she would make me take it back. I could not slip it in without her noticing. I sat still, listening to the whir of the engine at counterpoint to the clatter of Anula clearing the break-fast table, and suddenly a plan revealed itself to me.

I took the sari out of the bag, folded the bag so that it looked like there was something in it, and left it on the bed. Taking the sari with me, I went to the bedroom door and peered out. The hall was empty. I went into Sonali's room, which was next to my parents', and I crouched down on one side of the doorway. I took off my slippers and held them with the sari in my arms. The curtain in the open doorway of Sonali's room blew slightly in the breeze, and I moved farther away from it so that I would not be seen. After what seemed like an interminable amount of time, I heard Amma coming down the hallway to fetch me from her room. I crouched even lower as the sound of her footsteps got closer. From below the curtain, I saw her go into her room. As she entered, I stood up, pushed aside the cur-tain, and darted down the hallway. She came out of her room and called to me, but I didn't stop, and ran outside.

Thankfully the rear door of the car was open. I jumped in, quickly stuffed the sari into Sonali's sling-bag, and lay back against the seat, panting. Diggy and Sonali were looking at me strangely but they said nothing.

Soon Amma came out and got into the car. She glared at me, and I gave her an innocent look. I smiled at Sonali conspiratorially. Son-ali, my strongest ally, was doing her best to keep the bewilderment out of her face. By way of explanation, I said, with pretend gloomi-ness, "I can't play with you today. Amma says that I must play with the boys."

Sonali looked at me in amazement and then turned to Amma. "Why can't he play with the girls?" she said.

"Why?" Amma said and started up the car. "Because the sky is so high and pigs can't fly."

Amma sounded less sure of herself this time and a little weary. Looking in front, I saw that Diggy had turned in his seat and was regarding me morosely. I was reminded that the sari in the bag was worth nothing if I couldn't get out of the long day of cricket that lay ahead of me.

All the way to my grandparents' house, I gazed at the back of Diggy's head, hoping inspiration would come. The sound of his feet kicking irritably against the underside of the glove compartment confirmed that, however bad the consequences, he would follow Amma's orders. The sound of that ill-natured kicking made me search my mind all the more desperately for a way to escape playing cricket with the boys.

When the car turned down Ramanaygam Road, I still had not thought of anything. Meena was standing on top of the garden wall, her legs apart, her hands on her hips, her panties already dirty underneath her short dress. The boy cousins were on the wall on either side of her.

As we walked up the path to pay our respects to Ammachi and Appachi, I whispered to Sonali to keep the sari hidden and to tell no one about it. When we went into the drawing room, Her Fatness, who was as usual between Kanthi Aunty's knees, gave me a victorious look. A feeling of panic began to rise in me that no plan of escape had yet presented itself.

Once we had gone through the ritual of presenting our cheeks to our grandparents, we followed Amma outside to say goodbye.

"You children be good," Amma said before she got into the car. She looked pointedly at me. "I don't want to hear that you've given Ammachi and Appachi any trouble."

I watched her departing car with a sense of sorrow.

Diggy grabbed my arm. I followed reluctantly as he hurried across the road, still holding on to me, as if afraid I would run away.

The wickets had already been set up in the field in front of the house, and the boys and Meena were seated under a guava tree. When they saw us come towards them, they stopped talking and stared at us.

Muruges, who was on Diggy's team, stood up.

"What's he doing here?" he demanded, waving his half-eaten guava at me.

"He's going to play."

"What?" the others cried in amazement.

They looked at Diggy as if he had lost his mind.

"He's not going to play on our team, is he?" Muruges said, more a threat than a question.

"He's quite good," Diggy answered halfheartedly.

"If he's going to be on our team, I'm changing sides," Muruges declared, and some of the others murmured in agreement.

"Come on, guys," Diggy said with desperation in his voice, but they remained stern.

Diggy turned to Meena. "I'll trade you Arjie for Sanjay."

Meena spat out the seeds of the guava she was eating. "Do you think I'm mad or something?"

"Ah, come on," Diggy said in a wheedling tone. "He's good. We've been practicing the whole week."

"If he's so good, why don't you keep him yourself? Maybe with him on your team you might actually win."

"Yeah," Sanjay cried, insulted that I was considered an equal trade for him. "Why don't you keep the girlie-boy?"

At the new nickname "girlie-boy," everyone roared with laughter, and even Diggy grinned.

I should have felt humiliated and dejected that nobody wanted me on their team, but instead I felt the joy of relief begin to dance inside of me. The escape I had searched for was offering itself without any effort on my part. If Diggy's best team members were threatening to abandon him he would have no alternative but to let me go. I looked at my feet so that no one would see the hope in my eyes.

Unfortunately, the nickname "girlie-boy" had an effect which I had not predicted. The joke at my expense seemed to clear the air. After laughing heartily, Muruges withdrew his threat. "What the hell," he said benevolently. "It can't hurt to have another fielder. But," he added, as a warning to Diggy, "he can't bat."

Diggy nodded as if he had never even considered letting me bat. Since each side had only fifty overs, it was vital to send the best batsmen in first, and often the younger cousins never got a chance.

I glared at Muruges, and he, thinking that my look was a reaction to the new nickname, said "girlie-boy" again.

Diggy now laughed loudly, but in his laugh I detected a slight note of servility and also relief that the catastrophe of losing his team had been averted. I saw that the balance he was trying to maintain between following Amma's orders and keeping his team members happy was extremely precarious. All was not lost. Such a fragile balance would be easy to upset.

The opportunity to do this arose almost immediately.

Our team was to go first. In deciding the batting order, there was a certain system that the boys always followed. The captain would mark numbers in the sand with hyphens next to each and then cover the numbers with a bat. The players, who had been asked to turn their backs, would then come over and choose a hyphen. What was strange to me about this exercise was its redundancy, for when the numbers were uncovered, no matter what the batting order, the older and better players always went first, the younger cousins assenting without a murmur.

When Diggy uncovered the numbers, I was first, Diggy was second. Muruges had one of the highest numbers and would bat towards the end, if at all. "Well," Muruges said to Diggy in a tone that spoke of promises already made, "I'll take Arjie's place."

Diggy nodded vigorously as if Muruges had read his very thoughts.

Unfortunately for him, I had other plans.

"I want to go first," I said firmly, and waited for my request to produce the necessary consequences.

Muruges was crouched down, fixing his pads, and he straightened up slowly. The slowness of his action conveyed his anger at my daring to make such a suggestion and at the same time challenged Diggy to change the batting order.

Meena, unexpectedly, came to my defence. "He is the first!" she said. "Fair is fair!" In a game of only fifty overs, a bad opening bat would be ideal for her team.

"Fair is fair," I echoed Meena. "I picked first place and I should be allowed to play!"

"You can't," Diggy said desperately. "Muruges always goes first."

Meena's team, encouraged by her, also began to cry out, "Fair is fair!"

Diggy quickly crossed over to Muruges, put his arm around his shoulder, turned him away from the others, and talked earnestly to him. But Muruges shook his head, unconvinced by whatever Diggy was saying. finally Diggy dropped his hand from Muruges's shoulder and cried out in exasperation at him, "Come on, men!" In response, Muruges began to unbuckle his pads. Diggy put his hand on his shoulder, but he shrugged it off. Diggy, seeing that Muruges was determined, turned to me.

"Come on, Arjie," he said, pleading. "You can go later in the game."

"No," I said stubbornly, and, just to show how determined I was, I picked up the bat.

Muruges saw my action and threw the pads at my feet.

"I'm on your team now," he announced to Meena.

"Ah, no! Come on, men!" Diggy shouted in protest.

Muruges began to cross over to where Meena's team was gathered.

Diggy turned towards me now and grabbed the bat.

"*You* go!" he cried. "We don't need *you*." He pulled the bat out of my hands and started to walk with it towards Muruges.

"You're a cheater, cheater pumpkin-eater! I chose to bat first!" I yelled.

But I had gone too far. Diggy turned and looked at me. Then he howled as he realized how he had been tricked. Instead of giving Muruges the bat, he lifted it above his head and ran towards me. I turned and fled across the field towards my grandparents' gate. When I reached it, I lifted the latch, went inside the garden, and quickly put the latch back into place. Diggy stopped when he reached the gate. Safe on my side, I made a face at him through the slats. He came close and I retreated a little. Putting his head through the slats, he hissed at me, "If you ever come near the field again, you'll be sorry."

"Don't worry," I replied tartly. "I never will."

And with that, I forever closed any possibility of entering the boys' world again. But I didn't care, and just to show how much I didn't care I made another face, turned my back on Diggy, and walked up the front path to the house. As I went through the narrow passageway between the house and the side wall that led to the back, I could hear the girls' voices as they prepared for bride-bride, and especially Her Fatness's, ordering everyone around. When I reached the back garden, I stopped when I saw the wedding cake. The bottom layer consisted of mud pies molded from half a coconut shell. They supported the lid of a biscuit tin, which had three mud pies on it. On these rested the cover of a condensed-milk tin with a single mud pie on top. This was the three-tiered design that *I* had invented. Her Fatness had copied my design exactly. Further, she had taken upon herself the sole honour of decorating it with florets of gandapahana flowers and trails of antigonon, in the same way I had always done.

Sonali was the first to become aware of my presence. "Arjie!" she said, pleased.

The other cousins now noticed me, and they also exclaimed in delight. Lakshmi called out to me to come and join them, but before I could do so Her Fatness rose to her feet.

"What do you want?" she said.

I came forward a bit and she immediately stepped towards me, like a female mongoose defending her young against a cobra. "Go away!" she cried, holding up her hand. "Boys are not allowed here."

I didn't heed her command.

"Go away," she cried again. "Otherwise I'm going to tell Ammachi!"

I looked at her for a moment, but fearing that she would see the hatred in my eyes, I glanced down at the pound.

"I want to play bride-bride, please," I said, trying to sound as pathetic and inoffensive as possible.

"Bride-bride," Her Fatness repeated mockingly.

"Yes," I said, in a shy whisper.

Sonali stood up. "Can't he play?" she said to Her Fatness. "He'll be very good."

"Yes, he'll be very good," the others murmured in agreement.

Her Fatness considered their request.

"I have something that you don't have," I said quickly, hoping to sway her decision.

"Oh, what is that?"

"The sari!"

"The sari?" she echoed. A look of malicious slyness flickered across her face.

"Yes," I said. "Without the sari you can't play bride-bride."

"Why not?" Her Fatness said with indifference.

Her lack of concern about the sari puzzled me. Fearing that it might not have the same importance for her as it did for me, I cried out, "Why not?" and pretended to be amazed that she would ask such a question. "What is the bride going to wear, then? A bedsheet?"

Her Fatness played with a button on her dress. "Where is the sari?" she asked very casually.

"It's a secret," I said. I was not going to give it to her until I was firmly entrenched in the girls' world again. "If you let me play, I will give it to you when it's time for the bride to get ready."

A smile crossed her face. "The thing is, Arjie," she said in a very reasonable tone, "we've already decided what everyone is going to be for bride-bride and we don't need anyone else."

"But there must be some parts you need people for," I said and then added, "I'll play any part."

"Any part," Her Fatness repeated. Her eyes narrowed and she looked at me appraisingly.

"Let him play," Sonali and the others said.

"I'll play *any* part," I reiterated.

"You know what?" Her Fatness said suddenly, as if the idea had just dawned on her. "We don't have a groom."

That Her Fatness wanted me to swallow the bitter pill of humiliation was clear, and so great was my longing to be part of the girls' world again that I swallowed it.

"I'll take it," I said.

"Okay," Her Fatness said as if it mattered little to her whether I did or not.

The others cried out in delight and I smiled, happy that my goal had been at least partially achieved. Sonali beckoned to me to come and help them. I went towards where the preparations were being made for the wedding feast, but Her Fatness quickly stepped in front of me.

"The groom cannot help with the cooking."

"Why not?" I protested.

"Because grooms don't do that."

"They do."

"Have you ever heard of a groom doing that?"

I couldn't say I had, so I demanded with angry sarcasm, "What do grooms do then?"

"They go to office."

"Office?" I said.

Her Fatness nodded and pointed to the table on the back porch. The look on her face told me she would not tolerate any argument.

"I can't go to office," I said quickly. "It's Sunday."

"We're pretending it's Monday," Her Fatness replied glibly.

I glared at her. Not satisfied with the humiliation she had forced me to accept, she was determined to keep my participation in bride-bride to a minimum. For an instant I thought to refuse her, but, seeing the warning look in her eyes, I finally acquiesced and went up the porch steps.

From there, I watched the other cousins getting ready for the wedding. Using a stone, I began to bang on the table as if stamping papers. I noted, with pleasure, that the sound irritated Her Fatness. I pressed an imaginary buzzer and made a loud noise. Getting no response from anyone, I did so again. finally the other cousins looked up. "Boy," I called out imperiously to Sonali, "come here, boy."

Sonali left her cooking and came up the steps with the cringing attitude of the office peons at my father's bank.

"Yes sir, yes sir," she said breathlessly. Her performance was so accurate that the cousins stopped to observe her.

"Take this to the bank manager in Bambalapitiya," I said. Bowing again, she took the imaginary letter and hurried down the steps. I pressed my buzzer again. "Miss," I called to Lakshmi. "Miss, can you come here and take some dictation."

"Yes, sir, coming, sir," Lakshmi said, fluttering her eyelashes, with the exaggerated coyness of a Sinhala comic actress. She came up the steps, wriggling her hips for the amusement of her audience. Everyone laughed except Her Fatness.

When Lakshmi finished the dictation and went down the steps, the other cousins cried out, "Me! Me!" and clamoured to be the peon I would call next. But, before I could choose one of them, Her Fatness stormed up the steps.

"Stop that!" she shouted at me. "You're disturbing us."

"No!" I cried back, now that I had the support of everyone else.

"If you can't behave, go away."

"If I go away, you won't get the sari."

Her Fatness looked at me a long moment and then smiled. "What sari?" she said. "I bet you don't even have the sari."

"Yes, I do," I said in an earnest tone.

"Where?"

"It's a secret."

"You are lying. I know you don't have it."

"I do! I do!"

"Show me."

"No."

"You don't have it and I'm going to tell Janaki you are disturbing us."

I didn't move, wanting to see if she would carry out her threat. She crossed behind the table and walked towards the kitchen door. When she got to the door and I was sure she was serious, I jumped up.

"Where is it?" I said urgently to Sonali.

She pointed to Janaki's room.

I ran to Janaki's door, opened it, and went inside. Sonali's bag was lying on the bed, and I picked it up and rushed back out onto the porch. Her Fatness had come away from the kitchen door.

"Here!" I cried.

Her Fatness folded her arms. "Where?" she said tauntingly. I opened the bag, put my hand inside, and felt around for the sari. I touched a piece of clothing and drew it out. It was only Sonali's change of clothes. I put my hand inside again and this time brought out an Enid Blyton book. There was nothing else in the bag.

"Where is the sari?" Her Fatness demanded.

I glanced at Sonali, and she gave me a puzzled look.

"Liar, liar on the wall, who's the liarest one of all?" Her Fatness cried.

I turned towards Janaki's door, wondering if the sari had fallen out. Then I saw a slight smirk on Her Fatness's face and the truth came to me. She'd known all along about the sari. She must have discovered it earlier and hidden it. I realized I had been duped and felt a sudden rush of anger. Her Fatness saw the comprehension in my eyes, and her arms dropped by her sides as if in readiness. She inched back towards the kitchen door for safety. But I was not interested in her for the moment. What I wanted was the sari.

I rushed into Janaki's room.

"I'm going to tell Janaki you're in her room!" Her Fatness cried.

"Tell and catch my long fat tail!" I shouted back.

I looked around Janaki's room. Her Fatness must have hidden it here. There was no other place. I lifted Janaki's mattress. There was nothing under it, save a few Sinhala love comics. I went to Janaki's suitcase and began to go through the clothes she kept neatly folded inside it. As silent as a shadow, Her Fatness slipped into the room. I became aware of her presence and turned. But too late. She took the sari from the shelf where she had hidden it and ran out the door. Leaving the suitcase still open, I ran after her. The sari clutched to her chest, she rushed for the kitchen door. Luckily Sonali and Lakshmi were blocking her way. Seeing me coming at her, she jumped off the porch and began to head towards the front of the house. I leapt off the porch and chased after her. If she got to the front of the house, she would go straight to Ammachi.

Just as she reached the passageway, I managed to get hold of her arm. She turned, desperate, and struck out at me. Ducking her blow, I reached for the sari and managed to get some of it in my hand. She tried to take it back from me, but I held on tightly. Crying out, she jerked away from me with her whole body, hoping to wrest the sari from my grip. With a rasping sound, the sari began to tear. I yelled at her to stop pulling, but she jerked away again and the sari tore all the way down. There was a moment of stunned silence. I gazed at the torn sari in my hand, at the long threads that hung from it. Then, with a wail of anguish, I rushed at Her Fatness and grabbed hold of her hair. She screamed and flailed at me. I yanked her head so far to one side that it almost touched her shoulder. She let out a guttural sound and struck out desperately at me. Her fist caught me in the stomach and she managed to loosen my grip.

She began to run towards the porch steps, crying out for Ammachi and Janaki. I ran after her and grabbed the sleeve of her dress before she went up the porch steps. She struggled against my grip and the sleeve ripped open and hung down her arm like a broken limb. Free once again, she stumbled up the steps towards the kitchen door, shouting at the top of her voice.

Janaki rushed out of the kitchen. She raised her hand and looked around for the first person to wallop, but when she saw Her Fatness with her torn dress, she held her raised hand to her cheek and cried out in consternation, "Buddu Ammo!"

Now Her Fatness began to call out only for Ammachi.

Janaki came hurriedly towards her. "Shhh! Shhhh!" she said, but Her Fatness only increased the volume of her cry.

"What's wrong? What's wrong?" Janaki cried impatiently.

Her Fatness pointed to me.

"Janakiii! See what that boy did," she replied.

"I didn't do anything," I yelled, enraged that she was trying to push the blame onto me.

I ran back to where I had dropped the sari, picked it up, and held it out to Janaki.

"Yes!" Sonali cried, coming to my defense. "She did it and now she's blaming him."

"It's her fault!" Lakshani said, also taking my side.

Now all the voices of the girl cousins rose in a babble supporting my case and accusing Her Fatness.

"Quiet!" Janaki shouted in desperation. "Quiet!"

But nobody heeded her. We all crowded around her, so determined to give our version of the story that it was a while before we became aware of Ammachi's presence in the kitchen doorway. Gradually, like the bush that descends on a garrison town at the sound of enemy guns, we all became quiet. Even Her Fatness stopped her wailing.

Ammachi looked at all of us and then her gaze came to rest on Janaki. "How many times have I told you to keep these children quiet?" she said, her tone awful.

Janaki, always so full of anger, now wrung her hands like a child in fear of punishment. "I told them . . ." she started to say, but Ammachi raised her hand for silence. Her Fatness began to cry again, more out of fear than anything else. Ammachi glared at her, and, as if to deflect her look, Her Fatness held up her arm with the ripped sleeve.

"Who did that?" Ammachi said after a moment.

Her Fatness pointed at me, and her crying got even louder.

Ammachi looked at me sternly and then beckoned me with her index finger.

"Look!" I cried and held out the sari as if in supplication. "Look at what she did!"

But Ammachi was unmoved by the sight of the sari and continued to beckon me.

As I looked at her, I could almost hear the singing of the cane as it came down through the air, and then the sharp crack, which would be followed by searing pain. The time Diggy had been caned for climbing the roof came back to me, his pleas for mercy, his shouts of agony and loud sobs.

Before I could stop myself, I cried out angrily at Ammachi, "It's not fair! Why should I be punished?"

"Come here," Ammachi said.

"No. I won't."

Ammachi came to the edge of the porch, but rather than backing away I remained where I was.

"Come here, you vamban," she said to me sharply.

"No!" I cried back. "I hate you, you old fatty."

The other cousins and even Janaki gasped at my audacity. Ammachi began to come down the steps. I stood my ground for a few moments but then my courage gave out. I turned, and, with the sari still in my hands, I fled. I ran from the back garden to the front gate and out. In the field across the way, the boys were still at their cricket game. I hurried down the road towards the sea. At the railway lines I paused briefly, went across, then scrambled over the rocks to the beach. Once there, I sat on a rock and flung the sari down next to me. "I hate them, I hate them all," I whispered to myself. "I wish I was dead."

I put my head down and felt the first tears begin to wet my knees.

After a while I was still. The sound of the waves, their regular rhythm, had a calming effect on me. I leaned back against the rock behind me, watching them come in and go out. Soon the heat of the rocks became unbearable and I stood up, removed my slippers, and went down the beach to the edge of the water.

I had never seen the sea this colour before. Our visits to the beach were usually in the early evening when the sea was a turquoise blue. Now, under the midday sun, it had become hard silver, so bright that it hurt my eyes.

The sand burned my feet, and I moved closer to the waves to cool them. I looked down the deserted beach, whose white sand almost matched the colour of the sea, and saw tall buildings shimmering in the distance like a mirage. This daytime beach seemed foreign compared with the beach of the early evening, which was always crowded with strollers and joggers and vendors. Now both the beach and the sea, once so familiar, were like an unknown country into which I had journeyed by chance.

I knew then that something had changed. But how, I didn't altogether know.

The large waves, impersonal and oblivious to my despair, threw themselves against the beach, their crests frothing and hissing. Soon I would have to turn around and go back to my grandparents' house, where Ammachi awaited me with her thinnest cane, the one that left deep impressions on the backs of our thighs, so deep that sometimes they had to be treated with gentian violet. The thought of that cane as it cut through the air, humming like a mosquito, made me wince even now, so far away from it.

I glanced at the sari lying on the rock where I had thrown it, and I knew that I would never enter the girls' world again. Never stand in front of Janaki's mirror, watching a transformation take place before my eyes. No more would I step out of that room and make my way down the porch steps to the altar, a creature beautiful and adored, the personification of all that was good and perfect in the world. The future spend-the-days were no longer to be enjoyed, no longer to be looked forward to. And then there would be the loneliness. I would be caught between the boys' and the girls' worlds, not belonging or wanted in either. I would have to think of things with which to amuse myself, find ways to endure the lunches and teas when the cousins would talk to one another about what they had done and what they planned to do for the rest of the day.

The bell of St. Fatima's Church rang out the Angelus, and its melancholy sound seemed like a summoning. It was time to return to my grandparents' house. My absence at the lunch table would be construed as another act of defiance and eventually Janaki would be sent to fetch me. Then the punishment I received would be even more severe.

With a heavy heart, I slowly went back up the beach, not caring that the sand burned the soles of my feet. I put my slippers on, picked up my sari, and climbed up the rocks. I paused and looked back at the sea one last time. Then I turned, crossed the railway lines, and began my walk up Ramanaygam Road to the future that awaited me.

Sandip Roy

Auld Lang Syne

"Do you want sugar with your tea?" asked Sunil's mother from the kitchen.

"Of course I do, Ma," answered Sunil, looking up from the newspaper. "I always take two teaspoons of sugar with my tea. Have you forgotten everything?"

"Well, who knows what eight years in America can do to you. From what I read over there everything is low-this, low-that, no sugar, no fat. Tell me, does food have any taste anymore?"

She emerged from the kitchen with a cup of tea and set it down in front of him.

"Tell me," she said, "does it feel good to be back?"

He smiled and said, "Of course it does. It feels good to see you and all my aunts and uncles and friends."

"Talking of friends, have you called Bipin yet?"

"No."

"Aren't you going to?"

"Ma, I just got here last night. I'll call him, I'll call him."

"No need to get upset. I mean eight years ago you practically spent twenty-four hours together. And his mother tells me after you went to America you hardly ever wrote."

"I never was much of a letter writer."

"Still — at least you could have written something when I told you that he had a son."

"I meant to buy a card."

"Hmmph. Card. As if a card with your name scribbled hurriedly underneath can say anything except you are too lazy to write a letter. Anyway why don't you go to his house tonight?"

"Tonight?" he said stirring his tea.

"Why not — it will be a big surprise for him."

"Ma, let me settle down. I am going to be here for one month. There is plenty of time."

"Well actually I met his mother in the market and I said you'd go over. And she said she would not tell Bipin and it would be a great surprise. And anyway he is going away on tour on Wednesday."

Sunil put down his cup, stared at his mother and said, "So you've already planned it all for me anyway."

"Well if I didn't, you'd be meeting him for two minutes on your way to the airport."

Sunil seemed about to say something but thought better of it. Putting down the newspaper he said resignedly, "And what time have you told Bipin's mother I would be there?"

"Oh, around six. I have to go to my ladies' circle. And I thought I could drop you off on the way there. The driver will be here at five thirty. Now drink your tea before it gets cold."

Bipin's house still looked the same. It had been a dirty white eight years ago. Now it was a dirty yellow with green shutters streaked with crow droppings. The wizened old neem tree in front of the house was still there. The shops all around seemed to be crowding in on it even more. Sunil threaded past the gossiping maids and loitering cows and rang the doorbell. A crow perched on a half-open shutter cocked its head and inspected him solemnly. There was no answer. He pressed it again. Hard. He heard shuffling feet and an old grumbling voice.

"Oof oh. Coming, coming, I'm not deaf. Can't wait a second. What is it now? Ringing the bell like the world is on fire."

The door opened an inch and a wizened old face peered out.

"What is it? Whom do you want?" it demanded.

"Oh Mangala-di — how are you?" answered Sunil.

Mangala adjusted her thick, almost opaque glasses and peered at Sunil. Then her jaw dropped.

"Oh my goodness. If it is not little Sunil. After all these years. I thought this old woman would never see you again. Bouma, look who is here. Oh, that I lived to see this day." With that she started sniffling.

By the time Bipin's mother emerged Mangala was bawling. Sunil knew that soon after he left, Bipin's father had suddenly died of a heart attack. Even so, seeing his friend's mother in a widow's plain white sari made him start. Like his own mother, her hair was more silver than black and she seemed to have shrunk over the years. She smiled at him, wiping her hands on her sari.

"If it is not Mr. America-returned," said Bipin's mother. "Do you still remember us poor people?"

"Oh, what are you saying Auntie?" said Sunil, embarrassedly reaching to touch her feet. "How could I forget you. You were like my family to me."

"Let it be, let it be," said Bipin's mother, stopping him from touching her feet. "You are just back from America. No more of these old-fashioned customs."

"How tall he has grown," sniffled Mangala wiping her eyes. "Like a tree."

"Mangala-di," protested Sunil, "I was twenty-two years old when I left. I don't think I grew any taller."

"No, you can't fool your old Mangala-di. Then you were a boy. Now you are a man."

"So where is the wedding invitation?" said Bipin's mother.

"Wedding invitation?"

"Oh my goodness, don't you think it's about time? What are you waiting for — till my last few teeth fall out?"

Sunil smiled sheepishly and said, "Where is Bipin?"

"He just got back from the office and is changing. Come and sit down in the living room. Mangala, go tell Bipin to come down. But don't tell him who is here. And ask him to bring Abhisek too."

How well he remembered that living room. Time seemed to have stopped there. The old cuckoo clock that Bipin's father had brought back from a trip to Europe was still there. And the sofas still had the hideous green vinyl-like covering. In the corner stood the dark wooden display case jammed with Bipin's trophies and medals and little costume dolls all knocking each other over. The dolls were looking a little grubby these days, and Sunil was sure they were connected to each other by long strands of cobweb. The only thing new was a big portrait of Bipin's father looking very stern and professorial on the wall next to the cuckoo clock. Noticing him glance at it, Bipin's mother said, "It was so sudden. He had just come back from college. I was in the kitchen getting dinner ready. He said, 'I am not feeling so well. I think I'll go and lie down for a bit.' And next thing I knew Mangala was screaming, 'Bouma, Dadababu has fallen down.'" She sighed, glanced at Sunil, and then said, "Massive heart attack," with the air of a judge handing down a sentence. "Two days in intensive care but it was no use." She flung open a window and repeated, "Massive heart attack," with an air of grim satisfaction. Turning to Bipin, she said, "We had the best cardiac specialist, Dr. Biren Chandra. People even come from America to see him."

Now a little boy came hurtling into the room, took one look at Sunil and promptly ran behind the old lady. "Who is that, grandma?" he asked suspiciously.

"It's an uncle," she answered. "An uncle from far away. Where is your father?"

"Here," answered Bipin, walking into the room. Sunil turned around. Bipin's mouth fell open.

"You?" he said incredulously.

"Me," smiled Sunil.

Bipin was showing his years — mostly around the middle. His hair had started to recede and he looked astonishingly like his father. In those days he used to affect a beard (he called it his leftist look). But now he just had a very corporate trimmed moustache. He somehow seemed shorter. Perhaps he was just stouter. Sunil wondered what he looked like to Bipin after all these years. He stepped forward wondering if he should hug him. They paused awkwardly and then Bipin shook his hand.

"My God — when did you get to India? I did not even know you were coming."

"Who is this uncle, baba?" asked the little boy, inching out from behind his grandmother. "Grandmother says he is from far away."

"This is your uncle Sunil from America," answered his father. "We know each other from when I was hardly bigger than you."

"My friend Mintu says Mickey Mouse lives in America. And Rambo. Is that true?"

"That's right," answered Sunil. "And see what I got you from America." He held out a packet of Mickey Mouse colouring pens. The boy stepped forward. "Oh no — first you have to tell me your name."

"Abhisek Chatterjee," answered the boy.

"And how old are you, Mr. Abhisek Chatterjee?"

"I am six years old," intoned the boy, holding up six fingers as additional proof.

"And which school do you go to, Mr. Abhisek Chatterjee?"

"St. John's Collegiate School."

"Like father like son," said Sunil, looking at Bipin.

"Oh, he was lucky he got in. You can't imagine what it is like to get a boy into school these days. I had to take three days off work. They interviewed me and Mala. It was worse than getting a job."

"Are any of the old teachers still there?"

"A few — that Math teacher who joined right when we were about to leave and Miss Gomes who taught 3B. And Father Rozario died last year you know."

"Yes, I think my mother wrote me."

"Anyway, sit, sit," said Bipin, "and tell me how is America. Where are you now? Boston?"

"No, I moved to California two years ago."

"San Francisco or Los Angeles?"

"Well, about forty miles from San Francisco."

"Hmmm," said Bipin. "And how is the job?"

Sunil smiled. "It's all right. Busy. And yours?"

"Getting by. Getting by."

"Bipin got a promotion last month," interjected his mother. "He is now an assistant manager."

"Oh Ma," said Bipin flushing. "Sunil earns millions of dollars. Don't bore him with all this assistant manager nonsense."

Sunil smiled and said, "Hardly millions. And remember, if I earn in dollars I must spend in dollars too. So how are our friends — Madhu and Subir and . . ."

"I've kind of lost touch with most people," said Bipin. "Work keeps me so busy and I have to constantly go on tour. And when I am at home there's Abhisek's homework. You can't believe the amount of homework they give six-year-olds these days."

"I see," said Sunil. He suddenly didn't know what to say anymore. He didn't know anything about being a marketing executive in a pharmaceutical company and even less about homework for six-year-olds.

Bipin must have sensed what he was thinking, for he suddenly said, "You never wrote after the first few times."

"There wasn't much to write about. Everything was so different, so removed from what I'd known, it was very difficult to write about it. And then you got married and everything, and you know, our lives just didn't have much in common anymore. But my mother always kept me up to date with your news."

"How is she?"

"She is fine. She wants to invite you all over for dinner."

"Oh, I am in trouble," said Bipin. "She's going to say, 'Yes, now that Sunil's here you make an appearance. All these years. I could have been dead for all you cared.' But I swear man, I've meant to go, but I just don't have the time. So how long are you here for?"

"A month."

"Good, good. You must come over for dinner too. Mala is a wonderful cook. Abhisek, can you go and see if your mother is finished with the phone? Tell her to come down."

"I don't want to go," pouted Abhisek, who was trying out his new pens. "I want to sit here with Mickey Mouse Uncle."

"Mickey Mouse Uncle won't go anywhere," said Bipin, smiling. "Now hurry up and call your mother."

The boy ran off, hollering down the corridor.

"Wonderful things — children," said Bipin.

Sunil smiled. "You used to say for companionship you can get a puppy. Much more fun and much less headache."

"I used to say a lot of stupid things," said Bipin.

"When did you stop?"

"When I grew up," said Bipin, looking away. "But tell me, are you going to live in America for good?"

"Oh no, no," said his mother, "how can you say that? Who will look after your mother? No, no, you must come back and marry a nice girl. You have stayed there long enough. Enough of dollars and cars. Now you must come home. None of us is getting any younger. We need our sons near us."

"I don't know," said Sunil uncomfortably. "I haven't made up my mind."

"So who is this Mickey Mouse uncle?" said a young woman as she was dragged into the room by Abhisek. Sunil stood up, his hands folded in greeting. She was probably in her late twenties, dressed in a plain cotton sari, her hair loosely knotted in a bun.

"My wife Mala," said Bipin. "This is Sunil, my old friend."

Mala folded her hands in greeting and said, "The notorious Sunil from America?"

"Notorious?"

"Well, ever since you did not come for our wedding at least. Your friend here was distraught. It was like you were missing your own wedding."

"Oh well, I'd just changed jobs, no leave, you know."

"Anyway, do sit down. Let me get you some tea and sweets."

"Oh, don't bother with sweets."

"No, no, no," exclaimed Bipin's mother. "Coming here after all these years — you must sweeten your mouth. I will not hear otherwise. Mala see what we have, otherwise send Ramu to the store. See if they have those lemon sandesh — Sunil used to love those." Mala left the room ignoring Sunil's protestations.

"Oh," said Bipin, "how formal you have become. You never said no to sweets before. Or are you on some diet? I hear everyone in America is on a diet. Actually, you look quite fit."

"Well you have to take care of yourself, you know," Sunil replied. "We aren't getting any younger."

His mother laughed and said, "He has to keep trim because he is not married yet. Once you get married and taste your wife's cooking, all that exercise business ends. Look at Bipin here — used to do all that yoga and morning walks when you knew him. Now the only exercise he gets is climbing up the stairs and maybe a walk in the park at night."

"Really? What park?" asked Sunil.

"Oh just . . ." Bipin suddenly turned to his son and said, "Abhisek, go see if your mother is done with the tea. So tell me Sunil, you must have a car. What kind did you buy?"

Sunil laughed and said, "Unfortunately it's not a convertible. Remember we would always talk about buying convertibles in America? So is Maruti going to start a Maruti convertible here?"

Bipin said, "I don't think so. It's not really practical here. Just look at me. How can I get Ma and Mala and Abhisek and me into one convertible? Not to mention the driver when he is on duty. All that stuff only suits America. Here we need our old spacious Ambassadors — good old family cars. What kind do you have anyway?"

"It's just a Honda," said Sunil. "A hatchback. So when did the convertible lose its allure? I thought that was your big dream. Bipin, you've changed."

A shadow seemed to pass over Bipin's face. He fiddled with the copy of *India Today* on the table beside him. Then he turned around and said, "Well it's been a long time, Sunil. I don't know about you, but nothing stood still."

"Bipin just bought a Maruti," said his mother. "Red one. It was just getting too difficult with the old Ambassador. Was being repaired more than it was being used. And now even Mala is learning to drive. Of course we don't have such fancy cars like in America, but for me a Maruti is enough. Anyway, what American car would last on Calcutta roads — have you seen how bad they are getting?"

"Terrible," said Sunil. "The potholes look ten times bigger."

"They probably do to your American eyes. It's a poor country, you know. We can't afford to keep our roads shipshape," said Bipin.

"So is it a new Maruti?" said Sunil, changing track.

"New? Are you crazy? How can we afford new?"

"Well, it's only two years old," protested his mother.

"Very nice," said Sunil.

Bipin smiled, embarrassed, and said, "Oh, it's not much."

Mala came back inside bearing a tray with a teapot and four cups. They were part of a matching set — white with a pattern of pink peonies. Sunil had never seen peonies till he went to America. He had actually never been one to notice much about gardens anyway. Now he had a little kitchen garden. He was growing herbs there like basil and cilantro. On summer afternoons, he liked to sit around in his kitchen garden with friends. The smell of freshly cut grass, the sting of fresh lemonade and Russell making martinis with a flourish. It all seemed so far away. He wondered if all that really existed.

Mala placed a cup in front of him and said, "I didn't know how much sugar you wanted."

"Oh, two teaspoons."

"My goodness Mala," said Bipin, "where did that tea set come from? When I ask for tea I just get that old chipped cup. Look Sunil, what royal treatment you get for going to America."

"Oh well, if you went to my house you'd see none of my cups matched." He lied — he had a perfectly matching set of beautiful black ceramic cups with an octagonal teapot. But he felt obliged to lie.

"Well, if you got yourself a wife all that would get fixed. She would match your cups and saucers for you," said Bipin's mother relentlessly.

"Here," said Mala, giving Bipin his cup, "drink out of a matching cup too and quit complaining. Isn't it enough that you get tea when you come home from work without having the cup matching the teapot?

"Have some biscuits," she said holding a little plate with a matching peony pattern in front of Sunil. "I'm afraid we only had Horlicks biscuits. If you'd only let us know a little in advance. But Ramu has gone to get some sweets."

"Really," protested Sunil, "you shouldn't fuss so much over me."

"So," said Mala, sitting down, "tell us about America."

"Oh, no," replied Sunil, "what's your news? I have so much catching up to do."

"But tell me," said Mala, "doesn't it get lonely there — no wife, no children, no family? I can't imagine how you can live so far away all alone."

"Well," he replied, "one gets used to it. I have a lot of friends. Time just flies especially on the weekends. There's always something to do, a friend to visit or something. But it was lonely at first when I didn't know anyone. I would wish you were there, Bipin."

Bipin smiled but did not say anything.

"So are there many Bengali families where you are?" said Mala.

"There are several, but I have to admit I haven't been very good at keeping in contact with many of them. Or with the Indian community in general."

"Oh, but why?" asked Mala incredulously.

"Umm, I don't know," he said lamely. "Just no time I guess."

"Our classmate Paritosh is somewhere near San Francisco too," said Bipin.

"Yes, we talked once on the phone." He suddenly felt guilty that he had not kept in better contact with Paritosh, that he hadn't gone to the last Durga Puja celebration even though Mrs. Majumdar from the Bengali Cultural Association had personally called him.

Trying to change the subject from his social life, Sunil said, "Speaking of friends, I met Abhijit's brother once. He said Abhijit had died in an accident. I was thinking of visiting his mother."

As soon as he said it he knew something was wrong. Bipin, who had been stirring his tea, froze, his fingers still gripping the spoon.

"Accident?" he said dully, his voice so low it was almost a whisper.

"That's what his brother said," replied Sunil. "Something about falling off the roof."

Bipin just continued to stare at him.

"Abhijit committed suicide," said his mother quietly. "Of course his family had to say it was an accident. But everyone knows the truth. It was terrible. That poor young wife. They had been married less than a month. Thank God girls these days get educated. I hear she is teaching at some girls' school. But what a tragedy. His mother almost went mad. Bipin here did a lot for them. He was distraught too. Only natural. After all, you had all gone to college together. People said he had a love affair. I tell you these are modern times. He could have just told his mother and married her. I mean how bad could it be — maybe she was older than him or a different religion or something like that. Eventually his family would have adjusted. But to punish everyone like that." She shook her head.

"Oh," said Sunil. "I had no idea."

"You used to know him quite well — didn't you work with him on that college magazine of yours?" said Bipin's mother. "Did he have some secret romance? Was he depressed?"

"Ma," said Bipin, "let it be. It's all over now. Why dredge it all up?"

"No," said Sunil, slowly looking at her. "He never seemed depressed when we knew him. No more than any of the rest of us — worrying about college and exams and our futures. And whether we would make it as writers and change the world. Of course none of us write anymore. At least I don't."

Then turning to Bipin, he said, "So do you still write poetry?"

"Poetry?" laughed Mala incredulously. "You used to write poetry? You never told me that. My, my, I wonder what other hidden talents you have."

Bipin flushed and said, "It was just a stupid childish thing."

"No, no," protested Sunil. "You used to be quite good. I still have some of the poems you wrote when we once went on that trip to Manali."

"Oh Manali," said Mala. "Isn't that the most beautiful place on earth? I went there with my parents once and I thought to myself I must come back here with my husband someday. And walk under the pine trees down to the river. And those beautiful mountains and cherry orchards. I wanted to go there for our honeymoon but your friend here said, 'No, I've been there already with Sunil. I don't want to go there again.' My goodness — I thought if this man doesn't realize the difference between going to Manali with his friend and going there with his new wife, there is no hope for him."

"So where did you go?"

"Oh, Agra," she said, "and because of all the terrorist threats they weren't letting anyone go to the Taj Mahal at night."

"I want to go to Agra," said Abhisek, who was sitting on the floor drawing with his new pens.

"Do you know what's in Agra?" said Sunil smiling.

"Yes," he said, "the Taj Mahal. I have a picture of the Taj Mahal on my lunch box. A king called Shah Jahan built it."

"My goodness," said Sunil, "you know a lot for a six-year-old. Surely they are not teaching history to six-year-olds these days. How do you know about Shah Jahan?"

"Because sometimes my Ma calls me Shah Jahan because she says I was made in Agra."

"Made in Agra?" said Sunil, perplexed, and then noticed Mala was blushing furiously and casting desperate glances at Bipin, who was looking steadfastly at his tea.

"Yes," continued the boy undeterred, "my mother said Baba and she made me in Agra and so I am her little Shah Jahan."

"Oh," said Sunil as the light dawned on him. He saw Mala glance quickly at her mother-in-law and then hastily avert her gaze.

"That's enough, Abhisek," said Bipin, trying to regain control of the situation. "Why don't you show uncle your drawing book?"

There was an awkward pause as the boy left the room.

"Very bright boy," said Sunil a little weakly.

"Precocious," said Bipin's mother sharply. "Too precocious. That's what you get for being an only child. I keep telling Mala that she should have another child. For Abhisek's sake, if nothing else. It's not healthy for a child to grow up among adults and maid servants."

"Well Ma," protested Mala, with a sudden edge to her voice, "it's not enough just to tell me. I would love to have another baby, especially a little girl. But your son here thinks one is enough. He says look at all the trouble we went through to get this one into school."

"All his life he complained about being an only child. And now look at him," said his mother, shaking her head.

Sunil felt he had inadvertently wandered into well-worn old battlefields.

"Oh Ma," said Bipin a little testily, "you have a grandson to carry on the family name and all that. What more do you want from me?"

His mother just shook her head and said, "'Ma,' he used to say, 'why don't we go and get a little brother so I can have someone to play with?'"

"So," said Bipin, turning to Sunil, "tell me about your work."

This is what it comes down to, thought Sunil. After all those years we spent growing up together, all those secrets we shared, we can find nothing safe to talk about anymore other than our jobs.

"Is it a computers job?" said Mala.

"Mala here is taking a course in using PCs" said Bipin.

"Not that she needs to work," interjected his mother hurriedly. "But it's a good thing to learn, or so I hear."

"Tell me," said Bipin, "how much does a decent PC cost over there? I've been thinking of buying one."

"I have some magazines," said Sunil. "I'll give them to you next time I see you."

Abhisek had returned with his drawing book under his arm. He clambered up onto the sofa and settled down beside Sunil. "Look," he said, opening his drawing book with a flourish. There were pictures of lions and tigers and mountains and a village scene complete with a pond and palm trees.

"Have you ever seen a village?" said Sunil.

"Yes," said the boy, "from the train."

Then he turned the page. There was a picture of a wedding — a man with a moustache and a woman in a bright red sari sitting side by side.

"Who is this?" said Sunil.

"Ma and Baba getting married."

"How would you know?" teased Sunil. "Did you go to their wedding?"

"But I've seen pictures," protested the boy.

"That's not me," said his mother. "That doesn't look like me. Am I so beautiful and is my skin so golden?"

"That's you," protested the boy. "You are beautiful."

Mala laughed and stroked his head. Sunil glanced over at her. His gaze caught Bipin's, who looked away as if embarrassed. Mala was not really beautiful but she had a certain easy grace that gave her a quiet dignity. Her hair was knotted loosely in a bun and Sunil suddenly had a vision of it unravelling around her face like the black monsoon clouds that Tagore sang about in his songs. He wondered suddenly if Bipin still sang Tagore songs. Like he used to on summer nights when they were up on the roof. Sometimes there would be a power cut and everything would be dark — the houses dark shapes cut out of a dark sky. Downstairs Mangala would have lit an oil-lamp and he remembered the dim smoky light creeping up the stairways. From where he lay, smoking a cigarette, he could see the shadows of people downstairs — elongated and distorted like grotesque puppets. How hot and still it used to be on those nights — and lying there looking up he could very well believe that the stars were indeed made of fire. Burning fiercely in the sky, scarcely bigger than the glowing end of his cigarette. From a nearby house he would hear a woman laugh — the noise crystal clear like a glass breaking. And the hum of the city — the noises all melted together in the heat — a yapping street dog, the clangour of a bicycle bell as the rider weaved through the lane between pedestrians and rickshaw-pullers. And then perhaps Bipin would start to sing, softly at first like he was singing only for himself. Then his voice would get bolder and stronger.

"*Je raatey mor duarguli bhanglo jhorey*"

"On the night that my doors were broken by the storm."

He would lie there contentedly, watching Bipin singing with his eyes closed. About storms, and rain, and unrequited love. During the day they would often laugh at Tagore's poetry. Sunil always argued that it was too sickly and sentimental. But at night he was just content to lie there and let the notes and melodies wash over him and imagine that there was really a little storm starting up in the corner with the old neem tree. A storm that would break down the doors. And maybe the woman who was laughing in the flat next door had fallen silent listening to Bipin sing. He imagined her standing quietly at the window behind the curtain with the pattern of little flowers. Perhaps in one hand she still held the oil-lamp she had been about to light. And he would fall asleep and be woken up by Bipin stubbing out his burning cigarette.

"Silly," Bipin would say, gently mussing Sunil's hair, "do you want to set the world on fire?"

"Let's go into the room," Sunil would reply, stretching.

"Penny for your thoughts," said Mala brightly.

Startled, Sunil shook his head and smiled. "We learned that in school from our English teacher," she laughed. "We thought it was such a fashionable thing to say because Miss Cole had actually been to England."

"It's just this house. It brings so many memories back," said Sunil. Then turning to Bipin, he said, "Is the old room up on the roof still there?"

Startled, Bipin replied, "Yes, where would it go?"

"I want to see it."

"There's nothing to see — just junk and stuff."

"Still."

"No, really," said Bipin with a touch of irritation. "It's all dusty and no one's opened it in ages. I don't even know if the light still works. And I'd have to look for the key."

"But I know where it is, Baba," piped up Abhisek. "It's next to Ma's powder case. I'll take this uncle up to the roof."

"Now Abhisek — you have to do your homework."

"Oh, let him go up," said Mala. "It'll only take a minute. Why are you getting so worked up?"

"I am not worked up," said Bipin. "It's just that there's nothing there."

The little room was just as Sunil remembered it. The door cracked with the streaky green paint faded by the sun. Abhisek opened the door. Sunil reached round and turned on the light. The room was full of junk as Bipin had said. There were trunks and suitcases all covered with dust. Piles of yellowing newspapers and old mattresses and excess utensils. Something scampered away behind the newspapers making Abhisek jump.

"Did you and Baba play here?" asked Abhisek.

"Yes."

"What games did you play?"

"Oh, just games."

"Important games?"

"They seemed important then," smiled Sunil, ruffling the boy's hair.

"And why did you stop playing?"

"I don't know."

"Because we grew up," said Bipin appearing at the doorway. "Your mother is calling you Abhisek."

Abhisek scampered down the stairs.

The two men stood there watching the hustle and bustle of the neighbourhood. They could hear the impatient honks of passing buses and the cries of vendors. The TV next door was blaring the news and the radio was on full blast at the corner store.

"How little seems to have changed," said Sunil.

Bipin lit a cigarette and leaned his elbows on the parapet. Suddenly he turned around, and looked Sunil full in the face. "I had no choice."

"I wasn't blaming you," Sunil said.

"After Baba died suddenly, there was never any choice for me. I couldn't leave Ma and go abroad just like that."

"I never said you could."

"You don't have to — it's there in your face. I couldn't help it Sunil. You don't know what it's like. You got away. I got a job. Then I got married. That's just the way it is. It's just something that happened."

"I understand, Bipin."

"How is it there?" said Bipin. "Are you happy? Free?"

"It's, it's different. Yes, I think I am freer. But sometimes I look at you and feel perhaps you were right. You seem so much, so much safer. Are you happy?"

Bipin looked at him for a minute. Then he looked away and replied, "I have a good job. My mother is happy. She has a grandson. And I love Abhisek."

"But are you happy?"

Bipin didn't answer at once. He blew the smoke out and then said, "I don't think much about all that anymore. I'm contented, I guess."

"Don't you ever want to get out, away from all this like we used to plan up on this roof?"

"I told you Sunil, I'm at peace. Why should I torment myself needlessly about things I might have done? I get up. I go to work. I come home. Watch TV or . . ."

"Go for a walk in the park maybe," said Sunil quietly. "Which park do you go to, Bipu?"

"You have no right," said Bipin fiercely. "You have no right. Just let me be, Sunil. Why did you come back? To flaunt your San Francisco in my face?"

"You are right," said Sunil slowly. "I have no right. I lost that a long time ago."

"There you are," said a voice behind them. Turning around they saw Mala had come upstairs. Sunil wondered if she had heard anything. Smiling brightly she turned to Sunil. "You must stay for dinner. It won't be anything fancy, since I didn't get any warning. Just fish and rice."

"Oh no, some other time," said Sunil. "I promised Ma I'd be home for dinner and I think we have some cousins coming over. You know how it is when you come back after so long."

"Oh, you could call home or something," said Mala. Then turning to Bipin she said, "Ask him to stay, why don't you? After all he is your long-lost friend."

But Bipin did not say anything.

Jhumpa Lahiri

This Blessed House

They discovered the first one in a cupboard above the stove, beside an unopened bottle of malt vinegar.

"Guess what I found." Twinkle walked into the living room, lined from end to end with taped-up packing boxes, waving the vinegar in one hand and a white porcelain effigy of Christ, roughly the same size as the vinegar bottle, in the other.

Sanjeev looked up. He was kneeling on the floor, marking, with ripped bits of a Post-it, patches on the baseboard that needed to be retouched with paint. "Throw it away."

"Which?"

"Both."

"But I can cook something with the vinegar. It's brand new."

"You've never cooked anything with vinegar."

"I'll look something up. In one of those books we got for our wedding."

Sanjeev turned back to the baseboard, to replace a Post-it scrap that had fallen to the floor. "Check the expiration. And at the very least get rid of that idiotic statue."

"But it could be worth something. Who knows?" She turned it upside down, then stroked, with her index finger, the minuscule frozen folds of its robes. "It's pretty."

"We're not Christian," Sanjeev said. Lately he had begun noticing the need to state the obvious to Twinkle. The day before he had to tell her that if she dragged her end of the bureau instead of lifting it, the parquet floor would scratch.

She shrugged. "No, we're not Christian. We're good little Hindus." She planted a kiss on top of Christ's head, then placed the statue on top of the fireplace mantel, which needed, Sanjeev observed, to be dusted.

By the end of the week the mantel had still not been dusted; it had, however, come to serve as the display shelf for a sizable collection of Christian paraphernalia. There was a 3-D postcard of Saint Francis done in four colours, which Twinkle had found taped to the back of the medicine cabinet, and a wooden cross key chain, which Sanjeev had stepped on with bare feet as he was installing extra shelving in Twinkle's study. There was a framed paint-by-number of the three wise men, against a black velvet background, tucked in the linen closet. There was also a tile trivet depicting a blond, unbearded Jesus, delivering a sermon on a mountaintop, left in one of the drawers of the built-in china cabinet in the dining room.

"Do you think the previous owners were born-agains?" asked Twinkle, making room the next day for a small plastic snow-filled dome containing a miniature Nativity scene, found behind the pipes of the kitchen sink.

Sanjeev was organizing his engineering texts from MIT in alphabetical order on a bookshelf, though it had been several years since he had needed to consult any of them. After graduating, he moved from

Boston to Connecticut, to work for a firm near Hartford, and he had recently learned that he was being considered for the position of vice president. At thirty-three he had a secretary of his own and a dozen people working under his supervision who gladly supplied him with any information he needed. Still, the presence of his college books in the room reminded him of a time in his life he recalled with fondness, when he would walk each evening across the Mass. Avenue bridge to order Mughlai chicken with spinach from his favourite Indian restaurant on the other side of the Charles, and return to his dorm to write out clean copies of his problem sets.

"Or perhaps it's an attempt to convert people," Twinkle mused.

"Clearly the scheme has succeeded in your case."

She disregarded him, shaking the little plastic dome so that the snow swirled over the manger.

He studied the items on the mantel. It puzzled him that each was in its own way so silly. Clearly they lacked a sense of sacredness. He was further puzzled that Twinkle, who normally displayed good taste, was so charmed. These objects meant something to Twinkle, but they meant nothing to him. They irritated him. "We should call the Realtor. Tell him there's all this nonsense left behind. Tell him to take it away."

"Oh, Sanj." Twinkle groaned. "Please. I would feel terrible throwing them away. Obviously they were important to the people who used to live here. It would feel, I don't know, sacrilegious or something."

"If they're so precious, then why are they hidden all over the house? Why didn't they take them with them?"

"There must be others," Twinkle said. Her eyes roamed the bare off-white walls of the room, as if there were other things concealed behind the plaster. "What else do you think we'll find?"

But as they unpacked their boxes and hung up their winter clothes and the silk paintings of elephant processions bought on their honeymoon in Jaipur, Twinkle, much to her dismay, could not find a thing. Nearly a week had passed before they discovered, one Saturday afternoon, a larger-than-life-sized watercolour poster of Christ, weeping translucent tears the size of peanut shells and sporting a crown of thorns, rolled up behind a radiator in the guest bedroom. Sanjeev had mistaken it for a window shade.

"Oh, we must, we simply must put it up. It's too spectacular." Twinkle lit a cigarette and began to smoke it with relish, waving it around Sanjeev's head as if it were a conductor's baton as Mahler's Fifth Symphony roared from the stereo downstairs.

"Now, look. I will tolerate, for now, your little biblical menagerie in the living room. But I refuse to have this," he said, flicking at one of the painted peanut-tears, "displayed in our home."

Twinkle stared at him, placidly exhaling, the smoke emerging in two thin blue streams from her nostrils. She rolled up the poster slowly, securing it with one of the elastic bands she always wore around her wrist for tying back her thick, unruly hair, streaked here and there with henna. "I'm going to put it in my study," she informed him. "That way you don't have to look at it."

"What about the housewarming? They'll want to see all the rooms. I've invited people from the office."

She rolled her eyes. Sanjeev noted that the symphony, now in its third movement, had reached a crescendo, for it pulsed with the tell-tale clashing of cymbals.

"I'll put it behind the door," she offered. "That way, when they peek in, they won't see. Happy?"

He stood watching her as she left the room, with her poster and her cigarette; a few ashes had fallen to the floor where she'd been standing. He bent down, pinched them between his fingers, and deposited them in his cupped palm. The tender fourth movement, the *adagietto*, began. During breakfast, Sanjeev had read in the liner notes that Mahler had proposed to his wife by sending her the manuscript of this portion of the score. Although there were elements of tragedy and struggle in the Fifth Symphony, he had read, it was principally music of love and happiness.

He heard the toilet flush. "By the way," Twinkle hollered, "if you want to impress people, I wouldn't play this music. It's putting me to sleep."

Sanjeev went to the bathroom to throw away the ashes. The cigarette butt still bobbed in the toilet bowl, but the tank was refilling, so he had to wait a moment before he could flush it again. In the mirror of the medicine cabinet he inspected his long eyelashes — like a girl's, Twinkle liked to tease. Though he was of average build, his cheeks had a plumpness to them; this, along with the eyelashes, detracted, he feared, from what he hoped was a distinguished profile. He was of average height as well, and had wished ever since he had stopped growing that he were just one inch taller. For this reason it irritated him when Twinkle insisted on wearing high heels, as she had done the other night when they ate dinner in Manhattan. This was the first weekend after they'd moved into the house; by then the mantel had already filled up considerably and they had bickered about it in the car on the way down. But then Twinkle had drunk four glasses of whisky in a nameless bar in Alphabet City, and forgot all about it. She dragged him to a tiny bookshop on St. Mark's Place, where she browsed for nearly an hour, and when they left she insisted that they dance a tango on the sidewalk in front of strangers.

Afterward, she tottered on his arm, rising faintly over his line of vision, in a pair of suede three-inch leopard-print pumps. In this manner they walked the endless blocks back to a parking garage on Washington Square, for Sanjeev had heard far too many stories about the terrible things that happened to cars in Manhattan. "But I do nothing all day except sit at my desk," she fretted when they were driving home, after he had mentioned that her shoes looked uncomfortable and suggested that perhaps she should not wear them. "I can't exactly wear heels when I'm typing." Though he abandoned the argument, he knew for a fact that she didn't spend all day at her desk; just that afternoon, when he got back from a run, he found her inexplicably in bed, reading. When he asked why she was in bed in the middle of the day she told him she was bored. He had wanted to say to her then, You could unpack some boxes. You could sweep the attic. You could retouch the paint on the bathroom windowsill, and after you do it you could warn me so that I don't put my watch on it. They didn't bother her, these scattered, unsettled matters. She seemed content with whatever clothes she found at the front of the closet, with whatever magazine was lying around, with whatever song was on the radio — content yet curious. And now all of her curiosity centred around discovering the next treasure.

A few days later when Sanjeev returned from the office, he found Twinkle on the telephone, smoking and talking to one of her girl-friends in California even though it was before five o'clock and the long-distance rates were at their peak. "Highly devout people," she was saying, pausing every now and then to exhale. "Each day is like a treasure hunt. I'm serious. This you won't believe. The switch plates in the bedrooms were decorated with scenes from the Bible. You know, Noah's Ark and all that. Three bedrooms, but one is my study. Sanjeev went to the hardware store right away and replaced them, can you imagine, he replaced every single one."

Now it was the friend's turn to talk. Twinkle nodded, slouched on the floor in front of the fridge, wearing black stirrup pants and a yellow chenille sweater, groping for her lighter. Sanjeev could smell something aromatic on the stove, and he picked his way carefully across the extra-long phone cord tangled on the Mexican terra-cotta tiles. He opened the lid of a pot with some sort of reddish brown sauce dripping over the sides, boiling furiously.

"It's a stew made with fish. I put the vinegar in it," she said to him, interrupting her friend, crossing her fingers. "Sorry, you were saying?" She was like that, excited and delighted by little things, crossing her fingers before any remotely unpredictable event, like tasting a new flavour of ice cream, or dropping a letter in a mailbox. It was a quality he did not understand. It made him feel stupid, as if the world contained hidden wonders he could not anticipate, or see. He looked at her face, which, it occurred to him, had not grown out of its girlhood, the eyes untroubled, the pleasing features unfirm, as if they still had to settle into some sort of permanent expression. Nicknamed after a nursery rhyme, she had yet to shed a childhood endearment. Now, in the second month of their marriage, certain things nettled him — the way she sometimes spat a little when she spoke, or left her undergarments after removing them at night at the foot of their bed rather than depositing them in the laundry hamper.

They had met only four months before. Her parents, who lived in California, and his, who still lived in Calcutta, were old friends, and across continents they had arranged the occasion at which Twinkle and Sanjeev were introduced — a sixteenth birthday party for a daughter in their circle — when Sanjeev was in Palo Alto on business. At the restaurant they were seated side by side at a round table with a revolving platter of spareribs and egg rolls and chicken wings, which, they concurred, all tasted the same. They had concurred too on their adolescent but still persistent fondness for Wodehouse novels, and their dislike for the sitar, and later Twinkle confessed that she was charmed by the way Sanjeev had dutifully refilled her teacup during their conversation.

And so the phone calls began, and grew longer, and then the visits, first he to Stanford, then she to Connecticut, after which Sanjeev would save in an ashtray left on the balcony the crushed cigarettes she had smoked during the weekend — saved them, that is, until the next time she came to visit him, and then he vacuumed the apartment, washed the sheets, even dusted the plant leaves in her honour. She was twenty-seven and recently abandoned, he had gathered, by an American who had tried and failed to be an actor; Sanjeev was lonely, with an excessively generous income for a single man, and had never been in love. At the urging of their matchmakers, they married in India, amid hundreds of well-wishers whom he barely remembered from his childhood, in incessant August rains, under a red and orange tent strung with Christmas tree lights on Mandeville Road.

"Did you sweep the attic?" he asked Twinkle later as she was folding paper napkins and wedging them by their plates. The attic was the only part of the house they had not yet given an initial cleaning.

"Not yet. I will, I promise. I hope this tastes good," she said, planting the steaming pot on top of the Jesus trivet. There was a loaf of Italian bread in a little basket, and iceberg lettuce and grated carrots tossed with bottled dressing and croutons, and glasses of red wine.

She was not terribly ambitious in the kitchen. She bought preroasted chickens from the supermarket and served them with potato salad prepared who knew when, sold in little plastic containers. Indian food, she complained, was a bother; she detested chopping garlic, and peeling ginger, and could not operate a blender, and so it was Sanjeev who, on weekends, seasoned mustard oil with cinnamon sticks and cloves in order to produce a proper curry.

He had to admit, though, that whatever it was that she had cooked today, it was unusually tasty, attractive even, with bright white cubes of fish, and flecks of parsley, and fresh tomatoes gleaming in the dark brown-red broth.

"How did you make it?"

"I made it up."

"What did you do?"

"I just put some things into the pot and added the malt vinegar at the end."

"How much vinegar?"

She shrugged, ripping off some bread and plunging it into her bowl.

"What do you mean you don't know? You should write it down. What if you need to make it again, for a party or something?"

"I'll remember," she said. She covered the bread basket with a dishtowel that had, he suddenly noticed, the Ten Commandments printed on it. She flashed him a smile, giving his knee a little squeeze under the table. "Face it. This house is blessed."

The housewarming party was scheduled for the last Saturday in October, and they had invited about thirty people. All were Sanjeev's acquaintances, people from the office, and a number of Indian couples in the Connecticut area, many of whom he barely knew, but who had regularly invited him, in his bachelor days, to supper on Saturdays. He often wondered why they included him in their circle. He had little in common with any of them, but he always attended their gatherings, to eat spiced chickpeas and shrimp cutlets, and gossip and discuss politics, for he seldom had other plans. So far, no one had met Twinkle; back when they were still dating, Sanjeev didn't want to waste their brief weekends together with people he associated with being alone. Other than Sanjeev and an ex-boyfriend who she believed worked in a pottery studio in Brookfield, she knew no one in the state of Connecticut. She was completing her master's thesis at Stanford, a study of an Irish poet whom Sanjeev had never heard of.

Sanjeev had found the house on his own before leaving for the wedding, for a good price, in a neighbourhood with a fine school system. He was impressed by the elegant curved staircase with its wrought-iron banister, and the dark wooden wainscoting, and the solarium overlooking rhododendron bushes, and the solid brass 22, which also happened to be the date of his birth, nailed impressively to the vaguely Tudor facade. There were two working fireplaces, a two-car garage, and an attic suitable for converting into extra bedrooms if, the Realtor mentioned, the need should arise. By then Sanjeev had already made up his mind, was determined that he and Twinkle should live there together, forever, and so he had not bothered to notice the switch plates covered with biblical stickers, or the transparent decal of the Virgin on the half shell, as Twinkle liked to call it, adhered to the window in the master bedroom. When, after moving in, he tried to scrape it off, he scratched the glass.

The weekend before the party they were raking the lawn when he heard Twinkle shriek. He ran to her, clutching his rake, worried that she had discovered a dead animal, or a snake. A brisk October breeze stung the tops of his ears as his sneakers crunched over brown and yellow leaves. When he reached her, she had collapsed on the grass, dissolved in nearly silent laughter. Behind an overgrown forsythia bush was a plaster Virgin Mary as tall as their waists, with a blue painted hood draped over her head in the manner of an Indian bride. Twinkle grabbed the hem of her T-shirt and began wiping away the dirt staining the statue's brow.

"I suppose you want to put her by the foot of our bed," Sanjeev said.

She looked at him, astonished. Her belly was exposed, and he saw that there were goose bumps around her navel. "What do you think? Of course we can't put this in our bedroom."

"We can't?"

"No, silly Sanj. This is meant for outside. For the lawn."

"Oh God, no. Twinkle, no."

"But we must. It would be bad luck not to."

"All the neighbours will see. They'll think we're insane."

"Why, for having a statue of the Virgin Mary on our lawn? Every other person in this neighbourhood has a statue of Mary on the lawn. We'll fit right in."

"We're not Christian."

"So you keep reminding me." She spat onto the tip of her finger and started to rub intently at a particularly stubborn stain on Mary's chin. "Do you think this is dirt, or some kind of fungus?"

He was getting nowhere with her, with this woman whom he had known for only four months and whom he had married, this woman with whom he now shared his life. He thought with a flicker of regret of the snapshots his mother used to send him from Calcutta, of prospective brides who could sing and sew and season lentils without consulting a cookbook. Sanjeev had considered these women, had even ranked them in order of preference, but then he had met Twinkle. "Twinkle, I can't have the people I work with see this statue on my lawn."

"They can't fire you for being a believer. It would be discrimination."

"That's not the point."

"Why does it matter to you so much what other people think?"

"Twinkle, please." He was tired. He let his weight rest against his rake as she began dragging the statue toward an oval bed of myrtle, beside the lamppost that flanked the brick pathway. "Look, Sanj. She's so lovely."

He returned to his pile of leaves and began to deposit them by handfuls into a plastic garbage bag. Over his head the blue sky was cloudless. One tree on the lawn was still full of leaves, red and orange, like the tent in which he had married Twinkle.

He did not know if he loved her. He said he did when she had first asked him, one afternoon in Palo Alto as they sat side by side in a darkened, nearly empty movie theatre. Before the film, one of her favourites, something in German that he found extremely depressing, she had pressed the tip of her nose to his so that he could feel the flutter of her mascara-coated eyelashes. That afternoon he had replied, yes, he loved her, and she was delighted, and fed him a piece of popcorn, letting her finger linger an instant between his lips, as if it were his reward for coming up with the right answer.

Though she did not say it herself, he assumed then that she loved him too, but now he was no longer sure. In truth, Sanjeev did not know what love was, only what he thought it was not. It was not, he had decided, returning to an empty carpeted condominium each night, and using only the top fork in his cutlery drawer, and turning away politely at those weekend dinner parties when the other men eventually put their arms around the waists of their wives and girl-friends, leaning over every now and again to kiss their shoulders or necks. It was not sending away for classical music CDs by mail, working his way methodically through the major composers that the catalogue recommended, and always sending his payments in on time. In the months before meeting Twinkle, Sanjeev had begun to realize this. "You have enough money in the bank to raise three families," his mother reminded him when they spoke at the start of each month on the phone. "You need a wife to look after and love." Now he had one, a pretty one, from a suitably high caste, who would soon have a master's degree. What was there not to love?

That evening Sanjeev poured himself a gin and tonic, drank it and most of another during one segment of the news, and then approached Twinkle, who was taking a bubble bath, for she announced that her limbs ached from raking the lawn, something she had never done before. He didn't knock. She had applied a bright blue mask to her face, was smoking and sipping some bourbon with ice and leaf-ing through a fat paperback book whose pages had buckled and turned grey from the water. He glanced at the cover; the only thing written on it was the word "Sonnets" in dark red letters. He took a breath, and then he informed her very calmly that after finishing his drink he was going to put on his shoes and go outside and remove the Virgin from the front lawn.

"Where are you going to put it?" she asked him dreamily, her eyes closed. One of her legs emerged, unfolding gracefully, from the layer of suds. She flexed and pointed her toes.

"For now I am going to put it in the garage. Then tomorrow morning on my way to work I am going to take it to the dump."

"Don't you dare." She stood up, letting the book fall into the water, bubbles dripping down her thighs. "I hate you," she informed him, her eyes narrowing at the word "hate." She reached for her bathrobe, tied it tightly about her waist, and padded down the wind-ing staircase, leaving sloppy wet footprints along the parquet floor. When she reached the foyer, Sanjeev said, "Are you planning on leav-ing the house that way?" He felt a throbbing in his temples, and his voice revealed an unfamiliar snarl when he spoke.

"Who cares? Who cares what way I leave this house?"

"Where are you planning on going at this hour?"

"You can't throw away that statue. I won't let you." Her mask, now dry, had assumed an ashen quality, and water from her hair dripped onto the caked contours of her face.

"Yes I can. I will."

"No," Twinkle said, her voice suddenly small. "This is our house. We own it together. The statue is a part of our property." She had begun to shiver. A small pool of bathwater had collected around her ankles. He went to shut a window, fearing that she would catch cold. Then he noticed that some of the water dripping down her hard blue face was tears.

"Oh God, Twinkle, please, I didn't mean it." He had never seen her cry before, had never seen such sadness in her eyes. She didn't turn away or try to stop the tears; instead she looked strangely at peace. For a moment she closed her lids, pale and unprotected compared to the blue that caked the rest of her face. Sanjeev felt ill, as if he had eaten either too much or too little.

She went to him, placing her damp towelled arms about his neck, sobbing into his chest, soaking his shirt. The mask flaked onto his shoulders.

In the end they settled on a compromise: the statue would be placed in a recess at the side of the house, so that it wasn't obvious to passers-by, but was still clearly visible to all who came.

The menu for the party was fairly simple: there would be a case of champagne, and samosas from an Indian restaurant in Hartford, and big trays of rice with chicken and almonds and orange peels, which Sanjeev had spent the greater part of the morning and afternoon preparing. He had never entertained on such a large scale before and, worried that there would not be enough to drink, ran out at one point to buy another case of champagne just in case. For this reason he burned one of the rice trays and had to start it over again. Twinkle swept the floors and volunteered to pick up the samosas; she had an appointment for a manicure and a pedicure in that direction, anyway. Sanjeev had planned to ask if she would consider clearing the menagerie off the mantel, if only for the party, but she left while he was in the shower. She was gone for a good three hours, and so it was Sanjeev who did the rest of the cleaning. By five-thirty the entire house sparkled, with scented candles that Twinkle had picked up in Hartford illuminating the items on the mantel, and slender stalks of burning incense planted into the soil of potted plants. Each time he passed the mantel he winced, dreading the raised eyebrows of his guests as they viewed the flickering ceramic saints, the salt and pepper shakers designed to resemble Mary and Joseph. Still, they would be impressed, he hoped, by the lovely bay windows, the shining parquet floors, the impressive winding staircase, the wooden wainscoting, as they sipped champagne and dipped samosas in chutney.

Douglas, one of the new consultants at the firm, and his girlfriend Nora were the first to arrive. Both were tall and blond, wearing matching wire-rimmed glasses and long black overcoats. Nora wore a black hat full of sharp thin feathers that corresponded to the sharp thin angles of her face. Her left hand was joined with Douglas's. In her right hand was a bottle of cognac with a red ribbon wrapped around its neck, which she gave to Twinkle.

"Great lawn, Sanjeev," Douglas remarked. "We've got to get that rake out ourselves, sweetie. And this must be . . ."

"My wife. Tanima."

"Call me Twinkle."

"What an unusual name," Nora remarked.

Twinkle shrugged. "Not really. There's an actress in Bombay named Dimple Kapadia. She even has a sister named Simple."

Douglas and Nora raised their eyebrows simultaneously, nodding slowly, as if to let the absurdity of the names settle in. "Pleased to meet you, Twinkle."

"Help yourself to champagne. There's gallons."

"I hope you don't mind my asking," Douglas said, "but I noticed the statue outside, and are you guys Christian? I thought you were Indian."

"There are Christians in India," Sanjeev replied, "but we're not."

"I love your outfit," Nora told Twinkle.

"And I adore your hat. Would you like the grand tour?"

The bell rang again, and again and again. Within minutes, it seemed, the house had filled with bodies and conversations and unfamiliar fragrances. The women wore heels and sheer stockings, and short black dresses made of crepe and chiffon. They handed their wraps and coats to Sanjeev, who draped them carefully on hangers in the spacious coat closet, though Twinkle told people to throw their things on the ottomans in the solarium. Some of the Indian women wore their finest saris, made with gold filigree that draped in elegant pleats over their shoulders. The men wore jackets and ties and citrus-scented aftershaves. As people filtered from one room to the next, presents piled onto the long cherry-wood table that ran from one end of the downstairs hall to the other.

It bewildered Sanjeev that it was for him, and his house, and his wife, that they had all gone to so much care. The only other time in his life that something similar had happened was his wedding day, but somehow this was different, for these were not his family but people who knew him only casually, and in a sense owed him nothing. Everyone congratulated him. Lester, another coworker, predicted that Sanjeev would be promoted to vice president in two months maximum. People devoured the samosas, and dutifully admired the freshly painted ceilings and walls, the hanging plants, the bay windows, the silk paintings from Jaipur. But most of all they admired Twinkle, and her brocaded *salwar-kameez*, which was the shade of a persimmon with a low scoop in the back, and the little string of white rose petals she had coiled cleverly around her head, and the pearl choker with a sapphire at its centre that adorned her throat. Over hectic jazz records, played under Twinkle's supervision, they laughed at her anecdotes and observations, forming a widening circle around her, while Sanjeev replenished the samosas that he kept warming evenly in the oven, and getting ice for people's drinks, and opening more bottles of champagne with some difficulty, and explaining for the fortieth time that he wasn't Christian. It was Twinkle who led them in separate groups up and down the winding stairs, to gaze at the back lawn, to peer down the cellar steps. "Your friends adore the poster in my study," she mentioned to him triumphantly, placing her hand on the small of his back as they, at one point, brushed past each other.

Sanjeev went to the kitchen, which was empty, and ate a piece of chicken out of the tray on the counter with his fingers because he thought no one was looking. He ate a second piece, then washed it down with a gulp of gin straight from the bottle.

"Great house. Great rice." Sunil, an anaesthesiologist, walked in, spooning food from his paper plate into his mouth. "Do you have more champagne?"

"Your wife's wow," added Prabal, following behind. He was an unmarried professor of physics at Yale. For a moment Sanjeev stared at him blankly then blushed; once at a dinner party Prabal had pronounced that Sophia Loren was wow, as was Audrey Hepburn. "Does she have a sister?"

Sunil picked a raisin out of the rice tray. "Is her last name Little Star?"

The two men laughed and started eating more rice from the tray, plowing through it with their plastic spoons. Sanjeev went down to the cellar for more liquor. For a few minutes he paused on the steps, in the damp, cool silence, hugging the second crate of champagne to his chest as the party drifted above the rafters. Then he set the reinforcements on the dining table.

"Yes, everything, we found them all in the house, in the most unusual places," he heard Twinkle saying in the living room. "In fact we keep finding them."

"No!"

"Yes! Every day is like a treasure hunt. It's too good. God only knows what else we'll find, no pun intended."

That was what started it. As if by some unspoken pact, the whole party joined forces and began combing through each of the rooms, opening closets on their own, peering under chairs and cushions, feeling behind curtains, removing books from bookcases. Groups scampered, giggling and swaying, up and down the winding staircase.

"We've never explored the attic," Twinkle announced suddenly, and so everybody followed.

"How do we get up there?"

"There's a ladder in the hallway, somewhere in the ceiling."

Wearily Sanjeev followed at the back of the crowd, to point out the location of the ladder, but Twinkle had already found it on her own. "Eureka!" she hollered.

Douglas pulled the chain that released the steps. His face was flushed and he was wearing Nora's feather hat on his head. One by one the guests disappeared, men helping women as they placed their strappy high heels on the narrow slats of the ladder, the Indian women wrapping the free ends of their expensive saris into their waistbands. The men followed behind, all quickly disappearing, until Sanjeev alone remained at the top of the winding staircase. Footsteps thundered over his head. He had no desire to join them. He wondered if the ceiling would collapse, imagined, for a split second, the sight of all the tumbling drunk perfumed bodies crashing, tangled, around him. He heard a shriek, and then rising, spreading waves of laughter in discordant tones. Something fell, something else shattered. He could hear them babbling about a trunk. They seemed to be struggling to get it open, banging feverishly on its surface.

He thought perhaps Twinkle would call for his assistance, but he was not summoned. He looked about the hallway and to the landing below, at the champagne glasses and half-eaten samosas and napkins smeared with lipstick abandoned in every corner, on every available surface. Then he noticed that Twinkle, in her haste, had discarded her shoes altogether, for they lay by the foot of the ladder, black patent-leather mules with heels like golf tees, open toes, and slightly soiled silk labels on the instep where her soles had rested. He placed them in the doorway of the master bedroom so that no one would trip when they descended.

He heard something creaking open slowly. The strident voices had subsided to an even murmur. It occurred to Sanjeev that he had the house all to himself. The music had ended and he could hear, if he concentrated, the hum of the refrigerator, and the rustle of the last leaves on the trees outside, and the tapping of their branches against the windowpanes. With one flick of his hand he could snap the ladder back on its spring into the ceiling, and they would have no way of getting down unless he were to pull the chain and let them. He thought of all the things he could do, undisturbed. He could sweep Twinkle's menagerie into a garbage bag and get in the car and drive it all to the dump, and tear down the poster of weeping Jesus, and take a hammer to the Virgin Mary while he was at it. Then he would return to the empty house; he could easily clear up the cups and plates in an hour's time, and pour himself a gin and tonic, and eat a plate of warmed rice and listen to his new Bach CD while reading the liner notes so as to understand it properly. He nudged the ladder slightly, but it was sturdily planted against the floor. Budging it would require some effort.

"My God, I need a cigarette," Twinkle exclaimed from above.

Sanjeev felt knots forming at the back of his neck. He felt dizzy. He needed to lie down. He walked toward the bedroom, but stopped short when he saw Twinkle's shoes facing him in the doorway. He thought of her slipping them on her feet. But instead of feeling irritated, as he had ever since they'd moved into the house together, he felt a pang of anticipation at the thought of her rushing unsteadily down the winding staircase in them, scratching the floor a bit in her path. The pang intensified as he thought of her rushing to the bathroom to brighten her lipstick, and eventually rushing to get people their coats, and finally rushing to the cherry-wood table when the last guest had left, to begin opening their housewarming presents. It was the same pang he used to feel before they were married, when he would hang up the phone after one of their conversations, or when he would drive back from the airport, wondering which ascending plane in the sky was hers.

"Sanj, you won't believe this."

She emerged with her back to him, her hands over her head, the tops of her bare shoulder blades perspiring, supporting something still hidden from view.

"You got it, Twinkle?" someone asked.

"Yes, you can let go."

Now he saw that her hands were wrapped around it: a solid silver bust of Christ, the head easily three times the size of his own. It had a patrician bump on its nose, magnificent curly hair that rested atop a pronounced collarbone, and a broad forehead that reflected in miniature the walls and doors and lampshades around them. Its expression was confident, as if assured of its devotees, the unyielding lips sensuous and full. It was also sporting Nora's feather hat. As Twinkle descended, Sanjeev put his hands around her waist to balance her, and he relieved her of the bust when she had reached the ground. It weighed a good thirty pounds. The others began lowering themselves slowly, exhausted from the hunt. Some trickled downstairs in search of a fresh drink.

She took a breath, raised her eyebrows, crossed her fingers. "Would you mind terribly if we displayed it on the mantel? Just for tonight? I know you hate it."

He did hate it. He hated its immensity, and its flawless, polished surface, and its undeniable value. He hated that it was in his house, and that he owned it. Unlike the other things they'd found, this contained dignity, solemnity, beauty even. But to his surprise these qualities made him hate it all the more. Most of all he hated it because he knew that Twinkle loved it.

"I'll keep it in my study from tomorrow," Twinkle added. "I promise."

She would never put it in her study, he knew. For the rest of their days together she would keep it on the centre of the mantel, flanked on either side by the rest of the menagerie. Each time they had guests Twinkle would explain how she had found it, and they would admire her as they listened. He gazed at the crushed rose petals in her hair, at the pearl and sapphire choker at her throat, at the sparkly crimson polish on her toes. He decided these were among the things that made Prabal think she was wow. His head ached from gin and his arms ached from the weight of the statue. He said, "I put your shoes in the bedroom."

"Thanks. But my feet are killing me." Twinkle gave his elbow a little squeeze and headed for the living room.

Sanjeev pressed the massive silver face to his ribs, careful not to let the feather hat slip, and followed her.

Monica Ali

Dinner with Dr. Azad

Nazneen waved at the tattoo lady. The tattoo lady was always there when Nazneen looked out across the dead grass and broken paving stones to the block opposite. Most of the flats that closed three sides of a square had net curtains and the life behind was all shapes and shadows. But the tattoo lady had no curtains. Morning and afternoon she sat with her big thighs spilling over the sides of her chair, tipping forward to drop ash in a bowl, tipping back to slug from her can. She drank now, and tossed the can out of the window.

It was the middle of the day. Nazneen had finished the housework. Soon she would start preparing the evening meal, but for a while she would let the time pass. It was hot and the sun fell flat on the metal window frames and glared off the glass. A red and gold sari hung out of a top-floor flat in Rosemead block. A baby's bib and miniature dungarees lower down. The sign screwed to the brickwork was in stiff English capitals and the curlicues beneath were Bengali. NO DUMPING. NO PARKING. NO BALL GAMES. Two old men in white panjabi-pyjama and skullcaps walked along the path, slowly, as if they did not want to go where they were going. A thin brown dog sniffed along to the middle of the grass and defecated. The breeze on Nazneen's face was thick with the smell from the over-flowing communal bins.

Six months now since she'd been sent away to London. Every morning before she opened her eyes she thought, *if I were the wishing type, I know what I would wish.* And then she opened her eyes and saw Chanu's puffy face on the pillow next to her, his lips parted indig-nantly even as he slept. She saw the pink dressing table with the curly-sided mirror, and the monstrous black wardrobe that claimed most of the room. Was it cheating? To think, *I know what I would wish?* Was it not the same as making the wish? If she knew what the wish would be, then somewhere in her heart she had already made it.

The tattoo lady waved back at Nazneen. She scratched her arms, her shoulders, the accessible portions of her buttocks. She yawned and lit a cigarette. At least two thirds of the flesh on show was covered in ink. Nazneen had never been close enough (never closer than this, never further) to decipher the designs. Chanu said the tattoo lady was Hell's Angel, which upset Nazneen. She thought the tattoos might be flowers, or birds. They were ugly and they made the tattoo lady more ugly than was necessary, but the tattoo lady clearly did not care. Every time Nazneen saw her she wore the same look of boredom and detachment. Such a state was sought by the sadhus who walked in rags through the Muslim villages, indifferent to the kindness of strangers, the unkind sun.

Nazneen thought sometimes of going downstairs, crossing the yard and climbing the Rosemead stairwell to the fourth floor. She might have to knock on a few doors before the tattoo lady answered. She would take something, an offering of samosas or bhajis, and the tattoo lady would smile and Nazneen would smile and perhaps they would sit together by the window and let the time pass more easily.

She thought of it but she would not go. Strangers would answer if she knocked on the wrong door. The tattoo lady might be angry at an unwanted interruption. It was clear she did not like to leave her chair. And even if she wasn't angry, what would be the point? Nazneen could say two things in English: sorry and thank you. She could spend another day alone. It was only another day.

She should be getting on with the evening meal. The lamb curry was prepared. She had made it last night with tomatoes and new potatoes. There was chicken saved in the freezer from the last time Dr. Azad had been invited but had cancelled at the last minute. There was still the dhal to make, and the vegetable dishes, the spices to grind, the rice to wash, and the sauce to prepare for the fish that Chanu would bring this evening. She would rinse the glasses and rub them with newspaper to make them shine. The tablecloth had some spots to be scrubbed out. What if it went wrong? The rice might stick. She might over-salt the dhal. Chanu might forget the fish.

It was only dinner. One dinner. One guest.

She left the window open. Standing on the sofa to reach, she picked up the Holy Qur'an from the high shelf that Chanu, under duress, had specially built. She made her intention as fervently as possible, seeking refuge from Satan with fists clenched and fingernails digging into her palms. Then she selected a page at random and began to read.

To God belongs all that the heavens and the earth contain. We exhort you, as We have exhorted those to whom the Book was given before you, to fear God. If you deny Him, know that to God belongs all that the heavens and earth contain. God is self-sufficient and worthy of praise.

The words calmed her stomach and she was pleased. Even Dr. Azad was nothing as to God. To God belongs all that the heavens and the earth contain. She said it over a few times, aloud. She was composed. Nothing could bother her. Only God, if he chose to. Chanu might flap about and squawk because Dr. Azad was coming for dinner. Let him flap. To God belongs all that the heavens and the earth contain. How would it sound in Arabic? More lovely even than in Bengali she supposed, for those were the actual Words of God.

She closed the book and looked around the room to check it was tidy enough. Chanu's books and papers were stacked beneath the table. They would have to be moved or Dr. Azad would not be able to get his feet in. The rugs which she had held out of the window earlier and beaten with a wooden spoon needed to be put down again. There were three rugs: red and orange, green and purple, brown and blue. The carpet was yellow with a green leaf design. One hundred per cent nylon and, Chanu said, very hard-wearing. The sofa and chairs were the colour of dried cow dung, which was a practical colour. They had little sheaths of plastic on the headrests to protect them from Chanu's hair oil. There was a lot of furniture, more than Nazneen had seen in one room before. Even if you took all the furniture in the compound back home, from every auntie and uncle's ghar, it would not match up to this one room. There was a low table with a glass centre and orange plastic legs, three little wooden tables that stacked together, the big table they used for the evening meal, a bookcase, a corner cupboard, a rack for newspapers, a trolley filled with files and folders, the sofa and armchairs, two footstools, six dining chairs and a showcase. The walls were papered in yellow with brown squares and circles lining neatly up and down. Nobody in Gouripur had anything like it. It made her proud. Her father was the second wealthiest man in the village and he never had anything like it. He had made a good marriage for her. There were plates on the wall attached by hooks and wires, which were not for eating from but only for display. Some were rimmed in gold paint. "Gold leaf," Chanu called it. His certificates were framed and mixed with the plates. She had everything here. All these beautiful things.

She put the Qur'an back in its place. Next to it lay the most Holy Book wrapped inside a cloth covering: the Qur'an in Arabic. She touched her fingers to the cloth.

Nazneen stared at the glass showcase stuffed with pottery animals, china figures and plastic fruits. Each one had to be dusted. She wondered how the dust got in and where it came from. All of it belonged to God. She wondered what He wanted with clay tigers, trinkets and dust.

And then, because she had let her mind drift and become uncentred again, she began to recite in her head from the Holy Qur'an one of the suras she had learned in school. She did not know what the words meant but the rhythm of them soothed her.

"She is an unspoilt girl. From the village."

She had got up one night to fetch a glass of water. It was one week since they married. She had gone to bed and he was still up, talking on the telephone as she stood outside the door.

"No," said Chanu. "I would not say so. Not beautiful, but not so ugly either. The face is broad, big forehead. Eyes are a bit too close together."

Nazneen put her hand up to her head. It was true. The forehead was large. But she had never thought of her eyes being too close.

"Not tall. Not short. Around five foot two. Hips are a bit narrow but wide enough, I think, to carry children. All things considered, I am satisfied. Perhaps when she gets older she'll grow a beard on her chin but now she is only eighteen. And a blind uncle is better than no uncle. I waited too long to get a wife."

Narrow hips! You could wish for such a fault, Nazneen said to herself, thinking of the rolls of fat that hung low from Chanu's stomach. It would be possible to tuck all your hundred pens and pencils under those rolls and keep them safe and tight. You could stuff a book or two up there as well. If your spindle legs could take the weight.

"What's more, she is a good worker. Cleaning and cooking and all that. The only complaint I could make is she can't put my files in order, because she has no English. I don't complain though. As I say, a girl from the village: totally unspoilt."

Chanu went on talking but Nazneen crept away, back to bed. A blind uncle is better than no uncle. Her husband had a proverb for everything. Any wife is better than no wife. Something is better than nothing. What had she imagined? That he was in love with her? That he was grateful because she, young and graceful, had accepted him? That in sacrificing herself to him, she was owed something? Yes. Yes. She realized in a stinging rush she had imagined all these things. Such a foolish girl. Such high notions. What self-regard.

What she missed most was people. Not any people in particular but just people. If she put her ear to the wall she could hear sounds. The television on. Coughing. Sometimes the lavatory flushing. Someone upstairs scraping a chair. A shouting match below. Everyone in their boxes, counting their possessions. In all her eighteen years, she could scarcely remember a moment that she had spent alone. Until she married. And came to London to sit day after day in this large box with the furniture to dust, and the muffled sound of private lives sealed away above, below and around her.

Dr. Azad was a small, precise man who, contrary to the Bengali custom, spoke at a level only one quarter of a decibel above a whisper. Anyone who wished to hear what he was saying was obliged to lean in towards him, so that all evening Chanu gave the appearance of hanging on his every word.

"Come," said Dr. Azad, when Nazneen was hovering behind the table ready to serve, "Come and sit down with us."

"My wife is very shy." Chanu smiled and motioned with his head for her to be seated.

"This week I saw two of our young men in a very sorry state," said the doctor. "I told them straight, this is your choice: stop drinking alcohol now, or by Eid your liver will be finished. Ten years ago this would be unthinkable. Two in one week! But now our children are copying what they see here, going to the pub, to nightclubs. Or drinking at home in their bedrooms where their parents think they are perfectly safe. The problem is our community is not properly educated about these things." Dr. Azad drank a glass of water down in one long draught and poured himself another. "I always drink two glasses before starting the meal." He drank the second glass. "Good. Now I will not overeat."

"Eat! Eat!" said Chanu. "Water is good for cleansing the system, but food is also essential." He scooped up lamb and rice with his fingers and chewed. He put too much in his mouth at once, and he made sloppy noises as he ate. When he could speak again, he said, "I agree with you. Our community is not educated about this, and much else besides. But for my part, I don't plan to risk these things happening to my children. We will go back before they get spoiled."

"This is another disease that afflicts us," said the doctor. "I call it Going Home Syndrome. Do you know what that means?" He addressed himself to Nazneen.

She felt a heat on the back of her neck and formed words that did not leave her mouth.

"It is natural," said Chanu. "These people are basically peasants and they miss the land. The pull of the land is stronger even than the pull of blood."

"And when they have saved enough they will get on an airplane and go?"

"They don't ever really leave home. Their bodies are here, but their hearts are back there. And anyway, look how they live: just recreating the villages here."

"But they will never save enough to go back." Dr. Azad helped himself to vegetables. His shirt was spotless white, and his collar and tie so high under his chin that he seemed to be missing a neck. Nazneen saw an oily yellow stain on her husband's shirt where he had dripped food.

Dr. Azad continued, "Every year they think, just one more year. But whatever they save, it's never enough."

"We would not need very much," said Nazneen. Both men looked at her. She spoke to her plate. "I mean, we could live very cheaply." The back of her neck burned.

Chanu filled the silence with his laugh. "My wife is just settling in here." He coughed and shuffled in his chair. "The thing is, with the promotion coming up, things are beginning to go well for me now. If I just get the promotion confirmed then many things are possible."

"I used to think all the time of going back," said Dr. Azad. He spoke so quietly that Nazneen was forced to look directly at him, because to catch all the words she had to follow his lips. "Every year I thought, 'Maybe this year.' And I'd go for a visit, buy some more land, see relatives and friends and make up my mind to return for good. But something would always happen. A flood, a tornado that just missed the building, a power cut, some mind-numbing piece of petty bureaucracy, bribes to be paid out to get anything done. And I'd think, 'Well, maybe not this year.' And now, I don't know. I just don't know."

Chanu cleared his throat. "Of course, it's not been announced yet. Other people have applied. But after my years of service . . . Do you know, in six years I have not been late on one single day! And only three sick days, even with the ulcer. Some of my colleagues are very unhealthy, always going off sick with this or that. It's not something I could bring to Mr. Dalloway's attention. Even so, I feel he ought to be aware of it."

"I wish you luck," said Dr. Azad.

"Then there's the academic perspective. Within months I will be a fully fledged academic, with two degrees. One from a British University. Bachelor of Arts degree. With honours."

"I'm sure you have a good chance."

"Did Mr. Dalloway tell you that?"

"Who's that?"

"Mr. Dalloway."

The doctor shrugged his neat shoulders.

"My superior. Mr. Dalloway. He told you I have a good chance?"

"No."

"He said I didn't have a good chance?"

"He didn't say anything at all. I don't know the gentleman in question."

"He's one of your patients. His secretary made an appointment for him to see you about his shoulder sprain. He's a squash player. Very active man. Average build, I'd say. Red hair. Wears contact lenses — perhaps you test his eyes as well."

"It's possible he's a patient. There are several thousand on the list for my practice."

"What I should have told you straight away — he has a harelip. Well, it's been put right, reconstructive surgery and all that, but you can always tell. That should put you on to him."

The guest remained quiet. Nazneen heard Chanu suppress a belch. She wanted to go to him and stroke his forehead. She wanted to get up from the table and walk out of the door and never see him again.

"He might be a patient. I do not know him." It was nearly a whisper.

"No," said Chanu. "I see."

"But I wish you luck."

"I am forty years old," said Chanu. He spoke quietly like the doctor, with none of his assurance. "I have been in this country for sixteen years. Nearly half my life." He gave a dry-throated gargle. "When I came I was a young man. I had ambitions. Big dreams. When I got off the airplane, I had my degree certificate in my suitcase and a few pounds in my pocket. I thought there would be a red carpet laid out for me. I was going to join the Civil Service and become Private Secretary to the Prime Minister." As he told his story, his voice grew. It filled the room. "That was my plan. And then I found things were a bit different. These people here didn't know the difference between me, who stepped off an airplane with a degree certificate, and the peasants who jumped off the boat possessing only the lice on their heads. What can you do?" He rolled a ball of rice and meat in his fingers and teased it around his plate.

"I did this and that. Whatever I could. So much hard work, so little reward. More or less it is true to say, I have been chasing wild buffaloes and eating my own rice. You know that saying? All the begging letters from home I burned. And I made two promises to myself. I will be a success, come what may. That's promise number one. Number two, I will go back home. When I am a success. And I will honour these promises." Chanu, who had grown taller and taller in his chair, sank back down.

"Very good, very good," said Dr. Azad. He checked his watch.

"The begging letters still come," said Chanu. "From old servants, from the children of servants. Even from my own family, although they are not in need. All they can think of is money. They think there is gold lying about in the streets here and I am just hoarding it all in my palace. But I did not come here for money. Was I starving in Dhaka? I was not. Do they enquire about my diplomas?" He gestured to the wall, where his various framed certificates were displayed. "They do not. What is more . . ." He cleared his throat, although it was already clear. Dr. Azad looked at Nazneen and, without meaning to, she returned his gaze so that she was caught in a complicity of looks, given and returned, which said something about her husband that she ought not to be saying.

Chanu talked on. Dr. Azad finished the food on his plate while Chanu's food grew cold. Nazneen picked at the cauliflower curry. The doctor declined with a waggle of the head either a further helping or any dessert. He sat with his hands folded on the table while Chanu, his oration at an end, ate noisily and quickly. Twice more he checked his watch.

At half past nine Dr. Azad said, "Well, Chanu. I thank you and your wife for a most pleasant evening and a delicious meal."

Chanu protested that it was still early. The doctor was adamant. "I always retire at ten-thirty and I always read for half an hour in bed before that."

"We intellectuals must stick together," said Chanu, and he walked with his guest to the door.

"If you take my advice, one intellectual to another, you will eat more slowly, chew more thoroughly and take only a small portion of meat. Otherwise, I'll see you back at the clinic again with another ulcer."

"Just think," said Chanu, "if I did not have the ulcer in the first place, then we would not have met and we would not have had this dinner together."

"Just think," said the doctor. He waved stiffly and disappeared behind the door.

The television was on. Chanu liked to keep it glowing in the evenings, like a fire in the corner of the room. Sometimes he went over and stirred it by pressing the buttons so that the light flared and changed colours. Mostly he ignored it. Nazneen held a pile of the last dirty dishes to take to the kitchen, but the screen held her. A man in a very tight suit (so tight that it made his private parts stand out on display) and a woman in a skirt that did not even cover her bottom gripped each other as an invisible force hurtled them across an oval arena. The people in the audience clapped their hands together and then stopped. By some magic they all stopped at exactly the same time. The couple broke apart. They fled from each other and no sooner had they fled than they sought each other out. Every move they made was urgent, intense, a declaration. The woman raised one ·leg and rested her boot (Nazneen saw the thin blade for the first time) on the other thigh, making a triangular flag of her legs, and spun around until she would surely fall but didn't. She did not slow down. She stopped dead, and flung her arms above her head with a look so triumphant that you knew she had conquered everything: her body, the laws of nature, and the heart of the tight-suited man who slid over on his knees, vowing to lay down his life for her.

"What is this called?" said Nazneen.

Chanu glanced at the screen. "Ice skating," he said, in English.

"Ice e-skating," said Nazneen.

"Ice skating," said Chanu.

"Ice e-skating."

"No, no. No *e*. Ice skating. Try it again."

Nazneen hesitated.

"Go on!"

"Ice es-kating," she said, with deliberation.

Chanu smiled. "Don't worry about it. It's a common problem for Bengalis. Two consonants together causes a difficulty. I have conquered this issue after a long time. But you are unlikely to need these words in any case."

"I would like to learn some English," said Nazneen.

Chanu puffed his cheeks and spat the air out in a *fuff*. "It will come. Don't worry about it. Where's the need anyway?" He looked at his book and Nazneen watched the screen.

"He thinks he will get the promotion because he goes to the *pub* with the boss. He is so stupid he doesn't even realize there is any other way of getting promotion." Chanu was supposed to be studying. His books were open on the table. Every so often he looked in one, or turned a page. Mostly, he talked. *Pub, pub, pub.* Nazneen turned the word over in her mind. Another drop of English that she knew. There were other English words that Chanu sprinkled into his conversation, other things she could say to the tattoo lady. At this moment she could not think of any.

"This Wilkie — I told you about him — he has one or maybe two O levels. Every lunchtime he goes to the *pub* and he comes back half an hour late. Today I saw him sitting in Mr. Dalloway's office using the phone with his feet up on the desk. The jackfruit is still on the tree but already he is oiling his moustache. No way is he going to get promoted."

Nazneen stared at the television. There was a close-up of the woman. She had sparkly bits around her eyes like tiny sequins glued to her face. Her hair was scraped back and tied on top of her head with plastic flowers. Her chest pumped up and down as if her heart would shoot out and she smiled pure, gold joy. She must be terrified, thought Nazneen, because such things cannot be held, and must be lost.

"No," said Chanu. "I don't have anything to fear from Wilkie. I have a degree from Dhaka University in English Literature. Can Wilkie quote from Chaucer or Dickens or Hardy?"

Nazneen, who feared her husband would begin one of his long quotations, stacked a final plate and went to the kitchen. He liked to quote in English and then give her a translation, phrase by phrase. And when it was translated it usually meant no more to her than it did in English, so that she did not know what to reply or even if a reply was required.

She washed the dishes and rinsed them and Chanu came and leaned against the ill-fitting cupboards and talked some more. "You see," he said, a frequent opener although often she did not see, "it is the white underclass, like Wilkie, who are most afraid of people like me. To him, and people like him, we are the only thing standing in the way of them sliding totally to the bottom of the pile. As long as we are below them, then they are above something. If they see us rise then they are resentful because we have left our proper place. That is why you get the phenomenon of the *National Front*. They can play on those fears to create racial tensions, and give these people a superiority complex. The middle classes are more secure, and therefore more relaxed." He drummed his fingers against the Formica.

Nazneen took a tea towel and dried the plates. She wondered if the ice e-skating woman went home and washed and wiped. It was difficult to imagine. But there were no servants here. She would have to manage by herself.

Chanu ploughed on. "Wilkie is not exactly underclass. He has a job, so technically I would say no, he is not. But that is the mindset. This is what I am studying in the subsection on *Race, Ethnicity and Identity*. It is part of the sociology module. Of course, when I have my Open University degree then nobody can question my credentials. Although Dhaka University is one of the best in the world, these people here are by and large ignorant and know nothing of the Brontës or Thackeray."

Nazneen began to put things away. She needed to get in the cupboard that Chanu blocked with his body. He didn't move although she waited in front of him. Eventually she left the pans on the cooker to be put away in the morning.

After a minute or two in the dark, when her eyes had adjusted and the snoring began, Nazneen turned on her side and looked at her husband. She scrutinized his face, round as a ball, the blunt-cut thinning hair on top, and the dense eyebrows. His mouth was open and she began to regulate her breathing so that she inhaled as he did. When she got it wrong she could smell his breath. She looked at him for a long time. It was not a handsome face. In the month before her marriage, when she looked at his face in the photograph, she thought it ugly. Now she saw that it was not handsome, but it was kind. His mouth, always on duty, always moving, was full-lipped and generous, without a hint of cruelty. His eyes, small and beleaguered beneath those thick brows, were anxious or far away, or both. Now that they were closed she could see the way the skin puckered up across the lids and drooped down to meet the creases at the corners. He shifted in his sleep and moved on to his stomach with his arms down by his side and his face squashed against the pillow.

Nazneen got out of bed and crossed the hall. She caught hold of the bead curtain that partitioned the kitchen from the narrow hallway, to stop it tinkling, and went to the fridge. She got out the Tupperware containers of rice and fish and chicken and took a spoon from the drawer. As she ate, standing beside the sink, she looked out at the moon which hung above the dark flats checkered with lights. It was large and white and untroubled. She tried to imagine what it would be like to fall in love. She looked down into the courtyard. Two boys exchanged mock punches, feinting left and right. Cigarettes burned in their mouths. She opened the window and leaned into the breeze. Across the way the tattoo lady raised a can to her lips.

Numair Choudhury

Chokra

My sister was born in a kerosene drum. I was six years old when she was ready. Amma took me behind the railway tracks where rough men sat outside tea stalls and wooden slants. I could tell from her tight grip that I was to be silent. After much walking, we stopped outside a tin hut. The men here looked specially dangerous, and I began to fidget restlessly. This angered Amma and she stilled me with a sharp jerk. She spoke to them, asking for a Baba Mia. We were told to wait.

After a few minutes, a small man came out of the hut. He had a chilling stillness about him. He was Baba Mia. He led us inside. I sensed two things before we entered — a putrid smell and a strange humming sound. And as I followed my mother, I saw the drums. There must have been a hundred at least. Neatly stacked, each was covered with markings of white chalk. I realized that the stench and noise was coming from these small drums. The smell was that of rotting dampness. That of spoiling meat, like from a week old carcass. But much stronger. And the humming. Listening carefully, I could hear an undercurrent of scraping, moving and crying — as if there were a thousand noises in that hum.

The calm man walked over to a drum that had been pulled out from the rest and pointed to it. "Check the markings." Amma looked over it carefully and said, "It is mine." She ran shaking fingers over the chalk scribble. "Is she ready?"

"Yes. To wait any longer will kill her," he said softly. Amma nodded. The man then lifted the lid off the drum and reached inside with one hand. And he pulled out my three-year-old sister.

Today, it is raining. Munmun is cranky. She just sits in her trolley and makes faces at everything. She is not going to make any money for us this way, but when I tell her so, she just turns away. I don't know what to do. I hate the rain. I think we should move from here. Nobody is coming to the shops in this weather. The chokidar has also walked by twice, swishing his cane threateningly. We should not be here on his third round. And anyway, the downpour does not look like it will end anytime soon. There are many houses the next street over, I tell Munmun, maybe someone will let us use their porch. Maybe there will even be something to eat. But she only makes angry noises. I ignore her now. Tucking her wet clothes around her, I drape her with the piece of plastic. And I start to push. It is always difficult when the streets are wet. Mud cakes the tin-can wheels, making the trolley swerve wildly. Munmun flops uncontrollably, her shrivelled arms jutting out like disturbing branches.

When we reach the other street, I see that the houses here look poorer than I remember. It has been months since we begged here. Now I remember why. I search the length of the road, it is almost empty. Two dogs nose through a pile of garbage, and I chase them away to see if there is anything left, but they have done a thorough job. I push Munmun up to one door and knock softly. Almost immediately it opens to show a bare chested man tucking in his lungi. Seeing my outstretched hand near him and the two of us so close, he starts to raise a leg to kick at the cart, but I pull Munmun away. Just in time too. "Thieving beggars, out before I get my stick! Out!" He feigns a rush, but we are safe in the rain.

We try other houses — we are mostly yelled at and in a few cases, things are thrown at us. One angry man threw a chapati at us. We shared it, laughing. And then we got really lucky when a soft eyed woman opened the door to us, and then opened it wider. She let us in timidly, as if we were important guests. Her house is bare, but cool and dry of moisture. I feel myself steaming.

"Poor children. Sit down boy. It is bad for you to be outside." I sit on the earthen floor, resting my head on my folded knees.

"You have been in the wet for a long time?" I nod. She asks Munmun, "Are you brother and sister?"

I nod, "We are. She can't talk. She can understand though. Her name is Munmun."

"Munmun," the woman repeats slowly. "Poor Munmun. What has been done to you?" She removes the plastic and the layers of cloth I have draped, to look at my sister. She takes in the knotted stubs of what were legs and strokes mangled arm bones, making Munmun croon deep in her throat. "Huh Munmun? What have they done?" I look at this woman carefully and realize why she is so soft. There are no children in the house. We are the only ones there besides her. Women like her always help us, but they are rare and mixed blessings. For when it is time to leave, Munmun will cry for days. Because we always have to leave. Because she has never had a mother.

She feeds us soft rice and an egg each. I sense that this is a real treat, more than she can afford. Later she takes our clothes and soaks them in hot water. Munmun sleeps but I watch. The woman wants to talk.

"Why did you let them? Huh? Why? How long did they torture her?" She was not talking to me anymore — she knew these answers. She was just releasing her disappointment, like the man with the stick. Before, I used to wonder why the sight of Munmun and I angered people so much. It took a while before I understood. They could not stand our sight, we disgusted them; sickened them. Because we were what they might have to do themselves, one day, to their own children.

My head is becoming light with sleep, so I talk for a little. "I never knew what they took her for. Amma told me that Munmun had gone to be made new. To be made again, but different." I stopped here, laying down. "We have been on the streets for two years now. As it is, we have been hungry so many days. I don't know what we would have done if they hadn't changed her. But I would never let them take her away if I had known. I was small then."

"Don't you have anyone? In the villages?" she asked, but her eyes told me she was just making words, not sense. I shook my head. "I keep thinking that if we find someplace where they can fix her, we can look for work. But what work? And they say it costs much money for the operation. Millions. More than I can understand."

Later she tells me that we can stay the night there. I curl up to sleep. At some point, I wake to hear the woman crying. But I go back to sleep. Her tears mean nothing. She shakes my shoulder as the first streaks of light crack through the brick wall. Her husband is coming back from the factory: we should be gone soon. Munmun is already awake. She has that blank look on her face. Together, the woman and I dress her. Without a word I push the trolley out.

Outside the dust is gone after the long night's rain. But I see the ground is already dry, and I push happily. The street is murmuring with the sounds of five in the morning. And as we see the sun come up, from somewhere between green leaves and a building, I think it will be a bright day.

Acknowledgements

My first thanks go to Richard Teleky, who kindly recommended me to Patrick Crean as publisher of this anthology. I am also greatly indebted to Chelva Kanaganayakam at the University of Toronto for lending me his rare collection of South Asian fiction from the diaspora, and for carefully going through my introduction and making many valuable suggestions. Also thanks to Daniel Coleman at McMaster University for many discussions on the concept of diaspora, for pointing me in the direction of some great essays on the subject, and for reading my introduction and giving me some pointers. The following people suggested writers I should look at, or introduced me to people or resources that helped in my search: Frank Birbalsingh, Nurjehan Aziz (in Canada); Ali Smith, Rukhsana Ahmed, Melanie Abrahams (England); Muneeza Shamsie (Pakistan); Sneja Gunew, Vijay Mishra, Michelle de Kretser, Ivor Indyk, Chandani Lokuge (Australia). During my tenure as writer-in-residence at McMaster University, I had access to the valuable services of the

Interlibrary Loan Department. I am grateful to its staff for assiduously tracking down the most obscure story collections from the most remote libraries of North America. I am grateful to my partner, Andrew Champion, as always, for his support and love. Many thanks to Patrick Crean at Thomas Allen for giving me this wonderful opportunity. Special thanks to Sarah Williams, also at Thomas Allen, for shepherding this anthology through the quagmire of permissions, but also for her brilliant insights that helped the two of us narrow down an unwieldy list of short stories to a manageable anthology. Also Jim Gifford, at Thomas Allen, for all his input and editing. As always, I thank my agent, Bruce Westwood, and his assistant, Natasha Daneman.

Copyright Acknowledgements

Biographies

Mena Abdullah (b. 1930) was born at Bundarra in northern New South Wales, Australia. She was raised on a sheep property and gained her education at Sydney Girls' High School. Her short stories have been published in various anthologies. "The Time of the Peacock" (written in collaboration with Ray Mathew) was published in 1965.

Rukhsana Ahmad (b. 1948) is a writer, translator, and playwright who has written and adapted several plays for the stage and for radio, achieving distinction in both. Her first novel, *The Hope Chest*, was published by Virago. Alongside her theatre commitments she is currently working on her second novel.

Monica Ali (b. 1967) was born in Bangladesh and grew up in England. She studied politics, economy, and philosophy at Wadham College, Oxford. She has worked in publishing and design. Her first novel, *Brick Lane*, was released in 2003 and was shortlisted for the Booker Prize. Ali was named to *Granta*'s list of Best of Young British Novelists in 2003.

Numair A. Choudhury (b. 1975) was born in Bangladesh. He studied creative writing at Oberlin College, Ohio, and then at the University of East Anglia, Norwich. He is currently enrolled in the University of Texas at Dallas for his Ph.D. in Aesthetic Studies, where he continues work on his first novel.

Anita Desai (b. 1937) was born in India, the child of a Bengali father and a German mother. As a novelist Desai made her debut in 1963 with *The Peacock*. Since then she has written numerous novels including *fire on the Mountain*, *Clear Light of Day*, *In Custody*, *Fasting, Feasting*, and *Diamond Dust*, and has been shortlisted for the Booker Prize three times. She teaches creative writing at the Massachusetts Institute of Technology and spends one semester a year in the U.S.A and the rest of her time in India.

Chitra Fernando (b. 1935) was born in Sri Lanka and moved to Australia in the 1960s. She received an M.A. in Linguistics from the University of Sydney and a Ph.D. from Macquarie University, where she taught as a senior lecturer in English and Linguistics. She is the author of several collections of stories for children and two collections for adults, *Three Women* and *Between Worlds*. Her novel *Cousins* was published after her death in 1998.

Zulfikar Ghose (b. 1935) was born in Sialkot, Pakistan, and moved with his family in 1942 to Bombay. He later moved to London in 1952 where he was a cricket correspondent for *The Observer* and published some of his first work. He is the author of several collections of poetry and his autobiography, *Confessions of a Native-Alien*. Ghose moved to Austin, Texas, in 1969 where he became Professor of English at the University of Texas. His novels include *The Contradictions*, *The Murder of Aziz Khan*, *The Triple Mirror of the Self*, and the trilogy *The Incredible Brazilian*.

Romesh Gunesekera (b. 1954) was born in Sri Lanka, where he spent his early years. Before coming to Britain, he also lived in the Philippines. He now lives in London as a writer but travels widely. Recently he has been a writer-in-residence in Copenhagen, Singapore, and Hong Kong. His first novel, *Reef*, was shortlisted for the Booker Prize, as well as for the Guardian Fiction Prize. In the United States, he was nominated for a New Voice Award. He has published a collection of short stories titled *Monkfish Moon* and two other novels, *The Sandglass* and *Heaven's Edge*.

Aamer Hussein (b. 1955) was born in Karachi and has lived in London since 1970. He has published four collections of stories: *Mirror to the Sun, This Other Salt, Cactus Town,* and most recently the highly acclaimed *Turquoise.* He is an Associate Teaching Fellow at the Institute of English Studies (London University) and a Fellow of the Royal Society of Literature.

Ginu Kamani (b. 1962) was born in Bombay and later emigrated to the USA. An essayist and fiction writer, Kamani authored *Junglee Girl,* a collection of stories exploring sexuality, sensuality, and power. She has published fiction and essays in various anthologies, literary journals, newspapers, and magazines. She is Writer in Residence at Mills College, Oakland.

Farida Karodia (b. 1942) was born in South Africa and left for Canada in 1969. After working for many years in a variety of capacities, she took up writing full-time. She has published a number of novels and collections of short stories, including *Daughters of the Twilight, Coming Home and Other Stories, A Shattering of Silence,* and *Against an African Sky.* She currently lives in South Africa.

Hanif Kureishi (b. 1954) was born in Bromley, England. The product of an interracial marriage between a Pakistani immigrant and an English woman, he draws the inspiration for his work from his own life's trials and tribulations as a hybrid of two different races and cultures. He is the author of many plays, but is perhaps best known for his screenplays *My Beautiful Launderette, Sammy and Rosie Get Laid,* and *London Kills Me* and his works of fiction, *The Buddha of Suburbia, Intimacy, Midnight All Day, Love in a Blue Time,* and *Gabriel's Gift.*

Jhumpa Lahiri (b. 1967) was born in London and grew up in Rhode Island. She has travelled several times to India, where both her parents were born and raised. She graduated with a B.A. in English literature from Barnard College and an M.A. and Ph.D. from Boston University. Her debut collection, *Interpreter of Maladies,* received the Pulitzer Prize in 1999 and her latest novel, *The Namesake,* has been published to wide critical acclaim.

K.S. Maniam (b. 1942) is a leading writer in English from Malaysia. He has been recognized internationally in critical studies and recently received the Raja Rao Award for outstanding contribution to the literature of the Indian diaspora. Maniam's ancestors were indentured labourers from Tamil Nadu, and his first novel, *The Return* (1981), told in fictional guise the story of his grandmother's migration, his father's dreams of independence, and his own escape from servitude via English-medium schooling. He has written two novels, several collections of short stories, and a couple of very successful plays.

Rohinton Mistry (b. 1952) was born in Bombay and has lived in Canada since 1975. He is the author of *Tales from Firozsha Baag*, *Such a Long Journey*, *A Fine Balance*, and *Family Matters*. Mistry is the recipient of many prestigious awards, including the Giller Prize, the Commonwealth Writers Prize for Best Book, the Governor General's Award, and the Los Angeles Times Book Prize for Fiction. His three novels were all shortlisted for the Booker Prize. His work has also been shortlisted for the International IMPAC Dublin Literary Award and the Irish Times International Fiction Prize.

Rooplall Monar (b. 1947) was born in Guyana and grew up on a sugar estate. He has worked as a teacher, an estate bookkeeper, and a journalist. He is the winner of the Guyana Prize for literature. Amongst his numerous works of fiction are *Backdam People*, *Janjhat*, *High House and Radio*, and *Estate People*.

Shani Mootoo (b. 1957) was raised in Trinidad. She moved to Canada at the age of nineteen where she began a career as a visual artist and filmmaker. Her first book was a collection of short stories titled *Out on Main Street*. Her second book, *Cereus Blooms at Night*, was longlisted for the Booker Prize in 1997.

Bharati Mukherjee (b. 1940) was born in Calcutta, India. In 1961, she came to the United States on a scholarship from the University of Iowa, where she studied Creative Writing. She met and married the Canadian writer Clark Blaise and moved to Canada for a brief period before returning to the States. She is currently a professor at the University of California, Berkeley. Among the numerous works of fiction she has written are *The Tiger's Daughter*, *Wife*, *Days and Nights in Calcutta*, *Darkness*, *The Middleman and Other Stories* (winner of the National Book Critics Circle Award for Best Fiction), *Jasmine*, *The Holder of the World*, *Leave It to Me*, and *Desirable Daughters*.

Michael Ondaatje (b. 1943) was born in Colombo, Sri Lanka. He was educated in Colombo, London, and Quebec before receiving his B.A. from the University of Toronto in 1965. Ondaatje has been awarded many prizes for his work, including Canada's Governor General's Award, the Canada-Australia Prize, the Giller Prize, and the Kiriyama Pacific Rim Book Prize. His novel *The English Patient* won the Booker Prize in 1992. Among his other works of fiction and poetry are *Running in the Family*, *Coming Through Slaughter*, *In the Skin of a Lion*, *Anil's Ghost*, *The Cinnamon Peeler*, and *Handwriting*.

Raymond Pillai (b. 1942) is the great-grandson of an indentured labourer and was born in Ba, Fiji. After graduating from the University of the South Pacific, he taught in the university's English department and later in secondary schools. Since 1991 he has been living in New Zealand where he is involved in ESOL teaching.

Sandip Roy (b. 1966) was born in India and now lives and works in San Francisco as a journalist and editor for Pacific News Service. He hosts the radio show *UpFront* in San Francisco. His work has appeared in publications like the *San Francisco Chronicle*, *San Jose Mercury News*, *Newsday*, *India Currents*, *India Abroad*, and *Christopher Street*. His fiction and non-fiction have been featured in many anthologies, including *Contours of the Heart*, *Queer View Mirror*, and *Men on Men 6*.

Salman Rushdie (b. 1947) was born in India and moved with his family to England. He is the author of eight novels, including *Midnight's Children*, *The Satanic Verses*, *The Moor's Last Sigh*, and *The Ground Beneath Her Feet*; a collection of short stories; a book of reportage; two volumes of essays; and a work of film criticism. In 1981 he was awarded the Booker Prize for *Midnight's Children*, which later received the Booker of Bookers Prize (1993) as the best of the award's recipients in its 25-year history. He has also been awarded Germany's author of the year award, the French Prix du Meilleur Livre Etranger, the Whitbread Prize for Best Novel, the Writers Guild Award, the European Aristeion Prize for Literature, and the Austrian State Prize for European Literature.

Shyam Selvadurai (b. 1965) was born in Colombo, Sri Lanka. He came to Canada with his family at the age of nineteen. He has studied creative writing and theatre and has a BFA from York University. *Funny Boy*, his first novel, was published to acclaim in 1994 and won the W.H. Smith/ Books in Canada first Novel Award and in the United States the Lambda Literary Award, and was named a Notable Book by the American Library Association. His second novel, *Cinnamon Gardens*, was shortlisted for the Trillium Award, as well as the Aloa Literary Award in Denmark and the Premio Internazionale Riccardo Bacchelli in Italy.

Sam Selvon (b. 1923) was born in Trinidad to an Indian father and an Indian-Scottish mother. He immigrated to Britain in 1950, where his short stories and poetry were published in various journals and newspapers. He worked extensively with the BBC during the 1960s and '70s, producing television scripts and numerous radio programs. Among the many books he has written, he is best known for *The Lonely Londoners* and *A Brighter Sun*. He moved to Canada in 1978, and died in 1994.

Kirpal Singh (b. 1949) was born and raised in Singapore. He received his Ph.D. in English at the University of Adelaide. He is a poet, English-language expert, and culture critic. He currently teaches at the Centre for Cross-Cultural Studies, Singapore Management University. Among his books of poetry are *Palm Readings: Poems* and *Twenty Poems*.

M. G. Vassanji (b. 1950) was born in Nairobi, Kenya, and raised in Tanzania. When he was nineteen, Vassanji left for the United States, where he studied nuclear physics at the Massachusetts Institute of Technology, later earning a Ph.D. at the University of Pennsylvania. In 1980, Vassanji moved to Toronto and began writing his first novel, *The Gunny Sack* (winner of the Commonwealth Prize). Among his other works of fiction are *No New Land*, *Uhuru Street*, and *Amrika*. He won the Giller Prize for both *The Book of Secrets* and *The In-Between Life of Vikram Lall*.